Is he man enough for the ultimate job?

WANTED: FATHER FOR HER BABY

Three devastatingly handsome
potential daddies from three
beloved writers

We're proud to present

MILLS & BOON
SPOTLIGHT™

*A chance to buy collections of bestselling
novels by favourite authors every month –
they're back by popular demand!*

December 2009

Her Kind of Man

Featuring

Navy Husband by *New York Times*
bestselling author Debbie Macomber
A Man Apart by *New York Times*
bestselling author Joan Hohl
Second-Chance Hero by *USA Today*
bestselling author Justine Davis

Wanted: Father for Her Baby

Featuring

Keeping Baby Secret by Beverly Barton
Five Brothers and a Baby
by Peggy Moreland
Expecting Brand's Baby by Emilie Rose

WANTED: FATHER FOR HER BABY

New York Times bestselling author
BEVERLY BARTON

USA Today bestselling author
PEGGY MORELAND

EMILIE ROSE

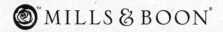

WANTED: FATHER FOR HER BABY © Harlequin Books S.A. 2009.

First published in Great Britain 2009
Harlequin Mills & Boon Limited,
Eton House, 18-24 Paradise Road, Richmond, Surrey TW9 1SR

The publisher acknowledges the copyright holders of the individual works, which have already been published in the UK in single, separate volumes, as follows:

Keeping Baby Secret © Beverly Beaver 2004
Five Brothers and a Baby © Peggy Bozeman Morse 2003
Expecting Brand's Baby © Emilie Rose Cunningham 2002

ISBN: 978 0 263 87169 2

64-1209

Printed and bound in Spain
by Litografia Rosés S.A., Barcelona

KEEPING BABY SECRET

BY
BEVERLY BARTON

Beverly Barton has been in love with romance since her grandfather gave her an illustrated book of *Beauty and the Beast*. An avid reader since childhood, Beverly wrote her first book at nine. After marriage to her own "hero" and the births of her daughter and son, Beverly chose to be a full-time homemaker, aka wife, mother, friend and volunteer. This author of over thirty-five books is a member of Romance Writers of America and helped found the Heart of Dixie chapter. She has won numerous awards, and has made several appearances on bestseller lists.

In loving memory of our cocker spaniel, Cole,
who was my faithful companion for nearly
fifteen years.

Prologue

Leenie checked the refrigerator for the third time. The bottles of milk were there, as she knew they would be. Just where she'd put them. But she simply had to check a final time, had to make sure nothing had been left undone. After all, this was a turning point in her life, a make-or-break night. As she hurried by the computer desk in her kitchen, she glanced at the list of phone numbers posted by the telephone. Emergency numbers, her cell number, her private number at work, as well as the switchboard number.

Rushing out of the kitchen and down the hall, her heartbeat rapid and her stomach painfully knotted, she wondered why this had to be so difficult. It wasn't as if she was the first woman in the world to go through this painful separation. Millions of women throughout the world had done what she was doing and most of them could probably sympathize with her feelings of guilt and fear.

As she neared the end of the hall, she slowed her pace, took a deep breath and told herself that she could do this. She was a strong woman. An independent woman. When she reached the nursery, she looked from Debra, who smiled compassionately, to Andrew, who lay sleeping peacefully in his bed, totally unaware of the trauma his mother was experiencing.

"Everything will be all right." Debra draped her arm around Leenie's shoulders. "You'll be gone only a few hours and he'll probably sleep the entire time you're away."

"But if he wakes and I'm not here…" Leenie pulled away from her son's nanny, walked over to Andrew's bassinet and watched her six-week-old baby as he slept. His little chest rose and fell softly with each tender breath he took. She reached out to touch his rosy cheek.

"If he wakes, I'll be right here," Debra assured her. "And if he's hungry, you left breast milk in the fridge. You aren't deserting him forever, you're just going to work."

"Maybe we should postpone this another week or so." Leenie couldn't bear the thought of being separated from Andrew, even for the four hours it would take her to drive to WJMM, do her two-hour midnight talk-show on the radio, set things up for her morning TV show and then drive home.

"No, we won't postpone it," Debra said firmly. "We can continue taking Andrew to the station every morning for your daytime show, but he shouldn't be dragged out of his bed every night." Debra crossed her arms over her chest and narrowed her gaze. "Go to work, Leenie. You do your job and let me do mine."

Sighing heavily, Leenie admitted her deepest fears. "But one of my jobs is being Andrew's mother and if you do your job too well, my son will bond with you and not me."

Huffing loudly, but following up with an understanding smile, Debra patted Leenie's arm. "Andrew has already bonded with you. He knows you're his mother. If I do my job well, and I'd like to think I've been doing that since the day we brought Andrew home from the hospital, then he'll think of me as a favorite aunt or as a grandmother."

"I'm being silly, aren't I?"

"No, you're being a good mother."

"Am I a good mother? I'm not sure what makes a good mother. As you well know, I didn't have one of my own. No mother at all raised me, good, bad or otherwise."

"Jerry and I were parents to over fifty foster kids in our thirty years of marriage." Debra sighed dreamily, as she always did whenever she mentioned her late husband, who had died two years ago at the age of sixty-three from a heart attack. "I've seen all kinds of mothers and I know a good one from a bad one."

"Yes, I imagine you do. You were certainly an excellent role model for me when I lived with you and Jerry. I learned by watching the way you were with all of us foster children what a good mother is." She had been fifteen when she'd been sent to live with Debra and Jerry Schmale, a young minister and his wife who'd been told they could never have children of their own and had decided they would give their love and time to unwanted, neglected kids of all ages. The three years she'd spent with the Schmales had been the best years of her childhood.

"You, Dr. Lurleen Patton, are a good mother," Debra said.

"Even though I'm a single parent? Even though I didn't provide Andrew with a father?"

"You told me that Andrew was the result of a very brief affair with a man you barely knew. A man who showed no interest in settling down. A man who was very careful to use protection each time y'all made love."

Leenie nodded. "One of those times, that protection failed. Otherwise, I wouldn't have gotten pregnant. But that wasn't Frank's fault."

"You made the decision not to tell Andrew's father about his existence because you felt it was the best thing for everyone concerned. Right?"

"Right."

"Have you changed your mind?"

No, she hadn't changed her mind. Although, truth be told, sometimes she wished she had called Frank the day she'd found out she was pregnant, called him and told him he was going to be a daddy. But she'd been so shocked herself that it had taken her weeks to figure out what to do. By the time she decided she wanted to keep her baby and raise it herself, she had also decided that the last thing Frank Latimer would want in his life was a child. Their entire relationship had lasted less than two weeks. Love hadn't been involved. Just a major case of lust.

"No, I haven't changed my mind. If Frank knew he had a child, it would simply complicate his life and mine, not to mention Andrew's."

Debra turned Leenie around, grasped her shoulders and all but shoved her out of the room. "If you don't leave now, you'll be late." Debra walked Leenie into the hallway and all the way to the back door. "Call me every thirty minutes, if that will make you feel better—but go. Now!"

Leenie sighed. "Thanks. I don't know what I'd do without you. Sometimes I think I need you even more than Andrew does."

Debra hugged her, then lifted Leenie's jacket and purse from where they hung on a coatrack near the door, handed them to her and said, "Drive carefully, call as often as you need to, have a great show tonight and I'll be waiting up for you when you come home."

Leenie slipped into her coat, draped her purse straps over her shoulder and opened the back door that led into the garage. She unlocked her new GMC Envoy SUV, a vehicle she'd purchased a month before her son's birth. Of course she'd kept her sports car, but hadn't used it since Andrew had been born because she never went anywhere without him. Use it tonight, she told herself. Get in your Mustang and fly off down the road.

After locking the SUV, she went over to the Mustang, unlocked it and got in, then revved the motor and hit the remote that opened the garage. Within minutes she was zipping along the highway that led from the suburbs of Maysville, Mississippi, into the downtown area where the studios for both WJMM radio and TV stations were located. She'd been doing a late-night radio talk show and a morning TV show for quite a few years and enjoyed being a local celebrity, a psychiatrist who doled out advice over the airwaves five days and nights a week.

When she'd been younger, she had longed to create a family of her own. Having grown up in a series of foster homes and remembering very little about her own parents, she had always felt so alone. Her mother had died when she was four and her father when she was eight. A skinny, gangly girl, who had talked too much and tried too hard to make others like her, she'd never had a real chance of being adopted. From eight to eighteen, she'd been shifted around from foster home to foster home. She'd felt unloved and unwanted all her life and by the time she hit thirty and Prince Charming hadn't entered her life, she'd pretty much given up hope for that fantasized happily ever after ending in her life.

Although she'd been around the block a few times, as the old saying went, she wasn't promiscuous. Each time she'd been in a committed relationship, she'd wanted it to be "the one." And she'd never had a one-night stand. Not until Frank Latimer entered her life. Or should she say breezed in and out of her life. And technically, he hadn't really been a one-night stand. More like a ten day mini-affair. She'd taken one look at the big lug and fallen hard and fast. They had set the sheets on fire and what she'd thought would be a one-nighter turned into a very brief, extremely passionate relationship.

Leenie wished it wasn't late November already so she could put the top down on her car and achieve that wild and free feeling it gave her to ride with the wind. Maybe that's what she needed—some cold night air to clear away the cobwebs. As hard as she tried to relegate Frank Latimer to the back of her mind, to put him into the past where he belonged, she found it difficult, if not impossible, to do. Although

Andrew had her blond hair and blue eyes, he resembled Frank or the way she was sure Frank had looked as a baby. And every time she looked at her son, she saw his father. How could she—a psychiatrist who'd been trained to understand the human psyche—have ever thought she'd be able to forget about the man who had fathered her child? Whether or not he was actually in her life, he'd always be a part of it. Andrew was the living, breathing proof of that.

She'd told Debra that she wasn't having any second thoughts about contacting Frank to let him know he had a child, but maybe she'd been lying to herself as well as Debra. Maybe she should call Frank, feel him out, see if there was somebody special in his life these days. Or maybe she should just fly to Atlanta and take Andrew with her. No, she couldn't do that, couldn't just show up on Frank's doorstep.

Stop debating the issue, she told herself. *You're not going to call Frank.* And she wasn't going to fly to Atlanta. If he had the slightest interest in renewing his relationship with her, he'd have called by now. After all, it was over ten months since he'd said goodbye and walked out of her life without a backward glance. She had to accept the fact that Frank wasn't her Prince Charming, accept the fact that there was no such animal. Just because he'd been different from the other men she'd known didn't mean she was as special to him as he had been to her. What they'd had wasn't love. It was just sex.

One

Leenie glanced across the table at Jim Isbell, a good-looking, likable guy. He had asked her out after their initial meeting last week when he'd appeared on her morning TV show in a segment about group therapy. Jim was a psychologist who worked with families in trouble—drugs, alcohol, infidelity and various other problems that plagued many people in today's complex modern society. This was their first date—one she'd been looking forward to eagerly. It was a simple workday lunch between friends. No strings attached. Nothing that would put pressure on either of them. Everyone who knew her, including Debra, had encouraged her to start dating again. After all, she hadn't been out with a man since she'd found out she was pregnant. Now Andrew was nearly two months old and adjusting beautifully to having a working mother. Debra brought him to the studio several days a week, but kept him home in his own bed at night. Although Leenie loved her job, her son was the center of her world.

"So, are you interested?" Jim asked.

"Hmm?"

"Dinner and a movie this weekend," Jim said.

"Oh, uh…yes. That might be nice." Nice. Such an odd word, with so many meanings. And often a bland word, one that conveyed very little emotion. *Oh, jeez, Leenie, don't overanalyze your response about the date. You meant the word nice in the…well, in the nicest way.* She smiled to herself. *You like Jim. Obviously he likes you. You've had a pleasant lunch, so why not follow up with a dinner date?*

Nice? Pleasant? Why not fantastic or great or fabulous or wonderful? What if Frank Latimer asked her out for a dinner date? *You wouldn't be using such lukewarm adjectives, now would you?* An inner voice taunted. *Stop it!* She shouldn't compare Jim to Frank. They were apples and oranges. Yeah, sure they were, but Jim was such a boring apple and Frank had been such an incredible orange.

Frank with the sexy gray eyes and hard, lean body. Frank, who had memorized every inch of her with his bedroom eyes, with his big hands and his mouth and tongue. Frank, who always looked like an unmade bed and had a way of curling her toes without even touching her.

"Lurleen?"

"Huh?" Apparently Jim had said something to which he expected a response and since she'd been thinking about another man, she hadn't heard a word Jim had said.

"You're a million miles away, aren't you?"

"Sorry, Jim, it's just that I—"

"No need to explain. You're thinking about your son, aren't you? New mothers tend to obsess about their babies. But you really should work your way through those typical feelings about neglecting and abandoning your child in favor of your career. You're too smart to believe that you have to be the most important person in his life right now. After all, you have a perfectly capable nanny, don't you?"

"Yes, a very capable nanny."

"I understand that you have an extra burden of guilt on your shoulders since you're a single mother."

Leenie stared at Jim as he continued talking, giving her his opinion about the correct way to rear children, especially a son without a father figure. Not one to take criticism or advice well, his comments aggravated her. Who was he to be giving her advice? Had she asked him to share his wisdom on the subject of raising children?

"Jim!"

With his mouth open midsentence, he stopped talking and looked quizzically at her. "Yes?"

She'd been about to lambaste him, tell him in no uncertain terms that her relationship with her son was none of his damn business. Instead she said, "Let's order dessert. Cheesecake."

He arched his eyebrows in a disapproving manner. "Are you sure you want the extra calories? After all, you probably still have some baby fat you want to lose."

He smiled at her in his good-natured manner. And she wanted to slap him. Baby fat, indeed! She weighed now precisely what she'd weighed before she'd gotten pregnant, having dropped twenty pounds when Andrew was born and another ten in the past two months. Everyone else she knew had marveled over how quickly she'd gotten back in shape.

"Right. No dessert." It wasn't the calories she could do without, it was the company. She gritted her teeth to keep from telling him off in no uncertain terms. "Look, I just remembered that I have a previous engagement this weekend, so I'll have to forego dinner and a movie." She shoved back her chair and stood.

Ever the gentleman, Jim stood up. "Perhaps lunch again next week, then?"

"Perhaps." She picked up her purse.

"I'll call you."

"Please do. I hate to run, but—"

"Work awaits," he said.

"Yes."

She didn't bother to contradict him, to tell him she was going home where she'd spend the afternoon and early evening with Andrew. Nodding, she forced a smile, then hurried away from the table, out of the restaurant and to her car. Once inside, she checked her watch. Two-fifteen. She'd go on home and be there in time to help put away groceries. About now Debra and Andrew were at Foodland on their weekly shopping excursion. Usually Leenie joined them for lunch on Fridays and afterward they bought groceries together, but today she'd had a date. A waste of time. Time she could have spent with her son.

Wonder if it's too late to join them at Foodland? She could buy one of those frozen cheesecakes and indulge at supper tonight. That's what she'd do. Eat cheesecake and forget about Jim Isbell. Out there somewhere was another guy who wouldn't bore her to tears. Someone as much fun as Frank. As sexy as Frank. As good in bed as Frank.

All right already. Enough about Frank!

Frank is the past. Jim Isbell was a dud. Think about Andrew. And cheesecake.

Frank Latimer stretched out as best he could in his seat, thankful that he was in first class and not stuck back in coach. Most of the time when he flew, it was on the luxurious Dundee jet, but when his latest job had ended today, the jet was already en route to Key West, taking a crew of Dundee's best for a top secret assignment. He was set for a week off and planned to do some fishing while he relaxed at Sawyer McNamara's Hilton Head vacation house. He'd been working practically nonstop for nearly a year now. When he'd left Maysville, Mississippi, eleven months ago, he'd taken a European assignment just to get him out of the country and as far away as was possible from a certain long and lean blonde. If there had been a flight to Mars eleven months ago, he'd have taken it.

"Would you care for another glass of tea, Mr. Latimer?" the attractive brunette flight attendant asked. He'd noticed her immediately, the minute he'd boarded his flight from Chicago to Atlanta. Ms. Gant was petite and slender, with big eyes and big boobs and a come-hither smile.

"No, thank you."

"Is there anything else I can do for you?"

Oh, yeah, there was something she could do for him all right. He was in bad need of a warm body in his bed. For months after his whirlwind affair with Leenie Patton, he hadn't touched another woman.

Then he'd convinced himself that what he needed to
get Leenie out of his system was a woman—actually
a lot of women. He'd tried that, but it hadn't worked.
No one had tasted like Leenie or felt like Leenie or
sounded like Leenie. So after gorging himself on
nameless, faceless bed partners, he'd sworn off
women altogether, at least until he could stop wanting
one particular lady—a sexy, wild woman he'd called
Slim.

"Mr. Latimer?"

"Huh?"

"Are you all right?"

"Yeah, sure. I'm fine."

No, he wasn't fine. He was tired. This last job had
lasted six weeks and he'd been shot at twice and
wound up in three fistfights. He badly needed some
major down-time. And Sawyer's luxurious home in
Hilton Head was just the ticket. If he could find a
gorgeous, sexy blonde to spend the week with him,
he'd have it made. It was time to end his months of
celibacy.

*The trouble is you don't want just any gorgeous,
sexy blonde. You want Slim. She's what you want. All
you want.*

So why not call her up when he landed in Atlanta?
And say what? *I've been thinking about you for
eleven months? Every time I slept with somebody else,
I wished she was you?*

"Hell, no!"

Frank didn't realize he'd cursed aloud until Ms.
Gant said, "Yes, Mr. Latimer, did you say something?"

"Just talking to myself," he told her. "That happens when you get old."

She giggled like a teenager and flashed him a brilliant smile. "You're hardly old."

"I'm forty," he admitted, feeling every year of it.

"That's not old. That's the prime of life for a man."

He chuckled. "I thought prime time for a guy was eighteen."

She moistened her lips. "A man of forty has experience that a younger man doesn't. I prefer experience."

She's putting it out there for you, Latimer, he told himself. All you have to do is take what she's offering. He was tempted. Damn tempted. Even if she wasn't a long-legged, willowy blonde.

Leaning down close to his ear, she whispered, "I'll be in Atlanta overnight."

"How about dinner?" He'd definitely been celibate long enough. Months of doing without wasn't his style. It was time he tried sex again. And past time to get Leenie Patton out of his system.

Two blocks from Foodland, Leenie heard the wail of sirens—police and ambulance—and couldn't help wondering if there had been a bad wreck somewhere nearby. The first thought that flashed through her mind was that Andrew and Debra had been involved in the accident. But she quickly dismissed the idea as nothing more than her tendency to worry much too much about Andrew whenever he was out of her sight. Of course she understood that her worries, concerns and fears were perfectly natural, that almost every new mother experienced these emotions whether she was a working mom or a stay at home mom. Naturally, being a single parent only added to her concerns about motherhood. With each passing day of Andrew's life, Leenie felt more and more guilty for not having contacted Frank to tell him about their child. She had given herself every reason not to call him, to keep Andrew's existence a secret from him, but in the end she knew, in her heart of hearts, that Frank had a right to know.

Admit it, she told herself, *you're scared to tell Frank the truth.* If she told him and he didn't want to be a part of Andrew's life, she'd wonder what kind of man he really was. On the other hand, if he wanted to be a part of his son's life, but didn't want her in the bargain, then she'd have to not only share Andrew, but she'd have to accept the fact that she'd never been special to Frank.

As she cruised down the tree-lined street at thirty-five miles an hour, she forced her mind off Frank Latimer and onto cheesecake. *Wonder if Foodland has any chocolate cheesecake?* she mused.

Suddenly the Lexus in front of her eased to a halt behind a line of other vehicles. Noting that the car's brake lights had come on, Leenie stopped her SUV and tried to see what lay ahead. Able to make out the whirl of blue flashing lights in the distance, she figured traffic had been stopped at the scene of the accident about a block ahead of her. If the wreck had just occurred, it could take quite a while to clear things up and get traffic moving again. Her lane was stalled and the other lane was empty, as if traffic had been stopped on the other side of the police car up ahead. She sighed. *I should have gone home instead of heading to Foodland to meet up with Debra and Andrew,* she thought. If she got stuck here for very long, she'd call Debra on her cell phone to let her know why she was delayed.

Tapping her fingers on the steering wheel, she hummed. And waited. Suddenly an ambulance flew by, its siren mournfully eerie. Once again, an odd sensation hit Leenie in the pit of her stomach. Don't do this to yourself, she cautioned. Stop thinking Debra's Saturn was involved in the wreck. Debra and Andrew were either still at Foodland or they were stalled on the other side of the accident and were waiting in line, just as she was.

As the minutes ticked by, Leenie tried to think of other things. Her boring lunch date with Jim. The topics she planned to discuss tonight on her midnight radio show before she took phone calls. Andrew's latest doctor's checkup when she'd been told he was absolutely perfect, something she'd already known, of course. Getting his two-month pictures made next week. He was such a beautiful child. He had her coloring. Blond hair and blue eyes. But he had Frank's mouth…and his little hands and feet were miniature replicas of Frank's. Odd that she could remember so well everything about a man she'd known for such a brief time.

A heavyset guy in the truck ahead of the Lexus in front of her got out and walked down the street, in the direction of the wreck. It never ceased to amaze her how curious people were about disasters, as if some weird inner force drew them to blood and gore.

She checked her watch. Less than five minutes had passed since she'd stopped. It seemed more like thirty. If there was one thing she hated, it was wasting time. Surely it wouldn't take that much longer before the police would get the traffic moving again, even if only in one lane.

A tow truck went by about the same time the man who'd gone to take a look at the scene came walking back up the street. Several people in other vehicles either got out to talk to him or rolled down their windows to ask him questions. A small crowd gathered in the middle of the road. Leenie rolled down her window, intending to holler and ask if the guy thought they'd be stuck here much longer, then she heard him say something that made her blood run cold.

"They were putting a gray-haired woman in the ambulance," he said. "It looked bad. Somebody had T-boned her Saturn on the driver's side and crushed it in." He shook his head. "I couldn't make out much, but there was a baby's car seat in back."

Leenie flung open the door, jumped out and ran, leaving the door open, her keys in the ignition and her purse lying on the seat. As she raced past the small crowd, they turned to stare at her, and one person even called out to her. She ignored everyone and everything. By the time she reached the scene of the accident, her breath was labored and her lungs ached. Fear consumed her. When she saw Debra's blue Saturn, she stopped dead still. While she stood there trembling, gasping for air, the ambulance drove past her. She reached out as if she could grab it and stop it.

Andrew! Debra! Her mind screamed their names.

A policeman approached her. "Ma'am, you need to move out of the way."

"Please, I have to—you don't understand."

"Ma'am are you all right?"

"Andrew and Debra. How badly were they hurt?"

"Do you know Mrs. Schmale?" he asked.

Numbness set in. Leenie nodded. "She's my nanny."

"Then you're Dr. Patton?"

"Yes, I'm Lurleen Patton."

The uniformed officer put his arm around Leenie's shoulders and led her out of the street and onto the sidewalk. Without protest, as if in a trance, she went with him.

"Mrs. Schmale is on her way to the hospital," he explained. "She has cuts, bruises, a broken arm and leg and possible internal bleeding. But she was conscious and able to tell us what happened."

"And Andrew?" Leenie asked.

When she noted the peculiar look on the policeman's face, her heart caught in her throat. Was Andrew dead? God, please, no. No! Surely he was all right. Debra always placed him in the regulation seat in the back of her car. And since it had been a driver's side collision...

"Your son...Andrew..." The officer paused, swallowed as if wishing he didn't have to deliver bad news, then said, "Mrs. Schmale told us that a white car came out of nowhere, crashed into her car and the driver jumped out and came to help her. Or so she thought. The driver—a woman—had Mrs. Schmale unlock the doors so she could get in on the other side. Before she realized what was happening, the woman got in the back seat and removed the baby from the car seat. Your nanny thought the woman was simply making sure Andrew was all right. But—"

Leenie swayed toward the officer, then grasped his shoulders and said, "Where is Andrew?"

"The woman took him, put him in her car and drove away," the policeman explained.

"What?"

"We've got an all-points bulletin out for the car—an older model white Buick—and the woman—medium height, weight, short brown hair, sunglasses."

The reality of the situation hit Leenie like a ton of bricks falling on her head. "Andrew was…was…" She couldn't bring herself to say the word, as if not voicing it aloud kept it from being a reality.

"I'm sorry, Dr. Patton, but your baby has been kidnapped."

Two

Leenie couldn't sit still. She felt as if a hundred-mile-an-hour freight train was surging through her. Nerves. Adrenaline. Fear beyond anything she'd ever experienced. Everyone kept telling her to go lie down, take a nap or just rest. Police Chief Ryan Bibb had suggested calling her doctor for a sedative. She knew the man meant well, but why couldn't he—and all the other people who had congregated at her house—understand that she didn't want her senses dulled, that she couldn't sleep or rest. Her baby had been kidnapped. Stolen from her by only God knew what sort of person. She'd overheard the local police surmising about the general identity of Andrew's abductor.

"She's probably some woman who either lost a baby or has a fixation about having a child," Chief Bibb had said. "And if that's the case, she'll take good care of Andrew."

Leenie supposed that believing the kidnapper was taking good care of her baby should be some comfort. It wasn't. Anyone capable of stealing a child had mental problems, whatever their reason.

"Why don't you let me fix you some tea?" Haley Wilson said, as she put her arm around Leenie's shoulder.

The plump brunette, who'd taken over as the manager of WJMM eleven months ago when Elsa Leone—now Elsa Devlin since she'd married—had moved to Knoxville, was a bubbly, energetic woman in her mid-forties and the mother of two teenage sons. From the minute Leenie and she met, they had bonded. Instant friendship. Haley had been the first person she'd called, the first person who'd come to mind when the police had asked her about a friend or family member to stay with her. Haley had dropped everything and rushed to Maysville Memorial, where Leenie had been waiting for Debra to come out of surgery. Haley stayed with her and they had prayed for Debra and for Andrew. Thankfully, Debra had come through the surgery to stop her internal bleeding with flying colors.

"Mrs. Schmale will be in intensive care for the next twenty-four hours," Dr. Brenner had explained. "But I expect a full and speedy recovery."

Knowing that Debra would be all right gave Leenie a great sense of relief. She loved Debra dearly, as a friend and mother figure. The police had said that Debra's ability to accurately describe the kidnapper and the car she'd been driving would be of immeasurable help in locating Andrew.

"Leenie." Haley shook her gently. "Come on in

the kitchen with me. You can sit down long enough for me to fix you some tea.''

''I don't want anything to drink.''

''Come in the kitchen with me anyway,'' Haley said. ''I'm going to prepare fresh coffee for those FBI people who just arrived and since it's nearly morning, maybe I should offer to make breakfast, too. Why don't you help me?''

Leenie stared at Haley, understanding what she'd said, but not comprehending.

Haley hugged her. ''You can't keep pacing the floor and you can't keep going into Andrew's room every ten minutes. You need something to do.''

''You're right. Staring at Andrew's crib in the nursery won't make him miraculously appear.'' Emotion lodged in Leenie's throat. *Don't cry,* she told herself. *Crying isn't going to help. You have to stay strong and in control.*

''They'll find him and bring him home to you.'' Haley hugged her again, then grasped her hand and tugged. ''Come on. Let's make us some tea first, then put on fresh coffee for the others. After that I'll take breakfast orders. And I expect you to eat. Even if it's just a few bites.''

Leenie followed her friend into the kitchen, thankful that she had someone with her, someone who understood what it meant to be a mother with a baby boy lost. No, not lost—stolen. Suddenly feeling as if they had become glued to the spot, her feet wouldn't move. The reality of Andrew's disappearance struck her once again, but harder this time, and she sensed that he was being taken farther and farther away from her.

''Leenie?''

"Oh, God, what if—what if—" Tears streamed down her cheeks.

Haley grabbed her and pulled her into her arms. "Cry, dammit. Cry your eyes out."

Leenie fell apart. She sobbed until she was spent. Was it seconds? Minutes? Hours? She didn't know. And all the while Haley held her and stroked her back and murmured soothing, comforting words that Leenie barely heard. As she gulped down the lingering sobs, she lifted her head and looked into Haley's kind hazel eyes.

Haley grasped her shoulders and offered her a fragile smile. "Go wash your face and when you get back, I'll have a cup of tea waiting for you."

Leenie nodded, but before she could turn around, the kitchen door opened and a tall, dark stranger entered. He wasn't one of the local police and he wasn't one of the three FBI agents who had arrived less than an hour ago.

"Dr. Patton?" The golden-eyed man looked right at Leenie.

"Yes."

When he came forward and held out his right hand, she noticed an onyx and diamond ring on his third finger. "I'm Special Agent Dante Moran. I'll be heading up this case."

She shook his hand. Warm. Firm.

"Could we sit and talk, Dr. Patton?" he asked.

"I've talked to the police and to the other FBI agents," she told him. "I don't know what more there is to say."

"No one has discussed possible scenarios with you, have they? Told you what we might be dealing with in Andrew's case?"

She shook her head.

He nodded toward the kitchen table. "Want to sit down?"

"No, I—I can't sit."

"All right." He shrugged. "We aren't sure what we're dealing with here. It's possible that whoever took Andrew simply wanted a baby. If that's—"

"Then she'll probably take good care of him," Leenie said sarcastically.

"Yeah, and I realize that doesn't make you feel any better. But it's better than the other possibilities."

"Which are?"

"He was taken for ransom."

"I'm not rich."

"Not rich, but wealthy," Moran said. "And you are a local celebrity."

"Hell."

"If Andrew was taken for a ransom, we'll be hearing from the kidnapper soon."

"And if he wasn't taken for a ransom?"

"He could have been stolen by someone who intends to sell him. There's a profitable market for stolen babies, especially WASP babies. Blond, blue-eyed. And then there's the other possibility." He looked Leenie square in the eyes. "The worst case scenario is—"

"Dammit, Mr. Moran, do you have to come right out and say it?" Haley practically screamed at the FBI agent.

"Sorry, ma'am." He glanced from Leenie to Haley and then focused on Leenie again. "Rest assured that we're going to do everything in our power to find Andrew and bring him home to you safe and sound."

"Yes, I—I know you will."

"What about Andrew's father?" Moran asked. "I understand you two aren't married, but don't you think that, under the circumstances, you should contact him to let him know his son has been kidnapped?"

Leenie didn't respond; she simply stared into Moran's yellow-brown eyes. After an endless moment, he shrugged. "Why don't you get some rest, Dr. Patton? We can talk again later. Special Agent Walker explained to you the procedure if the phone rings and that we'll screen anyone who comes to the door and—"

"He explained," Haley said.

Moran nodded, then walked out of the kitchen.

Leenie took a deep breath. *What about Andrew's father?* That question repeated itself over and over again inside her head. It wasn't as if she hadn't already asked herself the same thing several times during the night. She had been wrestling with indecision about whether to tell Frank about Andrew's existence since the day her baby was born. But now that Andrew had been abducted, it made the decision all the more difficult. What could she do, call Frank and say, "By the way, we have a baby boy and he's been kidnapped."

"I know what you're thinking," Haley said.

"Yeah, but do you know what I should do?"

"Oh, honey, that's a toughie. What's your heart telling you to do?"

Leenie groaned. "It's telling me that I need Frank, that somehow he can help."

"And what does your brain tell you?"

"That Frank is a Dundee agent, with the resources of the entire agency at his disposal, that he can do things the law can't do and that the Dundee Agency has strong ties to the FBI and—''

''Your heart and your mind are telling you to contact Frank Latimer,'' Haley said.

She sighed. ''How do I tell him about Andrew over the phone?''

''Good question. Is there someone else you could call, someone who could get Frank here under some other pretense so that you can tell him face-to-face?''

''I don't know—'' Leenie paused. ''Well there is Elsa. Maybe my old boss at WJMM, Elsa Devlin, could arrange it. Her husband used to be a Dundee agent. And she and I are good friends.''

''So call Elsa.''

''If I do, she'll come back to Maysville to be with me and she's pregnant and— No, I'm not going to upset Elsa. There was a female Dundee agent named Kate Malone who worked on Elsa's case with Frank. Maybe I could contact her.'' Agitated and uncertain, Leenie paced the floor. ''Oh, hell, maybe I'm complicating this much too much. Maybe I should just call Frank and tell him.''

''Then what are you waiting for?''

''For lightning to strike, I guess. For some sign that calling him is the right thing to do.''

''If you feel you can't call Frank, call this Kate Malone and ask for her help.''

''If she tells Frank that I have a child, he'll know or at the very least suspect the baby is his. Maybe it's better if I don't involve Frank. I don't think I can handle telling him. Not now. Not under these circumstances.''

Frank boarded the Dundee jet, Kate Malone at his side. This was a first for him—flying off on an assignment and not knowing where he was going. Kate had come to his apartment this morning and met the lovely flight attendant, Heather Gant, just as Heather was leaving. Although she hadn't said anything, Kate had lifted a judgmental eyebrow at Frank as the woman passed her in the hall. Ending his months of celibacy was reason for celebration, so he'd been feeling pretty good when Kate showed up.

"Shave and take a shower," Kate had told him. "We're off on an assignment as soon as we can get to the airport."

"No way, I've got vacation time coming."

"It's been canceled. You're needed on this job."

"Can't another agent handle it? Why me?"

"I'll fill you in on the plane," she'd told him. "We have a child kidnapping and the family wants Dundee involved."

"How does the FBI feel about us interfering?"

"Not thrilled. But our old friend Dante Moran is heading up the case, so he knows we won't work at cross purposes with his people."

So, he'd agreed to come along with Kate without putting up too much of a fuss. Although her reasons were apparently personal—and as a general rule none of his fellow agents nosed into other agents' past lives—everyone at Dundee knew that Kate always took a keen interest in any case involving a kidnapped baby. Shortly before leaving her job as Dundee's CEO, Ellen Denby had hired Kate, who was a former Atlanta P.D. officer, just as Ellen had been. And rumor was that they had worked together when Kate was a rookie.

Frank munched on a cheese danish, then washed it

down with black coffee. If he hadn't been such a
sucker for a sob story—single mother, overwrought
with fear, and an abducted two-month-old boy—he'd
be on his way to Sawyer's Hilton Head vacation retreat instead of being midair, flying off on an assignment that was sure to be pure hell on the nerves.
Dealing with overwrought mamas wasn't his speci-
ality. He'd leave coddling the abducted kid's mommy
to Kate.

He swigged on the coffee, then set aside the dark
blue mug with the gold Dundee emblem. "Exactly
where are we going?"

"South," Kate replied.

"Could you be more specific?"

"The deep South."

"Why all the secrecy? It's just a child abduction
case, isn't it? Nothing hush-hush."

"Yes."

An odd sensation hit him in the gut. Kate had
rushed him around so much at his apartment, assuring
him she'd give him all the info on their plane trip,
that he hadn't actually thought things through. But
something didn't feel right about this whole thing.

"We're working on the case as partners," he said.
"That means I need to know everything you know."

"Right."

"So fill me in."

"Okay, but I need to tell you things from the beginning. Or at least my beginning."

He nodded.

"Daisy got in touch with me this morning as soon
as she arrived at Dundee. A woman named Haley
Wilson had phoned her and asked specifically for me.
I returned Ms. Wilson's call because she had told

Daisy that we had a mutual acquaintance whose infant son had been kidnapped.''

''So this is personal for you?''

''In a way, but...''

Kate stared at him with a peculiar look of concern in her eyes, and Frank's gut tightened painfully. ''But what?''

''Ah, hell, Frank, there's no easy way to say this.''

''So, say it, will you?''

''The mutual acquaintance is Dr. Lurleen Patton.''

Although he'd thought about her, dreamed about her, cursed her for nearly destroying his love life, no one had mentioned her name in eleven months. ''Leenie?''

''Yes, Leenie.''

It took him a full minute to wrap his mind around the idea that Leenie had an infant son. ''Leenie has a baby?''

''A little boy.''

''How old?''

''Two months.''

He did the math quickly, but even before adding up eleven months since he'd been with Leenie, he'd known the truth. ''The baby's mine.''

''Yes.''

Then reality sucker punched him. ''Leenie's baby has been kidnapped?''

''Yesterday afternoon. Someone crashed their vehicle into the nanny's car. The nanny was injured, but she'll live. The woman who caused the wreck stole the baby from his car seat.''

''It is my baby, right?'' How was it possible? he asked himself. Yes, he and Leenie had had sex. Repeatedly. But not once had he forgotten to use a condom.

"The lady who called me, this Haley Wilson, is Leenie's best friend and she says the baby is definitely yours."

"Why the hell didn't she—God, Kate, I'm a father."

She reached out and put her hand on his shoulder, then squeezed. "Ms. Wilson said that Leenie is trying very hard to be strong and brave, but she's falling apart. She needs you."

"She needs me now. What about when she first found out she was pregnant? Or when the baby was born?" Frank growled the questions, outrage bringing his blood to a boil.

"And even now, with our child abducted, she's not the one who called and asked for me. Damn her!"

Leenie showered and changed clothes around noon, and at Haley's insistence lay down on the bed. She'd been staring up at the ceiling for the past hour. How could she sleep when she had no idea where Andrew was or what had happened to him? Didn't anyone understand that she was slowly going out of her mind? Although she'd tried to convince herself that it was only a matter of time before the FBI found her baby and brought him home to her, she hadn't been able to escape the wide-awake nightmares that plagued her. What if Andrew had been killed, maybe even tortured?

Keening mournfully, Leenie wrapped her arms around herself and rolled over in the bed. *Oh, God, please take care of Andrew. Don't let anyone hurt him.* Tears gathered in her eyes. She swallowed hard.

A sharp knock on the bedroom door gained her immediate attention. She sat straight up. "Yes?"

"Leenie, there's someone here to see you," Haley said through the closed door.

"I don't want to see anyone. Please tell whoever it is that—"

The door flew open. Frank Latimer stormed into her bedroom. Frank? Frank! What was he doing here? How had he found out about—?

He marched across the room to the bed, reached down, grabbed her by the arm and yanked her to her feet. They stood there staring at each other. Leenie's heartbeat accelerated at an alarming speed.

"Why the hell didn't you let me know I had a son?" he demanded.

Leenie trembled from head to toe, but she kept her gaze locked with his. "How did you—who told you about Andrew?"

"I did." Haley stepped into the bedroom, Kate Malone directly behind her. "Well, actually, I spoke to Ms. Malone and she told him about Andrew and what had happened."

"Leenie, we're here to help," Kate said. "You have all of Dundee's resources and manpower at your service. We're going to work with Moran…with the FBI to find your little boy." Kate came over and grasped Frank's arm. "And despite his less than pleasant greeting, Frank is here to help you." She shook his arm. "Aren't you, Frank?"

He broke eye contact with Leenie long enough to confront Kate. "How about you two let me talk to Leenie alone, without an audience."

"Is that all right with you?" Haley asked Leenie. She nodded.

Haley glared at Frank. "I'm the one responsible for your knowing about Andrew. Don't make me regret what I did." She hurriedly left the room.

After letting go of his arm, Kate hesitated. "The absolute worst thing that can happen when a child is kidnapped is for her—or his—parents to blame each other and be at each other's throats. What Leenie needs right now, Frank, is your understanding and your support."

He didn't reply, but he released his tenacious hold on Leenie's arm. Kate gave him a warning glare before leaving them alone. For several minutes the silence between them pulsated throughout the bedroom. A bedroom in which they had made mad, passionate love on more than one occasion. She couldn't help remembering and her body warmed as those luscious memories encompassed her. Frank's hard body pressing her into the mattress as he plunged into her. The feel of his strong arms holding her. His moist lips on hers, at her breasts. His fingers caressing, probing, tantalizing. For a millisecond she stopped breathing.

"I spoke to Dante Moran…briefly," Frank said, his voice tight and controlled. "The local police found the vehicle that crashed into your nanny's car. It was abandoned outside of town. Naturally there was no sign of the baby. Our baby."

"His name is Andrew," Leenie said.

He clenched his jaw, then said, "My middle name."

She nodded. "Andrew Latimer Patton."

Frank huffed, then frowned and shifted his shoulders. "Damn, Leenie, why didn't you tell me?"

"I don't know," she said. "Pride maybe. Too proud to ask for your help when I was perfectly capable of taking care of myself and a child without a father. Or maybe I was scared that you'd do the honorable thing and ruin all our lives. I don't know. We weren't even a couple, not really. We had a fling. No strings attached. We used protection. You left and never called or—''

''I thought about calling,'' he told her.

Had he? she wondered. She wanted to believe him, but it really didn't matter. He might have thought about it, but he hadn't called. Not once in nearly a year. ''Admit it, Frank, if Haley hadn't called Kate and you didn't know about Andrew, you'd never have gotten in touch with me.''

''We can't know that for sure, can we? Besides, that's a moot point now anyway.''

''Actually my not telling you about your child is a moot point.'' She wanted to touch Frank, to put her arms around him and beg him to hold her. ''Until we find Andrew, nothing else matters.''

''You're right. Finding our son is our only concern. Everything else can be sorted out later, once we bring him home.''

''For what it's worth…'' she paused and looked right at Frank ''…I'm glad you're here.''

Three

Frank had left Leenie in her bedroom and gone through the house, out the back door and onto the porch. For late November, it was unseasonably warm. Probably somewhere in the high sixties and not a rain cloud in the sky. He'd gotten away from Leenie as fast as he could because he'd sensed that she had wanted him to put his arms around her and hold her. But he hadn't. He couldn't. And not just because he was angry with her, that a part of him wanted to wring that long, smooth neck of hers for keeping his son a secret from him. He knew that if he touched her, she'd work that crazy magic spell on him and make him want to stay with her, hold on to her, make love to her and never let her go. When he'd left Maysville eleven months ago after his assignment ended, he'd sworn he'd never look back. The way Leenie turned him inside out had scared the hell out of him. He'd decided a long time ago that no woman was ever again going to do a number on him. No way was he going to let Leenie twist him around her little finger.

Yeah, well, Frank old buddy, maybe Leenie knew exactly how you felt. It wasn't as if he'd made a big secret of not wanting anything beyond a brief affair. He had told her he was not the type of guy for a committed relationship. Is it any wonder that when she found out she was pregnant, she didn't pick up the phone and call him? She probably had serious doubts he'd be thrilled to hear he was a father-to-be.

Okay, so maybe he had to accept part of the blame. Maybe he shouldn't take all his anger out on her.

The last time Frank had allowed anything to tear him apart inside had been twelve years ago when he'd walked in on his wife in bed with another man. They'd been married for two years and he'd been fool enough to think they were happy. He had been happy. Apparently Rita hadn't been. She'd decided she wanted more than Frank could give her and zeroed in on her married boss, a guy twice her age. Even now, after all these years, Frank could still remember how it felt seeing their naked bodies writhing on the bed. His bed, the one he'd slept in every night with Rita. And he could almost feel the power in the repeated punches he'd inflicted on Rodney Klyce. He'd beaten the hell out of the guy, but Klyce hadn't pressed charges. He'd wanted the whole thing kept quite because of his wife. But before Frank had packed his bags and left town, he'd called Mrs. Klyce. A bitter, vengeful thing to have done, but he'd never regretted it. He'd later heard she'd divorced Klyce and taken him for half his net worth. He'd also heard that Rita married Klyce, then divorced him a few years later and moved on to greener pastures. By now she'd probably gone through half a dozen husbands, and he could truthfully say he didn't give a damn.

He'd been a fool about Rita, a brown-eyed beauty with flaming red hair. She'd made him forget all about his solemn vow to never marry, to never repeat his parents' mistake. Their battle royale divorce when he was twelve should have proven to him how easily love can turn to hate and that eventually hate evolved into apathy. But learning that lesson a second time— firsthand—had seared it into both his conscious and subconscious. Love affairs were okay. Love was not. After Rita, he'd shut himself off from anything other than lust and sex. He'd thought that was all it had been with Leenie. Even when he'd realized he couldn't get her out of his mind, couldn't forget her, he'd halfway convinced himself that what he really couldn't forget was the fantastic sex.

You don't love her, he told himself. *You aren't capable of love.*

But the fact that he'd gotten her pregnant and she'd given birth to his child bonded them forever, marriage or no marriage. He had a son. A two-month-old son.

Frank cursed under his breath, then pounded his fist against the doorframe. He'd never given fatherhood a thought. When he'd sworn off love and marriage, naturally he'd assumed there wouldn't be any kids in his future and that had been fine with him. He was forty damn years old. Too old to become a first-time father.

The more he thought about the situation, the more he came to realize why Leenie hadn't told him about Andrew. If he'd been Leenie, he wouldn't have called him with the news. He was lousy father material. He needed to talk to her, apologize for acting like a jerk.

The woman had been traumatized enough by her baby's kidnapping and all he'd done was add to that trauma.

Just as he reached out to open the back door, Kate and Moran came outside onto the porch. He could tell by their expressions that the news wasn't good.

"What's happened?" Frank asked.

"Nothing new," Kate said. "But Dante has some information he's willing to share with you, not as Andrew's father, but as a Dundee agent who has certain government clearances and is deemed totally trustworthy."

"Cut the crap and lay it on the line," Frank told her.

"It's good news and bad news," she said.

"We're fairly certain we know who kidnapped your son," Special Agent Moran said.

"What?" Frank glared at Moran.

"Not the name of a person, but an organization," Kate said. "The good news is that the FBI is reasonably certain the woman who stole Andrew isn't some nutcase who'll kill him or keep him for herself."

"And just what makes the Feds so certain?" He looked to Moran for the answer.

"We unearthed information about an infant abduction ring several years ago," Moran said. "We're not sure how long it's been in operation, but we suspect at least ten years. We're on the verge of setting up a sting operation that will lead us right to the top, to the people making big money by stealing Caucasian babies and selling them to unsuspecting couples who'll gladly pay a hundred thousand or more for a cuddly blue-eyed, blond-haired baby."

"Hell. Are you telling me that you think Andrew was stolen by this baby abduction ring?"

"The odds are pretty high that he'll soon be sold to the highest bidder."

"Son of a bitch." Frank glowered at Kate. "And this is the good news?"

"At least there's a good chance they'll take care of him because he's worth a great deal of money to them."

In desperation Frank said, "What if we run an ad in the paper offering more than a hundred grand for Andrew's safe return?"

"These people aren't going to take any chances on getting caught," Moran said. "Selling these kids to adoptive parents is easy money because it's safe. The people who adopt these babies aren't going to ask too many questions about where their baby came from, now are they?"

"How close are you guys to nabbing them?"

"You know I can't tell you the details." Moran felt in his coat pocket, then patted his shirt pocket before letting his hand fall to his side. "I quit smoking nearly a year ago, but I can't kick the habit of reaching for one now and again."

"How close?" Frank repeated.

"Close."

"I want in on the sting."

"You know that's not possible."

"Who are these people and where do we find them?" Frank caught the sidelong glances Kate and Moran exchanged. "There's a good chance Andrew will be the next baby up on the auction block, so why not send me and Kate in as prospective parents?"

"We've got federal agents who can do that. Besides, you're the kidnapped boy's father. You're too close to this to—"

Frank grabbed Moran by his lapels and hauled him close so that they were eye-to-eye.

"If it were your kid, what would you do?"

Moran, cool as a cucumber, looked directly at Frank and said, "I'd want to go in myself and get my child and then I'd want to kill every bastard involved in the abduction ring…kill them with my bare hands."

Frank loosened his hold on Moran's suit, then released the lapels and took a deep breath. "And some stupid federal agent would stop you."

Moran's lips twitched with a hint of a smile. "You know it."

"How much can I tell Leenie?" Frank asked.

"Tell her about the abduction ring and our suspicions that Andrew was stolen by these slimeballs, but that's it. If and when we make a move, you can tell her afterward, hopefully when we bring her son home to her."

"She'll be mad as hell at all of us," Frank said.

"After the way you treated her in there, I'd say she's already mad as hell at you," Kate told him. "Maybe you should go back inside and talk to her, even apologize."

"Maybe you're right."

Kate smiled. "Could be there's hope for you yet, Latimer."

Leenie ran a comb through her hair, then opened her jewelry case and removed a pair of gold and diamond earrings. She'd been wearing these the first time she'd seen Frank. He'd come into WJMM as part

of the Dundee team sent to Maysville to protect Elsa
Leone against death threats nearly a year ago. He and
Kate had been the investigative team and they'd set
up shop in Elsa's office in the WJMM studio complex. The minute she'd met Frank, she'd wanted him.
And she'd had him in record time. She had thought
he'd be her first one-night stand; instead their encounter had turned out to be the first time she'd ever
had sex with someone she'd just met, someone little
more than a stranger. But with Frank it had seemed
right not to wait. The sex had been incredible. They'd
set the sheets on fire and sent off skyrockets. And the
more they had sex, the more they'd wanted it. They
couldn't get enough of each other.

Leenie slipped the earrings on, then slid her fingers
down the side of her neck, remembering the feel of
Frank's big, rough fingers caressing her.

While she stood staring at herself in the mirror, her
eyes glazed over with memories, Haley came in and
walked up behind her. "You haven't eaten enough to
keep a bird alive. Why don't you let me make you a
sandwich."

"Food won't help," Leenie said. "I feel as if I eat
a bite, I'll throw it up."

"How did things go with Frank?"

"You don't want to know."

"What did he do?"

"He hates me." Leenie sighed. "And I can't blame
him. He had every right to know about his son. He
doesn't understand why I didn't tell him I was pregnant."

A deep male voice said, "Yes, he does understand."

Leenie gasped when she saw Frank's reflection in

the mirror. Haley turned around and gave him a withering glare as she moved past him toward the door.

Haley paused, glanced over her shoulder and said, "See if you can get her to eat something. And if you say or do anything to upset her, you'll answer to me."

The minute Haley closed the door, Frank came up behind Leenie. Her breath caught in her throat. A part of her still wanted his arms around her; another part of her wanted to tell him to go away and leave her alone. She simply stood there, those stupid diamond earrings glimmering in the fading late afternoon sunlight coming through the sheer window curtains. Why had she put on these earrings? Had she thought he'd actually remember her wearing them?

"I'm sorry," he said.

She looked at his reflection in the mirror and plainly saw the sincerity of his words in the expression on his face. And in his eyes. Those stormy-sea gray eyes that spoke volumes.

Emotion tightened her throat. She couldn't speak, so she nodded.

He touched her then. Those big, hard hands tenderly clutched her shoulders. *Don't fall apart,* she told herself. *Don't crumble and fall into his arms. He's not here for you. He came because of Andrew.*

"I know you had your reasons for not telling me you were pregnant," he said. "You probably figured I wouldn't relish the news of impending fatherhood."

She inhaled deeply and exhaled slowly.

His hands tightened ever so slightly on her shoulders. "After the way we ended things, you had no reason to think I'd want to be a part of Andrew's life."

"I should have told you," she finally managed to say.

"It doesn't matter now. Finding Andrew and bringing him home is what matters. And I swear to you, Leenie, I'll move heaven and earth to do that."

She swallowed the tears choking her. Of its own accord her body swayed backward toward his and the minute it did, he slid his hands downward from her shoulders and wrapped his arms around her. Her back pressed against his chest and for the first time since Andrew had been kidnapped, she felt a sense of hope. Crazy as the notion was, her heart believed that Frank could keep his promise to bring their baby home to her.

"I love him so," she said. "He's everything… to…me." Her shaky voice grew softer with each word as she tried in vain to keep from crying. "At first I couldn't…cry. Now I—I can't…seem…to stop…crying."

Hugging her comfortingly, he lowered his head and pressed his cheek against her temple. "I wish I could cry. God knows I feel like it."

Startled by his comment, she stiffened in his arms. Frank Latimer crying? She couldn't imagine it. Was he saying that he cared about Andrew, even loved him? Was it possible that he was actually pleased about having a son? Or was his reaction strictly impersonal, the kind any normal person would have after learning a two-month-old baby had been kidnapped?

"I know what you're thinking," he said, his voice husky with emotion. "You're wondering what kind of man I am, if I'm pleased to be a father or horrified. You're thinking how dare he care now, after the fact.

Why didn't he call me after he left Maysville nearly a year ago? He's a day late and a dollar short.''

As the tension drained from her body, she allowed his strength to support her. Instinct told her that despite their past history, Frank was a man she could lean on, a man she could count on when the chips were down. And God knew she needed somebody strong right now, someone who felt what she felt—the panic and terror, the excruciating pain. Only Andrew's father could even begin to understand the depth of her feelings.

"How do you feel about having a child?" She avoided looking at his reflection in the mirror. She knew that no matter what he said, his true reaction would show on his face. She'd learned that much about him during their brief interlude. Frank Latimer did not have a poker face.

He turned her in his arms. "Look at me, Leenie."

She lifted her gaze to meet his and saw confusion in his eyes, as well as concern.

"I'm not sure how I feel," he admitted. "I never thought about being a father. I knew, after my divorce, that I'd never get married again. And I'm just old-fashioned enough to think a guy should get married before he fathers a child. I don't have unsafe sex. You know that."

"Condoms aren't foolproof," she told him. "And I wasn't on the pill. Most doctors recommend another form of birth control for women after they turn thirty-five."

"You don't have to explain. We thought we were being careful. Responsible. Accident's happen."

"Is that how you think of Andrew, as an accident?" Heat suffused her face as her temper rose.

"Don't put words in my mouth. All I'm saying is that Andrew's conception was an accident. I just found out today that I'm a father. Give me some time to figure out what I think about having a child. You had nine months of pregnancy and two months with Andrew to figure out how you feel. Did you know immediately when you found out you were pregnant that you wanted the child, that you loved him?"

Well, he had her there. No, of course she hadn't known immediately that she loved and wanted her baby. When she'd read the home pregnancy test, she'd panicked. And when the doctor had confirmed her condition, she'd stayed in a state of shock for days. She had even considered an abortion. But only for about two minutes.

"You're right. I was being unfair putting you on the spot that way."

He cupped her face with his hands. "I do know this—I care about Andrew. And I'll do whatever it takes to bring our son home to you. Once he's back in your arms, we'll figure out where to go from there."

"Fair enough." She swallowed fresh tears.

"I realize we're little more than strangers to each other. We had a whirlwind love affair and we spent most of our time making love, not getting acquainted."

She nodded.

"I'd like to learn more about Andrew, if you're willing to talk to me about him. It might help you. Hell, it might help both of us. But if you'd rather not, it's okay."

She pulled away from Frank, walked across the room and picked up the most recent photograph of her baby. "This was taken a few weeks ago. It's a picture of him I took with my digital camera. I enlarged it and framed it." She held it out to Frank.

He didn't move for a couple of minutes, as if he were afraid of the picture. Was he wondering how his first glimpse of his son would affect him?

"He's asleep in this picture, so you can't see his eyes." She moved toward Frank, the framed photograph in her hand. "He has blue eyes, like mine. And blond hair. Not much hair, mostly just baby-fine fluff." *He has your mouth, your chin and your hands and feet,* she wanted to say, but didn't. "He's big for his age. He weighed nine pounds, five ounces, when he was born."

Frank glanced down at the picture, then reached out and took it. He stared at the photo for what seemed like forever, then smiled and said, "He looks like you. Lucky kid."

Leenie clenched her teeth to keep from crying.

"I guess he'll grow up to be tall, huh, since I'm six-three and you're—what?—five-nine or ten." Frank looked at her.

She nodded. "He has big hands and big feet. Long toes and long fingers." She cast her gaze on Frank's hand holding the frame.

"Like me." He looked at Andrew's picture again, then handed it back to Leenie.

She placed the frame on the bedside table and slumped down on the edge of the bed. When she turned back to Frank, she noticed he was headed toward the door. *Don't leave me,* she wanted to cry, *please don't leave me.*

He glanced back at her. "I need to get my bag out

of the rental car. I'm going to stay here with you until we find Andrew, if that's all right.''

Her heart soared. ''Yes. Yes, it's all right with me.''

He offered her a forced smile, then opened the door.

''Thank you,'' she called.

He paused momentarily, but didn't turn or speak; then he left.

When Frank brought his bag in, Haley Wilson stopped him in the foyer. ''Are you planning on staying?''

''Yeah.''

''Good.''

''Look, Ms. Wilson, if you have something to say to me, just say it.''

''All right. Leenie is one of the strongest, most independent women I know. But she's vulnerable right now. Her whole life is hanging in the balance because Andrew *is* her life. I don't know if you can understand that, but as a mother myself, I do. So, no matter what your own feelings are or how you plan to deal with things when y'all get Andrew back, right now, Leenie needs you. She needs your support and your comfort.''

''I agree.''

Haley stared at him, a puzzled expression on her face. ''She hasn't slept since the night before last and she hasn't eaten since lunch yesterday. I've gotten her to drink a little tea, but that's all. Do you think you could get her to eat?''

''Is there any cheesecake in the house?'' Frank

asked, remembering how they had devoured cheese-cake at dawn, after a marathon lovemaking session.

Haley cocked her head sideways and smiled. "You do know a little something about her, don't you? As for the cheesecake—I had my husband stop by the bakery and drop one by here a little while ago."

Frank dumped his bag in the corner of the foyer. "I'll take her a piece and make sure she eats it." He looked directly at Leenie's friend. "I'm going to take care of her. I promise."

This woman had no way of knowing that Frank Latimer didn't make promises easily, that when he made one, he kept it.

Five minutes later, Frank entered Leenie's bed-room. He carried two slices of cheesecake and two cups of hot tea on a tray. Leenie glanced up at him from where she still sat on the edge of the bed. She clutched a damp, wrinkled handkerchief in her hand.

"Snack time." He walked over, placed the tray on the bed and sat beside her. "Cheesecake and hot tea. Remember?"

"Yes, I remember, but I'm surprised that you do."

He lifted one plate and fork and handed them to her. "Eat up."

"Frank, I'm not—"

"Eat." He picked up the other plate, sliced off a large chunk of cheesecake and slid it into his mouth. After chewing and swallowing, he sighed dramatically. "Nothing better than cheesecake, except—"

"Sex," she finished his sentence.

Grinning, he took a second bite before placing his plate back on the tray. He eased his hand under her hand to support her plate, then lifted her fork and cut off a piece of the cheesecake and lifted it to her mouth. She parted her lips; he slid the cheesecake into her mouth. As soon as she finished one bite, he gave her another, and then another—slowly, patiently—until three-fourths of her slice was gone.

"I can't eat anymore," she told him.

He set her plate on the tray, then handed her the tea. While she sipped the tea, he drank his, watching her all the while. After she drained her cup, he removed the tray from the bed and placed it on the floor.

Leenie was dead on her feet, worn out from lack of sleep and the stress of not knowing where Andrew was or if he was all right. Frank realized she needed more than cheesecake and tea. She needed to rest. He scooted up in her bed until his back hit the headboard, then he reached out, grasped Leenie's hand and tugged on it urging her to join him. They sat side-by-side in her bed, their backs resting against the headboard. Frank put his arm around her shoulders and cuddled her against him.

"Would you believe I had blond hair and blue eyes when I was a baby?" he said.

"What?" Turning her head sideways, she glanced over at him.

"I had blond hair and blue eyes like Andrew. So his eyes could turn gray later on and his hair might not stay blond like yours."

She laid her head on his shoulder. "I was bald when I was born. Well, actually, I think I had some white fuzz, but it wasn't much. I have a couple of baby pictures that a distant relative sent me when I contacted her after I grew up and started searching for any family I might have."

"That's right. You grew up in foster homes, didn't you?"

"Uh-huh. After my parents died, I got shuffled from one foster home to another, until I was fifteen and wound up with Debra and Jerry Schmale."

"Debra? The same Debra who's Andrew's nanny?"

"That's right." Leenie yawned.

"How's she doing after her surgery?"

"I spoke to her doctor earlier today and he said she should be able to go into a private room tomorrow. Debra's a wonderful person, the only real mother-figure I ever had that I can remember. My own mother died when I was four and I can barely remember her."

"I grew up in a fairly conventional family. Mom, dad and an older sister. Then when I was twelve my parents divorced. Ripped us to shreds. My sister went with Mom and I lived with Dad."

"It must have been difficult for you."

"Pure hell. You see, my mother had taken a lover and my father wanted to make her pay for her sins." Frank glanced at Leenie, her eyes shut, her lips slightly parted, her breathing soft and even.

"Did you hate your mother after that?" Leenie asked, her voice hushed.

"Yeah, I hated her for a long, long time, but that's all in the past now," Frank said, looking at the way Leenie's eyelids closed and realizing what she needed was sleep. He moved on to more mundane topics and Leenie melted against him as she began drifting off to sleep. He kept talking quietly until he knew she was fast asleep, then he eased her down into the bed so that her head rested in his lap. He pulled the folded quilt at the foot of the bed up and over her. While she slept, he watched her. Drank his fill of her.

He admitted to himself that he'd missed Leenie while they'd been apart. He'd missed seeing her, talking to her, having sex with her. She was the first woman since Rita who'd stirred something inside him other than lust.

But you don't love her, Frank told himself. *She's special. She's the mother of your child. But you do not love her.*

He caressed her hair and the side of her face tenderly. "Get some rest, Slim. I'm here now. You won't have to go through this alone."

Four

Andrew dangled helpless over the deep, dark well, a large hand holding him by the nape of his tiny neck. The hand loosened its grip and released the baby. His frightened cries echoed in the blackness as he fell down, down, down. God, no…no…no! Leenie tried to reach out and grab her son, but her efforts were useless. All she could do was scream in terror.

"Leenie…Leenie…wake up."

Strong masculine hands grasped her shoulders and shook her gently. She tried to fight him, fear spiraling through her alarmingly.

"Slim, it's me—Frank. Wake up. You were having a nightmare."

She opened her eyes suddenly and stared into Frank Latimer's concerned gray eyes.

"Oh, Frank, it was awful. Someone dropped Andrew into a deep well. He was crying...crying for me.''

Frank pulled her up off the bed and into his arms, his strength enveloping her. She clung to him, her mind and nerves rioting. ''It was just a bad dream,'' he told her.

''I know.'' She burrowed her head against his shoulder and closed her eyes. ''But he's out there— lost.'' She lifted her head and stared at Frank. ''We have to find him. Please, tell me that we can save him. Make me believe that he's not lost to me forever.''

Frank brushed loose strands of hair out of her face. His hand lingered, his fingertips caressed. And then he withdrew. She felt the emotional withdrawal as keenly as the physical release. He eased out of bed, his back to her, and said nothing for several awkward minutes.

''Frank?''

''I'll do everything I can, but...'' He turned halfway toward her, his jaw tense, his gaze unfocused as he glared off into nothingness. ''I don't make promises I can't keep. I've already sworn to you that I would move heaven and earth to bring Andrew home, and I meant it. I'll do everything humanly possible. But the honest truth is that even though I'd do anything to rescue Andrew, I can't promise you that I can bring him back to you safe and sound.''

Her heart lurched, then sank. This wasn't what she'd wanted to hear. She had thought he would reinforce his earlier vow to rescue Andrew and had longed to hear him say those comforting words. Even knowing Frank wasn't a miracle worker, she believed in him. He was her last best hope.

"What time is it?" she asked, needing the mundane to keep her sane, to take her mind out of the horrific abyss that sucked her in and kept repeating terrifying mental images of her baby's death.

Frank glanced at his wristwatch. "Nearly four-thirty."

"I slept quite a while." As she stretched, every muscle in her body cried from the tension that had played havoc on her physically, mentally and emotionally.

"You needed the rest. Your friend Haley said you haven't slept since Andrew's abduction." Frank glanced at the stacked empty dishes on the tray. "You should try to eat some supper later on."

"You're beginning to sound like a mother hen—telling me to rest and to eat."

"It's the training," he told her. "Part of the regimen for looking after someone is making sure they take care of themselves. A Dundee agent is an all-around bodyguard. He or she tries to not only protect the client, but see to their well-being."

"And am I a client? Is that how you think of me now?"

"You're putting words in my mouth again, Slim."

"I'm only interpreting what I hear you say."

"You're misinterpreting," he said. "And you're being argumentative. Why? Are you angry with me for some reason?"

Was she angry with him? Yes. No. Maybe.

Leenie got out of bed, rubbed the back of her sore neck and slipped on her shoes. Had Frank taken her shoes off after she'd fallen asleep? More of his all-around bodyguard duties? Was that it—the reason she suddenly felt so hostile toward him? Because he'd acted as if his kindness to her wasn't anything personal?

"I'm angry with the world right now," she admitted. "Besides, I believe that should be my question, not yours. After all, you're the one who has every right to be angry and upset with me for keeping Andrew's existence a secret from you."

He shot her a quick glance, then looked away before he replied, "I told you before that now is not the time for us to be at cross purposes, that once Andrew is safely home will be time enough to—"

"To what? For you to tell me what you really think, how you really feel?"

"I don't know how I feel. I don't want to dig too deep right now." He looked at her. "You're hurting enough for both of us. I need to stay as detached and as unemotional as possible."

"Can you do that? Can you be unemotional when it comes to Andrew?"

Could he actually remain detached where his own child was concerned? If so, then he certainly wasn't the man she'd thought he was. But then again, she didn't really know Frank Latimer. He was a stranger with whom she'd had a passionate fling. She knew without a doubt that he was an incredible lover. Considerate. Attentive. She knew he liked his coffee black, his whiskey straight and his loving frequent. But beyond the obvious, she knew nothing, except what little he'd told her today. And the same held true for him—he didn't know who the real Lurleen Patton was.

When the silence between them became more than she could bear, she said, "Can't you answer me?"

"What do you want me to say? Yes, I care about

my son. I'm not a heartless bastard. But for God's sake, Leenie, I haven't even seen him or touched him or held him. And I've known that I'm a father for only a few hours.''

''I'm sorry. I—''

''No, I'm sorry,'' he told her. ''Sorry I can't say whatever it is you need for me to say. But the more unemotional and detached I can be, the clearer my thinking, the more logical I'll act and react. Don't you see—''

''I see. I see a man who's afraid to feel. You don't want to love Andrew. You don't want to love anybody because sometimes love hurts.''

Clenching her teeth in an effort not to burst into fresh tears, Leenie rushed toward the door, wanting to get away from Frank. But he caught up with her just as she reached for the doorknob. He grasped her arm. She stopped and glared at him.

''There it is again,'' he said. ''Anger. You're angry with me. Want to tell me why? I've tried to be honest with you, so how about being honest with me?''

She jerked her arm loose and took a step backward, but she kept her gaze boldly glued to his. ''You want honesty? All right. I kept Andrew a secret from you because I didn't know how you'd react. I was half afraid you'd want to take him away from me and half afraid you'd tell me you didn't give a damn. But your reaction is somewhere in between and I can't figure you out. I feel like a fool for having gotten myself pregnant by a man I don't even know. And a part of me is angry because on some completely stupid female level I needed you to care—really care. Not just about Andrew, but about me. I needed you to *not* be detached and unemotional.''

They stood there staring at each other for several minutes until the silence stretched tautly and the tension mounted.

A solid, repetitive knock on the door snapped the tension and ended the silence.

"Frank?" Kate Malone called.

Frank opened the door. "Yeah, what is it?"

"Moran wants to talk to you and Dr. Patton."

"Has something happened?" Leenie asked.

"No bad news," Kate said. "He just wants to go over some things with y'all."

Frank held the door open while Leenie walked into the hall and joined Kate, then he followed behind them, down the hall and into the living room. Only Dante Moran occupied the room, which made Leenie wonder where the other FBI agents were and if Haley was still here.

"Come on in," Moran said. "Please. We need to talk."

"Is Haley—?"

"Mrs. Wilson went home," Kate replied. "She said if you need her, to call her. The house was getting a little crowded, what with two Dundee agents and several FBI agents."

"Where are the other agents?" Leenie asked.

"From here on out, they'll work in shifts. We have your phone tapped and we're fully prepared to act at a moment's notice," Moran said. "The crucial first twenty-four hours has ended." When Leenie stared at him quizzically, he continued. "If the kidnapper is going to demand a ransom, the family usually hears something within the first twenty-four hours."

Kate answered Leenie's next question before she asked it. "Which means that more than likely Andrew was not kidnapped for ransom money, but for another reason.''

"How will we know if the woman who stole him kept him, that she wanted him for herself?'' Wasn't that the best case scenario for a kidnapping? Leenie wondered.

"We can't know for sure.'' Moran cut a sideways glance at Frank. "Did you tell her about the abduction ring?''

"What abduction ring?'' Leenie's heart skipped a beat.

Frank shook his head. "I didn't get a chance to tell her.''

"What abduction ring?'' Leenie repeated her question.

"The bureau is aware that there is an infant abduction ring operating in the South and it is possible that your baby was taken in order to sell him,'' Moran told her.

"Sell him? You mean—''

"Sell him to people who desperately want to adopt a child,'' Kate explained. "Unfortunately there is a shortage of white infants and some people are willing to pay an exorbitant amount in order to procure a child through any means necessary.''

"They're willing to buy a child that's been stolen from a loving home?'' Leenie looked from Kate to Moran, but she couldn't bring herself to make eye contact with Frank.

"In all fairness, these people are told that the children have been willingly given up by parents who don't want them and these adoptive parents want a child so much that they kid themselves into believing whatever they need to believe.'' Kate put her hand on Leenie's shoulder. "Don't give up hope. Don't ever give up hope."

Having noted a peculiar tone in Kate's voice, Leenie studied her for several moments. The two women exchanged silent confidences and unspoken pain. Without truly understanding, Leenie knew that at some time in her life Kate Malone had suffered an intolerable loss, perhaps the loss of a child. She reached up and covered Kate's hand with her own. "I won't give up." She squeezed Kate's hand, then turned to Frank. "From now on, please don't keep anything from me. I'm not some weak, trembling female who can't handle the truth. Yes, I've been crying a great deal and I'm scared out of my mind and I'll gladly lean on anybody who'll let me. But do not treat me as if I'm a child myself. Do I make myself clear?"

Frank glowered at her for a split second. "Yeah. Crystal clear." Looking as if she'd slapped him, Frank darted a glance from Moran to Kate, then grumbled, "I need a breath of fresh air."

"And I need a smoke," Moran said, "but I'll settle for some of that cold fresh air outside."

As soon as the two men disappeared into the kitchen, presumably to go out on the porch or into the backyard, Kate turned to Leenie and offered a comforting smile.

"Cut Frank some slack," Kate advised. "Basically he's a good guy. It's just that discovering he's a father has thrown him for a loop. You may think Andrew's kidnapping isn't as hard on him as it is you, but it probably is. Maybe even more so."

"How do you figure that?"

"Because he's thinking that if—just if, mind you—

Andrew isn't rescued, then he'll never see his son or hold him or get the chance to love him."

"And I have seen him and held him and loved him."

"Look, this is none of my business. Not really." Kate clicked her tongue. "Want some advice from a busybody?"

Leenie wanted to ask Kate the question that hung heavily between them—did you lose a child?—but she didn't ask. "I'm taking my frustration out on Frank, aren't I? And I shouldn't. Isn't that what you were going to say?"

"Something like that." Kate nodded. "Frank's not the enemy."

"Who is the enemy? Someone who might still call and ask for ransom? Some crazy woman who stole my baby for herself? Some maniac who kills babies? Or the money-hungry abduction ring who steals babies and sells them?"

"We don't know which. Not yet."

"When will we know?"

Kate closed her eyes for a millisecond as if she'd suddenly experienced a pain too agonizing to bear, then she took a deep, cleansing breath and replied, "I don't know the answer to that either. We may find out tomorrow. Or next week. Or maybe never." She reached out and grabbed Leenie's shoulders. "But no matter how long it takes, do not give up. Don't ever let anyone convince you to give up."

Before Leenie could respond, Kate released her and walked away, mumbling something about needing to go to the bathroom as she disappeared down the hall.

Leenie sank down into the nearest chair, leaned over, propped her elbows on her knees and cupped her face with her open palms. Sitting there alone, the house eerily quiet, she said one more prayer.

Please, dear God, keep Andrew safe and bring him home to me. Home to me and Frank.

Kate handed Moran a cup of coffee, then poured one for herself and sat down across the kitchen table from him. "Where did Frank go?" she asked.

"For a walk down the street. He said to tell you he'd be back in a little while."

Kate studied Dante Moran, a dark, compellingly handsome man, with danger written all over him. She didn't think she'd ever met such a cool character and she'd known her share of self-confident, powerful men. Her ex-husband had been rich, powerful and arrogant in a way only someone born and bred into wealth and power can be. Most of the time she managed not to think about Trent Winston. Trenton Bayard Winston IV. But this kidnapping case had brought back all the old and painful memories. It was only natural that she'd think about Trent, wasn't it, and wonder how he was doing? She hadn't seen him in nearly eleven years. Not since—

"How's she holding up?" Moran nodded toward the living room.

"Dr. Patton? She's doing okay, considering her child is missing and that child's father is trying to help her and probably saying and doing all the wrong things."

"Men are like that." Moran's lips twitched with a hint of humor.

"Yes, you are. All of you."

"Including your ex?"

"How'd you know— You didn't, did you? Not until I reacted. And before you ask, I do not want to talk about him or about it.''

''It?'' Moran cocked an inquisitive eyebrow.

''It. The divorce. What about you, Moran—got an ex-wife and a less than pleasant divorce you don't want to talk about?''

''No marriages. No divorces.''

''Hmm-mmm.''

''And before you ask—''

''Why is a guy who's decidedly over thirty-five never been married?''

''Yeah, that's the question I don't want you to ask.'' He actually grinned.

''Being a woman, my guess would be either unrequited love and you're still hoping to eventually woo and win her...or you loved and lost and—'' A flicker of something incomprehensible danced in Moran's black eyes, coming and going so quickly that she could have imagined it. But she hadn't. Loved and lost. That was it. Moran's *it* that he couldn't bear to talk about, the way her divorce from Trent was her unbearable *it*.

Moran sipped on his coffee. Kate did the same.

The phone rang and both of them tensed.

He got up and rushed into the living room. Kate quickly followed. Leenie stood by the phone, allowing it to ring, and looked to Moran for direction the minute she saw him. He nodded and motioned for her to answer the phone.

Although Leenie's hand trembled as she lifted the receiver, her voice was steady when she said, ''This is Dr. Lurleen Patton.'' Tears gathered in the corners of her eyes. She gasped, then responded, ''No, thank you, I'm not interested in a free vacation.'' She slammed down the receiver.

Kate released the breath she'd unknowingly been holding. ''It's after five. Why don't I put together some sandwiches for us?''

''I—I'll help you,'' Leenie offered. ''God knows I need something to do. I'm on the verge of losing my mind.''

''Do you need anything from the store?'' Kate asked. ''If you do, I'll give Frank a call on his cell phone and tell him to—''

''Is Frank not back yet?'' Leenie asked.

''Not yet,'' Kate told her.

''Then please call him. I'd like to speak to him.'' Leenie motioned for Kate to come with her into the kitchen.

''You two go ahead,'' Moran said. ''I should check in with headquarters.''

Once they were in the kitchen, Kate dialed Frank's cell number. He answered on the first ring.

''Latimer.''

''Frank, it's Kate.''

''What's up? Anything wrong?''

''Nothing new. But Leenie wants to talk to you.''

''She does?''

''Yes, she does.'' Kate held out the phone to Leenie.

She grasped the phone, inhaled and exhaled then said, ''Kate and I are going to make sandwiches for supper. They should be ready in about fifteen minutes. Would you please come home and eat with us. Afterward, I want to show you Andrew's photo album and if you'd like to know more about him, I want to tell you about your son.''

Kate turned her head and willed herself not to cry. It had been ages since she'd shed a tear. At one time she had thought she'd cried herself dry, that there were no more tears left in her. But every once in a while something happened—usually a case involving a kidnapped child—that stirred long dead emotions within her. Years ago when she'd been a rookie cop on the Atlanta P.D., she'd worked with Ellen Denby and marveled at how the woman could keep a cool head and deal with the toughest cases involving children. But as the years went by and she and Ellen had exchanged confidences, she had learned that they shared a similarly tragic experience which enabled them to understand each other in a way no one else could. Just as Kate understood Leenie as only a mother who'd also had a child stolen from her could understand.

Kate offered to clear up the dishes and surprisingly Moran stayed in the kitchen to help her. Leenie felt as if she'd made a new friend in Kate and understood on an unspoken level that perhaps Kate had suffered once just as she suffered now. She realized she could be wrong about Kate, but her feminine intuition—her gut instincts—told her she was right. Sometime in her past, Kate Malone had lost a child.

Frank had been awfully quiet while they ate sandwiches, chips and cheesecake. She couldn't remember the last time she'd eaten cheesecake twice in one day. Oh yes she did remember—it had been the last time she'd made love with Frank. They'd had cheesecake for breakfast and again for lunch.

Alone together in the living room, Frank and she sat side by side on the sofa while she opened Andrew's baby book, filled with photographs and memorabilia from her pregnancy and Andrew's first two months of life. When Frank made no effort to close the gap between their bodies—the two feet that separated them—she took the initiative and scooted up next to him, hip-to-hip. He flinched, then stiffened. What was wrong with him? She wasn't going to attack him, for pity's sake. She laid the book in her lap and flipped it open so the other side dropped down on his thigh.

"Here's a picture of me at my baby shower," Leenie said. "Elsa came back to Maysville to help Haley host the event."

Frank glanced at the picture, but said nothing.

"I was big as a barrel there. I gained thirty pounds."

"Elsa and Rafe knew you were pregnant?"

"Yes, they knew. And before you get all huffy at Rafe, Elsa threatened him with divorce if he called and told you. She tried to talk me into getting in touch with you, but once she realized she couldn't persuade me, she promised me that neither she nor Rafe would call you because it wasn't their place to tell you."

"You're right. It was your place."

"I thought we'd already agreed that I made a mistake in not informing you I was pregnant with your child. Do we have to continue beating a dead horse?"

Frank glanced at the photo again. "You look happy."

"I was happy." She tried to smile. "Fat and happy."

"You were beautiful pregnant. Fat and beautiful." He grinned, but didn't make eye contact.

"I got even fatter," she told him. "I was only

seven and a half months in that picture.'' She flipped through the pages, slowing on each page long enough for him to glance at it. When she reached the page with Andrew's birth announcement and the first photo of him taken at the hospital, Frank clamped the page open with his big hand.

''Were you alone when he was born or did—''

''Haley was with me.''

''I should have been with you.''

''Yes. And it's my fault you weren't.''

''No, it was only partly your fault. And it was partly my own damn fault.''

''Well, at least we can agree on something—that there's enough blame to share.''

When Leenie heard a phone ring, she tensed. It had to be either Kate's or Moran's cell phone since the ringing came from the kitchen and it wasn't her private line.

''It's not necessarily bad news,'' Frank told her.

''I know. It's just that I—''

The kitchen door swung open; Kate walked in and looked right at Frank. ''Moran wants to see you in the kitchen for a minute.''

''What's wrong?'' Leenie asked. ''And don't tell me it's nothing. I can sense something has happened.''

''You're right,'' Kate admitted, then called into the kitchen. ''We're telling them both, Moran. Leenie needs to know, too. Right now.''

Oh, God, what was it? What had happened?

Moran came out of the kitchen and stood in the open doorway. He glanced from Frank to Leenie, shuffled his feet and said, ''I got a call from Chief Bibb.''

"And?" Frank asked.

Moran hesitated. "They…er…they found a body."

Leenie gasped. Frank put his arm around her waist and held her.

"A baby?" Frank asked.

"Yes. An infant. A boy. Age estimated at one to three months."

"Oh, God, no!" Leenie screamed and suddenly everything went black.

Five

Frank wasn't the type of man easily affected by a woman's tears, swooning spells or temper tantrums. He'd seen it all as a kid—watching his mother, who'd been an expert in feminine wiles, manipulate his father time and again. And he'd learned from that very same father how to harden his heart and shut off his emotions. The only time he'd ever let his defenses down had been with Rita. Bad mistake. Not one he'd repeated. But damn it, catching Leenie in his arms when she fainted dead away had stirred up some unwanted emotions inside him. She wasn't playing him, wasn't putting on an act in an effort to control him. Her actions were real, brought on by true and honest feelings. All he'd wanted to do at that moment was hold and comfort her, protect her from the ugly truth and reassure her that she wasn't alone. And here they were an hour later at the police morgue and still all he wanted to do was protect her, take care of her, shield her from more pain. Already this woman—the mother of his child—had somehow managed to sneak past his defenses and make him vulnerable. He hated feeling vulnerable; it was an alien concept to him.

"You shouldn't have come down here." Chief Bibb cleared his throat as his gaze dropped from Leenie's pale face to the tile floor beneath his feet. "We can get an ID on the body without—"

Leenie gasped quietly. When he felt her stiffen, Frank tightened his grip on her waist. "Andrew's pediatrician or even Haley Wilson could ID the child," Frank said softly. "Why put yourself through this ordeal when it might not even be Andrew?"

"Either way, I have to do this," Leenie said.

Frank studied her, noting the tension in her body and the grave expression on her face.

"No, you don't have to do this." If Frank had been given the chance to know his son, a chance to have been a father from the moment Andrew was born, then he could have come on his own to ID the infant's body. He assumed that in most cases such as this, the father was the one who went to the morgue and put himself through hell in order to protect the child's mother. If only he could do that for Leenie. But he couldn't.

"Yes, Frank, I do have to do this," Leenie told him. "If it isn't Andrew, I need to see that for myself. And if it is…if it is, then I'll know he's dead. I won't spend the rest of my life wondering."

"But if it is Andrew, you'll never be able to forget—"

Kate laid her hand on Frank's back. "Don't try to stop her. She has to do this." Kate reached over and patted Leenie's arm. "I understand how you feel. It's worse not knowing one way or the other, holding on to hope when everyone tells you there is none, than it is having to face the certainty of your child's death."

Leenie clenched her teeth tightly, barely containing her overwrought emotions, then nodded agreement to Kate's comment.

"We're ready," Frank told the coroner, a bald, middle-aged doctor named Huggins.

Securing his arm around her waist, Frank walked with Leenie into the cold, dimly lit room. Dr. Huggins, who had preceded them, walked over to the steel table where a white sheet covered the tiny body. Silence permeated every square inch of the area. Frank heard only his own breathing moments before Leenie sighed aloud. He tightened his grip on her hand. She looked at him, fear and uncertainty in her eyes.

"We'll do this together," he told her.

She nodded.

"All right," Frank said to Dr. Huggins.

The coroner removed the sheet, revealing the small, lifeless body. Frank wanted to pull Leenie back, to rush her out of the room and away from the possible heartache facing her. But she forged ahead, then stopped abruptly to gaze down at the infant's discolored corpse.

Leenie's hand flew to her mouth as she gasped loudly. "Oh, God. God!"

Frank's heart lurched to his throat. His pulse accelerated. *No, please, no,* he prayed silently, the plea a gut-level reaction. But he couldn't bring himself to look at the infant.

Leenie gasped for air. "It's not him. It's not Andrew."

Frank had never known such overwhelming relief. It was then—in that unparalleled moment of thankfulness—that he experienced a personal epiphany. Without ever having seen or held his child, he knew he loved Andrew. And he wanted a chance to be a father to his son.

Kate uttered a loud, gasping sigh. Frank blew out a deep breath. Leenie turned to Frank, a bittersweet smile on her face, and flung herself into his open arms. He held her, stroking her back, comforting her, as she clung to him for dear life. She wept. Only for a few moments. Quietly. But her body trembled uncontrollably long after she stopped crying.

Finally Frank managed to turn her around and head her toward the door. "Let's go home."

She allowed him to escort her from the room and into the outer office where Chief Bibb and Special Agent Moran waited.

"I'll get the car and bring it around to the front door," Kate said as she hurried away.

No one said another word as Frank led Leenie across the room. When they reached the door, she paused and spoke softly to the police chief. "Ryan, when you find out the child's identity, would you please let us know. I—I want to send my condolences to the family."

As long as she lived, she would never forget the image of that tiny infant lying on the cold, steel table. Somewhere out there another mother had lost a child. The only difference between that woman and Leenie was that this other woman had no hope. Her baby boy was dead.

Frank probably didn't understand why she'd pulled away from him the moment they returned to her house or why she'd hurried into the bathroom and locked the door. He had called to her several times, asking her if she was all right and if there was anything he could do for her. But she hadn't responded. Wouldn't. Couldn't. As much as she needed Frank, as desperately as she wanted him close, she had to be alone right now. Alone to cry. Alone to die a thousand deaths in her heart and soul. Alone to work through the wild, mixed emotions she could barely control.

Even before the unknown infant's body had been found, Leenie had felt as if she were on the verge of losing her mind. Although Frank and Kate and Haley had forced her to go through the motions of living, she really didn't feel alive. She felt numb one minute and on fire with terror the next. She wanted to crawl into a hole and die. And at the same time she wanted to run and scream and beat her fists against the wall. It was as if she were dead and alive. Numb and oversensitive. Subdued and crazed. All simultaneously.

After closing the lid, Leenie sat down on the commode and crossed her arms over her chest. She sat there and cried. Soft sobs. A steady stream of tears cascaded down her face. There was an ache inside her that hurt so bad she could barely breathe.

''Oh, Andrew…Andrew.''

Frank lifted his hand to knock on the bathroom door again. He'd knocked several times half an hour ago and pleaded with Leenie to answer him, to let him help her. But when she hadn't responded, he'd finally left her alone. He had talked to Kate for a few minutes, then spent the past twenty minutes alone in his son's nursery. He had run his fingers over the hand-painted mural on the wall—a Noah's Ark scene. The walls were a pale blue, the ceiling covered with fluffy clouds and a host of stuffed animals and infant toys lined the floor-to-ceiling shelves. A magic room for a much-loved baby boy.

"Leave her alone." Kate stood in the doorway to Leenie's bedroom.

Frank whirled around to face Kate. "What?"

"Leave Leenie alone. She'll come out when she's ready. You'll have plenty of time to comfort her then, when she needs you. Right now, she needs to hide away."

He didn't know Kate all that well, but had heard the speculations about her that abounded around the Dundee office. "What makes you the expert?" he asked.

"I'm a woman."

"Okay, if being a woman makes you an expert on all things female, then tell me this—why is it that Leenie pulls me to her with one hand and pushes me away with the other? She's blowing hot and cold. I don't know what she wants."

"Believe me, you men are just as big a puzzle to us as we are to you." Kate motioned for him to come toward her. "Let's wait for Leenie in the living room. Eventually she'll come out and that's when you can play knight in shining armor again. Just wait for the signals. A smart man knows when to advance and when to retreat."

"I'm not smart when it comes to women," Frank

admitted, following Kate down the hall and into the living room. "I'm bad at relationships."

They sat down on the sofa. Kate curled up sideways, her waist and lower back supported by the sofa arm. Frank pressed his shoulders into the back of the couch, then crossed one leg over the other knee.

"Your personal life is none of my business. But if you care about Leenie, and I think you do, then ask yourself just how serious you are about a relationship with her. Don't let her believe she can count on you for the long haul if you're just in this until we find Andrew."

Good advice. Hell, great advice. "What if I don't know how I feel or what I want for the future? For now, I want to bring Andrew home. I want to protect Leenie and support her through this ordeal. But..." He shook his head. "I want to be a father to my son."

Kate looked him right in the eye. "But not a husband to your son's mother?"

"You're not one for being subtle, are you?"

"No. I think there's no use beating around the bush. Right? Let's call a spade a spade. You no doubt have your reasons for being afraid of love, of committed relationships. And whatever those reasons are, I don't want or need to know. But Leenie has a right to know why."

"Maybe Leenie doesn't care," Frank said. "You're assuming she wants something permanent with me. Just because we had a child together and right now she needs me doesn't mean she wants a future with me."

"Have you ever thought of just asking her?"

Frank shook his head. "Nope. I've found the direct approach seldom works with women."

Kate made a face, then huffed. "What sort of women have you been dating? Or did one woman do a number on you years ago and now you paint us all with the same brush?"

The truth stung just a tad, but Frank managed to halfway smile at her comment.

Kate opened her mouth, but before she could speak, Frank's cell phone rang. Grateful for the reprieve—he'd figured Kate was about to dish out some more feminine advice or dig deeper into his past personal life—Frank whipped the phone from his pocket and hit the on button.

"Latimer here."

"Yeah, this is Special Agent Moran. We've got a possible break in the Andrew Patton case."

Frank went stiff, his body tense, his breathing momentarily halted. "Have you found him?"

"Sorry, no," Moran replied. "But the abduction ring we've infiltrated is putting up a new infant for adoption. In Tennessee. Memphis to be exact. The baby is male. Blond hair. Blue eyes. Approximately two to three months old. We're making plans now to send in a couple of agents as prospective parents."

"You can't nab the kid right then and there can you?"

"You know we can't. So maybe it's better if you don't share this info with Ms. Patton, unless you're sure she can handle it."

"I'll talk things over with Kate before I decide whether or not to tell Leenie," Frank said. "Keep us posted, will you?"

"Yeah, I will. I know he's your kid and…well… I'll keep you updated."

"Thanks."

Frank understood that these agents, disguised as hopeful, adoptive parents, would simply go in for a first meeting, but wouldn't make any arrests or do anything to alert the top bananas in the abduction ring that the feds were on to them. From what Moran had told Frank, the bureau had been building this case for quite some time, working toward the moment when everything fell together just right. They wanted more than the peons in this dirty business—they wanted the kingpins. The only way to shut down the ring permanently was to destroy it from the top.

After returning his cell phone to his pocket, Frank turned to Kate. "Moran says there's a new infant on the adoption block. Words out from the association the Feds have been investigating that they have a blond-haired, blue-eyed infant ready for adoption."

Kate sucked in her breath. "And they're sending in federal agents posing as a couple desperate to adopt a child, right?"

"Right."

Rubbing the back of his neck, Frank paced around the room. His paternal instincts warred with his logical, trained warrior mind. As a father, he didn't give a damn about anything but rescuing his son. But the Dundee agent in him, as well as the Army Special Forces training that was such a fundamental part of him, acknowledged that the mission outweighed any personal needs. The FBI's mission was not only to return Andrew Patton—unharmed—to his parents, but to destroy a malicious infant adoption ring that had been operating in the Southern states for over a decade.

"She won't understand, will she?" Frank said, his back to Kate.

"No, she won't understand."

"Then I shouldn't tell her. Moran thinks it best not to tell her."

"Moran doesn't have anything personal to lose by not telling Leenie." Kate said. "You do."

"Do I?"

"You tell me."

"I'm willing to bet that once Andrew is back in her arms safe and sound, she'll be willing to forgive me for just about anything."

"Don't count on it. If she ever finds out—"

"If I ever find out what?" Leenie's voice rang out loud and clear from the other side of the room.

Frank snapped around to face her. A wide-eyed Kate glanced from Frank to Leenie and then back to Frank.

"Is it something about Andrew?" Leenie asked, hope in her voice.

Frank grimaced. "Nothing concrete."

"What does that mean?"

Frank looked at Kate, wanting her to say something—anything—to defuse this ticking time bomb before it exploded. One of them had to give Leenie an explanation. Kate looked at him, her expression telling him that she thought it should be him.

Hell, now what was he supposed to do? "It means that the FBI have a lead in the case, but—"

"What sort of lead?" Leenie entered the living room, her face freshly washed, her eyes slightly swollen.

She'd been crying, Frank realized. And now she was approaching him, all but begging him with every look, every move, every word to give her a thread of hope to cling to. "A blue-eyed, blond infant has been put up for adoption in Memphis. His general description fits Andrew—''

''We have to go to Memphis right now,'' Leenie said emphatically. ''Where do they have him? Has Special Agent Moran sent someone to get him? Oh, Frank, this is wonderful news. Andrew is safe and—''

Frank grabbed her by the shoulders. She gasped as her startled gaze met his.

''We don't know that it's Andrew,'' Frank said.

''But it might be.'' She offered him a fragile smile. ''It has to be.''

''We'll know soon enough.'' He squeezed her shoulders, then eased his hands down her arms, caressing and comforting.

''How soon? Tonight? First thing in the morning? How long do we have to wait?''

''It could be a while.'' His gut instincts told him that this was not going to go well. Leenie was in no mood to listen to reason. Hell, who could blame her?

She jerked free of his hold and glared at him. ''How long is a while? And why do we have to wait? If it's Andrew—and I have to believe that it is—why won't the FBI bring him home to me immediately?''

Frank let out a sigh of relief when Kate injected, ''Things are never that simple with the feds. There are procedures to follow, agendas that have to be—''

''No, I don't want you to explain.'' Leenie held up her hand in a stop signal. ''I want Frank to tell me why he isn't moving heaven and earth to get his hands on Andrew and bring him home to me.'' Narrowing her eyes to slits, she skewered Frank with her angry glare.

Frank cleared his throat, then took a step toward Leenie. Easing backward, she held both hands in front of her, a gesture that warned him not to come any closer.

"Dammit, Slim, don't you think I want that baby to be Andrew? Don't you think I want to drive to Memphis and be the one to go in there and tell those slimeballs that I want to adopt the baby and then get him away from them as quickly as possible?"

"Then why don't you? Why can't we pose as the people wanting to adopt Andrew, then—"

"Moran will send in a couple of federal agents," Frank told her.

Leenie nodded. "All right. And if the baby is Andrew?"

"If these people supposedly representing the birth parents have the baby with them, they're not going to release him immediately to the adoptive couple. A price will have to be agreed on and a second meeting set up to sign legal documents and exchange cash for the infant."

"What are you not telling me?"

Frank swallowed. Damn! She wasn't going to let this go until she knew everything. "It's complicated. The feds have a major case going on, something they've been putting together for quite some time. In order to bring down the ringleaders of the infant abduction ring, they can't do anything that might tip off these people and that includes grabbing this particular infant before the time is right. The entire procedure could take several days, maybe even several weeks."

"I see."

No, she didn't. She didn't see, didn't understand. And she hated him. It was all there in her eyes, in the cold, distant expression.

"Leenie…"

"The FBI has its own agenda and if Andrew gets lost in the shuffle, too bad. He's just one baby out of hundreds, right? What difference does it make if they lose him as long as they save all the others?"

"That's not the way it is." Frank held out his hands to her.

"Yes, it is. You don't have a problem going along with Special Agent Moran's plans, do you? You see the big picture, whereas I see only the little picture. Andrew. My son is all that matters to me. Call me selfish and uncaring of other people's feelings, but all I want is my baby! And if Andrew meant a damn thing to you, he would be all that mattered to you."

"Leenie, give Frank a break," Kate said. "His hands are tied. Moran is in charge and no matter how much Frank and I would like to rush in and grab this baby—be he Andrew or not—we can't. We won't. If we did, we might not only jeopardize the child's life, but we would definitely jeopardize the bureau's operation that is on the verge of—"

"To hell with the bureau's operation. I want my baby! And I'm going to get him." She glowered at Frank. "With or without your help."

Frank glanced at Kate. God help them, Leenie was irrational.

When Leenie ran into her bedroom, Frank turned to Kate. "What do I do now?"

"Be patient and understanding."

"Should I go in there and—"

"No, leave her alone. Let her calm down. I'll check on her in a little while."

Two minutes later Leenie came barreling out of her bedroom. Wearing a black winter coat and carrying her black shoulder bag, she stormed past Kate and Frank on her mad dash to the front door.

''Where are you going?'' Frank called to her.

''Where do you think? I'm going to Memphis!''

Frank groaned. Damn it! She'd completely lost it. She wasn't thinking straight. She had no idea where Moran was or where the meeting tomorrow would take place.

''Leenie, come back,'' he told her when she yanked open the front door.

Ignoring him completely, she rushed outside. Frank ran after her, catching up with her on the sidewalk. When he grabbed her arm, she turned on him, a snarl on her lips and maternal rage shining in her eyes.

''Don't do this,'' he said. ''Slim, pull yourself together. You have no idea where to go in Memphis. And Moran is not going to tell you or me or Kate. Whether we like it or not, all we can do is wait.''

''No, dammit, no!'' She hurled herself at him, her fists pounding against his chest. ''I want my baby. I want Andrew.''

He allowed her to vent her anger, frustration and fear by pummeling him repeatedly. When her blows became nothing more than unsteady, weak strikes, he grabbed her and pulled her into his arms. She sank into him. Exhausted. Soul weary. He held her with a fierce protective strength, wanting nothing more in life than to ease her pain.

''We'll get him back,'' Frank said.

Burrowing against him, her head on his shoulder, she clung to him. And after several minutes, she lifted her head just enough to gaze into his eyes. He hadn't realized he'd gotten emotional until she reached up, caressed the side of his face and then wiped away a lone tear from his cheek.

Six

Making love should always be this wonderful, this intense. Every fiber of her being felt Frank's touch. What had begun with soft gentleness quickly progressed to ravaging hunger. She needed him—wanted him—as a woman wants only that one special man. For her, Frank Latimer was that man.

His mouth was hot and demanding. His tongue probed, then plunged. The kiss consumed her, possessed her. Her body surrendered to the pleasure, reveling in the luscious abandonment. How long had she waited to be with him again? It seemed like forever. Frank was special, different from any other man she'd ever known. They fit together so perfectly and had from the first time they'd made love, as if they were old lovers who had long ago memorized every inch of each other's bodies. He had touched her physically and emotionally on a level she'd never experienced.

He rose up and over her, his big naked body magnificent, his erection projecting outward boldly. As he settled between her thighs, she caressed his sex. He shuddered. She smiled, loving the power she possessed to arouse him unbearably. He allowed her to pet him for a few moments, then eased out of her grasp and probed her body, seeking entrance. Opening herself up to his invasion, she cried out when he entered her, the sensation so satisfying. She loved the feel of him inside her. Big. Hard. Hot.

She looked up at him. He tossed back his head and closed his eyes. Instinctively she lifted herself and wrapped her legs around his hips, bringing him deeper inside her, increasing his pleasure and hers. He groaned. She sighed.

"I can't get enough of you, Slim." He whispered the words as he nuzzled her ear.

"I know the feeling." She kissed his neck.

He withdrew, then plunged deep and hard, burying himself completely inside her. He alternated deep thrusts with heated kisses and damp, demanding forays to her breasts. She tingled from inside out, on fire for him. The tension inside her built gradually, increasing with each earthy, erotic word he spoke. His grunts and moans mingled with an occasional, barely discernable graphic phrase. He told her what he wanted and what he was going to do to her. She responded with incoherent mumbles and escalating desire.

The urges inside her grew in intensity. *Not yet, I want it to last longer,* a part of her begged, while another part of her demanded, *Now, damn it, now. It's too good to wait.*

What was that ringing noise? she wondered. And

where was it coming from? Hadn't she unplugged the phone in her bedroom as she usually did when she and Frank were together? Go away, she wanted to scream. Leave us alone. We've waited such a long time to be together again.

The ringing continued.

Leenie's eyelids popped open. She groaned when she realized she'd been asleep and only dreaming of being with Frank. It had seemed so real, so breathtakingly real.

Suddenly the telephone stopped ringing. Groggy, her mouth dry as cotton, her head filled with cobwebs, she forced herself into a sitting position. She still wore the clothes she'd had on the evening before, including her shoes.

What time was it? How long had she been asleep? Leenie glanced at the lighted digital clock on the bedside table—7:40 a.m.

As she slid her feet off the bed and onto the floor, yesterday's events flooded her memory. She and Frank had argued about rescuing Andrew. She had been damned and determined to go to Memphis, totally irrational, uncaring that she wouldn't have known where to go once she arrived there.

She had taken her frustration and rage out on Frank. She had actually hit him. Repeatedly. And he'd just stood there and let her vent, let her pound his chest with her fists. How could she have done such a thing? She'd never been a violent person.

Oh, Frank, I'm sorry. I'm so sorry.

She vaguely remembered him lifting her up into his arms and carrying her back into the house and… What had happened next? He had laid her on this bed, then Kate had sat with her, talking softly, assuring her that everything possible would be done to bring Andrew home. And then someone gave her an injection? Who? Had Frank called a doctor? Why couldn't she remember clearly?

An insistent rapping on the closed door drew Leenie's attention. "Yes?"

"May I come in?" Kate Malone asked.

"Yes, please." She needed to ask Kate some questions and find out what had happened to her yesterday evening.

Looking like morning sunshine in her brown dress slacks and gold sweater set, her long blond hair neatly restrained in a loose bun at her neck, Kate entered the bedroom. "How are you feeling this morning?"

"Like I've been drugged."

"You were."

Leenie lifted a questioning eyebrow.

Kate smiled. "Forgive us?"

"What are you asking forgiveness for?" Leenie asked.

"You were hysterical, then emotionally wiped out. We couldn't get you to stop crying, so Frank and I agreed that you needed a doctor. We phoned Haley Wilson and she arranged for her physician to make a house call."

"It was Haley's doctor who came to the house? I guess that's the reason I didn't recognize him."

"She tried your doctor first, but he was out of town."

"What did Haley's doctor give me—an elephant tranquilizer?"

Kate chuckled. "Are you that hungover?"

Leenie rubbed either side of her forehead with her

fingertips. "I feel as if I've been run down by a Mack truck."

"Despite that fact, are we forgiven?"

Somehow Leenie managed to get up. When Kate came toward her, she nodded. "You're forgiven. And I'm okay. I don't need any help. However, I do need a shower." She glanced down at herself. "And I need a change of clothes."

"We thought it best to just let you—"

"We? You and Haley? Or you and Frank?"

"All three of us."

"Where is Frank?"

"That was him on the phone. I tried to get to it before the ringing woke you, but—"

"Frank isn't here?"

"No, he left last night, as soon as you went off to sleep."

"I guess I can't blame him for leaving. I said some terrible things to him."

Kate reached out and took Leenie's hands in hers. "He didn't leave because of anything you said or did. And he's coming back later today. He went to Memphis."

Had she heard Kate right? "Frank went to Memphis?"

"He phoned Moran last night and asked if he promised to stay out of the way, could he just be there in town, at FBI headquarters, and wait around for word on Andrew."

Emotion tightened Leenie's throat. She had accused Frank of not caring about Andrew. But he did care, didn't he? Why else would he have gone to Memphis.

"Do you know what time the meeting is today?" Leenie asked.

"The agents are set to go in posing as adoptive parents at ten o'clock."

Leenie pulled her hands from Kate's and hugged herself, determined not to fall apart again. "Why did Frank call? Is there a problem?"

"He called to check on you," Kate said. "When he left here last night, he was worried sick about you."

"Was he?"

"Yes, he was. You've got to know that despite the emotional barrier Frank has erected to keep the world at bay, that man cares about you. It's so obvious to anyone watching him when he's around you that he's in love."

"Kate Malone, I do believe you're a romantic. Otherwise you'd never think Frank was in love with me. I doubt he's capable of falling in love."

"He is. He just doesn't know it yet." Kate looked Leenie square in the eyes. "You're in love with him, aren't you?"

Leenie sighed.

"I know it's none of my business, but—"

"Yes, I'm in love with the big lug. I'm so in love with him that it hurts."

Kate smiled. "Why don't you take a shower while I fix us some breakfast?"

"Sounds like a plan to me."

Kate turned and headed for the door, then paused, glanced over her shoulder and said, "Frank will call us as soon as he knows anything. If the agents get to see the baby, they should be able to tell if it's Andrew or not from all the photos the feds have of him."

"Even if they can't take him away from those horrible people today, I pray that it is Andrew. At least then, I'll know he's safe."

Frank held his breath, a heartfelt plea repeating in his head, when Special Agents Currie and Rushing returned to the field office on Humphreys Blvd. He waited impatiently while Moran spoke privately to the two agents who had posed as potential adoptive parents. Despite all his training and the lifelong habit of employing logic before emotion, right about now Frank was thinking like a father. A father whose son had been kidnapped.

The office door opened and Moran came out alone to meet Frank. Please, God, please, let that baby be Andrew.

"Sorry it took so long," Moran said.

"Is he or isn't he Andrew?"

Moran shook his head. "No."

Frank felt as if he'd been sucker punched.

"The baby Rushing and Currie was shown is six months old, has reddish blond hair and has a small birthmark on his right arm," Moran explained. "Definitely not Andrew Patton."

"Which means Andrew is still out there, his fate unknown. He might not have been kidnapped by this abduction ring y'all are investigating."

"Just because this baby wasn't your son doesn't mean he won't come up on the auction block in a few days or few weeks."

"I'm not sure his mother can hold it together for a few more days, let alone a few more weeks."

"Dr. Patton seems like an amazingly strong woman to me," Moran said.

"Even the strongest person can break under the kind of pressure Leenie is living with on a daily basis. That baby—our baby—means everything to her. If I can't give her some kind of hope that I'll be able to bring him home to her…"

Moran nodded, then glanced down at the floor. "Yeah. Well…yeah."

Uncomfortable discussing such an emotionally personal issue, Frank changed the subject. "How much time before this operation comes to a head?"

"That's confidential info."

"I don't want specifics. No date, time, place. Just a general idea. I think I've got clearance for that much, don't you?"

"A week. Ten days tops. But possibly sooner."

"How soon?"

"A few days."

Frank drew in a deep breath and released it slowly. "Once the operation's in motion, would you let me know? Just in case Andrew is caught up in things."

"Are you sure you want to know before it's all over and done with?"

"I probably don't want to know, but I'd appreciate a call beforehand anyway." What Frank didn't say, but suspected Moran knew anyway was that he needed time to prepare himself in order to be strong for Leenie if the worst happened.

Moran clamped his hand down on Frank's shoulder. "There's always a chance we'll find Andrew. Tell her that. Give her that much hope."

"False hope?" Frank asked.

"I honestly don't know."

Somehow knowing it was Frank, Leenie grabbed the telephone when it rang at two-thirty that afternoon. Her hand trembled as she placed the receiver to her ear.

"Hello." Her voice quivered.

"Leenie…"

"I've been waiting for your call."

"I know and I'm sorry I didn't call sooner. I'm on the road, heading back to Maysville. I should be there soon."

She knew the news was bad; if it had been good, he'd have already told her. "The baby wasn't Andrew, was he?"

"No, honey, it wasn't Andrew. I'm sorry."

"Me, too." She swallowed. Tears welled up inside her, but did not surface. She was all cried out.

"Moran said that there's a good chance another baby will come up for adoption soon. Maybe in a few days. The next one could be Andrew."

"Yes, it could be."

"Please don't give up hope."

She closed her eyes and willed herself to remain totally in control. Crying wouldn't change anything. Hysterics wouldn't help Andrew. And blaming Frank only hurt them both.

"I won't give up hope," she told him. "You shouldn't either."

"You're right."

"Frank?"

"Huh?"

"Thank you for going to Memphis to be there when… I'm sorry I was so rough on you yesterday. I couldn't see beyond my own hurt to—"

"It's okay, Slim. Honest. I didn't mind being your

whipping boy, if it helped you. God knows I'm not able to do much else to help."

"That's not true. Your being here helps."

He didn't respond for several minutes.

"Frank?"

"Yeah, I'm here. Just wishing I was already in Maysville with you. I'd really like to hold you in my arms right now."

"Me, too. I sure could use a hug."

"Give me about forty-five minutes and I'll hug the life out of you."

"Is that a promise?"

"Damn right it is."

Kate had made herself scarce after telling Leenie she thought she'd go into town for dinner and a movie. "I need a break, if you think you'll be okay here alone until Frank gets back." She hadn't fooled Leenie for a minute. Kate had left so that Leenie and Frank could be alone. But now that she heard Frank's car pulling up in the driveway, Leenie wasn't sure she wanted to be alone with him. She was so needy right now, so desperate to be held and comforted. What if Frank's actions were rooted in his desire to take care of her? She didn't want him being kind to her. She wanted him to love her.

Bracing her shoulders and willing herself to be calm, she opened the front door and waited for him. The moment she saw him, her stomach did a wicked flip-flop and sexual awareness zinged along her nerve endings. Their gazes met and held for an instant and then Frank was there, grabbing her and pulling her into his arms as he walked her backward into the house. Using his foot, he slammed the door shut. He clutched the back of Leenie's head, his big fingers spearing into her hair. She gasped half a second before his mouth came down on hers.

He ate at her mouth, his hunger desperately obvious. She wrapped her arms around him and returned his kiss with equal fury. Rational thought ceased to exist. For her. And she suspected for him, too. They wanted each other. Needed each other.

Help me make the world go away was her last coherent thought before she tore at the buttons on Frank's shirt. He released her only long enough to shrug off his jacket, then he shoved her backward and onto the sofa. She all but ripped off his shirt and buttons flew everywhere. They shared kiss after passionate kiss as he yanked her sweater over her head and hurriedly removed her bra. She gazed up at him when he came down over her. He blocked out the rest of the world. Life itself began and ended with Frank Latimer and with this moment out of time.

When his mouth took hold of her breast to suckle and tease, Leenie bucked up against him. His hands dipped under her to lift her hips so that she felt his pulsating erection pressing into her mound. She slid her hand between them and cupped his sex.

"I wanted to make slow sweet love to you," he told her in a hungry, whispered rush of words. "But I don't know if I can wait."

"I don't want slow and sweet." She rubbed herself provocatively against him, naked breasts to hairy naked chest. "I need it fast and dirty."

Her slacks landed on the floor, followed quickly by his. Her panties flew through the air and perched on a nearby lampshade. His briefs sailed off and onto the coffee table, atop a copy of *Psychiatry Today*.

His tongue lunged into her mouth just as he hoisted her hips upward to meet his hard, conquering thrust. He hammered into her. She went wild. Blind to everything except Frank. Deaf to everything except the beating of their hearts. Speechless, their only sounds those of grunts and groans and moans of powerful pleasure.

As they went at each other, hot, hungry passion ruling their actions, they toppled off the sofa and onto the floor. Frank rolled her over and placed her on top of him. She rode him at a frenetic pace until she came. Her climax hit her like a tidal wave. Fierce and overwhelming, wiping her out completely. Just as she cried with release, he took the dominant position and with one final stab sent himself over the edge. Growling ferociously, he jetted inside her, not giving a damn that he'd forgotten all about using a condom.

While ripples of the sexual aftermath glided through their bodies, Frank and Leenie lay in the living room floor and held each other. Naked, sated, tension drained from their bodies, he touched her tenderly as she caressed him. Those unbearably sweet moments after the loving prolonged their escape from harsh reality.

Leenie cuddled close. Frank cocooned her in his big, strong arms. She felt safe and protected. And loved.

Please, God, even if he doesn't love me, let me hold on to that hope for a little while, just as I'm clinging to the precious hope that You will keep Andrew safe.

Frank kissed her temple. "Should we talk?"

"No. Not now. Later."

He stood, then held out his hand to her. She rose to her feet and together they gathered up their scattered clothing and walked arm-in-arm into Leenie's bedroom.

"How long did Kate say she'd be gone?" Frank asked.

"Long enough for an early dinner and a movie."

He tossed his clothes on a nearby chair. She did the same.

Frank led her to the bed. She went with him willingly.

She needed Frank as she'd never needed him before, as she'd never needed another human being. Only he could share her every thought, her every feeling. He offered her solace and sweet moments of forgetfulness. Apart, their fears and worries were more than either could bear. But together, holding on to each other for dear life, they could manage to survive a few more hours…a few more days.

Seven

Leenie awakened early the next morning and for a few seconds remembered nothing except the pleasure she had experienced with Frank. He hadn't stayed the night in her bed. After they'd made love for a second time, they had showered together, fixed sandwiches together and talked about Andrew. Being able to share this horrific experience with Andrew's father somehow comforted her in a way she had never dreamed it could. Although there had been no promises exchanged, no words of love spoken between them, Leenie truly believed that Frank cared about her. And about Andrew. Perhaps Kate had been right. Was it possible that Frank loved her and just didn't know it?

After slipping into her thick velour robe, Leenie ventured into the hallway. Silence permeated the house at this early hour. Perhaps Kate and Frank were both still asleep, after all it was only half past five and still dark outside. Wintertime dark. As she made her way into the kitchen, a chill racked her body. Was it a sense of foreboding or simply the chilliness of the house? She'd turn up the thermostat after she set the coffeemaker.

If only Frank had stayed in bed with her all night. Even without sex, it would have been such a comfort to have him within arm's reach, to have been able to reach out and feel his strong presence beside her. How many times had she longed for him during her pregnancy?

Expecting the kitchen to be empty, Leenie gasped when she opened the door and found Frank sitting at the table reading the morning newspaper and drinking a cup of coffee.

"Morning," He glanced up at her and smiled.

She returned his smile, even if it was somewhat tentative and uncertain. "Good morning." She had no idea what last night had meant to him. Had it been nothing more than sex? Just a way to relieve the unbearable tension?

"Sleep well?" he asked.

"Yes, as a matter of fact I did." She looked away from him and toward the coffeemaker on the counter. "Coffee. Wonderful. I could use a shot of caffeine."

When Frank didn't respond, she walked past him, lifted a mug from the mug rack and poured a cup of black coffee. "Is Kate still asleep?" she asked, her back to Frank.

"As far as I know. She's still in her room." Frank set his coffee mug on the table.

"She stayed out pretty late last night, didn't she?

She probably didn't get to sleep until well past eleven.''

"Closer to midnight," Frank said. "She and I stayed up for a while and talked about things.''

"About Andrew?''

"About the feds' case involving the infant abduction ring. Kate is more than just a little interested in it, maybe even a little obsessed. I've never seen her quite so involved in a Dundee assignment. She's taking your situation personally, almost as if—''

"As if she understands what it's like to have a child kidnapped?''

Frank closed the newspaper, folded it in half and laid it aside, then looked at Leenie as she pulled out a chair and sat across from him. "Kate is a complex lady. She's warm and friendly, but she never allows anyone to get too close." Frank chuckled. "I can't fault her on that, can I?''

"Maybe her relating to my predicament is nothing more than her having an empathic heart. She seems like a very kind person. I liked her when we first met last winter." Leenie took a sip of coffee, then placed her mug on the table. "Tell me, Frank, why is it that you won't allow anyone to get too close to you? I know your marriage ended in divorce, but—''

"I made a fool of myself over Rita.''

A surge of uncontrollable jealousy rose up inside Leenie. She hated Rita, sight unseen. "So Rita hurt you so badly that you decided to never risk being hurt again.''

"You make it sound melodramatic. It wasn't. Just an old familiar tale. I cared more for her than she did for me. She found someone she liked better. Or should I say she met someone whose money she liked better.''

"You loved her madly, of course.''

"Of course.''

Hearing him admit it so freely stung Leenie terribly, as if he'd stabbed her in the heart with a very sharp knife. "Do you still?''

"Do I still what?''

"Love Rita.''

"Good God, no.''

"But you let what she did to you affect every aspect of your life,'' Leenie said. "Even if you don't love her now, she certainly still has a tremendous influence in your life, doesn't she?''

Frank glared at Leenie, tension etching the lines around his eyes and across his forehead. "Look, Slim, don't try to psychoanalyze me. And don't try to change me. I am what I am. Yeah, in part that's thanks to Rita. And in part thanks to my mother, who was quite a bit like Rita as a matter of fact. And part of who I am is thanks to my own survival instincts. A guy who makes the same mistake twice is a fool.''

"And Frank Latimer is nobody's fool.''

Their gazes collided, exploded, then when the metaphorical smoke cleared, he looked down at the newspaper and tapped it with his index finger. "It's going to rain today. We might even get a little sleet.''

"Kate knows there's something between us,'' Leenie said. "That's why she left us alone yesterday evening…why she stayed gone so long. You could have spent the night in my bed and she wouldn't have been surprised.''

"If you're trying to say something, just say it.''

Not making eye contact with her, he picked up his mug, stood and went to the coffeemaker for a refill.

"Why didn't you stay with me, Frank? We made love. Twice. It's obvious that you care about me, that you care about our son. What are you so afraid of? Did you think sleeping with me all night would have been some sort of commitment, that I'd take it the wrong way and believe there was more to our relationship than there is?"

Full coffee mug in hand, he turned to face her, a somber expression on his face. "What do you want me to say?"

"Just tell me the truth. I think I deserve that much, don't I?"

"The truth is—yeah, I care about you. I did last winter. I do now. The last thing I want to do is hurt you and if I allow you to believe we have a future together... I want to be good to you. I want to help you through this ordeal. I want to bring Andrew home to you. And I want a chance to get to know my son."

Leenie sucked in a deep breath. Even without him saying it, she knew Frank already loved Andrew.

"When Andrew comes home, and he will, you and I will work out an arrangement so that you can be a part of his life." Her pride in need of bolstering and not wanting Frank to suspect that he'd just broken her heart—again—Leenie forced a smile. "And don't think that if we have sex again or even if we sleep all night together some night that I'll start hearing wedding bells and ordering a picket fence to put up around this place. Heck, Frank, I'm the quintessential free spirit who has lost count of the men I've been with over the years. I don't want to be tied down to one man any more than you want to get trapped by some woman.''

God would get her for those lies, Leenie told herself, all the while managing to keep her phony smile in place. She certainly wasn't a simpering virgin, but she was hardly a good-time girl either. She remembered the names of her former lovers because there actually hadn't been all that many and each time she'd been in a relationship, she had hoped he would be "the one." But the biggest lie of all was that she didn't want marriage. She did. Now more than ever. And not marriage to just anyone. She wanted Frank.

He narrowed his gaze as he studied her closely, as if trying to gauge the truth of her declaration. "Let me give you a little advice about men, Slim. A guy never likes to hear about a woman's former lovers. And he especially doesn't like to hear that there have been so many she can't remember their names.''

Leenie laughed spontaneously. Frank was jealous. But he had no idea that he was. Why would a man be jealous of other men in a woman's life unless he loved that woman? "Thanks for the advice. I'll remember not to mention my former lovers to my next boyfriend.''

Frank growled quietly, then cleared his throat.

He was so jealous! It was apparent that he hated the idea of her being with another man. Past. Present. Or future.

Don't do this to yourself, Leenie's inner voice cautioned. *Even if Frank does love you, he may never be able to admit it to himself, let alone to you.*

Coming to an understanding, of sorts, they relaxed around each other. The tension between Frank and her should have eased up, and it had—to a certain extent. Beneath the calm alliance binding them together as Andrew's parents lay an ever smoldering sexual edginess. Neither could escape a basic truth—they were in lust, if not in love. And lust was a potent motivator, not as enduring as love, but equally as powerful.

The hours passed slowly, turning the day into night and into day again. During the daylight hours, Kate and Frank kept Leenie busy and occasionally, for brief periods of time, she became so absorbed in whatever she was doing that the ache in her heart diminished a fraction. Those were moments when her entire focus was not on Andrew. But those moments were few and far between. The nighttime hours were the worst, when she lay alone in her bed, longing to hold her baby in her arms. And needing Frank at her side. It had been two days and nights since they'd made love and although he was tender and caring, he had not come to her again.

Leenie kept telling herself that he was afraid of her, of the way she made him feel. He didn't want to love her, didn't want a future with her, but the passion between them was something he could not ignore.

The waiting was wearing on her nerves. How much longer could she hold it together without falling completely apart again? Special Agent Dante Moran had called and talked to her. He'd told her to be patient, to keep hoping for the best, that it could well be only a matter of time before Andrew surfaced as an adoptive infant. So she clung to that hope because it might well be the only hope she had. If her baby had been taken by some woman wanting a child, she might never see him again. And if some lunatic had kidnapped Andrew, her baby was probably already dead.

Leenie shook her head, an effort to dislodge all morbid thoughts. Andrew was alive. He would come home to her. Frank kept repeating those words to her over and over again, as if he was trying desperately to convince himself as well as her.

"Are you ready to go?" Frank asked.

She nodded. "Yes, I'm ready."

The first thing on the keep-Leenie-busy schedule for today was a visit to the hospital to see Debra, who was now resting comfortably in a private room. The doctors had said Debra might be released in a week or less. She had recovered remarkably well for a woman of sixty.

"Stay as long as you'd like," Kate told them as they headed for the front door. "As a matter of fact, why don't you two go out for lunch after your visit to Mrs. Schmale. I can hold down the fort here and if I get any news, I'll phone y'all immediately."

"I'd like to run by the station," Leenie said. "Haley suggested that I might want to give a statement about Andrew's abduction and make a personal plea for his return. I simply haven't been up to doing something like that before now. WJMM has been broadcasting Andrew's photograph periodically, with the news about his kidnapping, but Haley thinks a message from me might actually influence his abductor to return him."

"Since Moran has given you the okay to make a public statement, I see no reason why you shouldn't," Frank said.

"Just so long as you don't mention the infant abduction ring," Kate reminded her. "You don't want to do anything that might alert them that the feds are on to them."

Leenie sighed. "God, I hope Andrew was taken by those damn people. It's the one sure chance we have of getting him back, isn't it?"

Frank put his arm around Leenie's shoulders. "Come on, Slim, let's go see Mrs. Schmale, then I'll take you out for lunch. I'm in the mood for...a greasy hamburger and fries. And maybe a chocolate milk-shake."

Leenie smiled. "Just thinking about that kind of food has already put five pounds on me, mostly on my hips."

Frank's arm slipped down her back and encircled her waist. One hand slid down to cup her hip. "Five pounds won't hurt you. Hell, ten pounds wouldn't."

"Frank Latimer, you know just what to say to a girl to make her happy, don't you?"

"I try," he said, sincerity and a touch of sadness in his voice.

Frank liked Debra Schmale and could see why Leenie had hired her as Andrew's nanny. She possessed a kind disposition and maternal love oozed from her pores. The woman's hospital room looked like a florist. Floral arrangements of every size and kind filled the small private room and four balloon bouquets floated in the air, held in place by ribbon streamers tied to both chairs in the room and to the knobs on the closet doors.

Leenie hugged Debra, careful not to squeeze too hard and hurt the healing patient. "It's good to see you looking so well. I've been worried about you."

"I'll be just fine...once we get Andrew back. I feel so guilty for—"

"Hush that kind of talk," Leenie said. "You have nothing to feel guilty about."

"If only I could have stopped that woman from taking Andrew."

"Mrs. Schmale, you had no way of knowing that the woman had deliberately crashed into your car so that she could kidnap Andrew. You did exactly what anyone would have done," Frank told her as he walked over and stood directly behind Leenie.

"Please, call me Debra." She offered him a warm, genuine smile. "I'm so glad that you're here with Leenie. She needs you, now, more than ever."

Leenie gasped softly. Frank realized that Mrs. Schmale—Debra—knew he was Andrew's father, which made him wonder just how much Leenie had told her about him.

"In case you're wondering, Leenie told me very little about you, not even your name," Debra said, as if reading his mind. "She didn't offer the information and I didn't pry.

"Then how did you know—?" Leenie asked.

"Haley told me about Mr. Latimer. She's been a frequent visitor. And she is as pleased as I am that Andrew's father is by your side during this terrible ordeal."

When Debra looked at Frank, she smiled, but he felt her disapproval and understood she was wondering why he had gotten Leenie pregnant and walked out of her life. Women of Debra Schmale's generation expected a man to do the right thing, to make an honest woman of his child's mother.

"You and Haley are a couple of busybodies," Leenie said jokingly. "And just so you won't badger

Frank, you should know that he plans to be a part of Andrew's life...once we have him back with us.''

"There's no news, then?" Debra asked.

Leenie shook her head.

Frank put his arm around Leenie's waist and pulled her close. "We have every reason to hope that no news is good news, at least for now. The FBI thinks Andrew will be found unharmed. Leenie and I are clinging to that hope."

Debra eyed Frank's arm around Leenie.

The telephone on Debra's bedside table rang. She reached out for it, but Leenie grabbed it to save Debra the effort.

"I've gotten a dozen calls already today," Debra told Frank. "Everyone in Maysville must know I'm out of ICU and in a private room now."

"Debra Schmale's room," Leenie said.

Frank glanced at Leenie, who paled instantly.

Leenie looked at Frank and said, "It's Kate and she wants to speak to you."

The muscles in Frank's belly knotted painfully. He reached out and took the receiver from Leenie. "Yeah, Kate, what's up?"

"Moran just called," Kate said.

"Tell me it's good news."

Leenie grasped Frank's arm.

"It could be," Kate told him. "Two new infants have come up for adoption. Both fit Andrew's description."

"When is he sending in a couple of agents?" Frank asked.

"What is it?" Leenie demanded, tugging on Frank's arm. "Is it news about Andrew?"

"Everything is set up for tomorrow," Kate said.

"Moran wanted me to tell you something. He made me repeat it twice."

"What?"

"He said to tell you that it's sooner rather than later."

"God!" The FBI operation that had been in the works for several years was coming together. Sooner rather than later. Possibly tomorrow? Was that what Moran was trying to tell him? Was it all going to happen tomorrow, right when Andrew—if he was one of the two infants—would be smack dab in the middle of everything? What if when the feds made their arrests, the two babies were whisked away before being rescued? What if they lost Andrew? What if there was gunplay?

"I'll bring Leenie home right away," Frank told Kate. "We'll skip going to WJMM today."

"Moran knows you'll come back to Memphis."

"Damn straight about that." Frank replaced the receiver and turned to Leenie, who was squeezing the life out of his arm. "Good news. A couple of infants have been found and it's possible one of them is Andrew." He glanced at Debra Schmale and smiled, then gave Leenie a sharp glare, hoping she'd understand why he couldn't be totally forthcoming with Debra.

"This is wonderful news," Debra said.

"Keep it to yourself for now, okay?" Frank smiled at her.

"Absolutely." Debra folded her hands together in a prayerlike gesture.

"We need to go," Frank told Leenie.

She kissed Debra on the forehead and said her goodbyes, then rushed out of the room with Frank.

When they were alone in the elevator, she didn't wait for him to explain.

"Two more infants have come up for adoption, right?" she asked.

"Right."

"In Memphis?"

"Yeah."

"You're going to Memphis tonight, aren't you?"

"Yeah."

"And you want me to stay here in Maysville and wait."

"Yeah."

The elevator doors swung open and they emerged on the first floor. Frank grabbed her arm and hurried her outside to the parking lot. She walked quickly to keep up with his long-legged gait. When they reached his rental car, she halted and dug in her heels.

Before she could speak, he grabbed her by the shoulders and said, "Dammit, Slim, stay here in Maysville, will you? Let me be the big, strong man. Let me be your man."

"You want to be a buffer between me and the big bad world, don't you?"

"Something like that. After all, I am Andrew's father. I wasn't around when you were pregnant or when you gave birth. I should have been. You needed me and I let you down.

"I need to do this for you. Hell, I need to do it for myself. Let me be the one to handle things, and if it is Andrew, I want to be the one to bring him home to you."

"And if it isn't Andrew?"

"Then I should be the one to tell you. We're Andrew's parents. And if we've lost him, we should share that grief together.''

Leenie swallowed, then offered Frank a fragile smile. Tears gathered in the corners of her eyes. ''You go to Memphis. I'll wait here in Maysville for you…and Andrew.''

He cupped her face with his hands, then kissed her.

Eight

Frank had left for Memphis around eight-thirty last night and called after he arrived at the hotel. Leenie and Kate had sat up until after two this morning, watching television, talking, looking through magazines, listening to Leenie's substitute on WJMM's late-night talk show. They had done anything they could think of to kill time. At midnight, while listening to the radio, they made fudge and devoured a third of what they'd prepared. As if by silent agreement, they hadn't mentioned Frank or Andrew. At two, they'd gone to their separate bedrooms and Leenie had tried her best to sleep. She had tossed and turned for hours. Finally giving up hope of getting any rest, she'd flipped on the bedside lamp and searched for a romance novel in her stash of to-be-read paperbacks. As entertaining as the book was, Leenie simply could not concentrate enough to do the story justice, so around four-thirty, she'd taken a shower and put on jeans and a sweatshirt.

As she passed the floor-to-ceiling mirror in the hallway, she caught a glimpse of her image. She looked bleary-eyed and somber. Her damp hair was secured in a loose ponytail. Faded jeans hugged her hips and legs. A comfy green fleece sweatshirt with an enormous sunflower in the center gave her otherwise pale appearance a touch of color. All-in-all, she was a pitiful sight.

She wondered if Frank had gotten any sleep last night. Probably not. If only she'd gone with him, at least they'd be together right now. But Frank had needed to make the trip to Memphis alone. She understood. And deep in her primitive feminine heart, she loved him all the more for wanting to play the role of her protector.

How was it possible that her whole world had become condensed into one event—into what happened this morning in Memphis, at some immoral, money-hungry lawyer's office? Two FBI agents would once again pose as prospective parents, but would they get to see the two infants who were available for adoption? Would one of those babies be Andrew? If Andrew hadn't been kidnapped in order to sell him to the highest bidder, then she might never know his fate. Could she live that way, never knowing?

When Leenie entered the kitchen, she glanced at the wall clock. Five-fifteen. The meeting was set for nine o'clock this morning. Less than four hours from now. But how long would it take the agents to report back to Moran if they did get to see the babies? It was possible that even after the meeting, they still wouldn't know if Andrew was one of the two infants.

While preparing the coffee machine, she stared at the telephone. She wanted to talk to Frank, to hear his voice. But he might be asleep. She shouldn't disturb him.

She reached out and jerked the receiver from the wall phone, then glanced at Frank's cell number, which he'd jotted down on the bulletin board by the telephone. After dialing, she suddenly had second thoughts and started to hang up, but Frank answered on the second ring.

"Latimer here."

"Frank?"

"Leenie? Honey, are you all right?"

"I'm okay. I didn't sleep much."

"You didn't sleep at all, did you?"

"No, I didn't," she admitted. "I'll bet you didn't either."

"I closed my eyes a few times, but... We'll both sleep once I bring Andrew home."

"I—I want you to know that if neither baby is Andrew—" Emotion tightened her throat. She swallowed. "It won't be your fault, so don't blame yourself."

"We can't lose hope, even if neither baby is Andrew. He's out there somewhere. We'll keep searching."

"I'm going to hang up now." Her voice quivered. "Before I start blubbering."

"Yeah, we don't want that, do we? If you start, I might, too. And that would blow my macho image to hell and back."

"Nothing could destroy your macho image, least of all crying for your lost son."

"Leenie...I...keep praying, will you?"

"Mmm-hmm."

"I'll call you as soon as I know anything."

"Yes...please..."

"Bye, Slim."

"Bye."

With the dial tone humming in her ear, Leenie stood there and forced back the tears that ached inside her. These next few hours were going to be the longest of her life.

By the time Leenie downed her second cup of coffee and was munching on a slice of buttered toast, Kate entered the kitchen. Wearing a pair of flame-red sweats, her hair hanging loosely around her shoulders, Kate looked like a teenager, all fresh-faced and glowing with good health.

"How long have you been up?" Kate asked, as she headed for the coffeepot. "Or should I say how long have you been in the kitchen? I figure you've been up most of the night."

"I came in the kitchen about forty-five minutes ago."

"Hmm-mmm." Kate poured herself a cup of coffee, then sat across from Leenie.

"I called Frank."

Kate raised an inquisitive eyebrow.

"He's going to call back the minute he knows something," Leenie said.

Kate took a sip of coffee, clutched the mug with both hands and looked right at Leenie.

"I hope and pray one of those baby boys is Andrew. But while you're hoping for the best, you have to prepare yourself for the worst."

"I don't know if I can do that. I don't want to think about what it'll mean if—"

"It doesn't mean you have to give up hope. As long as you don't have proof that Andrew is dead, then no one can take your hope away from you," Kate said emphatically.

Leenie stared at Kate, puzzled by the fierceness in her voice, by the resolute certainty of her statement. "What is it that you still hope for, Kate?"

Gripping the mug she held as if it were her anchor in a stormy sea, Kate closed her eyes for a split second, then opened them and looked directly at Leenie again. "I hope that out there somewhere, my little girl is alive and well and somebody is loving her and taking good care of her."

Rendered speechless by Kate's honesty, Leenie gaped soundlessly, her heartbeat drumming in her ears. Although she had suspected Kate had lost a child, hearing her admit it tore at Leenie's heart. "Was your child…your daughter kidnapped?"

"Yes. Mary Kate was barely two months old when it happened."

Kate inhaled and exhaled slowly. Leenie figured the deep breathing technique was a tool Kate used to keep her emotions in check. Despite her in-control-at-all-times facade, Kate occasionally let her vulnerability show. And Leenie liked her all the more for those tiny lapses.

"Mary Kate was kidnapped eleven years ago," Kate said. "At the time, we thought she'd been taken for ransom because my husband—my ex-husband now—is a member of a very wealthy and prominent family."

"But she wasn't taken for ransom?"

Kate shook her head. "The FBI was brought in, of course, and we waited for the call or the letter to tell us how much money the kidnappers wanted. But there was no call. No letter. Trent hired a private firm to search for our daughter, but they never found her, of course. And after a while, Trent convinced himself that Mary Kate was dead.''

''What made him think she was—''

''Nothing in particular. I believe it was the only way he could cope with what had happened. He loved her as much as I did. We just coped with her loss in different ways.'' Kate set the mug on the table and laid her hands flat against the wooden surface on either side of the mug. ''We argued about it day and night. I told him he was wrong to give up hope and he told me I was living in a fantasy world if I thought we'd ever find Mary Kate, that she was dead.''

''It's apparent that you never changed your mind, that you still believe your child is alive. Did your ex-husband ever come around to your way of thinking?''

''No. And that, along with his family's interference and Trent's feelings of guilt and my feelings of guilt…and the endless arguments, destroyed our marriage. We've been divorced ten years now. And I haven't seen him since the divorce became final.''

''But you still love him, don't you?''

Kate laughed, the sound mirthless, stilted. ''Now who's the romantic?''

''You've never remarried, have you? That means something.''

''It means I'm afraid of being hurt,'' Kate admitted. ''Besides, most men want children and I know that I could never have another child and risk losing her or him. The pain is too great.'' Kate gasped. ''Oh, God, Leenie, I'm sorry. I shouldn't have—''

Leenie reached across the table and grasped Kate's

hand in hers. "We haven't lost Andrew. Just as you have somehow managed to keep the faith for eleven years, I'm not giving up hope. Not now, after only a few days. And not ever. If I keep telling myself over and over again that one of those babies the abduction ring is putting up for sale is Andrew, then it will be. It has to be!"

Kate squeezed Leenie's hand. "Yes, it will be."

"And someday you'll find your daughter."

"I believe Mary Kate is alive. If she weren't, I'd know it, wouldn't I? In my mother's heart. Wouldn't you know if— Oh, damn, I keep saying all the wrong things."

"No, you don't," Leenie assured her. "I understand what you mean. But I honestly don't know if my believing Andrew is alive is because I'd know in my heart if he wasn't, or if it's because I simply cannot accept the possibility that..." Leenie paused, her emotions so raw she feared bursting into tears. "I can't even say it."

"Then don't say it. Don't even think it."

"I wouldn't want to live in a world without Andrew." Leenie clenched her teeth tightly, determined not to cry.

Kate squeezed her hand again. They looked at each other, tears misting their eyes, their deepest, darkest fears kept just below the surface.

Frank paced the floor in the Memphis FBI office on Humphreys Blvd. He'd drunk the equivalent of three pots of coffee since he'd arrived this morning and he'd all but worn a hole in the floor. It was nearly three-thirty. Where the hell was Moran? The last word they'd had from the agents involved in the operation was around noon and Frank had been privy to the information only because Moran had personally okayed it. All Frank knew was that the two male infants had been taken into FBI custody and were being checked by a local pediatrician. From overhearing snippets of conversation that the office personnel didn't share with him, Frank had figured out that arrests were being made, the ringleaders of the abduction ring gathered up, along with the lawyers involved in the illegal adoptions.

As much as Frank appreciated the importance of the bureau's great victory in this case, what mattered most to him was finding out if one of those babies was his son. Leenie's son. If only there was some way to find out, if only there was something he could do. But all he could do was wait. And hope. And pray. He'd done more praying these past few days than he'd done all his life. But he supposed when things seemed hopeless was the time a man was most likely to turn to prayer. Frank had known hopelessness before, but not helplessness.

He knew that the feds weren't deliberately keeping any pertinent information about his son from him. During this case, Moran had shared more confidential info than was probably legal and Frank appreciated that fact. And he believed that Moran would let him know something about the babies just as soon as either could be identified as Andrew, or both could be ruled out as his and Leenie's son. The federal agents had regulations and procedures they had to follow and even though Moran had bent a few rules lately, he couldn't give Frank information he didn't have. Not yet. But soon. It was only a matter of waiting on a definite ID for both baby boys.

A flurry of activity occurred outside Moran's office where Frank had been waiting impatiently. Doors slammed, voices rose and suddenly Moran came barreling into his office, a wide smile on his face.

"We got 'em," Moran said. "Every slimy, fat-cat, freaking bastard. We took them down from the top. We arrested twenty people, including the four masterminds and three of their lawyers." He slapped Frank on the back. "By God, it's over. And now we've got ourselves one hell of a mess."

"Where are the babies?" Frank asked. "Is one of them—"

"We've got nearly twelve years of adoption records. Confiscated. Records of children who were probably all abducted from their parents and sold to adoptive families. Do you have any idea what that means? Biological parents and adoptive parents and hundreds of children caught in the middle. It's not only a legal nightmare, but a moral dilemma for everyone involved."

Frank grabbed Moran's shoulder. "Damn it, I'm interested in one child. My son. Where the hell are those babies? Is one of them Andrew?"

"Dr. Tomlin's office hasn't called?" Moran asked as he eased out from under Frank's tenacious grasp.

"Who's—is he the pediatrician in charge of the babies? If so, then no, he hasn't called. Or if he has no one has bothered to tell me."

"The agents who went into this morning's meeting as adoptive parents weren't able to positively ID either child they were shown, but one of the babies fit Andrew's description to a tee." Moran walked over to his desk and picked up the telephone. "I'll make arrangements to take you to Dr. Tomlin's office. Both babies are being kept there for the time being. If one of them is positively identified as Andrew, I'll see to it that you can take him home to his mother this evening.''

"What the hell are you waiting for? Make the call. Now!"

The telephone rang. Kate and Leenie jumped simultaneously. They exchanged quick glances, then Kate shot up off the sofa and grabbed the receiver. Before she could even say hello, Frank spoke.

"I've got him," Frank said. "All fourteen pounds of him. Can you hear him squalling. He's not sure whether or not he likes his old man."

Kate smiled. She'd never heard Frank Latimer enthusiastic about anything, never heard such pure joy in his voice. "Calm down and tell me what's going on."

"Is it Frank?" Leenie asked as she came toward Kate.

Kate nodded and mouthed the word yes.

"Look, I've got to change his diaper and I'm not sure I even know how. Just tell Leenie that I'm bringing Andrew home to her tonight. And tell her he's fine."

"Wait!" Kate barely had the word out of her mouth when the dial tone buzzed.

"Does he have Andrew?" Leenie asked.

"He said to tell you that he has Andrew and—"

"Oh, God!" Leenie grabbed Kate, who still held the telephone in her hand. "Thank you, God."

Kate eased the phone back on the hook and wrapped her arms around Leenie. "Frank said that

Andrew is fine. He's bringing your son home to you tonight.''

''I wanted to talk to him, to ask him a dozen questions. Why did he hang up so quickly?''

''I believe Andrew needed an immediate diaper change and Frank was feeling a little overwhelmed by the daunting task. I don't think he's ever changed a diaper before.''

Leenie's joyous laughter was contagious and within seconds she and Kate were giggling and hugging and dancing around the room like a couple of adolescents. And when they'd exhausted themselves, they fell onto the sofa, all smiles and giddiness.

''I'll never ask for anything again as long as I live,'' Leenie said. ''All my prayers have been answered.''

''You're very lucky,'' Kate told her. ''You're getting your son back and I have a feeling it's only a matter of time before Frank realizes that he wants to spend the rest of his life with you and Andrew. You should have heard him on the phone. The guy was delirious with fatherly pride.''

Leenie sighed. ''Loving Andrew and loving me are two different things. I can't expect Frank to want me on a permanent basis just because he wants to be a father to Andrew.''

''Ready for some more unsolicited advice?''

''Sure. Advise away.''

''Don't put any pressure on Frank. Let him do things his way, in his own time. When he brings Andrew home, just enjoy the time y'all have together and don't worry too much about the future.''

''Kate, I wish…well, I know you must be thinking about Mary Kate and wondering why I'm getting my son back so quickly and your little girl has been missing for eleven years.''

Kate shrugged. ''Life's a mystery. Why I haven't found Mary Kate after over a decade of searching and why your Andrew is being returned to you only days after losing him is one of those mysteries.'' Kate patted Leenie's hand. ''Somehow, someway, someday, I'll find out what happened to my daughter. But for now, for tonight, you just concentrate on celebrating Andrew's return.''

Frank hadn't had a clue that he'd go ga-ga over a two-month-old kid. But the minute Dr. Tomlin's nurse put Andrew in his arms, Frank had melted like ice in the July sun. His little boy had looked at him with Leenie's big blue eyes and he'd been a goner on the spot.

''Is this Andrew Patton?'' Dante Moran had asked, pointing to the child Dr. Tomlin's nurse held.

''We've matched his footprint to Andrew Patton's footprint taken at birth and they're a perfect match,'' Dr. Tomlin had said. ''This young man is definitely Andrew.''

Yes, he certainly was. Andrew. His son. Frank had inspected the kid from top to bottom and seen himself or Leenie in every feature. Odd how he loved the child instantly, and not just because Andrew was his, but because Andrew was Leenie's.

Glancing in the rearview mirror of the rental car he was driving, Frank caught a shadowy glimpse of his son asleep in the carseat Dr. Tomlin had provided. Poor little guy, Frank thought. He'd worn himself out bellowing. Apparently Andrew hadn't inherited Leenie's sunny disposition. Of course, Andrew had been through a traumatic experience, being snatched away from the security of his mother's arms and the loving care of Debra Schmale.

"It's okay, kid," Frank said to the sleeping child, "I'm taking you home to your mama. We should be there in a few minutes. And as for your inheriting my grumpy disposition, don't worry about it. Women seem to go for surly, brooding men."

When Leenie's house came into view, Frank's gut tightened. Because of the bad weather—rain mixed with sleet—he'd driven much slower than his usual speed, so it had taken longer than it should have to make the drive from Memphis to Maysville. But he didn't want to take any chances with Andrew on-board. From now on, his top priority was going to be keeping his son safe. He didn't want Leenie to ever again have to endure the anguish she'd suffered these past few days.

The minute he pulled into the driveway, the front door flew open and Leenie ran outside, off the porch and into the yard. By the time he stopped the car, she was yanking on the back door handle. Frank unlocked the doors, undid his seat belt and got out, but before he could even say hello, Leenie was removing a sleeping Andrew from the carseat. She wrapped him in the blanket she'd brought with her and took him out of the car. She turned to Frank then and smiled as tears streamed down her cheeks. He put his hand on the small of her back and together they hurried into the house. Kate stood just inside the foyer, a warm smile on her face.

Suddenly Andrew let out a loud yowl. Leenie flung the damp blanket to the floor and crushed her baby to her chest. That one yowl turned into a screaming fit. Leenie held him away from her and looked at him, then spoke to him softly, a mother's tender rambling words to soothe her fretful child. Andrew didn't respond immediately, but Leenie kept talking to him and caressing him. Within minutes his crying diminished and soon stopped altogether. He focused his big blue eyes on his mother.

"Hello, my darling," Leenie said, then covered his little face with kisses.

Andrew whimpered, then cooed.

Frank thought he'd lose it right then and there. Hell, he couldn't remember the last time he'd cried. After his father's funeral? Yeah, that had been the last time. When he'd been alone. But seeing his son safe in Leenie's arms was enough to bring a grown man to his knees. She had a magic touch, the ability to soothe Andrew's surly Latimer disposition. Why should that surprise him? Hadn't she been able to work that same magic on him?

"I'm so happy that everything turned out this way," Kate said. "I'm going to make myself scarce so y'all can have this time alone with your son."

Cuddling Andrew close, Leenie said, "No, Kate, you don't have to—"

"This is family time—mother, father and baby time." Kate headed toward the guest bedroom. "I'll see y'all in the morning."

Frank followed Leenie into the living room and sat down beside her on the sofa. He lifted his arm and put it around her shoulders, encompassing her in his embrace as she did Andrew. They sat there together, the three of them, Andrew secure in his mother's arms. Frank couldn't remember ever feeling so good.

"You brought him home to me, just the way you

said you would.'' Leenie kissed the top of Andrew's head. The baby's eyelids drooped.

"He's a beautiful child,'' Frank told her. "Just perfect. And that's amazing considering I'm his father.''

Leenie laughed. And dear God, how strongly her laughter affected him. He'd never heard a sweeter sound.

"Has he been fed? Did you give him a bottle or—''

"I've changed his diaper twice and given him a bottle. Dr. Tomlin, the pediatrician the FBI used in Memphis, gave me three bottles of formula.''

"I breast-fed him, you know. I'd just weaned him onto a bottle when the wreck happened and he was taken...'' Leenie gulped down a sob.

Frank hugged her closer. "He's home. He's safe. The nightmare is over.''

"I don't think I'll ever let him out of my sight again as long as I live.''

Frank chuckled. "Yeah, I know the feeling, but I think Andrew will object when you start going out on his dates with him.''

"He's not even three months old and you're already talking about him dating.''

"Hey, if he takes after his old man, he'll have a girlfriend in kindergarten. Actually, he'll have half a dozen girlfriends.''

"I will not allow my son to be a ladies' man.'' Leenie tore her gaze away from Andrew to look at Frank. "But I won't mind if he takes after you in other ways. You, Frank Latimer, are quite a man and I'm glad you're my son's father.''

An embarrassing flush warmed Frank's face. No one had ever told him anything that affected him so strongly. His masculine pride doubled instantly. He leaned over and kissed Leenie, a gentle, fleeting kiss. "He's the luckiest kid in the world having you for a mother."

Nine

Frank locked up and set the security alarm after Leenie went to her bedroom, a fast-asleep Andrew cradled in her arms. These past few days had been the longest, most grueling days of his life, and he knew they'd been even worse for Leenie. He loved watching her with Andrew, the way she touched their child, the way the sound of her voice soothed him. For all her sexy, sophisticated, career-woman exterior, Leenie was a mother at heart. Of course, one was not exclusive of the other. He figured Dr. Lurleen Patton was what people might call a multifaceted woman. And he sure as hell had never known anyone like her. She wasn't anything like his mother, who'd never done a selfless thing in her life, who had put her own needs above her son's and daughter's needs time and again. And Leenie bore no resemblance to his former wife. What had he ever seen in Rita, beyond her flashy good looks?

Listen to yourself, Latimer, you sound like a man in love. No way! Even if he did like Leenie, even care about her deeply, he wasn't fool enough to fall in love. Never again. Once had been one time too many. Okay, so Leenie was as different from Rita as night is from day. It didn't matter. Love was no guarantee of happiness. And what could start out as a wonderful relationship—like he'd thought his marriage to Rita was—could turn out to be very wrong. There were too many unknowns between two people. He had seen a lot of promising relationships end up in the gutter, a couple battling it out in the divorce courts. He and Leenie were too smart to make forever promises, to risk not only messing up their lives, but Andrew's too. Wasn't the kid better off with two parents who liked and respected each other and shared the responsibilities of raising him than parents who'd been madly in love and ended up fighting over who was going to get custody of him when they split?

Frank turned out all the lights, except the one lamp in the corner of the living room. He removed his cell phone from his pocket and dialed Sawyer Mac-Namara's private number. He could easily wait until morning to call his boss, but now that he'd made his decision to keep things friendly but not committed between Leenie and him, he wanted to forge ahead with his plans to become acquainted with his son. He needed some time off, some time to spend with Andrew. And during that time, he and Leenie could figure out how they wanted to handle their joint parenthood. Right now, with Andrew a baby, he probably needed Leenie more than he needed Frank. But as he grew older, he might need Frank more. He could suggest to Leenie that they take things a year at a time and see how things worked out as their son matured.

Sawyer answered his phone on the third ring. "McNamara here."

"Yeah, it's Frank Latimer."

"I spoke to Moran earlier and then to Kate. I'm glad to know everything worked out and you were able to take the baby home to his mother. Kate tells me that the child is well."

"Andrew is fine, now that he's with his mother." Frank paused for a moment, then made his request. "I need some time off. A week, maybe ten days. Leenie…Dr. Patton and I have some things to work out about Andrew. And I'd like a chance to get to know my son before I head back to Atlanta and go out on another case."

"A week, even two, can be arranged," Sawyer said. "And if you need more time—"

"Ten days, tops."

"Good thing I hired Geoff Monday. He can pick up some of the slack and fill in for you and Kate until you're both back on the job."

"Kate's taking time off, too? Why? I thought she'd be flying back to Atlanta tomorrow."

"She asked for a leave of absence for personal reasons. I figured she might have told you what those reasons were."

"She hasn't said a word to me."

"Okay. So, we'll see you back at the office in a couple of weeks."

"A week to ten days," Frank corrected.

"Fine. A week to ten days. Good luck, Frank. I

hope you and Dr. Patton can come to an amicable agreement about your son.''

''Thanks. I see no reason why we can't. Leenie is a reasonable woman. And being a psychiatrist, she knows how important it is for a child to have two parents who have an amicable relationship.''

''Sounds like you've got it all worked out, at least from your point of view.''

''Yeah. I do.''

After he finished talking to Sawyer, doubts started creeping into his mind. Maybe Leenie wouldn't be cooperative, maybe she wouldn't like the idea of sharing Andrew. After all, she hadn't let him know she was pregnant, hadn't informed him after Andrew was born that he had a son. If Andrew hadn't been kidnapped, would she have ever told him about his child's existence?

Rubbing the back of his neck as he stretched, Frank groaned. He was tired and sleepy. And confused. He needed a good night's sleep. Then in the morning, he'd be able to think straight.

As he walked down the hall, he noticed Leenie's bedroom door stood open. He couldn't resist peeking in on her and Andrew. He stopped in the doorway. His gut clenched when he saw Leenie, in her pink silk gown, lying in bed, her long hair fanned out on her pillow, and Andrew, in his blue terrycloth pajamas, cuddled against Leenie's chest. Mother and child.

His son.

His woman!

Damn, why couldn't he stop thinking of Leenie as his. These past few days he'd become much too possessive of her. How could they build separate lives if he kept laying claim to her?

Face the facts, he told himself. Eventually Leenie was going to start dating again. There would be other men in her life. Other men in Andrew's life, whether he liked it or not. No! He didn't want other men parading in and out of his son's life. But who was to say that Leenie wouldn't find one special guy and get married. It could happen. And then Andrew would have a stepfather.

He had to stop doing this to himself. Don't start making decisions based on what ifs, he told himself.

As he watched Leenie and Andrew sleeping, he was so drawn to them that he couldn't resist the temptation to be near them. It wasn't as if he was invading her privacy. She'd left the door open, hadn't she? She'd probably expected him to check on them before he turned in for the night. Leaving the door open the way she had was an invitation, wasn't it?

Frank walked quietly into the room, not stopping until he reached the bed. What would it hurt if he stayed here with them? Just for tonight. After all, it was Andrew's homecoming. But if he lay down beside them, he might waken Leenie and God knew she needed her rest after all she'd been through. But he could not bring himself to leave. Glancing around the semidark room, he noticed the comfy overstuffed chair in the corner. He could rest comfortably there without disturbing Leenie and Andrew and at the same time, he could be with them, keep watch over them.

Frank made his way to the chair, sat, adjusted his body until he was fairly comfortable, then dragged the knitted lavender afghan from the back of the chair and spread it out over him. A tad short for his long frame, it covered him from shoulders to knees.

For quite a while he sat there, his gaze glued to the woman and infant in the bed. But finally exhaustion overcame him and his eyelids drooped. He yawned, then closed his eyes and gave in to sleep.

Andrew was crying.

It's all right, baby. Mother's here. You're safe.

Leenie woke with a start. When she found Andrew wriggling against her, his little nose and mouth rooting at her breast, she sighed contentedly. *Thank you, God. Thank you for keeping my baby safe and bringing him home to me.*

"Hush, my darling," Leenie whispered. "Mommy will get you a bottle. It won't take a minute."

She got out of bed, then reached down and lifted a whimpering Andrew up and into her arms. Just as she turned around, she noticed Frank in the chair in the corner. She gasped. When had he come into her bedroom? He roused groggily from sleep and stood.

"Is he all right?" Frank asked, his voice husky.

Leenie had left the door to her room open, hoping Frank would come to her—come to her and Andrew and be a part of Andrew's homecoming. Apparently she'd fallen asleep before he'd joined them.

"He's fine. Just hungry." How was it that a man who needed a haircut and a shave and whose clothes always looked as if he slept in them could be so damned attractive? she wondered. And in the middle of the night, no less. "I have several bottles in the refrigerator. I'm taking Andrew with me to get one and warm it in the microwave."

"You stay here," Frank told her. "Let me get Andrew's bottle."

"All right. Thank you." Leenie began walking the floor with her whiny little boy. "But hurry, will you? Your son won't be patient for long. He wants what he wants when he wants it."

"Not unlike his father." Frank grinned. "By the way, how long do I heat the bottle in the microwave?"

"About forty-five seconds, then test it on the inside of your wrist. It should be warm, but not hot."

When Frank disappeared out into the hall, Leenie paced the floor, crooning to Andrew. How wonderful to hold him again. She kissed his little head. Ah, she loved his sweet smell.

By the time Frank returned—in three minutes flat—Andrew's whimpers had grown louder.

Her son had a big appetite and little patience.

"Here you go." Frank held out the bottle to her.

"Would you like to feed him?"

"Me?"

"You've already fed him once, right? You're an old pro now."

"Yeah, sure. I—"

"Sit back down in the chair and I'll hand him to you."

Frank did as she'd instructed. Then she placed Andrew in his arms. At first Andrew cried, apparently not happy about leaving his mother's arms. But when Frank stuck the nipple in his mouth, Andrew latched on and began sucking. Frank looked up at Leenie and smiled triumphantly.

"You're a natural," she told him.

"Am I?"

Her heart did a crazy rat-a-tat-tat. She wanted to wrap her arms around Frank and hug the life out of him. Didn't he have any idea how wonderful he was? Couldn't the big lug figure out that he was meant to be a family man? He was gentle, kind, loving and had so much to give to a woman and child. If only he wasn't so scarred from bad experiences with a selfish mother and an unfaithful wife. If only the two most important women in his life hadn't crippled him emotionally.

"The way you are with Andrew, a person would think you had vast experience with babies," Leenie said.

"I have zero experience with babies. It's Andrew. The way I feel about him makes it so easy to just—" Frank lifted his gaze from his son to Leenie. "I want to be a part of his life from now on."

She nodded. Emotion welled up inside her. Why hadn't she called Frank and told him the minute she found out she was pregnant?

"I called my boss at Dundee and asked for some time off. A week. I thought…that is if it's okay with you, I'd like to stay and get to know my son."

"Of course it's okay with me. I want you to be a part of Andrew's life."

"You won't have to put up with me permanently. Just for the next week or so." Frank looked down at Andrew. "I know a baby needs his mother, but when I'm between assignments, I'd like to come for visits. And maybe when Andrew is older, you might let him visit me in Atlanta."

Leenie clenched her teeth, then forced a smile, even though her heart was breaking. What had she expected? Not some confession of undying love. Not from Frank Latimer. He might love his son, but by God, he wasn't going to ever trust his heart to another woman, not even his son's mother. Not even to a woman who loved him so damn much that she could hardly stand it.

Smiling like an idiot, Leenie nodded and willed herself not to cry. She swallowed hard, then said, "Absolutely. You'll be welcome here any time. I want you to be a father to Andrew."

"Thanks, Slim." With Andrew nestled against him, Frank held the bottle securely in place while he leaned down and kissed his son's forehead.

Kate answered her cell phone on the first ring. She'd been waiting all night for this call.

"Hello."

"Kate?"

"Yes."

"I'm sorry it's taken me so long to get back to you, but I've had a lot going on here in Memphis. I guess Frank told you something about—"

"Frank doesn't really care about the FBI's great success," Kate said. "Andrew is all that matters to him."

"Yes, of course. That's understandable." Dante Moran hesitated for several moments. "I'm afraid I'm puzzled as to why you left me a message to call you. Is there some information Dundee needs in order to close out the case?"

"This wasn't an official Dundee case. This was a personal matter for Frank. Sawyer McNamara sent me along because...well, to be honest with you, Sawyer thought I might have a special interest in Andrew Patton's kidnapping."

"You've lost me. I don't understand why—"

"Eleven years ago my daughter was kidnapped and to this day I don't know what happened to her. I've searched for her for over a decade without any success. What I want to know is this—did y'all confiscate any files on the abducted children? Things like where they were born. State? Town? And dates. Dates of births? Dates they were adopted? Who adopted them?"

"You're asking me to divulge official FBI business," Moran said.

"All you have to say is yes or no."

"Yes."

Kate sucked in her breath. "How far back do those files go?"

"Rephrase that so I can give you a yes or no reply."

"Do they go back eleven years?"

"Yes."

Kate's heart lurched to her throat and for a moment she couldn't breathe. "Is there any way I can get a look at those files?"

"No."

"What if Sawyer McNamara—"

"No."

"You don't understand." Kate didn't mind begging. She'd gladly get down on her hands and knees and plead with him if she thought it would get her what she wanted. "Please. If there's even the slightest chance that my daughter was taken by the same abduction ring that stole Andrew—"

"I can't promise you anything. But I'll pull the files from ten years ago and take a look. I can't give you permission to see the files, but if you'll give me all the information on your daughter—"

"Mary Kate Winston. She was two months old. Blonde. Brown-eyed. Kidnapped from Prospect, Alabama. I can fax you all the details."

"You do that."

"How long—?"

"It could take days to find something...if there's anything to find."

"I'm coming to Memphis," Kate told him. "I'll give you the details of Mary Kate's abduction when I get there."

"I'll be expecting you."

"Moran?"

"Huh?"

"Thanks."

"Don't thank me. I haven't done anything."

"Oh yes you have. You've given me just a tiny bit of hope. I'm not sure why you're doing this for me. I don't think it's because you're such a nice guy, is it?"

"Hell no. Anybody who knows me will tell you I'm a real hard-ass."

"Then why?"

"Don't look a gift horse in the mouth."

"I'll leave for Memphis as soon as I can get packed."

Leenie and Frank stood in the doorway, Andrew in Leenie's arms, and waved goodbye to Kate as she walked toward Frank's rental car parked in the driveway.

"Be careful driving in this rain," Leenie cautioned.

"The roads are probably still slippery from last night's sleet."

"I'll be very careful," Kate called back as she opened the car door.

"Call us when you get to Memphis," Frank said.

"Becoming a father has certainly turned you into the paternal type, hasn't it," Kate said jokingly, then slammed the door and started the car.

As soon as Kate backed out of the drive, Frank closed the door and turned to Leenie. "She'll be all right. I'm sure the roads are mostly clear by now. It's nearly ten o'clock."

"I'm not as concerned about her arriving safely to Memphis as I am about what she'll find out while she's there. If there is no information about her daughter in those files the FBI confiscated, she'll be heartbroken. She's been searching for her little girl for eleven years."

Frank slipped his arm around Leenie's shoulder, then tickled Andrew under his chin. "Everybody at Dundee knew there was something tragic in her past and some even speculated it had to do with a child, but none of us knew exactly what had happened."

"I can't imagine how she's stayed sane all these years," Leenie said. "And not only stayed sane, but actually functioned, kept a job, lived a fairly normal life and all. If I'd lost Andrew that way—"

"You didn't. He's right here, safe in your arms." Frank hugged her and their son to him. She slipped her free arm around Frank, trapping Andrew between them.

When Frank leaned over and kissed her on the mouth and then kissed Andrew on the top of his head, Andrew fussed loudly.

"I think we're crowding him," Frank said, a wide grin on his face. "So, Mama, what's the next thing on the agenda for today? Andrew's had his morning bottle and a diaper change, so what's next?"

"A bath. Want to give Andrew his bath?"

"Me?"

"Yes, you."

"Sure. No problem. How hard can it be to give a two-month-old a bath?"

Leenie smiled. Frank had a great deal to learn about babies.

Ten

Leenie prepared Andrew's bath, placing everything Frank would need in easy reach. Then she handed her son over to his father. Frank grinned confidently and laid Andrew on the changing table in the corner of the bathroom. Although Andrew whined softly, Frank managed to remove his son's sleeper and diaper before Andrew bellowed loudly.

Frank lifted Andrew in his arms, the baby's fat little naked body wriggling. "What's the matter big boy? Did Daddy not do it right? Is Mommy better at this than I am?"

When Andrew yelled even louder, his face turning red and tears pooling in his eyes, Frank turned to Leenie, who stood in the bathroom doorway. "Maybe you'd better—"

"No way." Leenie shook her head. "You can't change your mind at the last minute just because this is turning out to be a bit more difficult than you'd anticipated.'' When Frank frowned at her, she smiled. ''Remember, you're going to be around for only a week, so you need to cram a lot of experiences with Andrew into the time you'll have with him.''

Leenie was proud of herself for being able to joke with Frank about him leaving soon. Her pride demanded that he not know how much she wanted him to stay. If he didn't love her, she would be better off without him, wouldn't she? And she certainly wasn't going to use Andrew to hang on to a man who didn't want her.

Frank nodded. ''You're right.'' He carried a less-than-happy Andrew over to the bathroom sink filled with lukewarm bathwater, then shifted his son around in his arms several times. Once again he looked at Leenie. ''Maybe you'd better show me how to do this.''

Not budging an inch, Leenie said, ''Use your arm to support him, then ease him down into the water. The liquid soap and washcloth are right there on the vanity. And so is the shampoo. I usually wash his hair first, but if you prefer to leave that until last, it's okay.''

''No, we'll do this the way you always do it.''

Going by Leenie's instructions, Frank eased his son into the sink. Andrew quieted, but continued sniffing tiny sobs while Frank talked to him. Nonsensical words. Baby talk. It was all Leenie could do not to burst out laughing. If only the other Dundee agents could see him now, trying to support a baby in his bathwater with one arm while struggling with his other hand to open a bottle of shampoo. Finally after several attempts Frank managed to squirt a generous amount of shampoo into his hand.

"You know a guy needs at least four hands to do this." Frank wiped half the shampoo off on the vanity counter, then rubbed the rest into Andrew's hair.

Leenie watched while Frank scrubbed Andrew from top to bottom. And he was doing a pretty good job, too. Andrew cooperated fully, enjoying his bath—until Frank started to rinse the shampoo from his hair. The minute several drops of soapy water trickled down on his face, Andrew started screaming and thrashing. Water splashed everywhere. All over the vanity. Across the mirror behind the sink. And onto Frank, drenching his shirt and dampening his jeans.

"Help!" Frank called out. "I need reinforcements."

Chuckling softly, Leenie rushed in to assist him. "Here, let me take over."

The minute Leenie eased her arm around Andrew, Frank pulled back and moved out of her way. "Mommy to the rescue," Frank said to his son. "It's a good thing we've got her, isn't it?"

With practiced ease, Leenie soothed Andrew, then rinsed his hair and body thoroughly before lifting him up and out of the sink. Holding him with one hand, she picked up the hooded towel and wrapped him in it, covering his head with the hood. She turned to show Frank how easily the job had been accomplished, but instead stopped dead still and sucked in her breath.

Oh, jeez! Frank had stripped out of his shirt, leaving him bare to the waist. It just wasn't fair that he looked so damned appealing. Some men looked better with their clothes on. Not Frank Latimer. He definitely looked better without clothes. As a matter of fact, he was downright irresistible.

When he caught her ogling his muscular chest, he grinned. An electrified awareness passed between them. Leenie forced her gaze from his chest to his face.

"He's probably gotten you wet to the skin, too," Frank said, pointedly staring at her shirt, his gaze quickly zeroing in on the exposed right side of the damp cloth sticking to her breast. Andrew lay pressed to the left side, effectively concealing the other breast.

She swallowed. Her nipples tightened. "Why don't you put on a dry shirt while I get Andrew dressed." That said, she hurried out of the bathroom and straight to Andrew's nursery.

Escape! her mind screamed. *Get the hell away from Frank before he figures out how much you want him.* It was ridiculous the way her body reacted to him, to nothing more than him staring at her breast. If she gave in to her desires, she'd jump Frank the minute Andrew went down for a nap.

So, would that be so bad? she asked herself. *Yes, the logical part of her brain responded, you'd be a fool to fall into the sack with him. The guy's leaving in a week, running off to God knows where on his next assignment.* If she was smart, she'd keep Frank out of her bed and find a way to rip him out of her heart. When he left Maysville, he'd return to his life back in Atlanta. And that meant he'd be dating other women.

Gritting her teeth, Leenie growled inwardly, with only a murmured whine audible. She hugged her baby before laying him in the middle of his crib.

By the time Frank joined them in their son's room a few minutes later, she had dressed Andrew for the day in navy blue corduroy overalls and a light blue cotton knit shirt. Just as she pulled on his light blue socks and white booties, Frank came up behind her and looked over her shoulder. She felt the heat from his body as he stood there so very close, his chest brushing against her back. When she glanced over her shoulder to speak to him, she gasped when she realized he'd lowered his head so that they were nose to nose, only inches separating them. She sucked in her breath. They stared at each other, both momentarily transfixed. And then he gave her a quick kiss, a kiss that was over before she had a chance to react. Frank slipped his arm around her waist, then looked down in the crib at Andrew. Using his free hand, he reached out and tickled Andrew's belly.

"I hope you'll give your dad another chance," Frank said. "If Mommy will let me, I want to try giving you a bath tomorrow."

Clearing her throat, Leenie responded. "Of course you can try again tomorrow. You can do anything you want for and with Andrew while you're here. You can bathe him and give him his bottle. You can rock him, sing to him, walk the floor with him. And change his diapers. Both the wet ones and the dirty ones."

Frank groaned. "I'm not sure about the dirty ones. I might leave those to you."

"Ah, don't be a chicken. You want to teach your son to be brave, don't you? How's it going to look to him if years from now he finds out you were afraid of a dirty diaper?"

"Being a man himself, I figure he'll understand."

"Andrew will not be a chauvinist. He's going to

be the type of man who shares all the responsibilities for childcare with his wife.'' The moment she made the statement, she wished back the words. She couldn't retract what she'd said, no matter how much she'd like to. Had Frank misconstrued her perfectly innocent comment? Would he think she was hinting for a marriage proposal?

When Frank didn't say anything, was in fact extremely quiet, Leenie took a deep breath and said, ''That's a generalization, of course. I'm assuming Andrew will be married before he becomes a father.''

Frank cleared his throat. ''Yeah. We—er—it'll be a case of do as I say, not do as I did.''

Leenie groaned. ''Look, let's just lay our cards on the table, okay?'' She reached up and wound the Noah's Ark musical mobile hanging above the crib. ''We've been dancing around each other, around the subject of marriage and sharing custody of Andrew and his future…our futures.''

''I didn't want to rush you into making decisions right away.'' Frank stepped back, putting some distance between their bodies. ''I thought I was doing the right thing by not pushing you, by giving you time to recover from everything you've gone through lately.''

With Andrew contentedly gurgling and cooing as he watched the colorful animals circling above him and listening to the soft lullaby the mobile's music box played, Leenie turned to Frank. ''Let's step out in the hall.''

Frank stared at her with a puzzled expression on his face.

''Babies pick up on the moods of the adults in their

life, especially their mother's mood. In case either of us gets upset or talks a little too loud or—"

"Are we going to have an argument?"

"No, of course not. It's just...well, we might not agree on everything. And I'd rather Andrew not be exposed to our differences of opinion. Not now. And not in the future."

Frank nodded. "I agree."

When Leenie walked out of the nursery and down the hall, Frank followed her. After pausing a few feet shy of her bedroom door, she confronted Frank.

"I don't want you to get the wrong impression," she told him. "Or read anything into the comment I made."

"What wrong impression?"

"About marriage."

"I didn't read anything into your comment," he said. "I hope Andrew is married when he becomes a father. It'll make his life and his child's much easier." Frank's gaze met hers. "Not to mention his child's mother."

"Hmm-mmm." Leenie blew out a long, huffing sigh. "Let me be honest with you." *Yeah, sure, you're going to be honest with him.* Her conscience laughed at her lie. Okay, so she'd be honest with him, up to a point.

"By all means." Frank leaned closer, placed his open palm on the wall behind Leenie's head and looked directly into her eyes. "Be honest with me."

Leenie's knees went weak. Her heartbeat accelerated. "I'm very fond of you. And I like you." *Oh, get real, Leenie. You're fond of him? You like him? You're not being exactly honest are you? Okay, so*

I'm hog-wild crazy about him. I love the big lug so much it hurts.

"I'm very fond of you, too." He didn't take his eyes off her. "And I've been surprised by the fact that I like you so much. Really like you. More than any woman..." He cleared his throat. "Let's just say I admire you."

He admired her? Well, at least that was something. "Ideally, I'd like to be married to my son's father, but—"

"That would be ideal for Andrew, for any kid, to have his parents married to each other. But having parents who are not married is much better than having married parents who fight all the time. Believe me, I know. My parents hated each other and my sister and I paid the price for every one of their battles."

"You're right, of course. Parents who don't love each other shouldn't be married."

"Sometimes even love isn't enough to keep people together. I loved Rita, but—"

"It usually is when both of them are in love."

Frank removed his hand from the wall and stood up straight. "Yeah, I suppose that's true."

The rather sad look on Frank's face touched her heart. She wanted to hug him to her and tell him that she'd never betray him the way Rita had, that he could trust her with his love.

"We don't have to rehash any of your bad memories. Your parent's horrible marriage. Your breakup with Rita. And I won't bore you with how many years I looked for Mr. Right and kept finding one Mr. Wrong after another. Nor will I go to great lengths to make you understand how important a family is to me since I grew up without a real family. But you do need to know that Andrew is the most important thing in my life and although I'm willing for you to be a part of his life—''

''But since we aren't married, I'll never be a full-time dad. You'll be his primary caretaker and some-day if...when you marry, your husband will be a full-time dad to my son.''

She stared at Frank, her mind trying to understand his reasoning. ''You've given this quite a bit of thought, haven't you?''

Frank stuck his hands in his pockets as if he needed to do something with them. ''Since we're being honest with each other...'' He grimaced, as if what he had to say pained him. ''The truth of the matter is that I hate the idea of Andrew having a stepfather.''

Leenie nodded. ''I understand. Believe me, I'd hate him having a stepmother.''

Frank grabbed her by the shoulders, his big, long fingers holding her firmly. ''I hate the idea of you with another man.''

Her eyes rounded in surprise. Her stomach muscles tightened. ''Frank?''

His mouth came down on hers possessively, claim-ing her completely. She responded immediately, re-turning his passion. When she lifted her arms to en-circle his neck, his hands skimmed either side of her waist and moved downward, settling on her hips. He pressed her against him. She gasped when she felt his erection.

Stop this while you still can, the sensible part of her mind told her. But it felt so good to be in Frank's arms, to have his mouth devouring hers, to know that he wanted her as desperately as she wanted him.

However, just because he didn't want another man to have her didn't mean he loved her. Remember that, she told herself.

If she succumbed to Frank every time he came back to Maysville to visit Andrew, she'd wind up living in limbo, always waiting for Frank, accepting him on his terms, taking whatever he was willing to give her. She simply couldn't live that way. She wanted more. Hell, she deserved better.

Ending the kiss, she shoved against his chest. He didn't stop immediately, but when she gave him a second and much harder shove, he halted, pulled back and glared at her.

"I can't," she told him.

"Leenie…"

She held both hands up between them, warning him off. "It's not that I don't want you. God knows I do. I want you so much. But even though you're Andrew's father and have every right to come in and out of his life from now on, I can't put my life on hold waiting for your visits, no matter how frequent they might be. I want more than a part-time lover, more than an on-again-off-again affair."

The vein in Frank's neck throbbed. His gaze narrowed as he studied her face intently. "Do you think holding out on me will make me propose? Is that it? You want me to marry you and you think I want to have sex with you so much that I'll—"

How dare he! To think he'd judge her so harshly, that he'd believe her capable of doing such a despicable thing. Leenie saw red. "Why you egotistical bastard, you!" She flung back her hand, instinctively preparing to attack.

Catching her by the wrist, Frank aborted the slap

midair. "I won't be manipulated, honey. I've played the puppet fool for women more masterful at the art than you. My mother led my father around by the nose for years and she used me and my sister to torment the hell out of him. And Rita—"

"Rita, Rita, Rita!" Leenie jerked free of his hold. "God, Frank, grow up, will you? Do you think you're the only person who had a rotten childhood? Do you think you're the only man who's ever let a woman make a fool of him? I made a mistake thinking you were strong and brave and fearless. Under that Dundee agent guise of yours, you're a coward. You're scared of me. You don't have the guts to love me, let alone marry me."

Frank opened his mouth to respond, but before he could, she tapped her finger on his chest repeatedly and shouted, "I wouldn't marry you if you were the last man on earth. Do you hear me, Frank Latimer? You're lousy husband material." She whirled around and ran to her bedroom.

Frank stood in the hallway, so stunned that he couldn't move or speak for several minutes. By the time he recovered, Leenie had slammed her bedroom door in his face and Andrew was crying at the top of his lungs.

Frank cursed softly under his breath as he stared at the closed door. Women! Hadn't she said she wanted them to be honest with each other? Apparently she hadn't meant what she'd said. Leenie wasn't any different from other women. All that mattered to her was what she wanted, what she needed. Well, he didn't want to get married and he sure as hell didn't need her. He didn't need any woman.

Andrew's cries grew louder. Frank banged on Leenie's bedroom door. "Andrew's crying."

"I'm not deaf," she shouted through the closed door.

"Aren't you going check on him?"

"You're his father, aren't you? You go see why he's crying."

"All right, I will."

Frank stomped off down the hallway, went into the nursery, marched over to his son's crib and looked down at the red-faced infant. "What's the matter? Did you hear your mother screaming at me?" Frank leaned over the crib, then reached down and lifted Andrew up and into his arms. He laid his son on his shoulder and patted his back lovingly. "It's all right. Don't cry. I think I just made a big mistake and I don't know how I'm going to fix it."

After several minutes of being petted and soothed, Andrew stopped crying and lay peacefully against his father.

"You might as well know it now, son—you'll never understand women."

After sulking in her room for a good fifteen minutes, Leenie eased open the door and peeked outside, making sure Frank wasn't waiting around for her. Since Andrew had stopped crying, she assumed Frank had managed to soothe their son.

Their son.

Frank was right about one thing—about the way squabbling parents had an adverse effect on kids. If they were going to work out an arrangement to share Andrew—and whether she wanted to or not, she knew it was the right thing to do—they had to find a way to be friends. Just not friends *and* lovers. She could not deal with an on-again-off-again affair.

Could she?

No! Absolutely positively not!

Opening the door wide, she scanned the hallway and saw no sign of Frank. She walked quietly down the hall to the nursery. The door was open, the room empty. Frank must have taken Andrew downstairs, she thought. He'd probably realized Andrew was hungry and he'd taken him to the kitchen to prepare a bottle.

Do what you have to do, she told herself. *Go find Frank and settle things with him. Convince him that you don't expect him to marry you, that it's not what you want. Lie to him? Yes, lie to him, if that's what it takes to make peace. For Andrew's sake.*

Leenie went to the living room, through the dining room and into the kitchen, but saw no sign of Frank and Andrew. Where were they? Surely Frank hadn't gone outside with Andrew, not in this freezing weather.

"Frank?" she called.

No response.

She rushed from room to room, searching the entire house, calling out Frank's name repeatedly. Realizing they weren't anywhere inside, Leenie grabbed her coat off the rack and rushed into the backyard. Empty. A few birds searched the frozen ground for food. A lone squirrel scurried across the fence and onto a low hanging limb.

"Frank Latimer, where are you?" she cried.

Silence.

She raced to the front yard. No sign of them. Then she opened the garage and stopped dead still when she saw her SUV was missing. Frank had taken Andrew! He'd put her baby in his car seat inside the Envoy and driven off with him. Without saying one word to her. Where the hell had Frank gone? How dare he run off with Andrew!

Calm down, Leenie, she told herself. *Frank has not kidnapped Andrew. You're overreacting. Take some deep breaths. Andrew is safe. He's with his father.*

Leenie sat down on the front step, pulled her knees up to her chest and hugged her arm around her legs as she rocked back and forth. *How could you do this to me, Frank?* she asked silently. *What were you thinking, taking Andrew without asking me?*

Andrew is all right. Frank will bring him back. Andrew is all right. Frank will bring him back. As she sat there, the frigid winter wind chilling her to the bone, Leenie kept reassuring herself. But deep down inside fear ate away at her, gradually eroding her belief that Frank would never actually take Andrew away from her.

The minute he turned the SUV into the driveway, Frank saw Leenie sitting on the steps and wondered why she was there instead of inside. It couldn't be much more than thirty-nine or forty degrees, with a wind chill factor of well below freezing. So what was she doing outside? Was something wrong? When she saw him, she jumped up and came running toward the Envoy, waving her arms and screaming something. Good God, what had happened? Instead of pulling into the garage as he'd planned, he stopped the vehicle in the driveway and rolled down his window.

"Where is Andrew?" Leenie cried."

"Shh." Frank put his index finger to his lips to

indicate silence, then nodded to the back seat where a sleeping Andrew rested comfortably in his car seat. "Don't wake him."

"Don't you dare tell me what to do!" she screeched at Frank as she jerked on the backdoor handle. "Open this damn door. I want my son!"

"What the hell's the matter with you?" Frank hit the button to unlock the doors, then opened his door and got out just as Leenie flung open the back door. He grabbed her half a second before she dove inside the SUV.

When he hauled her out of the Envoy, she fought him like a wild woman for a couple of seconds. He yanked her to him, then reached around her and closed the door quietly before her tirade woke Andrew.

"Tell me what's wrong?" he asked when she glared at him.

"You took Andrew away and I had no idea where you'd gone or if...if you'd bring him back. How dare you—"

Frank grasped her shoulders and shook her gently. "Calm down. You're nearly hysterical."

"I am not hysterical. How dare you take Andrew without telling me. You should have—"

"I left a note on the refrigerator. Didn't you see it? God, Slim, you're overreacting a bit, aren't you?"

"Overreacting my ass, you unfeeling, uncaring bastard! My son was kidnapped and for days I had no idea if he was dead or alive. And you just take him with you, without telling me. What was I supposed to think?"

Ah, hell. When she put it that way, she made sense. Frank hadn't given it a thought, taking Andrew with him to pick up lunch. He'd hoped that the meal could be a peace offering, had believed she'd see him providing lunch as a caring thing to do. The last thing he'd intended was to frighten Leenie. No wonder she was so upset.

He loosened his tight grip on her shoulders and looked into her teary eyes. "I'm sorry. God, honey, I'm so sorry. I didn't think. You have a right to call me every name in the book. I went to pick up lunch for us and since Andrew was a little fussy, I just took him and a bottle with me. I knew if I knocked on your bedroom door, you'd just holler at me again, so—"

"I panicked when I realized you'd taken Andrew. I didn't see the note you'd left."

"What I did was thoughtless. It was stupid."

"I—I did overreact."

He pulled her into his arms, then kissed her temple. "I'm sorry about all the things I said to you earlier. I know you'd never do what I accused you of doing. You're nothing like my mother or my ex-wife. Let's face it, I'm an idiot."

"You're not an idiot. You want us to be lovers and when I said no, you went with your gut reaction and thought I was trying to pull a fast one on you. I wasn't. I'd never do that."

"Yeah, I know. And you're right. I have a major problem with trusting a woman. And you're right about my wanting us to be lovers. But I'll settle for our being friends."

"Oh, Frank, don't you see—we can't be just friends. The sexual chemistry between us is too strong. We're already using Andrew as an excuse to bicker, when what we should do is—"

"Get married?"

"What? No, I mean—"

"Are you saying that if I asked you to marry me, you'd say no?"

"Yes. No. Oh, damn it, Frank, don't do this. You don't want to get married. Not to me. Not to anyone."

"I want to be a full-time father to Andrew. I want to be a full-time lover to you. Do you have another solution, other than marriage?"

Eleven

"Let's postpone this talk until later," Leenie had told Frank. "Right now, all I want is to take Andrew inside and put him in his bed. I need to see him safe and sound in his own room, with me watching over him."

Frank had opened the door, removed Andrew from his car seat and handed him to her. "I'm sorry I upset you. I swear it'll never happen again. I won't even take Andrew from one room to another without asking you, if that's what you want."

How could she stay angry with Frank when he was so apologetic? And sincerely so. If she had trusted him, the thought that he might have taken Andrew away from her would never have entered her mind. But that was one of the problems between them—she and Frank didn't trust each other. He didn't trust women in general, and understandably so, after the numbers his mother and Rita had done on him. And trust was an issue with her, too. She didn't trust Frank not to hurt her, and he would, even though it really wouldn't be his fault. He couldn't help it if he didn't love her.

They spent the rest of the day together as a family. She and Frank had shared the chicken salads and freshly baked croissants he'd gone to the deli and bought for their lunch. And they'd talked about the future, about the pros and cons of marriage versus finding a way to share joint custody of Andrew. But they hadn't reached a decision, hadn't agreed on a solution to their problem. They both wanted what was best for Andrew, but couldn't decide exactly what that was.

When Andrew woke from his nap, Frank had changed his diaper and given him a bottle while she telephoned Debra to check on her progress.

"I should be able to leave the hospital the day after tomorrow," Debra had said. "Are you sure my coming to your house won't be a problem since Frank's still there?"

"Frank and I can sort through our problems just as easily with you here as we can alone."

"What's wrong? I hear something in your voice."

"Frank thinks maybe we should get married."

"That's wonderful," Debra had said.

"He thinks we should get married for Andrew's sake."

"That's not so wonderful."

No, that wasn't so wonderful. She loved Frank and wanted to be his wife. She'd like nothing better than to have him around all the time, for him to be a full-time father to his son. But what sort of life would it be for them? How long would it take before Frank started feeling trapped? And how long would it be before he realized she was madly in love with him? Sooner or later, she'd want more than great sex and his admiration. And eventually her neediness would push him further and further away from her.

The sun set early in December, making the days short. Darkness descended somewhere around five o'clock. While Frank sat on the floor beside Andrew, who lay on a quilt staring up at his infant jungle gym, and watching as his father played with the toy, Leenie went around closing all the blinds and turning on lamps throughout the house.

''Are you hungry?'' she asked, standing across the room watching Frank entertaining his son. ''Want me to open some cans and put together a bite of supper?''

''Yeah, I'm getting hungry, but why don't we just order pizza?''

''Okay. What do you like on yours?''

''The works. Everything but anchovies.''

''All right.''

When Frank smiled at her, she returned his smile. Suddenly the telephone rang. Leenie jumped.

''Want me to get it?'' he asked.

''No, I'll get it. I'm just jittery from days of hoping and praying the phone would ring and we'd hear good news.'' She went over to the portable phone resting on the desk near the windows, picked up the receiver and said, ''Hello, Patton residence.''

''Leenie?''

''Haley?''

''Hey, girl. When can I come over and see my godson?''

"Anytime you'd like. I was wondering why you hadn't already dropped by."

"I thought you and Frank might need some time alone with Andrew," Haley said. "Besides, I'm having some problems here at the station and I'll be stuck here until I can find a replacement for your replacement on tonight's show."

"What happened to Dr. Bryant?"

"An emergency appendectomy around two this afternoon."

"What about Megan Vickers?"

"Called her office. She's out of town."

"You know, Haley, I could come in just for tonight."

"Could you? No. Forget it. You're not ready to come back to work."

Frank eased Andrew out from under the plastic jungle gym and lifted him into his arms.

"What's wrong?" he asked.

"Wait just a minute, will you, Haley?" She placed her hand over the mouthpiece and looked at Frank. "Dr. Bryant had an emergency appendectomy this afternoon and Haley can't find someone to do my talk show tonight. Do you think you can handle Andrew alone for about three hours so I could—"

"Do you trust me to look after him?"

Their gazes met and locked. Good question. Did she trust Frank? Did she trust him to take care of Andrew? Did she trust him to not run off with their son?

"Yes, I trust you," she told him.

For a fraction of a second she noticed something in Frank's eyes, in his expression, something that made her heart flutter and her stomach do flip-flops.

The smile playing at the corners of his mouth widened into an ear-to-ear grin.

"If you'd rather, Andrew and I can come to the station with you."

"Oh, that would be— No, that's unnecessary. It's freezing cold outside and Andrew will be asleep by eight and...no, you keep him here."

"All right. Tell Haley you'll do the show tonight."

She removed her hand from the mouthpiece. "Haley, I'll be at the station by eleven-thirty."

Andrew went to sleep early. At seven-twenty. Odd, she thought, since her son was a little creature of habit and took his naps at regular times, ate on schedule and went to sleep for the night between eight and eight-fifteen every evening. He'd been doing this for weeks before the kidnapping. There's nothing to worry about, she told herself. Being stolen from Debra's car and taken care of by strangers for days on end was the probable cause in his change of habit.

Frank, who'd been holding Andrew when he fell asleep, laid their baby down in his crib, then turned to Leenie. "If there's anything you need to do to get ready for tonight's broadcast, go ahead. I'll listen for Andrew in case he wakes up."

"Thanks. I'd like a long, hot soak in the bathtub. I need to come up with a topic to present tonight. Although it's been only a week since I did my last show, it feels as if it's been months."

"Go take your bath," he told her. "I'm going to watch a little TV. But I'll keep the baby monitor with me so I can hear Andrew if he so much as whimpers."

"You know what I wish you'd do before you settle down in front of the TV?"

"What? Just name it."

"Call Kate."

"She said she'd call us if…when she found out something."

"I know, but I just want to hear from her. And I want her to know that we're thinking positive thoughts for her."

"Okay, I'll see if I can get in touch with her."

Leenie slipped into her gold silk robe and matching house slippers after drying off and wrapped a towel around her wet hair. She'd decided that her topic for tonight's radio show would be "Dealing with Issues of Trust." She'd present a list of facts stated by other professionals from their various published works and then she'd give the listeners a chance to call in. It was during those discussions with her audience that the programs came alive. And in all honesty, it was when she came alive, too. God, she loved her job.

After towel drying her hair, she tossed the towel into the hamper and exited the bathroom. The house was quiet, almost too quiet. When she opened her bedroom door, she heard humming, then singing. A deep baritone voice crooning softly. Had Andrew awakened and Frank was trying to get him back to sleep? Leenie walked down the hall until she reached the open nursery door.

Shirtless and shoeless, Frank stood in the middle of the room, a half-awake Andrew pressed against his naked chest. Leenie stood there, spellbound, her gaze glued to Frank's face. He was looking at his son with such overwhelming love. And fascination. It was so obvious that he was in awe of the child they had created together.

Leenie's heart caught in her throat.

Frank kept humming and kept staring adoringly at Andrew, completely unaware that Leenie was watching him. After a good four or five minutes, Andrew's eyes closed completely and Frank laid him down in his crib. He leaned over and kissed Andrew. And tears lodged in Leenie's throat.

Frank turned around, then halted abruptly when he saw Leenie standing in the doorway. "He woke up and fretted a little bit, so I gave him a bottle and tried rocking him. But he kept fighting going back to sleep. When I started walking around with him and singing to him, he quieted down."

"You're spoiling him."

"Is that a bad thing?"

"No, it most certainly isn't. I think a little spoiling is essential for every child, don't you?"

"Absolutely."

Frank kept his gaze linked with hers as he walked toward her. "We created something pretty great when we made that little boy."

"Yes, we did. He's the best of both of us, isn't he?"

Frank reached out and caressed her cheek. "Leenie, I—"

It was happening again, just like it did every time he touched her. All that wild and crazy magic between them couldn't be controlled. But she had to control it or she'd wind up giving in to him, and not just for tonight. If she wasn't careful, she'd wind up agreeing to marry him and then where would they be? She'd be deliriously happy for a while and maybe

Frank would be, too. But he'd be marrying her for the wrong reason and eventually he'd want out. Wasn't it better to end things now than later, after she and Andrew had grown accustomed to having Frank in their lives all the time?

"Did you call Kate?" Leenie asked, determined to ease the sexual tension sizzling between them.

"Uh, yeah, I called. She said to tell you hi and to give Andrew a hug from her."

"Has she found out anything?"

"Nope. She told me that Moran has promised he'll share any information he finds that might be linked to Mary Kate, but it could take weeks to find anything. And there's always the chance that Kate's daughter wasn't taken by the infant abduction ring."

"Poor Kate. When I think about what she's gone through—"

Frank cupped Leenie's face with his hands. "Don't think about it. Just be grateful that we got Andrew back so quickly, that he's safe here with us. With his mother and father."

Don't look at me that way, she wanted to shout at him. His gaze devoured her hungrily, as if he was starving and she was a bountiful feast laid out before him. Every feminine instinct within her cried out for him to take her, to make her his. But logic dictated the exact opposite. If she wanted to save herself, she needed to get away from him. Now!

"Go back to watching TV," she told him as she turned away and headed down the hall. "I have things to do—"

He caught up with her, grabbed her arm and whirled her around to face him. "I know all the reasons why we shouldn't, but I don't give a damn. I want you, Slim. And I know you want me.''

''Oh, Frank. Of course I want you, but—''

He placed his index finger over her lips to silence her.

She looked pleadingly into his eyes.

His broad shoulders lifted and fell. He nodded, then released her and turned away, without saying a word. She stood there and watched him leave her. And that's what it felt like—it felt like he was leaving her, not just at this moment, but forever.

''Frank!''

He halted, but didn't turn around, simply standing at the end of the hallway.

She blurted out, ''I know I'll regret it later, but…''

He turned to face her, a hopeful expression on his face.

She ran toward him. He caught her in his arms and lifted her off her feet. She flung her arms around his neck and held on as he lowered his head to kiss her. Maybe she was a fool—a fool in love—but she didn't care. *Don't think about tomorrow,* she told herself. *Don't worry about the future. You have this precious moment. Don't waste it.*

Frank carried her into her bedroom, slid her down his body and onto her feet. With nervous need, she touched his chest. Kissed him. Tasted him. Smelled him. When she reached his jeans, she popped the snap and lowered the zipper, then slid her hand inside to fondle his sex. He was hard. Ready for her. He helped her get rid of his jeans and briefs, then stood very still when she ran her hands over him from hips to knees and slowly made her way back up. Leenie dropped to her knees in front of him. He held his breath when she touched him intimately. When her tongue replaced her fingertips, he groaned with pleasure. She laved him from root to tip, then took him into her mouth. Frank speared his big fingers through her hair and held her head in place while she titillated him.

And when he was on the verge, he yanked her to her feet, ripped open her robe and gazed at her breasts, at her flat belly and at the thatch of golden hair between her thighs. Her body tingled, her nerves zinging with anticipation. Her femininity clenched and unclenched as moisture gathered in preparation. He slid the robe off her shoulders. The gold silk pooled at her feet.

Frank kissed her neck, her throat and each shoulder, before lowering his head to first one breast and then the other. Already aroused unbearably, Leenie keened when he suckled her breast, his tongue tormenting her nipple. Her back arched. She grasped his muscular biceps and her nails bit into his flesh. His mouth on her breasts, moving back and forth from one to the other, drove her mad. He cupped her hips and pulled her up and against his erection. Pure electricity shot through her when he drove his tongue into her mouth at the same time he lifted her by her hips so that he could thrust up inside her. Yowling with earthshattering intensity, she wrapped her legs around his waist.

With their bodies joined intimately, Frank walked backward toward the bed, then toppled them over and onto the plush cotton sheets. He hammered into her repeatedly. Leenie responded with upward lunges, wild with her own need. They went at one another with animalistic passion. Kissing. Licking. Nipping.

The tension wound tighter and tighter inside Leenie
until she thought she'd splinter into a million pieces,
but each time she reached the brink, Frank would pull
back just enough to stop the inevitable. And after she
had a chance to catch her breath, he'd begin the sensual attack again until she was out of her mind, wanting, needing, begging him for release.

He lifted her buttocks, bringing her as close as possible and then plunged to the hilt, burying himself
deeply inside her. She clung to him, maneuvering herself so that each jab gave her pleasure and suddenly
with one final thrust, she came apart. Fulfillment burst
inside her. The sensations went on and on, until only
the sweet aftershocks remained. And as those remaining tingles floated through her body, Frank increased
his speed, pounding harder and faster. He growled,
then shuddered as he jetted into her.

Afterward he slid to her side and they lay there
together, breathing hard, staring up at the ceiling. He
inched his hand over to hers and clasped it firmly.
She sighed with contentment. And in that moment she
realized that lovemaking would never be this way
with anyone else. Only with Frank. Because she loved
Frank, as she would never love another man.

Twelve

After Leenie left for the studio, Frank wandered around the house, returning again and again to Andrew's nursery. He wanted to take care of his son, wanted to provide for him. And he wanted to make sure that even if something happened to him Leenie and Andrew would be provided for. He wasn't a multimillionaire by any means, but when his father died, he'd inherited close to half a million dollars, which he'd divided between investments and one-hundred-percent-safe certificates of deposit. The first thing he wanted his lawyer to do was set up a college fund for Andrew. After that he needed to adjust his will. All of this could wait till morning, of course. He intended to call his lawyer first thing tomorrow and let him get busy on the paperwork. He'd have to fly back to Atlanta sooner than he'd planned to sign the papers, to lease his apartment and to hand in his resignation.

Sawyer might release him immediately, if he wasn't needed on another assignment. If that were the case, he'd use the final assignment as the equivalent of his two weeks' notice.

He might be jumping the gun a bit by making all these plans. Leenie hadn't agreed to marry him. Not yet. But she hadn't been able to come up with an arrangement that made more sense. If anyone had told him that he'd ever even remotely consider remarrying, he'd have told them they were crazy. He'd sworn to himself that after the fiasco with Rita, he'd stay single to his dying day. But that was before Andrew.

Admit it, Latimer, Andrew is only a part of this equation. You actually want to marry Leenie. You like the idea of being with her every day for the rest of your life.

So what would it take to persuade Leenie to accept his proposal? Would he have to get down on bended knee?

Come to think of it, he never did actually propose. He'd asked her if she knew another solution to their problem other than marriage. That sure hadn't been romantic. No wonder she hadn't been overly thrilled by his suggestion. Women liked romance. Leenie probably expected a diamond and a fancy dinner and— He'd have to take care of those things, too, when he went to Atlanta. But he wanted everything to be a surprise. So, how was he going to work it? He'd have to figure out something so she wouldn't suspect what he had planned.

And what will you do if after all your best laid plans, she tells you thanks but no thanks? He'd camp on her doorstep and wear her down, that's what he'd do. He had no intention of taking no for an answer.

Leenie woke at ten-thirty the next morning when the telephone rang insistently. Where's Frank? she wondered. She'd arrived home from the station at two-forty this morning and found Frank asleep in the rocker in Andrew's room. She hadn't had the heart to wake him, but sometime before dawn, he'd crawled in bed with her and snuggled close. They'd made slow, sweet love and then had fallen asleep.

Damn, why didn't he answer the phone? She came awake groggily, reached over and picked up the receiver from the bedside phone.

"Hello?"

"May I speak with Frank Latimer?" a male voice asked.

"Who may I say is calling?"

"Steve O'Neal. I'm his lawyer."

Leenie's eyes popped wide open. "And this is in reference to?"

"Is this Ms. Patton?" the man asked.

"Yes, it is."

"Then I'm sure Frank's told you about his plans for Andrew."

Frank had plans for Andrew? What plans? "Yes, of course he's told me."

"I have to admit that I was totally surprised by Frank's news that he's a father. Never saw old Frank in that role. But he doesn't seem to have any doubts about being a full-time father to his son."

Leenie's heart sank. Frank intended to be a full-time father? When had he gotten in touch with his lawyer? Had he called this Mr. O'Neal and told him that he wanted full custody of Andrew? No! Frank wouldn't do that. But what other reason would Frank

need a lawyer to handle anything concerning Andrew?

"Hold on, please, Mr. O'Neal, and I'll get Frank."

Leenie laid the phone on the nightstand, got out of
bed, slipped into her robe and searched from room to
room. She found Frank in the kitchen scrambling eggs
and frying bacon. Safe in his infant carrier placed in
the middle of the kitchen table, Andrew contentedly
watched his father.

"What are you doing?" she asked.

"Morning, Slim. I'm fixing your breakfast. I had
planned to bring it to you on a tray, but now that
you're up, I'll serve it to you at the table."

"Didn't you hear the phone ringing?"

"Yeah, but I sort of had my hands full, so I figured
I'd let the answering machine get it." His broad, in-
fectious smile prompted an involuntary smile from
her. "Damn, I didn't unplug the phone in the bedroom, did I? I'd meant to do that, so if it rang it
wouldn't wake you, but—"

"The call is for you," she told him. "It's a Mr.
O'Neal."

"Oh, yeah. He's a, uh, er, a friend from Atlanta."

Leenie kept her smile in place by sheer force of
will. If Frank had nothing to hide, why hadn't he
admitted that Mr. O'Neal was his lawyer? Whatever
business about Andrew he needed to discuss with his
attorney apparently was something he didn't want her
to know about. So what could she construe from that?

"Look, honey, everything's ready—even the coffee. All you have to do is put the bacon, eggs and
toast on a plate. I won't be on the phone long. You
enjoy breakfast and I'll clean up when I get back."

He gave her a hurried kiss as he passed by her on

his way out of the kitchen. The minute he went out the door, she slumped into a kitchen chair and turned to her son.

"I think your father might be up to something." Leenie sighed. "The problem is I'm not sure what. If I trusted him, I wouldn't be filled with all these doubts, would I? When he comes back, I'll ask him. I'll come right out and tell him I want to know what's going on."

Andrew gurgled and cooed. Leenie groaned. Would she have to marry Frank to stop him for trying to get custody of Andrew? Maybe he'd contacted a lawyer because he wanted partial custody. But that wasn't what he'd told her. He'd agreed that while he was an infant, Andrew needed to be with her. So, what had changed Frank's mind? Did he intend to give her a choice—either marry him or he'd take Andrew away from her?

Don't be ridiculous, she told herself. Frank would never— She had to trust him. Had to believe in him. But could she marry him, knowing he didn't love her? It's what she wanted, wasn't it? Wasn't it possible that he'd fall in love with her after they married? It could happen, couldn't it?

Frank came back in the kitchen ten minutes later, after talking to Steve and then placing a call to Sawyer, who'd accepted his resignation over the phone and wished him the best of luck.

"I'm flying back to Atlanta this afternoon," Frank had told Sawyer. "I've got some legal papers to sign and an engagement ring to buy. And there's my apartment, I need to get rid of it, but I doubt I'll be able to get out of my lease."

"Geoff Monday's looking for a place," Sawyer had said. "He'd probably be glad to sublet the apartment from you until your lease is up."

Leenie sat at the table sipping coffee and pushing her scrambled eggs around on the plate. It didn't look as if she'd eaten a bite.

"What's wrong, Slim, aren't you hungry?" Frank asked. "Or don't you like my eggs?"

She offered him a fragile smile. "Just not hungry, I guess."

"Hey, look, I've got something to tell you."

Her smile widened. "Yes, what is it?"

"I have to fly back to Atlanta this afternoon."

"What?"

"I'll be gone only a couple of days," he said. "I'll be back before you know I'm gone."

"Why do you have to leave? I thought you planned—"

"Plans change. I—I've got some business for Dundee to take care of and—"

"Does Mr. O'Neal have something to do with your change of plans?"

"In a way." Frank came up behind her chair, leaned over, lifted her hair and kissed the nape of her neck. "Miss me a little while I'm gone."

"Frank, maybe we should talk some more about getting married. We never did resolve the issue, did we? I've been thinking about all the reasons I'm reluctant to rush into marriage and—"

"We can talk about our future plans when I get back from Atlanta." He gave her shoulders a caressing squeeze. "If I'm going to catch my plane, I need to hustle."

"I wish you didn't have to go."

"I'll be gone two days, tops."

She looked up at him with those shimmery blue eyes of hers and he thought he'd lose it. She had to be the prettiest thing on God's green earth. And if he played his cards right and didn't screw up again, she just might be his for the rest of their lives. But he had to do this thing right. He had to prove to her that they could make a lifelong commitment work. Okay, so she wanted romance and lovey-dovey stuff and he wasn't good at playing Prince Charming. But he could damn well try, couldn't he? And even if all they had going for them was great sex and Andrew, that would be enough, wouldn't it? Who knew, maybe love would come later for both of them.

"How about you and Andrew go with me to the airport?" he asked, wanting to be with them as long as possible. What he really wanted was to ask her to bring Andrew and come to Atlanta with him. But he'd be so damn busy that she might feel neglected.

"Why don't you just call a cab," she suggested. "We can say our goodbyes here and I won't have to get Andrew out in the cold."

"Sure." There was something bothering Leenie, but he couldn't imagine what. Maybe he should ask her about it. No, he'd just let it wait until he came back. If he didn't get a move on, he'd miss his flight and the sooner he went to Atlanta and set his house in order, the sooner he could come back to Leenie and Andrew.

Leenie had been stewing for two and a half days. Frank had called a couple of times each day and he'd been all sweetness and light, telling her how much he missed Andrew and her. And for the entire time he'd been gone, she had fought her inner demons—distrust and fear.

She had come to realize that it wasn't so much that she didn't trust Frank as that she wouldn't allow herself to believe that everything would work out all right for them. She'd had such rotten luck in her life. First her mother had died and a few years later her father. She'd been bounced around from foster home to foster home until she'd been sent to live with the Schmales. And in the happily ever after department, her love life had been a dismal failure. She'd had her heart battered and bruised several times before Frank Latimer finally broke it in so many pieces that it could never be mended.

Leenie was afraid to believe anyone could love her. And that's what it all boiled down to in the end. Frank was afraid to love because love had hurt him so badly in the past. And despite what her brilliant, logical mind told her, Leenie had somehow convinced herself that no man would ever truly love her. Certainly not Frank.

"Come on tater-tot," Leenie said as she lifted Andrew into her arms. "Your daddy is coming home today and we're going to the airport to meet him."

Ever since Frank had telephoned her to let her know he'd be arriving in Maysville around two-thirty, she had been debating what to do.

"I wish you'd come to the airport to meet me. You and Andrew. I'm flying in on the Dundee jet," he'd told her.

Not knowing what to expect when she arrived at the airport, Leenie buckled Andrew into his car seat in the back of her Envoy. Debra stood in the doorway, waving and smiling, as if she were seeing them off on some fabulous adventure. As a matter of fact, Debra had been entirely too cheerful since she'd come home from the hospital and whenever Leenie had complained about Frank's behavior, Debra had defended him. Was it because Debra wanted Leenie to marry Frank? Debra was just old-fashioned enough to think that a child's parents should be married. Or did Debra know something she didn't know?

Fifteen minutes after leaving her house, Leenie pulled into a parking slot at Maysville's small airport. What would she do if Frank asked her to marry him? What if he gave her only two choices—marry him or he'd take her to court over Andrew's custody?

"Let's go find out what Daddy's got up his sleeve." Leenie removed Andrew from his car seat, pulled the hood of his quilted coat over his head and took him out of the SUV.

After wrapping Andrew in a thick blanket to block out the crisp December wind, she hurried into the airport terminal and checked at the arrival desk to see if the private Dundee jet was expected to be on time.

"Yes, ma'am, that aircraft will be landing in approximately four minutes. By the way, are you Dr. Patton?"

"Yes, I'm Lurleen Patton."

"The pilot radioed ahead to ask that Dr. Patton—" the clerk smiled at Andrew "—and her son be escorted to the airplane."

"Oh, I see." Frank had been awfully sure she'd show up, hadn't he? "Well, all right. Exactly what do we do?"

"Just follow me. You'll be driven out on the runway and personally taken to the plane."

"I don't understand, but—"

"Come along. By the time we get outside, the plane will have landed."

Keeping Andrew cuddled against her, Leenie went along for the ride. Literally. In less than five minutes, when she stepped out of the cart that had delivered them to the Dundee jet, Frank Latimer appeared at the top of the steps. He waved at her, then rushed down the steps toward her.

She gasped when he wrapped his arm around her and urged her toward the steps. "Come on, Slim, I want to show you and Andrew the Dundee jet."

"Frank, what's going on? Nothing has made any sense to me since the day you left."

"Just come on board and I'll explain everything." When she eyed him skeptically, he said, "I promise."

She allowed him to escort her up the steps and into the airplane. Once inside, she skidded to a halt. The sleek, luxuriously decorated interior had been filled with flowers. Soft music wafted through the lounge. A bottle of champagne chilled in a silver bucket, flanked by two crystal flutes.

"What—what is all this?" she asked.

"It's a romantic setting," Frank told her.

"Yes, I guess it is, but—"

Frank reached out and took Andrew from her, removed their son's coat and placed him in an infant carrier lying in one of the ultraplush seats. "You sit there and be quiet for a few minutes, okay, pal? Daddy's got something very important to do."

Frank came back to Leenie, knelt down on one knee in front of her and clasped her hand. She felt as if her head was spinning.

"Leenie, will you marry me?"

"What?"

"I want you to marry me. I want us to build a life together."

He was proposing to her. Wasn't this what she'd wanted? And he'd set the scene for his proposal. He'd thought of just about everything.

"You want us to get married for Andrew's sake," she said.

Frank dug in his rumpled jacket pocket, pulled out a midnight blue velvet box and flipped open the lid. A sparkling diamond solitaire glistened against the dark blue bed.

"I went to half a dozen jewelers in Atlanta before I found the right one." He removed the ring from the box, lifted Leenie's left hand and slid the ring on her finger. She looked at the two-carat diamond and then stared down into Frank's smiling face.

"What will you do if I say no?" she asked, and held her breath waiting for his reply.

He laughed. "I'd die of a broken heart," he said jokingly.

"No, Frank, I'm serious." She tugged on his shoulders, urging him to stand.

His smile vanished. "I thought you—"

"If I refuse to marry you, what will you do?"

"Leenie, I'm confused by your question."

"I know that Steve O'Neal is your lawyer and that whatever legal matters he was taking care of for you had to do with Andrew. Do you plan to take me to court to get your rights as Andrew's father? Is that what you'll do if I won't marry you?"

Frank stared at her as if she'd suddenly grown an extra head. "I had Steve set up a college fund for Andrew. And I revised my will, leaving the estate I inherited from my father to Andrew and you." He grasped Leenie's shoulders. "Have you been fretting ever since I left Maysville thinking I was going to… My God, Slim, how could you think I'd ever try to take Andrew away from you?"

"I'm sorry. I—I just didn't know what to think."

"Don't you know I'd never do anything to hurt you? Hell, look at me, will you? I quit my job at Dundee, I sublet my apartment, I arranged my financial affairs so you and Andrew would be taken care of if anything ever happened to me. And I borrowed the Dundee jet to whisk us off to Las Vegas to get married. I bought out half a florist shop and spent a small fortune on that ring." His gaze jumped from the ring to Leenie's face. "What does that tell you?"

"It tells me that you really want to marry me."

"Is that all it tells you?"

"That you wanted everything to be romantic and special for me?"

"And?" He shook her gently. "Damn it, woman, don't you know when you've won?"

She jerked away from him. "Exactly what have I won? Marriage to you? Does that mean you've lost? If you think for one minute that I'm going to marry you just because—"

He grabbed her and kissed her, effectively ending her tirade.

When they finally came up for air, Frank said, "You're going to make me say it, aren't you?"

Leenie gasped silently as realization dawned. Frank Latimer was hers. She could see it in his eyes. He hadn't proposed simply because he wanted to provide a family for their son.

"Say what?" she asked, grinning, barely able to keep from laughing.

"Hell, Slim, you won my heart. Not that it's such a grand prize, but it's yours. All yours."

She slipped her arms around his neck, then lifted her left hand to look at her engagement ring. "If I've won your heart, does that mean you love me?"

Frank cleared his throat. "Yeah, I guess it does."

"Tell me."

"I just did."

"No you didn't. I want to hear the words."

"What about you?" he asked.

"What about me?"

"Do you love me?"

Leenie laughed. Joyously. Closing her eyes for just a second, she said a silent thanks to God. "Of course I love you, you big lug. I've been head over heels in love with you since the first time we made love."

Andrew gurgled loudly several times. Frank and Leenie looked at their son.

Frank shook his head. "Okay, son, okay. I know what I've got to do." Frank pulled Leenie close, gazed down into her eyes and said, "I love you, Leenie. But I have no idea how long I've loved you or when I realized that I did. I'm not sure. Maybe it was when I was in Atlanta whirling around, making plans. Or maybe it was just a few minutes ago when I saw you again."

"I think you've been in love with me since that first night." She brushed his lips breezily.

"Maybe I have."

"Maybe." She kissed him again. "We're going to have a wonderful life—you, me and Andrew."

"If we don't, it won't be for lack of trying." He kissed her. "We've got everything going for us."

"Including love."

"Especially love."

Epilogue

Leenie and Frank celebrated their first anniversary in style, surrounded by family and friends in their new house. They had designed the house themselves and worked with the contractor for eight long months until their dream became a reality. And during that time, Frank had designed several other projects, from a new garage for Haley and her husband to an addition for the pastor's home. While Leenie found job fulfillment in her TV and radio shows on WJMM, Frank was putting to use his heretofore unused college degree in architecture.

They had moved into their sprawling, bilevel, modern brick-and-glass structure shortly after Andrew's first birthday a little over two months ago. The day this house became their home, they'd had their own private party in front of the fireplace in their bedroom, a night neither of them would ever forget.

This year with Frank had been the happiest of her life. He let her know every day how much he loved her. An affair that had begun as a one-night stand had miraculously turned into a love affair that had healed two wounded souls and mended two battered hearts.

When Debra produced a piece of the wedding cake she had saved from the reception Leenie's friends had given them upon their return from their Las Vegas wedding, Frank accepted the plate and fork. He sliced off a piece of cake and put it in Leenie's mouth, then took a bite himself. Their guests clapped and cheered and Haley called for a speech.

Frank looked to Leenie. She shrugged. He leaned down and murmured in her ear, "Do you want me to tell all these people that I'm the happiest man on earth?"

Leenie slid her arm around his waist and hugged her husband. "You could, if you want to," she whispered. "But I think they already know that. Just as they know I'm mad about you and I'm deliriously happy."

"I could tell them that Andrew is the best-looking, smartest, most athletic one-year-old in the world, but that wouldn't be news either, would it?"

"Nope. Andrew's perfection is a well-known fact here in Maysville."

"Then we really don't have a speech to give them, do we? There's nothing we can tell them that they don't already know."

Leenie kissed Frank in front of their guests, which

actually made him blush and brought another round of cheers from their friends. ''I have a secret that I can tell you and then you can share it with everyone else.''

''You've got a secret?'' Frank said, not bothering to keep his voice low.

''Mmm-hmmm.''

''What's your secret?'' Haley Wilson shouted.

Once again Leenie whispered in her husband's ear.

''We're what?'' Frank said rather loudly. ''Are you sure?''

Smiling exuberantly, Leenie nodded.

''Hey, everybody, we're going to have another baby,'' Frank announced. ''In about six and a half months.'' When he calmed down a bit, he hugged Leenie to him and said softly, ''It happened the first night we spent in this house, didn't it?''

''Probably.''

Frank hugged her again. ''Are you all right? Is everything okay? With you and the baby? Is there anything I need to do for you?''

''I'm fine. The baby's fine. But I won't mind getting lots of TLC from my husband. After all, being pregnant at forty—''

''Slim, I'm going to give you enough TLC with this pregnancy to make up for what you missed when you were carrying Andrew. This time around, you can count on me every minute of every day. I'm not going to miss anything. I promise that I'll—''

Leenie covered his mouth with her open palm to quiet him, then reached down and took his hand in hers. "Just promise me that you'll love me forever. That's all I want. All I'll ever want."

"I'll love you forever," he vowed.

And Leenie knew he meant what he'd said. She trusted Frank as he did her. Trusted him with her heart, believing fully that at long last they had been blessed with the happily ever after love that neither of them had thought they'd ever find.

* * * * *

FIVE BROTHERS
AND A BABY

BY
PEGGY MORELAND

Peggy Moreland published her first romance in 1989 and continues to delight readers with stories set in her home state of Texas. Winner of the National Readers' Choice Award, a nominee for the *Romantic Times* Reviewer's Choice Award and a two-time finalist for the prestigious RITA® Award, Peggy's books frequently appear on the *USA TODAY* and Waldenbooks bestseller lists. When not writing, you can usually find Peggy outside, tending the cattle, goats and other creatures on the ranch she shares with her husband. You may write to Peggy at PO Box 1099, Florence, TX 76527-1099, USA, or e-mail her at peggy@peggymoreland.com.

One

The room the Tanner brothers gathered in was like everything in Texas. It was *big*. Rough-hewn logs felled and notched by the first Tanner to settle in the Texas Hill Country in the 1800s framed three sides of the room; a stone fireplace, broad and deep enough to barbecue a whole steer, spanned the fourth. Photographs framed in tooled leather covered the walls, depicting the family's climb in both prosperity and power.

Though considered large even by Texas standards, the room seemed to shrink in size as the current generation of Tanners filed inside. Death had brought the brothers together again, but it was duty that bound them now. Duty to a father who had single-handedly driven them away with his careless and wild ways from the home and ranch where they were raised and, ultimately, from each other.

Ace, the oldest, seated himself behind their father's desk, assuming the position as head of the family—a job, he knew, his brothers were more than willing to relinquish to him. Woodrow, four years Ace's junior, took a seat on the leather sofa opposite the desk, while Rory, the youngest, dropped down on the opposite end. Ry, the second-born, paced.

His expression grim, Ace met each of his brothers' gazes in turn. "I guess y'all know he's left us one hell of a mess to deal with."

Woodrow snorted. "So what's new?"

Ace nodded, understanding his brother's sarcasm. "The old man did seem to thrive on stirring up excitement."

Rory, the most laid-back of the four, stretched out his long legs and folded his hands behind his head. "Excitement, hell," he drawled. "*Trouble* would be more like it."

Ry stopped pacing to shoot his brother a quelling look. "There's no need to be disrespectful. This *is* our father we're talking about."

"And just about everybody else's in the county," Woodrow muttered under his breath.

Though Woodrow's comment was an exaggeration, not one of his brothers challenged him on it. With his tomcatting ways and his secretiveness, the old man could have populated a town twice the size of Tanner's Crossing and they never would have known it.

"Ry's got a point," he said, hoping to steer the conversation back toward the purpose of the meeting. "We're not here to judge the old man. Our job is to untangle the mess he's left us with."

Ry glanced impatiently at his watch. "Then let's get on with it. I need to get back to Austin. I've got a full surgery schedule in the morning."

Woodrow snorted a breath. "And we certainly wouldn't want to keep the good doctor from making another million or two, now would we?"

Primed for a fight since the day he'd arrived, Ry lunged

for Woodrow, caught him by the lapels of his Western suit and dragged him to his feet.

Rory jumped up to separate the two. "Come on, guys. You can beat each other's faces in later. Right now we've got business to tend to."

Ry glared at a Woodrow a full second, then gave him a shove that sent him sprawling back on the sofa. Ace nailed him there with a steely look, before he could leap back up.

"The old man didn't leave a will," Ace said, hoping to refocus his brothers' attention on the business at hand, before another fight broke out. "So it's going to take awhile to settle the estate. In the meantime, we've got a ranch to run."

Ry whipped his head around. "We?" he repeated. "I can't work the ranch. I'm a surgeon. I've got a practice to maintain."

"We *all* have other obligations," Ace reminded him. "But it's going to take all of us, chipping in what time we can, to keep this place going. At least, until we decide if we're going to sell it."

Woodrow shot to his feet. "We can't sell the Bar-T! This is Tanner land and always has been."

"And hopefully it'll remain Tanner land," Ace told him. "But we won't be able to make that decision until the estate is settled and we know what we're dealing with, both financially and legally."

Sobered by the reminder that their father was as secretive about his business dealings as he was his personal life, Woodrow and Rory sank back down on the sofa.

Ry crossed to frown out the window. "What about Whit?" He glanced over his shoulder at Ace. "He should be in on this."

"I left him a message on his machine, asking him to meet us here. If he gets it in time, he'll come."

Woodrow grunted. "He didn't show up for the old man's funeral. What makes you think he'll come here?"

"Why should he?" Ry returned. "The old man treated him like dirt."

"Whit was at the funeral."

Woodrow turned to look at Rory. "Where? I didn't see him."

"That's because he didn't want to be seen."

Chuckling, Woodrow shook his head. "That damn kid. He always was a sneaky little bastard."

"Quiet," Ry corrected. "Not sneaky."

"Is that a professional diagnosis?" Woodrow shot back. "And here I thought you were a plastic surgeon for the rich and famous, not a psychiatrist."

Though Ry tensed at the verbal jab, he didn't respond to it, an act of control that Ace would thank him for later. With all they had to deal with, both known and unknown, Ace knew fighting among themselves would only complicate matters more. He quickly directed the conversation back to the purpose of their meeting.

"Since I'm currently between photo assignments, my schedule is the most flexible, so I'll stay here at the ranch until the estate is settled. But I can't run the ranch alone. I'll need all of you to pitch in. We'll need to—"

The doorbell chimed, interrupting him, and Ace pushed to his feet. "That's probably Whit now."

"More likely a neighbor coming to pay their condolences," Woodrow grumbled, unwilling to let go of his anger.

Ace stopped in the doorway and slowly turned back around. "Whoever it is," he said evenly, "I expect the three of you to be on your best behavior. Understood?"

Woodrow and Rory rolled their eyes and looked away, but Ry met Ace's gaze squarely almost defiantly, as if to let Ace know he wasn't a little kid any more who could be bossed around by his big brother.

Pushing a disgusted hand at the lot of them, Ace headed for the front entry, praying it was Whit at the door, so they could get this business settled once and for all. The sooner he could get away from Tanner Crossing, the better. Being on the ranch again and in the town named for his family, was already beginning to wear on his nerves.

But when he opened the door, instead of his stepbrother Whit, he found a woman standing on the porch. Dressed in faded jeans and a bright blue T-shirt, she clutched a blanket-wrapped bundle against her chest—a bundle that looked suspiciously like a baby. Ace glanced behind her at the beat-up car parked on the drive. Not recognizing the woman or the vehicle, he peered at her curiously. "Can I help you?"

"You can, if you're one of the Tanner brothers."

The bitterness in her voice surprised him. This was no neighbor coming to offer her condolences, that was for sure. "Ace," he informed her, and stepped out onto the porch. "Ace Tanner. The oldest. And you are?"

"Maggie Dean."

He stole a glance at the blanket-wrapped bundle, then shifted his gaze back to hers. The defiant gleam in her eyes immediately put him on guard. "And what business do you have with the Tanner brothers, Ms. Dean?"

She shoved the baby at him. "I'm bringing you what's yours."

Ace fell back a step, shooting his hands up in the air. "Whoa. Wait a minute. That baby's not mine."

"By law it is."

"What law?" he snapped, suddenly impatient.

"Any law."

"Now just a damn minute. I—"

A wail rose from the depths of the blanket and Ace winced at the irritating noise.

The woman tipped up a corner of the blanket. "There, there, precious," she soothed. "Everything's all right. He wasn't yelling at you."

Ace planted his hands on his hips. "Look, lady," he said, having to raise his voice to make himself heard over the crying infant. "I don't know who you are or why you chose to stop here, but that is *not* my baby." He pointed to her car. "Now, you get yourself and that squalling brat of yours off Tanner land, before I call the law."

She jerked her chin up, her face flushed with fury, her eyes blazing with it. "I'll be happy to get off your land, but the baby stays."

With that, she thrust the crying infant against Ace's chest. He caught the bundle instinctively as the woman whirled away. Stunned, he stared after her. Something struck his chest and he glanced down to find two tiny fists had worked free of the blanket and were flailing the air. As he watched, the folds of the blanket parted and a miniature-sized face appeared, its features too small and too perfect to be real. Vivid blue eyes leaking crystal tears that glimmered in the sunlight; a little pink nose no bigger than one of the buttons on his shirt; a tiny circle of a mouth, open birdlike.

But the sound pouring from that tiny mouth was certainly real enough.

He looked up again to find the woman had made it to her car and was jerking items from the backseat and tossing them out onto the grass. "Hey!" he yelled. "What are you doing? You aren't leaving this kid here."

She slammed the car door and turned, shoving the strap of a large duffel bag over her shoulder. "She's not a *kid*," she said through clenched teeth. "She's a *baby*." She stooped and grabbed the handle of some of kind of contraption, then straightened. "And she *is* staying."

Since anger had gotten him nowhere with the woman, Ace tried reason. "Look," he said, struggling for patience. "Obviously you're in trouble and need help." He shifted the baby to one shoulder and held it there as he worked his wallet from his rear pocket. He flipped it open one-handed and held it out to her, revealing a thick wedge of bills tucked inside. "Take what you need. Take all of it, if you want."

She slapped his hand away, sending the wallet flying from his grasp. "You're just like your father," she accused bitterly. "You think money solves everything. Well, it doesn't! What this baby needs is family. Someone to take care of her, to love her."

Ace's mind registered nothing after the word *father*. Suddenly he felt weak, sick. "This is my father's baby?"

"Yes, she's your father's!" she cried. "That's what I've been trying to tell you since you opened the door."

Ace hauled in a breath, trying to still the dizzying sensation that threatened to force him to his knees. "My father's," he repeated.

She pursed her lips. "Yes, your father's."

Ace caught her by the arm and dragged her to the porch. "We need to sit down. Talk about this."

She stumbled after him, the portable playpen knocking against her legs, impeding her movement.

When he reached the porch, Ace pushed her down onto a step, but changed his mind about sitting, as well. Instead, he paced, absently thumping a wide hand on the baby's back. He didn't bother to ask the woman for proof that the infant was his father's. It was a wonder this scenario hadn't taken place before.

But Ace was at a loss as to what to do. He'd never had to deal with his father's indiscretions before. In the past, if one of the old man's lady friends, as his father referred to the women he became involved with, kicked up a fuss and started making demands the old man dealt with them himself…and usually by buying the woman off.

"If it's a matter of money," he began.

Groaning, the woman dropped her forehead against her hands and fisted her fingers in her hair. "I've already told you I don't want your money. What I want is for you to give this baby a decent home."

"Hell, you're the kid's mother! You give it a home."

She jerked up her head, her hands balled against her thighs. "She's not a *kid*. She's a *baby*. And I'm *not* her mother."

Ace stared, more confused than ever. "Then who is?"

Dropping her gaze, she rubbed the heels of her hands up and down her thighs. "Star. Star Cantrell."

"So why doesn't she provide a home for the kid?" he demanded to know, his anger spiking again.

"She's dead."

She said it so softly, Ace wasn't sure he'd heard her correctly. But then he saw a fat tear drop to splatter on the back of her hand. "Dead?" he repeated.

She nodded, then dashed a hand across her cheek, wiping at the tears. "Yes. A little over a week ago. Something went wrong after the birth. She began to hemorrhage and—" She waved away the explanation, as if the cause of death wasn't important. Not any longer. "I worked with Star. At the Longhorn. We were…friends. She made me promise if something happened to her, that I'd bring the baby here. Give her to your father."

She forced a swallow, then shook her head. "I didn't want to. I'd met your father. But I'd promised Star. Then I heard that your father had died. I wanted to keep her myself, but—"

She looked up then, and Ace wished she hadn't. He

couldn't remember ever seeing a face more ravaged by grief, by regret in his life.

She lifted a hand, then let it fall helplessly. "I can't keep the baby." She dropped her gaze and shook her head. "She deserves more than I can give her. That's why I brought her here."

Ace stared, aware of the faded jeans the woman wore, the work-reddened knuckles of the hands she held fisted against her thighs, the beat-up car she arrived in. What the woman was saying was that she couldn't afford to keep the child. "Surely there's someone else," he said. "Star must have had family somewhere. A mother. Sister. Aunt. Somebody."

She shook her head. "No. She was an only child. Her parents died in an automobile accident when she was a teenager."

Before he could think of another solution, she pushed to her feet.

"Everything you'll need is here," she said, gesturing at the duffel and portable playpen. "Diapers. Bottles. Formula. Clothing. She sleeps in the playpen, though you'll probably want to get her a crib fairly soon."

She turned to look at him...or rather, at the baby, and tears flooded her eyes. "Star named her Laura. I hope you won't change it. That's the only thing she'll ever have that was given to her by her mother."

Ace looked down at the baby, only now aware that the infant had stopped crying. She slept, one cheek turned against his shoulder. The lashes that brushed the upturned cheek were spiked with tears.

When he lifted his head, the woman was gone. He spun and ran after her, trying not to jostle the baby overmuch. "Hey! Wait!"

She turned, one hand on the door handle of the old car. He stopped, breathing heavily, more from panic than exertion. "Listen. I know this isn't your problem, that you're just doing what you were asked to do, but you can't leave this kid here. My brothers and I all have jobs, careers, responsibilities. We can't take care of a baby. We wouldn't even know how to begin."

He watched her face as she shifted her gaze to the baby, seeing the hesitation, the uncertainty, her obvious affection for the infant. Then she firmed her lips and pulled open the car door.

"You'll figure it out," she said, as she slid behind the wheel and started the engine. "I did."

Ace grabbed for the door. "No! You can't—"

Before he could demand that she take the baby with her, she stomped down on the accelerator and sped away, ripping the handle from his grasp.

The slam of the door reverberated through Ace like a death knell, as he watched the car disappear from sight.

Maggie made it five miles down the road, before she was forced to pull to the shoulder, blinded by tears. Giving in to them, she dropped her forehead against the back of her hands and wept. She wept for the baby who would grow up without ever knowing her mother. For Star, the baby's mother, and a life cut so tragically short.

And she wept—selfishly, she knew—for the loss of the baby she'd grown so attached to, for the inequities in life that made it impossible for her to keep the child herself. And while she wept, she sent up prayers, beseeching God to look after the baby, to keep it safe. To soften the hearts of the Tanner brothers so they would accept the baby into their home and into their lives.

When she was done, when there were no more tears to be shed, she tugged the hem of her T-shirt from the waist of her jeans and mopped her face, blotted her eyes. Then, with a sniff, she put the car in gear and pulled back onto the road.

It's best this way, she told herself, as she made the drive home. She had a hard enough time keeping a roof over her own head and food in her belly to even consider taking on the responsibility of an infant. With the Tanners, Laura would have a chance at a better life. They had a castle-size home, butt-loads of money and even a town named after them. With them, Laura would never have to worry about being evicted for late rent payments, where the money for medical expenses would come from or whether she could afford to go to college. And she'd have the opportunity to socialize with people with real class and not have to live around the kind of scum Maggie had lived with all her life.

But there was one thing that Maggie knew she could have given Laura in spades.

Her love.

The four Tanner brothers flanked Ace's bed, two on each side, staring down at the baby Ace had placed in its center.

Ace glanced over at Ry. "Take her with you to Austin. You're the one with a wife."

"Ex-wife," Ry reminded him. "Or soon will be."

Scowling, Ace looked at Rory. "What about you? Couldn't you get one of the ladies who works in your chain of Western stores to baby-sit for awhile?"

Rory shook his head. "No way. It's summer and vacation time. I'm already down to a skeleton staff as it is."

He looked back across the width of the bed at Woodrow.

Woodrow held up a hand. "Uh-uh. Don't even ask. The only experience I've had with babies was when my dog Blue had a litter of pups."

Ace tossed up his hands. "Well, what the hell am I supposed to do with the kid? I don't know any more about babies than the rest of you."

Ry gave him a pat on the back, as he turned to leave. "You can handle it."

"Yeah," Woodrow agreed, backing from the room. "You always were good at handling things, Ace."

Ace clamped a hand on Rory's arm, stopping his brother before he could follow the other two from the room. "Where do you think you're going?"

"Uh...to get the baby a bottle? Yeah, a bottle. She's probably hungry."

Ace slowly relaxed his grip. "All right. But make it fast. I don't want her to start crying again."

"Sure thing, bro," Rory promised...then turned and ran.

Ace heard the front door slam behind all three of his brothers, the rev of three engines.

And swore.

Bleary-eyed, Ace jostled the squalling infant on his shoulder as he watched the pan, willing the water to boil.

"Come on, kid," he begged pitifully. "Give me a break. I'm doing the best I can."

When the baby only cried louder, he snatched the bottle from the pan, shook a couple of drops of milk onto the inside of his wrist, testing the temperature, then used his foot to drag a chair out from the table.

Easing down, he shifted the baby to cradle in the crook of his arm and stuck the bottle in her mouth. She latched on to the nipple and sucked, as if she hadn't eaten in a week, which he knew wasn't the case, since she'd gotten him up a minimum of three different times during the night to give her a bottle.

With the baby occupied for the moment—and quiet—he reached for the phone book and drew it to the edge of the table, desperate to find someone to take care of the kid. He'd already called every child care facility listed in the Yellow Pages and been told by each that they didn't accept newborns. His only hope was to locate the woman who'd dumped the kid on him in the first place and try to hire her.

And he'd do that just as soon as he remembered her name.

It started with a D, he recalled, and was short. He quickly flipped pages to the D section and began to skim. Daily. Dale. Davis. Day. Dean. That was it! Dean. Maggie Dean. Relieved, he skimmed the listings, searching for her name, but didn't find anything that came even close. Unwilling to give up, he pushed aside the phone book and reached for the portable phone. He quickly punched in the number for directory assistance.

"Information. May I help you?"

"I hope so," he said with a weary sigh. "I'm looking for a listing for Maggie Dean." He frowned when the operator asked for the city. "I don't know. Some place in Texas, I'd guess."

While he waited, he thumbed a line of milky drool from the corner of the baby's mouth and wiped it down the leg of his jeans.

"I have a listing for a Maggie Dean in Killeen."

Recognizing the town as one near Tanner Crossing, Ace went almost weak with relief. "That's bound to be her." He tucked the phone between shoulder and ear, while he grabbed a pencil.

As he wrote down the number, it occurred to him that it might be better if he talked to Maggie face-to-face, rather than over the phone, figuring it would be harder for her to refuse him in person.

"Do you have an address?" he asked. He jotted that down, as well, then thanked the operator for her help and punched the disconnect button.

"Well, kid," he said, pleased with himself. "Looks like we're fixing to take us a little ride through the country."

* * *

To say Maggie lived in a low-rent district would be an understatement, Ace thought, as he drove slowly down her street.

Wood-framed houses lined the narrow, potholed road, each less than spitting distance from its neighbors. Junk cars were parked along the curb and on the postage-stamp-sized lawns, while cast-off furniture and appliances seemed the decorative choice for sagging porches.

As he searched the fronts of the jammed-together houses for her address, he found himself remembering the clunker of a car she had driven, the worn jeans, her work-roughened hands.

He spotted the faded numbers of the address he'd jotted down and pulled to the curb in front. Like the other cookie-cutter houses surrounding it, it was sorely in need of repair. Peeling paint; missing shingles; a silver strip of electrical tape stretching across a broken windowpane. A sidewalk shot in a straight line from the street to the porch. Halfway up to the house there was a hump in the walk where the concrete had broken and the parched earth had forced it to buckle.

But unlike the neighboring houses, no cars were left abandoned on Maggie's lawn. No ratty furniture or rusted appliances cluttered her small porch. Though her attempts at improving the place were meager, the pride she took in her home was obvious. A sprinkler turned lazily beneath an already blazing sun, casting badly needed water over clumps of newly planted plugs of grass. From the porch eaves hung wire baskets filled with a colorful array of cas-cading flowers. On the front door, a wooden sunflower with the word Welcome hand-painted in the flower's center greeted guests.

Ace tried to name the emotion that suddenly crowded his throat. Pity? No, he thought. Not pity. It was more an overwhelming sadness at her feeble attempts to make the dump a home. Which was stupid, he told himself, as he reached to unbuckle the seat belt from around the infant carrier. He didn't want to feel anything for this woman but relief when she agreed to return to the ranch with him and take care of the kid.

He hooked an arm around the car seat and climbed down from his truck. Silently praying he could convince Maggie to see things his way, he strode for the front door. He rapped his knuckles on the wood just above the Welcome sign, then shifted the carrier to a more comfortable position on his hip and waited. The faint sound of music came from somewhere inside. Country, he noted with relief, not that god-awful heavy metal so many favored these days.

The door opened and he quickly stuck a foot in the opening before she could slam it in his face.

Narrowing her eyes at him through the crack that remained, she kept a firm grip on the door. "What do you want?"

"Your help." When she tried to shut the door again, he put a shoulder against it. "Please. Just hear me out."

She glared at him for a good five seconds, then dropped her gaze, noticing the infant for the first time. She gulped, staring, then set her jaw and released her hold on the door. "Make it fast," she said, as she turned back into the room. "I have to go to work."

Ace quickly pushed his way past the door, before she changed her mind about letting him inside. "Ten minutes, max," he promised. He glanced around, noting the cleanness, if scantiness, of her furnishings. "Mind if I sit down?"

Folding her arms beneath her breasts, she tipped her head toward the sofa beneath the front window, but kept her lips pressed tightly together. Her silence didn't worry Ace. He planned on doing most of the talking anyway. He plunked the carrier down on the sofa, then rolled his arm, lengthening the cramped muscles, before dropping down beside it.

Stretching his arms out along the sofa's back, he focused his gaze on her. Another time, he might have taken a moment to admire the length of long legs exposed by the short denim shorts and the swell of breasts beneath the red bandanna print cropped shirt, but at the moment he was more interested in finding a baby-sitter for the kid than he was the anatomy of a good-looking woman. "I've got a proposition for you."

"If you're here to try to persuade me to take the baby, you're wasting your time. I've already told you I can't keep her."

He shook his head. "No. Actually, I came to offer you a job."

She rolled her eyes. "I have a job. Now, if you don't mind—"

Ace held up a hand, cutting her off. "Just hear me out. My brothers and I are willing to take responsibility for the ki—" At her arched brow, he amended quickly, "I mean baby. But, as I said before, we're just a bunch of bachelors and don't know the first thing about caring for an infant. The obvious solution, as far as I can see, is to find a relative of Star's who'd be willing to take the baby in. I plan to hire a private detective to track down Star's family, but in the meantime…" He lifted his hands. "Someone's got to take care of the baby."

"And you want me to be that someone."

"You seem the perfect choice. You obviously developed an affection for the baby while you had her, and you're already familiar with her routine."

"I have a job," she reminded him. "Plus, I go to college part-time. I don't have the time or energy to take on anything else."

"I'm not asking you to. What I'm proposing is that you quit your job, take a break from your classes. Work full-time for me. As a nanny of sorts." He watched her face and was sure that he saw a change in her expression. Interest? "How much money do you make as a waitress?" he asked.

Her chin came up. "That's none of your business."

"I wasn't being nosy. Just trying to establish a base. How about if I offer to pay you say...six hundred a week."

Though she didn't say a word, he could tell by the rounding of her eyes that his offer was a hell of a lot more than she currently earned waiting tables. "And free room and board," he added, hoping to sweeten the pot a little more. "Does that sound like a fair offer to you?"

He watched her throat convulse in a swallow and knew she was close to saying yes. In hopes of tipping her over the edge, he pulled his cell phone from his shirt pocket and tossed it to her. "Call your boss. Tell him you quit. We can use my truck to haul whatever you want to take with you to the ranch."

She slowly flipped open the cover of the phone. She'd punched in at least four numbers, before she stopped. "I can't."

He pushed out a hand, urging her to complete the call. "Sure you can. Once you've given your notice, we're outta here."

"But what happens to me if you're able to locate Star's family? I'll be out of a job." Pressing her lips together, she snapped the cover on the cell phone back into place. "I won't do it. Jobs are too hard to come by. You'll have to find someone else."

Ace leaped to his feet. "Dammit! There isn't anyone else! I've already called every child care facility in town and was told they don't take newborns."

Awakened by Ace's shouting, the baby began to whimper. He dropped his head back and groaned. "Please, don't start squalling again," he begged. "My nerves can't take any more."

In the blink of an eye, Maggie had tossed aside the phone and was across the room, snatching the baby from the car seat.

"She's been crying?"

"Yeah," he said cautiously, watching her. "Most of the night."

Her face creased with worry, she gently laid the baby on the sofa and began to examine her. "Did you feed her?"

"Yeah. Three or four times."

"Change her diaper?"

He shuddered upon being reminded of that disgusting task. "Yeah. And she's definitely not constipated, if that's what you're worried about."

Maggie picked up the baby and held her against her shoulder, as she began to pace. "Did she sleep at all?"

"Some, I guess. At least, I assume she was sleeping, when she wasn't screaming."

Maggie continued to pace, while frantically patting the baby on the back. "It's okay, precious," she soothed. "Maggie's got you now."

Ace watched, kicking himself for not thinking of just handing over the baby when he'd first walked in the door, instead of waving money in front of Maggie's face. It appeared the kid was much more of an inducement than a big salary.

There was a loud burp and Maggie jerked to a stop to look at the baby in surprise. She turned slowly, narrowing her eyes suspiciously at Ace. "Did you burp her?"

"Burp her?"

"Yes. At least twice while she was having her bottle."

He lifted a shoulder. "Didn't know I was supposed to."

"Seven hundred."

Ace looked at her confusion. "What?"

"Seven hundred a week. And I'll need at least one day off."

Though he hoped this was the last time he ever had to touch the kid, Ace pried the baby from Maggie's arms. "Seven hundred it is." He nodded toward the cell phone she'd dropped. "Now why don't you make that call so we can get this kid home before she needs another feeding."

Maggie took the baby right back from him. "No. I'd rather give my notice in person."

"How long will that take?" he asked in frustration.

"I don't know. A half hour or so. But there's no need for you to wait." She clutched the baby tighter against her chest. "Laura can ride along with me."

Two

___

When a woman doesn't own much, it doesn't take her long to pack. Maggie completed the task within fifteen minutes of Ace's departure. Within thirty, she was standing in front of the Longhorn Restaurant and Saloon, the baby in her arms, taking one last look at the place she'd worked for the past four years.

After sundown, when the oversized neon horns above the entrance were lit and the parking lot was jammed full of vehicles, the Longhorn didn't look half bad. But in daylight, with the cracks on the stucco facade as glaring as varicose veins on an aging woman's legs, and the sidewalk and the parking lot littered with empty beer cans and debris, it looked shabby, cheap.

But Maggie was used to shabby and cheap. She'd lived with both all her life. She intended to see that Laura didn't have to do the same.

Pressing a kiss against the top of the baby's head in a

pledge to fulfill that promise, she headed for the rear of the building. Finding the delivery door locked, she used her key to enter. The hallway she stepped into was dark, as were the kitchen and public rest rooms she passed, but ahead she could hear Tammy Wynnette's soulful whine coming from the jukebox in the bar. She followed the sound and found Dixie Leigh, the Longhorn's owner, perched on a tall bar stool, studying her liquor order for the day, her eyes squinted against the thin column of smoke curling from the tip of the cigarette she held clamped between her teeth. With her bottle-red hair teased high, false eyelashes and skin tight jeans, Dixie looked much the same as the building she owned—faded and cheap.

But beneath the layers of heavy makeup and too-tight clothing, Maggie knew lay a heart of solid gold.

"Hey, Dixie," she called softly.

Dixie jumped, then snatched the cigarette from her mouth and scowled. "Girl, don't you know how to knock? You almost made me swallow this thing."

Biting back a smile, Maggie approached the bar. "Shouldn't smoke."

"Shouldn't do a lot of things," Dixie grumbled, "but there you are." She shifted her gaze to the baby, her frown deepening. "I thought you took that kid to the Tanners?"

"I did. Ace brought her back this morning."

"Ace? He'd be Buck's oldest. The wildlife photographer."

"He didn't mention his line of work."

Dixie grunted. "Guess he was too busy dumping the kid and hightailing it to take time for any small talk. A shame, too, since all the Tanner men are blessed with such pretty faces."

Maggie couldn't vouch for all the Tanner men, but if the rest of them looked anything like Ace, they'd been blessed with more than just pretty faces. They had the bodies to go along with them. "I really didn't notice," she said vaguely.

Scowling, Dixie tamped out her cigarette. "Which is more the shame." She fluttered her fingers, motioning for Maggie to bring her the baby. After settling the infant in the crook of her arm, she lifted the blanket back from its face. Her lips trembled as she looked down at the sleeping infant. "Ain't she just the prettiest little thing," she murmured. "The spittin' image of her mama."

Maggie heard the tears in Dixie's voice and felt her own throat constrict. "Yes, she is."

Dixie shook her head with regret. "Seems like I should've been able to do something to prevent all this. The minute Star walked into the Longhorn, I knew that girl was headed for a bad end. Had tragedy written all over her."

"She needed a job and you gave her one," Maggie said in her employer's defense. "What Star did with her free time was her choice and no fault of yours."

Dixie sighed wearily. "I suppose." She stared down at the baby a moment longer, then glanced up at Maggie. "So you're going to keep her, after all?"

"Oh, Dix. You know I can't."

"Then what are you going to do with the child?"

Maggie avoided Dixie's gaze, knowing her employer probably wouldn't approve of her plans. "That's what I came by to talk to you about."

Dixie narrowed her eyes. "Why do I get the feeling that I'm not going to like what you have to say?"

Maggie lifted a shoulder. "Probably because you're not."

"Well, you might as well spit it out," Dixie snapped irritably. "Dragging out the telling isn't going to make it any easier for me to swallow."

"Ace has asked me to work for him as Laura's nanny."

For a moment, Dixie could only stare. "You're quitting your job here?"

"I'd rather think of it as taking a leave of absence," Maggie said, hoping to soften the blow—and at the same time leave a door open for herself should she need it. "If you'll let me, I'd like to come back once Ace locates Star's family."

"Star didn't have family," Dixie reminded her drolly.

"No," Maggie agreed. "At least, not that she mentioned to us. But Ace is convinced she has a relative somewhere. An aunt or a distant cousin, maybe, who'd be willing to take the baby. He's hiring a private detective to track them down."

"And you think this private eye's gonna find someone?"

Maggie shook her head. "I think if Star had any family, she would've told me."

"Then why are you letting the Tanners waste good money chasing folks who don't exist?"

"They can afford it. Besides, it'll give Laura some time."

"Time for what?"

"To win them over." Curving a hand around the top of the baby's head, Maggie smiled down at the sleeping infant. "A few weeks with this sweet little angel and they won't be able to let her go."

"Ace has already told you they don't want her."

"No," Maggie corrected, straightening. "He said they didn't know how to take care of a baby. With me there to see to her needs, that won't be a problem."

Dixie eyed her suspiciously. "You see yourself in this kid, don't you? You think by sticking with her, you can prevent happening to her what happened to you."

Maggie stiffened defensively. "I'm only doing what Star asked me to do."

"You've already done what Star asked of you. You delivered her baby to the Tanners."

"She asked me to take the baby to Mr. Tanner. His death made that impossible."

"So you did the next best thing. You delivered the kid to his heirs. And what about your schooling?" Dixie went on, not giving Maggie time to argue. "You've worked too hard toward that nursing degree to give up on it now."

"I'm not giving it up. Once things are settled for Laura, I can pick right up where I left off."

Her expression melting to one of concern, Dixie cupped a hand on Maggie's cheek. "Oh, honey. I know you're only trying to do what's best for the baby. But if you don't cut your ties to her now, you're going to get your heart broke for sure. And, God knows, you've had it broken enough times as it is."

Gulping back tears, Maggie closed her hand over Dixie's and held it against her cheek. "I'm just giving her a chance, Dix. The same as you gave me."

Dixie pressed her lips together. "I gave you a job when you were down on your luck. Nothing more."

"You gave me a lot more than a job. You gave me back my pride, my self-confidence, the opportunity to make something of myself."

Dixie snatched her hand from beneath Maggie's. "I gave you a *job*," she repeated stubbornly. "Whatever else you've done with your life, you've done on your own."

"I couldn't have done anything, if you hadn't given me a break when I needed it. And that's what I want to give Laura. She deserves a decent home and a shot at a halfway normal life. With the Tanners' name and money behind her, she'll get both."

Dixie eyed Maggie, her lips pursed in annoyance. "You've already made up your mind about this, haven't you?"

"Yes."

She eyed her a moment longer, then heaved a sigh of defeat. Sliding an arm around Maggie's waist, she hauled her up hard against her side. "Then you be careful, you hear? Those Tanner men can be dangerous."

"Dangerous?" Maggie repeated in alarm.

Dixie drew her arm back to tuck the blanket beneath the baby's chin. "Not in the way you might think. But a handsome face and a smooth tongue can be as deadly a weapon as any gun."

"You don't have to worry about me," Maggie assured her. "My only interest in Ace Tanner is his ability and willingness to provide Laura with a decent home."

Dixie humphed. "For now, maybe," she conceded grudgingly. "But mark my words. Before this is over, you'll be singing a different tune. I've yet to meet the woman who didn't fall head over bloomers for a Tanner, once he took a notion to seduce her."

Ace sat reared back in his father's chair, his boots propped on the desk's oak surface, the phone held loosely at his ear, as he briefed his stepbrother Whit on the meeting he and his brothers had held the day before.

"Since the old man didn't leave a will," he finished, "we've got a hell of a mess to sort through."

"I don't know why you're telling me all this. Even if the old man had left a will, he wouldn't have named me in it."

Ace heard the bitterness in his stepbrother's voice and understood it. What Whit said was true. The old man probably wouldn't have included him in his will. Buck Tanner might've adopted Whit, but he'd never treated him as a son.

But, in Ace's mind at least, Whit was a Tanner and would inherit his share of the old man's estate, the same as Ace and his brothers would. By *not* leaving a will, the old man had unknowingly given Ace the opportunity to right some of the wrongs Whit had suffered at the old man's hand.

"But he didn't leave a will," Ace reminded him pointedly. "Which means that his estate will be split equally between his heirs. Since he adopted you, by law you're entitled to a full fifth."

"I don't care what the law says," Whit said stubbornly. "I want nothing that was his."

"Now, Whit," Ace began.

"No," Whit said, cutting him off. "I'll do what I can to help y'all settle the estate, but not for any personal gain."

Ace knew it would be a waste of his time to press the issue…for the moment, at least. But Whit would get his fair share of the old man's estate, as would the half-sister he'd known nothing about. Ace would see to that.

"I appreciate your offer of help," Ace told him, opting to focus on the positive portion of Whit's reply. "We can certainly use it."

"Well, you've got it, though I don't know how much help I'll be. I know next to nothing about the laws pertaining to estates."

"It isn't your legal advice we need," Ace assured him. "We've got a string of attorneys on retainer to handle that. What we need is your help here on the ranch."

"Why? The ranch hands ought to be able to handle whatever needs to be done. They've been working on the place for years."

"What ranch hands?" Ace said wryly. "The bunkhouse is empty and has been since the day I arrived."

"What?" Whit said, sounding surprised. "The hands wouldn't just up and leave because the old man died. Not when there's livestock needing tending."

"I wouldn't have thought so, either," Ace replied. "But

the fact is, they're gone. You knew most of the men who worked here. Maybe you can do some checking. See if you can track them down, persuade them to come back.''

"Hell, Ace. You know how cowboys are. They drift with the wind. No telling where they are by now.''

"If anybody can find them, you can.''

"Maybe,'' Whit said doubtfully. "But it's liable to take me awhile.''

Ace frowned. "Unfortunately, we don't have a lot of time. God only knows where the cattle are or what condition they're in.''

"Dry as it is, I'd imagine they've scattered, searching for grass and water.''

"Yeah, I'd imagine so,'' Ace agreed. "I'm planning to ride out this afternoon and—'' The chime of the doorbell had him lifting his head. "Hang on a minute, Whit,'' he said into the receiver. "Somebody's at the door.'' He clamped a hand over the mouthpiece and yelled, "Come on in! It's open!'' then drew the phone back to his mouth.

"Like I was saying,'' he said, continuing his conversation with Whit. "I'm riding out this afternoon to see if I can locate any of the herds.'' He glanced up and saw Maggie hovering uncertainly in the doorway. With the car seat balanced on one hip and her shoulder weighted down by a large duffel bag, she looked more like a pack mule than a nanny...although Ace couldn't remember ever seeing a pack mule built quite like Maggie was. Still dressed in the getup she'd had on earlier, she could've easily posed as a model for one of the cowgirl pinup calendars he'd seen in Rory's store.

He hesitated a moment, debating whether he should jump up and hug her for showing up as promised or tell her he'd changed his mind about hiring her to take care of the kid. Having a good-looking woman in the house might present more problems than it solved, and Ace had enough problems to deal with at the moment.

One glance at the baby convinced him that he'd rather take his chances on another problem arising, than have to deal with the kid.

He waved Maggie in and pointed to the sofa. "Keep me posted on how many of the ranch hands you're able to locate," he said to Whit. "If you have to, promise them a bonus to get them to sign back on with the Bar-T."

"Sure thing, Ace."

"In the meantime, we're going to have to round up the herds and see what kind of shape they're in. Plan on meeting here at the ranch, say, a week from Saturday at daybreak. That'll give me a good ten days to get a handle on things around here. I'll call Ry, Woodrow and Rory and let 'em know we're gonna need their help, too."

Ace opened his mouth to say something else, but Maggie chose that moment to bend over and set the car seat on the sofa. He totally lost his train of thought as he watched the denim shorts ride up higher on the back of her thighs, accentuating the cheeks of a well-shaped butt and legs that seemed to stretch on forever. His mind dulled by the view, he said to Whit, "I'll be in touch," and broke the connection.

As he leaned to replace the receiver, Maggie straightened, moaning softly, her hands pressed low on her back. Letting the strap of the bag slide down her arm, she hunched her shoulders to her ears, then turned and sank down on the sofa with a weary sigh.

Her change in position put Ace at eye level with her chest and an interesting—if miserly—peek of cleavage. Disappointed that the cropped shirt wasn't cut a little lower, he lifted his gaze higher and found her looking at him through narrowed eyes.

Since he'd been caught red-handed, Ace didn't see much

point in trying to deny his guilt. He lifted his hands. "What can I say? I'm a healthy, red-blooded, all-American male."

Reaching behind her, she gave the shirt a tug, snatching the top up higher on her chest. "That's the lousiest excuse for voyeurism I've ever heard."

He shrugged. "A woman wears an outfit like that, a man is bound to look."

She gave her chin an indignant lift. "It's my uniform. All the girls at the Longhorn are required to wear them."

"Let me guess," he said, having to bite back a smile. "The Longhorn's clientele is predominantly male."

"Killeen's a military town, so the men outnumber the women just about everywhere you go. But if you're thinking the Longhorn's some kind of titty bar," she was quick to inform him, "you're wrong. Dixie serves up the best chicken fried steak in Texas and books the most popular country and western bands the area has to offer. *That's* what draws the men to the Longhorn. Good food and good music. Not the waitresses."

If the woman thought food held more appeal to a man than the scantily-clad women delivering it, Ace didn't see why he should be the one to tell her otherwise. Keeping his expression impassive, he leaned back in the chair and laced his fingers over his middle. "This Dixie sounds like an astute businesswoman."

"She's that and more."

"Did she give you any trouble about quitting on such short notice?"

"No, but I didn't actually quit. I asked for a leave of absence, instead. That way, once I'm done here, I'll still have a job."

He snorted a laugh. "You don't believe in burning any bridges, do you?"

She shrugged. "Can't afford to. Like I told you before, jobs are hard to come by."

Her comment brought to mind her broken-down car and the rundown neighborhood she lived in, which made him wonder about her background. He'd been so desperate to get her to agree to come to the ranch and take care of the baby, he hadn't asked anything about her personal life, an oversight he figured he should rectify before they went any further.

"Since you were able to pick up and leave so quickly, I assume you're not married."

She gave him a withering look. "A little late for an interview, isn't it, since you've already hired me for the job?"

"Just trying to get to know you a little better. What's the harm in that?"

Though he could tell she resented doing so, she complied.

"Single white female. Twenty-eight. Divorced. No hobbies. Not looking for male companionship, sexual or otherwise." She lifted a brow. "And you?"

Since she'd tossed his question right back at him, Ace responded in the same personal-column-ad manner in which she'd revealed her stats.

"Single white male. Pushing forty. Divorced. Enjoy fishing and hunting when I have the time." He waited a beat, then added with a wink, "And I'm *always* looking."

He wasn't sure why he'd tossed in that last bit, but considering the attitude she was sporting, he would've sworn it would've gotten a rise out of her. When she remained silent, her gaze steady on his, he cleared his throat and plowed on. "So...who wanted out of the marriage? You or your ex?"

"I guess I'd have to say he did, since he was the one who left, taking with him our only means of transportation and owing three months back rent."

Ace puckered his lips in a silent whistle. "Nice guy."

"Yeah. A real angel. Who gets the blame for yours?"

"Mutual agreement." At her doubtful look, he held up a hand. "Swear to God. Though the official decree states irreconcilable differences as grounds for the divorce."

"That's certainly original," she said dryly.

"The judge who granted the divorce didn't seem to have a problem with it."

"I doubt he would, you being a Tanner and all."

Ace stiffened at the insinuation. "And what's that supposed to mean?"

She lifted a shoulder. "From what I've heard, your family practically owns the town. I'd imagine they own the politicians, as well."

Her interference to the Tanners' power in the town hit a nerve. A sore one. "The Tanners don't own Tanner's Crossing," he informed her, to set the record straight. "Yes, we own several businesses and substantial real estate holdings here, but we do not own the town."

"Then why is it called Tanner's Crossing?"

"Because it was a Tanner who settled here first, and Tanners who built the town." Hoping to distract her from pursuing the subject further, Ace steered the conversation away from his family and back to her. "You said you were going back to work at the Longhorn, once we've located Star's family."

"If you find any."

"Everybody's got relatives."

"I don't. But even if Star does, there's no guarantee that whoever you find will want to take her baby."

Ace had thought about that possibility—and promptly discarded it, not wanting to think about what that would mean to him and his brothers. For some reason, hearing Maggie voice the possibility annoyed the hell out of him. "Are you always this pessimistic?" he asked irritably.

She lifted a shoulder. "Just thought I should point out what problems you might encounter."

Scowling, he dropped his feet to the floor and stood. "Well, don't. I've got enough trouble to deal with, without you borrowing more."

At the mention of trouble, Maggie tensed. "Trouble?" she repeated, keeping her gaze on him as he rounded the desk. "What kind of trouble?"

He picked up her duffel and turned for the door without responding. She hopped up and grabbed the car seat, hitching it on her hip as she charged after him.

"What kind of trouble?" she asked again, having to trot to keep up with his longer stride.

"None that concerns you."

She firmed her lips. "Look, Slick. If I'm going to be living with you, I think I have a right to know if you're in some kind of trouble."

"There aren't any warrants out for my arrest, if that's what you're worried about."

"And that's supposed to make me feel better?"

Heaving a sigh, he turned to face her. "It's more like problems than trouble. The old man left us with a butt-load of 'em, not the least of which is a ranch to run and no ranch hands to do the work."

"What happened to the ranch hands?"

"That's the million-dollar question."

"Your father never said anything to you about firing them or them quitting?"

"The old man and I never talked."

Her eyes rounded in amazement. "Never?"

"Never."

"Why not? I mean, he *was* your father. Seems like you would've at least checked up on him every now and then, especially considering his age and the fact that he lived alone."

"Buck Tanner was healthy as a horse and more than capable of taking care of himself."

"Well, he couldn't have been all that healthy," she said wryly. "He died, didn't he?"

"Of a heart attack, which I couldn't have prevented even if I'd been here."

"But you were his son," she persisted. "Didn't you worry about him at all?"

"Look. If all this is to make me feel guilty, you're wasting your breath. Not where the old man is concerned. Now if you don't mind," he said, and tipped his head toward the door on his left. "I've got things to do."

Not at all satisfied with the answers he'd given her, Maggie gave him a sour look as she passed by him. Two steps beyond the threshold, she stopped short, her eyes rounding, as she got her first look at the room he'd shown her to. It wasn't luxurious. Not by modern-day standards. But it was the most beautiful room she'd seen outside the covers of a decorating magazine.

Opposite her, a four-poster mahogany bed, covered with an heirloom-quality, hand-crocheted spread, stood between two floor-to-ceiling windows. Angled in the corner was a chaise lounge upholstered in a dusty pink velvet, an ecru chenille throw draped across its back. To her left, a porcelain pitcher and bowl rested on the marble top of a washstand. On her right, a tall linen press stretched almost to the ceiling. Beside it was an open doorway through which she could see the tip end of a old-fashioned footed tub. All the furnishings appeared to be genuine antiques, probably passed down from one generation of Tanners to the next.

And Maggie intended for Laura to be a part of the next generation of Tanners to enjoy this rich heritage.

"If you don't like this room," Ace said from behind her, "there are others."

She swung her head around, having forgotten his presence. "Oh, no," she said quickly, then slowly turned back to stare. "It's just that it's so—" She laid her palm over the dainty roses covering the cream-colored wallpaper. "Feminine," she finished, unable to think of a better word to describe the room.

He strode by her and dropped her duffel at the foot of the bed. "My stepmother's doings. And before you ask why I haven't asked her to take care of the baby, she's deceased, killed by a drunk driver years ago. As to the decorating," he went on, "she claimed she had to have one room in the house with a little fluff, since she was forced to live in an all-male household outfitted more like a hunting lodge than a home. Threatened us within an inch of our lives if we put so much as a foot inside."

Figuring a woman would have to be pretty tough to issue an ultimatum like that and expect a houseful of males to obey, Maggie crossed to the washstand and ran a hand lightly over the marble surface. Surprised at the amount of dust she gathered, she held up her hand to show Ace. "Did her warning include the housekeeper?"

He shrugged. "I figure the housekeeper left about the same time as the ranch hands. The whole place could stand a good cleaning."

She dragged her palm across the seat of her shorts. "I'll take care of it."

"Now wait a minute," he said. "I wasn't suggesting that you take on the cleaning chores. I hired you to take care of the baby. Period."

"I don't mind. Besides, it'll give me something to do while Laura naps."

He eyed her a moment, as if wanting to argue, then sighed and gestured to the adjoining bath. "Towels are in the linen closet. Extra pillows and blankets are on the top shelf of the closet. If you're hungry, there's plenty of food left over from the funeral meal in the refrigerator. If you need anything else, you can make a list and give it to me later.'' He turned for the door. ''I'm saddling up and riding out to see if I can locate any of the cattle. Probably be gone most of the afternoon.''

''I'll need Laura's playpen,'' she called after him. ''She'll want a nap soon.''

''It's in my room. I'll get it.''

While Ace went after the playpen, Maggie set the car seat on the bed and lifted the baby out. Unable to resist, she dropped a kiss on the infant's cheek before laying her down on the bed. Cooing softly to the baby, she unwound the receiving blanket from around her legs. Laura kicked and waved at the air, obviously enjoying the freedom of movement, after being confined in the infant carrier for so long. Laughing at her antics, Maggie glanced up as Ace returned, carrying the playpen.

''Look,'' she said. ''She's doing aerobics.''

He glanced the baby's way, as he set the playpen at the foot of the bed and frowned. ''Needs to. I've seen bigger legs on a malnourished bird.''

Maggie caught the baby's foot and placed a kiss on her toes. ''Don't you listen to him,'' she lectured gently. ''He's just jealous because your legs are prettier than his.''

''Since you've never seen my legs, how would you know?''

Smiling down at the baby, Maggie pressed a finger lightly to the end of the infant's nose. ''I wouldn't. But I've seen your eyes and Laura's are the same shade of blue.''

''All babies' eyes are blue,'' he muttered disagreeably, but eased closer for a better look.

Taking his curiosity as a sign of interest, Maggie decided this might be the perfect time to start establishing a relationship between the two. ''Not necessarily. Do your brothers have blue eyes?''

"Yeah. Except for Whit. His are brown. But he's a step-brother, so I guess he doesn't count."

"Stands to reason then that Laura's will be blue, too." Scooping the baby up, she held her along the length of her arms, angling her so that Ace had a better look. "What about her nose?" she asked, studying it thoughtfully. "Do you think she has the Tanner nose?"

When he didn't immediately reply, she glanced over and saw that he was looking at her and not at the baby. His frown told her that he'd seen right through her act.

"Don't even try," he warned.

Feigning innocence, she turned away to lay the baby back on the bed. "Try what?"

"To make me feel a connection to the kid. It's not going to work. No amount of family resemblance is going to persuade me to keep her."

When she didn't reply, he hooked a knuckle beneath her chin and forced her face around to his. "Understand?"

Maggie knew he expected a response from her. But for the life of her, she couldn't seem to push the one-syllable word past her lips. Not when his face was so close to hers she could count the squint lines that fanned from the corners of his eyes.

Dixie was wrong, was all she could think. There was nothing pretty about *this* Tanner's face. Pretty was reserved for mild-tempered men, with dimpled cheeks, who spent their evenings playing the piano for their mothers.

Ace was handsome. Yes. She couldn't argue that. But his was a rugged handsomeness, heightened at the moment by the dark stubble of beard that shadowed his jaw and the steely blue eyes leveled on hers.

When she didn't immediately respond, he increased the pressure on her chin, tipping her face up a fraction higher, as if to remind her he was waiting for—and expected—an answer. Though the movement was subtle, she sensed the strength behind the finger that held her face to his, the stubbornness in the blue eyes fixed on hers, and knew she was dealing with a man who was accustomed to having his way.

It would be so easy to knuckle under to him, she thought, feeling herself weakening.

Easier still to be seduced by him.

A whimper from the baby reminded her why she could afford to do neither.

Stiffening her spine, she set her jaw. "I understand perfectly. But you need to understand something, too."

"And what's that?"

She closed a hand over his wrist. "No man touches me, without my permission."

She felt a swell of satisfaction at the surprise she saw flare in his eyes...but it was short-lived.

"Oh, I'll remember," he assured her, biting back a smile. "But the same doesn't go. In fact," he said, "you can touch me anytime, anywhere and you won't hear a complaint out of me."

He bumped his knuckle against her chin to close her gaping mouth, then shot her a wink, turned and strode from the room.

Maggie stood, rooted to the spot, staring after him until he'd disappeared from sight.

Touch him anytime, anywhere?

Because the image of doing so came much too easily to mind, she sank down on the side of the bed and buried her face in her hands.

"Oh, God," she moaned. "What have I gotten myself into?"

Three

By the time Maggie had finished feeding the baby and putting her down for her nap, she'd convinced herself that Ace had said what he'd said to drive her crazy.

...you can touch me anytime, anywhere...

Why else would he say such a thing, if not to drive her nuts?

And if that was his purpose, he'd certainly done a good job of it. Twice, while feeding the baby, she'd actually caught herself imagining doing what he'd suggested. Framing her hands at his face and tracing the sharp ridge of his sculpted cheekbones with the tips of her fingers. Smoothing her palms over those strong, broad shoulders. Splaying them over the muscled expanse of his chest, the hard, flat plane of his abdomen.

The images alone were enough to have her thinking of sweaty bodies and tangled sheets.

Which was exactly what he'd hoped her reaction would be, she was sure.

Furious with herself for letting him get to her so easily, she snatched up her duffel and marched to the linen press to unpack.

It wasn't as if she hadn't known that something like this could happen, she reminded herself as she jerked clothes from her duffel and stuffed them into drawers. She knew that sharing a house with a man required a careful balancing act in order to keep the relationship platonic and the two from toppling into bed together.

Especially, it seemed, when the man was a Tanner.

Not that Maggie had had any personal contact with the Tanner brothers prior to delivering Star's baby to their ranch. But she'd certainly heard enough stories about them from the women who hung out at the Longhorn to know they were legends in this part of Texas. According to the gossip, they were all rich, handsome and eligible—three traits that apparently made them irresistible to the female population, considering the number of women who had claimed to have slept with one or more of them.

But Maggie had no intention of being charmed out of her panties by a Tanner. She'd let lust overrule good sense once in her life and she certainly didn't intend to make that mistake again. Lust she'd learned to deal with. And she'd learn to handle Ace Tanner, too, she promised herself, as she stuffed her empty duffel into the bottom of the linen press. It was just a matter of keeping her mind focused on her purpose for being in his home...*and* keeping a safe distance from him.

Confident that she could accomplish both, she changed from her waitress uniform into a pair of jeans and a T-shirt. With nothing else to do until the baby awoke, she decided to explore the rest of the house. She felt a moment's unease at snooping around without asking Ace's permission first, but dispensed with it by telling herself that since she'd offered to clean the house, she'd need to be familiar with its layout.

As she wandered from room to room, she began to understand what had motivated Ace's stepmother to claim a space as a feminine escape for herself. The house *did* have the look and feel of a hunting lodge, just as Ace had claimed. Though there were gorgeous antiques scattered throughout, the bulk of the furnishings and accessories leaned toward a more rustic, western-style. Most of the upholstered pieces were covered in leather, varying in hue from warm golds to dark, distressed browns, while others sported western print fabrics, as did many of the throw pillows tossed about. The art she found displayed on the walls and tabletops ranged from bronze statues of cowboys galloping on horses to priceless oil paintings of Texas landscapes to ornately carved silver objects.

And over it all lay a thick layer of dust.

Some might find the prospect of cleaning such a large house daunting, if not depressing. But not Maggie. She'd never had much, and what she did have she'd picked up at garage sales, tag sales and a few successful Dumpster dives. The thought of putting the shine back on a house like the Tanners'…well, for her, it would be more pleasure than work.

Anxious to get started, she headed for the kitchen. Obviously added on by one of the later generations of Tanners, the kitchen appeared to have undergone a fairly recent remodeling and offered every modern convenience imaginable. A brick arch above a commercial-sized range complemented the home's rustic theme, giving the appliance the look and feel of a working fireplace. Terra-cotta Mexican tiles covered the floor, while dark slabs of slate spanned the countertops. A long island, topped with butcher block on one end and beautifully veined granite on the other, created a convenient food prep area.

Dazzled by the grandeur of it all, Maggie crossed to the built-in refrigerator to check out its contents, assuming she'd be responsible for the cooking, as well as the cleaning. Her chin nearly hit the floor when she saw the number of covered bowls and casserole dishes crammed onto the shelves, apparently the leftovers from the funeral meal Ace had mentioned. Certain that she wouldn't have to cook for a month, she closed the door and rolled up her sleeves, ready to get to work. She attacked the kitchen first, using the cleaning supplies she unearthed from beneath the farm-style sink.

An hour later, with only the floor left to be mopped, she took a break to check on the baby. Finding the infant still sleeping peacefully, she returned to the kitchen and gave the tile floor a good scrubbing.

Just as she was putting the mop away in the mudroom, she caught a glimpse of Ace through the window, walking back toward the house. Wondering why he was on foot instead of horseback, she crossed to the window to peer out.

He certainly doesn't look much like a wealthy playboy, she thought with more than a little resentment, as she watched his approach. He looked more like a rough and tumble cowboy, returning home after a long cattle drive. The slow ambling gait with just a bit of a swagger. The dust-covered boots and jeans. The sweat-stained cowboy hat pulled low over his brow. If his face was visible, she knew it would only enhance the image more. With his flint-like blue eyes and sharply defined features, he could easily play the part of a gunslinger from the Wild West. All that was needed to complete the picture was a holster riding low on his hips and a six-shooter gripped in each hand.

Finding the sight of him a little too appealing, she turned away with a sniff of disdain. As she did, out of her peripheral vision, she saw him stumble. Frowning, she moved back to the window and watched as he shoved back his hat and dragged his arm across his brow. Noticing that the shirt sleeve was torn, she stepped to the door and pushed it open.

"Ace?" she called uncertainly. "Are you all right?"

At the sound of her voice, he dropped his arm and looked up. Her breath caught in her throat, when she saw that blood smeared half his face and dripped from his chin. Forgetting her vow to keep a safe distance, she flung open the door and flew down the steps, across the yard.

By the time she reached him, he was bent over, his hands braced on his knees, gulping air. Fearing he was about to pass out, she slid an arm around his waist to support him. "What happened?" she asked in alarm.

He dragged in air through his nose, puffed his cheeks and slowly blew the breath out through his mouth. "Horse spooked. Pitched me off a mile or two back. Had to walk home."

"Are you hurt?"

He pressed a hand gingerly against his rib cage. "Don't know," he said, wincing. "Might've busted a rib or two."

"And you walked home?" she cried in dismay, then clamped her lips together. "Never mind," she said, and urged him into motion. "We need to get you inside before you fall flat on your face."

He tried to shake free of her hold. "Never fainted in my life," he grumbled.

She tightened her grip on him. "Well, you better hope you don't start now, because I'm sure as heck not carrying you."

She managed to get him to the back door and used her hip to hold it open, while she maneuvered him inside. Once in the kitchen, she half pushed, half dragged him to a chair at the table and eased him down. Dropping to her knees between his sprawled legs, she looked up to examine his face more closely. Beneath the dust and blood, high on his left cheek was a puncture-type wound the size of a bullet hole.

"There's a contusion beneath your left eye."

He lifted a hand to the spot and flinched, when his finger touched the broken skin. Setting his jaw, he shook his head. "Some antibiotic cream and it'll be okay."

She pursed her lips. "That's going to need more than antibiotic cream." She reached for his hand. "Let me see your arm."

He tensed, watching as she carefully peeled back the tattered sleeve, exposing more blood and dirt and two more deep cuts.

"I must've landed on a rock or something when my horse pitched me," he mumbled.

She closed her eyes, gulped, then forced them open again. "We need to get you to a doctor."

He yanked his arm from her grasp. "No way. You're not hauling me to a sawbones over a couple of scrapes."

"These are more serious than scrapes," she argued. "You have two lacerations on your arm, one of which will likely require stitches. And that gash on your cheek might, too," she added, shifting her gaze to frown at it. "Plus, you said you might've broken a couple of ribs. You'll need X-rays to be sure."

He reared back in the chair, lengthening his chest in an obvious effort to relieve the pressure on his ribs. "Probably just bruised. There's a first aid kit in the mudroom. Top drawer of the chest. Get it for me, would you?"

She wavered uncertainly, wanting to refuse, but finally pushed to her feet, knowing it would be a waste of her time.

"You have to be the stubbornest man I've ever had the misfortune to meet," she muttered, as she strode for the mudroom.

"If you'd met my brother Woodrow," he called after

her, "You wouldn't say that. Woodrow, now he wrote the book on stubborn."

She returned with the first aid kit. "If he did," she said, as she passed by him on her way to the sink, "he had a handy case study in you." After filling a bowl with water, she knelt in front of him again, positioning the bowl and first aid kit on the floor beside her. "Take off your shirt."

"Is that an invitation or an order?"

She glanced up, surprised by the teasing in his voice. But she saw the shadow of pain that clouded his blue eyes, the deep lines of it that etched his mouth and knew that his teasing was nothing but a ruse to hide how much he was truly hurting.

It was in Maggie's nature to soothe, to heal. If he were anyone else, she would have reached up and brushed back the lock of damp hair that had fallen across his forehead, gently thumbed away the dust that had gathered in the squint lines that fanned from the corners of his eyes and teased him right back.

But this was Ace Tanner she was dealing with. The man who had given her his permission to touch him anytime, anywhere. Remembering that—as well as how tempting she found that offer—she dropped her gaze and opened the first aid kit.

"An order," she replied stiffly, as she began to lay out the supplies she'd need.

Eyeing her warily, he tugged the tail of his shirt from his jeans. "I hope the hell you know what you're doing."

"I'm training to be a nurse, so I've had some experience dealing with scrapes and bruises."

He shrugged the shirt from his shoulders, grimacing as he eased his injured arm from the tattered sleeve. "A nurse, huh?" he said, sweat popping out on his brow. "What is it they say about nurses? They do it with patients?"

Maggie recognized his need to keep talking as yet another means of distracting himself from the pain. She might have responded to that need, if he hadn't chosen that moment to drop his shirt, exposing the most incredible chest she'd ever seen in her life. A mat of dark hair swirled tightly around his nipples and arrowed down his flat stomach to disappear behind the waist of his jeans.

Tearing her gaze away from the tempting sight, she plunged a cloth into the bowl of water, struggling to find the detachment she needed to respond.

"'Nurses call the shots.' 'Nurses do it with gloves on.'" She looked up and gave him what she hoped was a patronizing smile. "You can save the jokes. I've heard them all."

"I'll bet you haven't heard this one. 'Nurses are here to save your ass, not kiss it.'"

Kiss his ass? Oh, Lord, she thought. She didn't dare even think about that! Sure that her cheeks were flaming, she dropped her gaze to his arm and frantically began to cleanse the dirt and debris that clung to the wound. When she was sure she could speak without stammering like a fool, she laid the cloth aside and picked up the bottle of antiseptic. "As a matter of fact, I've considered having that one embroidered on my nurse's cap when I graduate."

He snorted a laugh, then choked on it when she tipped the bottle over his arm, flushing out the cuts. "Damn!" he swore. "That stuff burns like hell."

She blew to cool the stinging sensation. "Better a little discomfort than an infection."

He closed his free hand over the edge of the chair's seat as if prepared to endure whatever tortures she had planned for him. "Spoken like a true medical professional," he grumbled.

"It's a required class for all nursing students. Handy Retorts for Whiners 101."

Tipping his head back, he closed his eyes. "Handy Retorts for Whiners," he mumbled, then chuckled weakly. "If it isn't a class, it ought to be. I'd imagine a nurse takes a lot of grief from her patients.''

"Sometimes. But nursing can be a very gratifying career, too.''

Puzzled by her comment, Ace lifted his head to peer down at her. "How would you know if you've never worked as one?''

She pulled a strip of tape over the cut, measuring the length she needed to close the wound. "I've done volunteer work as a nurse's aid in the hospital. An internship for one of my classes,'' she explained, then warned, "this might hurt a little.''

Clamping his teeth together, he watched as she pulled the torn flesh together and applied tape over it. He was surprised to find that, in spite of her prickly and sour disposition, she had the touch of an angel. "What made you want to be a nurse?''

She measured off another strip of tape. "Taking care of my mother before she died. She didn't have insurance and had to rely on indigent care. The staff at the hospital where she was admitted was less than courteous to her and sometimes careless with the medical treatments they dispensed.'' She lifted a shoulder, as she pressed the strip into place. "I guess they figured since she couldn't afford to pay, she didn't deserve the same quality of care as those who could.'' She lifted her shoulder again. "Anyway, that's when I decided to become a nurse.''

Ace thought of his own mother's hospital stays during her brief but painful fight against cancer and the five-star treatment she'd received there, and suspected that Maggie was right. "How old were you?'' he asked curiously.

"Sixteen.''

"Wow. Your mother must've died awfully young.''

"She was thirty-one.''

"Thirty-one!" he exclaimed. "But that would've made her—"

"Fifteen when she had me," she finished for him, then looked up and met his gaze squarely. "And, no, she wasn't married."

Judging by the defiant gleam in her eyes, Ace figured she was a bit touchy about her illegitimacy. "I don't recall asking whether she was married or not."

She dropped her gaze and pressed the last strip into place. "Most people do."

Ace stared at the top of her head, feeling a bit guilty because the question had been on the tip of his tongue to ask. Though he wanted to quiz her more about her mother, he decided it best, considering her touchiness, to keep his questions to himself. "So you've wanted to be a nurse since you were sixteen," he said instead.

She wound the gauze back onto the roll. "That's right."

"If you knew what you wanted to do with your life, what took you so long to begin your studies?"

She stretched to place the gauze back inside the first aid kit. "Money. Circumstances."

"What kind of circumstances?"

She rocked back on her heels to look at him in frustration. "What is this? Twenty questions?"

"Just curious."

Pursing her lips, she bent to gather the bowl and cloths. "My ex thought boozing it up with his buddies was more important than me getting an education."

Not wanting to answer any more questions about her past, Maggie rose and headed for the sink.

She took her time rinsing out the cloths and refilling the bowl with fresh water, but when she turned, she found that Ace was watching her, his eyes narrowed thoughtfully.

Uncomfortable, she looked away as she crossed back to

the table and set down the bowl. "If you'll lean your head back and close your eyes, it'll make this a lot easier."

Though she half expected him to grill her with more questions, he tilted his head back and closed his eyes. Breathing a quiet sigh of relief, she eased closer to examine the cut.

Confronted with the dried mixture of dust, sweat and blood that covered most of his face, she wished that she'd had the forethought to insist that he take a shower before she began treating his wounds. And a good shampooing wouldn't have hurt, either, she thought, shifting her gaze to his hair. Thick and jet-black, it lay plastered against his head, flattened there by the cowboy hat he'd shoved off when he'd first sat down.

Cupping a hand at the back of his neck to hold his head in place while she cleaned his face, she paused, her heart softening a bit, as she looked down at him. A part of her yearned to comb her fingers through his thick, dark hair, lift the wayward lock that had fallen across his forehead and smooth it back into place.

Another wiser part knew what a mistake that would be.

Forcing herself to focus on the task at hand, she pulled the cloth from the bowl, squeezed the water from it and began to wash his face. She gently wiped the cloth across his forehead and down his cheek, removing as much of the blood and dirt as possible without causing him any more pain. As she drew the cloth along the line of his jaw, she couldn't help but notice again how prominent his features were, what a manly ruggedness they added to an already handsome face. The thick dark eyebrows. The high slash of cheekbone. The strong, square jaw. A slight crook in his nose was all that saved him from perfection.

And his mouth…

She dipped the cloth into the water again and smoothed it over his dry, parched lips, moistening them. Hearing his low moan of gratitude, she found her mind straying again, this time to wonder what his lips would feel like pressed against hers. She was sure his kisses would be hard, demanding, seductive, much like the image he projected. Mesmerized by the shape of his mouth, his lips' texture, she stilled her hand at the bow of his upper lip and stared, all but able to taste the salty sweat that beaded the skin above it, feel the rasp of his day-old beard chafing against her skin.

Heat flooded her cheeks and pooled in her belly, as the image grew. She quickly plunged the cloth into the water again, determined to keep her mind focused on his wounds. Though it was difficult, she made herself finish cleansing his face, then plucked a gauze pad from the kit and soaked it with antiseptic.

"I'm going to put on the antiseptic now," she warned.

"Do it quick. That stuff burns like—"

Before he could say more, Maggie squeezed, drizzling the liquid over his cheek.

He sat bolt upright, his eyes flipping wide. "Holy sh—!" Groaning, he clamped an arm around his middle and sank weakly back against the chair.

Knowing how much pain that movement must have caused him, Maggie laid a sympathetic hand on his shoulder. "Sorry."

"Blow," he begged. "Please."

Without questioning the wisdom of that act, she leaned over and blew softly over the cut. His relief was almost immediate, evidenced by his sigh. She felt the moist warmth of it against her cheek, heard the low, throaty sound that accompanied it in the gust of air that wafted past her ear.

Sure that the stinging sensation had eased by now, she started to draw away, but he cuffed a hand at the back of her neck, stopping her.

"Again."

Though she knew it would be wiser to refuse, the husky plea in his voice, the desperate clasp of his fingers around her neck had her inhaling a deep breath. As she blew, his scent swirled around her, filled her. The musky, masculine odors of sweat, leather and horses tangled together, clouding her mind and forming a knot of keen awareness that settled low in her belly.

It would be so easy to kiss him right now, she thought. They were so close. A slight turn of the head…a pucker. Then she'd know what his kiss was like, his taste.

Even as the tempting thought formed in her mind, she felt his fingers tighten on her neck, sensed the tensing of his body. Mortified that he had somehow read her thoughts, she snapped her gaze to his and saw that his eyes were open and focused on her. In the blue depths she saw the same heat, the same question that burned behind hers.

His gaze slid to her mouth, and heat seared her chest, her cheeks, her throat, quickened her pulse. Unconsciously, she wet her lips, and he groaned, his eyes following the arc of her tongue. Slowly he raised his eyes to meet hers.

"You know what a mistake this would be."

She didn't need to ask what he meant by *this*. Gulping, she nodded. "Yes…I know."

With his gaze on hers, he drew her face to his. He touched his mouth to hers once, briefly, withdrew, and inhaled deeply, as if to savor the flavors he'd found there. Then, with a groan, he opened his mouth over hers and covered hers, capturing her lips, her very soul. The heat was instantaneous, blinding, debilitating. Closing her eyes against it, she braced her hands against his shoulders to keep from sinking weakly to her knees.

His kiss was everything she'd imagined it to be. Hard, demanding…yet gloriously seductive. His teeth nipped, his tongue soothed. Greedy, yet at the same time tender, captivating. She knew she should turn away or, at the very least, put up a halfhearted struggle, but found she couldn't. She wanted the kiss to go on and on and never end.

He cupped a hand at her hip. "Closer," he murmured, as he urged her down to his lap.

She'd barely settled there, before he was pushing her hair back over her shoulder to bury his face in the curve of her neck.

"Better," he said, with a sigh, as he dragged his tongue along the narrow channel above her collar bone.

Rocked by the sensations that flooded her, frightened by them, she dug her fingers into his shoulders. "Ace," she gasped. "You have to—"

Before she could tell him to stop, demand that he do so, he brought his mouth back to hers, silencing her. With her hips gripped between his hands, he slid down lower on the chair and stretched out his long legs, shifting her around until they were positioned chest-to-chest, groin-to-groin, thigh-to-thigh. Holding her hard against him, he thrust his tongue between her lips and stole her breath, along with whatever power she had to stop him.

Gradually she became aware of his erection thickening and lengthening between them. She could almost hear the blood rushing into it, making it swell, feel the heat that fired it, forging it into a thick shaft of steel between them. An ache throbbed to life between her legs and she rolled her hips over his erection, desperate to ease it. She heard his low groan, felt the painful dig of his fingers into her buttocks, and was sure he was suffering the same frustrations as she.

Dizzy with need, for a moment she felt as if she were falling, but was sure she was only imagining the sensation. A split second later her bottom struck the tile floor with enough momentum to jar her teeth. Stunned, she blinked open her eyes to find Ace standing over her, his arms vised around his chest, his head flung back, his teeth bared.

Fury shot through her at him treating her so carelessly.

But it drained away just as quickly, when she realized the expression on his face was one of pain. Alarmed, she scrambled to her feet. "Oh, my God, Ace! Did you hurt your ribs?"

He dropped his chin to glare at her. "*I* didn't. *You* did."

She fell back a step. "Me?"

"Yes, you. With all that thrashing and grinding you were doing, if my ribs weren't busted before, they sure as hell are now."

Stunned, for a moment she could only stare. Then the anger came, filling her with a blinding rage.

"I wouldn't have been anywhere near your ribs, if you hadn't dragged me down onto your lap!"

"How the hell was I supposed to know that you were so starved for sex that you'd paw me half to death?"

Her mouth dropped open, then slammed shut with an indignant click of teeth. Taking a threatening step toward him, she stabbed a finger against the middle of his chest. "*You're* the desperate one. All I did was blow on your cut, just like you asked me to do. The rest was *your* doing."

He shoved her hand away. "And what the hell did you expect me to do, with you rubbing yourself all over me and blowing in my ear?"

"I was blowing on your cheek!"

"Same damn thing. You were—"

Cocking her head toward the hall, she threw up a hand to silence him and listened. Dropping her arm, she glared at him. "Now look what you've done."

"What?" he cried in frustration.

She spun on her heel and marched for the door. "You woke up the baby."

"Me!" he shouted after her. "You were yelling just as loud as I was!" When she didn't respond, he gave the chair an angry kick, then flopped down on it and glared at the empty doorway, his blood boiling at all the injustices that kept piling up on him.

First his old man up and dies, leaving him an estate to settle with no will to use as a guide and a ranch to manage with no ranch hands to do the work. If that wasn't bad enough, he then gets stuck with a baby he doesn't want and winds up hiring the nanny from hell to take care of the kid.

She didn't ask for the job, a small voice reminded him. *You all but bulldozed her into taking it on. And, she was right about you starting all this. You were the one who pulled her down on your lap.*

Ace squirmed uncomfortably at his conscience's prodding.

Okay, he admitted reluctantly. So maybe he was partially to blame for what had happened. But what man wouldn't have reacted the same as he had, if caught in a similar situation? Having a woman rubbing her hands all over you and blowing her hot breath in your ear, when you'd spent the last six months alone on a photo shoot in the remote mountains of Central America, where the closest you'd come to female companionship was an overly friendly donkey, who stole your food out of your backpack? Hell, it was a wonder he hadn't thrown Maggie down on the floor and taken her right then and there!

But sex complicated things. Always did. Ace knew that. And he sure as hell wasn't going to take a chance on getting physically involved with Maggie. He needed her to take care of the kid a lot worse than he needed an outlet for his sexual frustrations.

Exhausted from the lack of sleep he'd gotten the night before, as well as the long, hot trek back to the house, he leaned his head back with a sigh and closed his eyes, vowing a life of celibacy.

At least where Maggie was concerned.

Four

Ace wasn't sure how much time had passed before he heard Maggie's footsteps, signaling her return. Minutes? Hours? Could've been either, because he'd lost all sense of time the second he'd closed his eyes.

Too tired to rouse himself, he asked groggily, "Was the kid okay?"

"She was fine."

He felt something soft brush his chest, a strange warmth, followed by the scent of talcum powder. Opening his eyes, he looked down to find the baby on his chest and Maggie guiding his hand to the infant's back.

He tried to wrench his hand free. "What do you think you're doing? I'm not holding this kid!"

"I can't very well hold her and wrap your ribs, too."

He narrowed an eye at her. "Like I'm gonna let you anywhere near my ribs."

Folding her arms across her chest, she looked down her

nose at him. "So you've changed your mind about going to see a doctor?"

"I'm not going anywhere. Now get this kid off me."

She plucked a roll of elastic bandage from the first aid kit. "I will as soon as I've wrapped your ribs."

"But she's naked!"

"Oh, she is not," Maggie fussed. "She has a diaper on. I just took her gown off, so she could air out for awhile."

"Well, let her air out someplace else."

She looked around the room. "And where would you suggest I put her? In the refrigerator?" Frowning, she shook her head. "No, it's too full. She'd never fit. How about the sink?"

"Very funny."

"I'm not trying to be funny. I'm *trying* to make you see that there's no place else to put her but on your lap. You really should buy one of those infant swings. She'd like that. Tell me if this hurts," she said, and pressed her fingers lightly against his ribs.

Her touch, though light, sent pain lancing through his side. Ace would have jumped up and howled like a wounded dog, if he hadn't been afraid he'd drop the kid.

He curled his lip in a snarl. "First thing tomorrow morning I want you to go to town and buy a damn swing and whatever else this kid needs."

She fluttered her eyelashes at him. "How could I possibly refuse, with you asking so sweetly?" Losing the fake smile, she waved an impatient hand. "Now hold her out of the way, so that I can bandage your chest."

When he didn't make a move to comply, she huffed a breath, plucked his hand from the baby's back and picked the baby up herself. Unable to resist, she took a moment to nuzzle Laura's cheek before draping a blanket over Ace's legs and laying the infant, stomach down, across his thighs.

She reached for his hand again, but he snatched it away.

"I know the drill," he growled, and spread his fingers over the baby's back, holding her in place.

With a shrug, Maggie picked up the roll of elastic bandage and placed an end in the middle of Ace's chest. "Lean forward a little," she instructed, as she moved to his side and began wrapping the tape around him.

When she'd finished, she stepped back to admire her work. "Not bad, even if I do say so myself."

"Great. Now would you please get this kid off me?"

She held up a finger. "Just give me a second to put these things away."

She quickly gathered the first aid supplies and put them back into the kit, then turned for the mudroom to return it to the chest. As she did, she shrieked and jumped back, knocking against Ace's shoulder.

"What the hell's the matter with you?" he shouted. "You almost made me drop the kid."

"There's a man—"

Before she could tell him there was a man outside the door, peering through the glass, the man in question opened the door and stepped inside.

"Did I scare you?" he asked Maggie, but was grinning as if he knew he had and thought her reaction funny.

Ace's back was to the door, making it impossible for him to see their visitor, but he must have recognized the voice.

"A face like that would scare the hell out of anybody," he grumbled.

Tossing his hat onto the counter, the stranger crossed to Maggie, his hand extended in greeting. "Rory Tanner, ma'am." He tipped his head toward Ace. "I'm this old cuss's younger and much more handsome brother."

Up close, Maggie could see the resemblance between the two, though Rory was leaner than Ace and seemed to have been blessed with a much more pleasant disposition. Releasing the breath she'd been holding, she accepted his hand. "Maggie Dean. I'm Laura's nanny."

When she tried to withdraw her hand, Rory held on. Smiling, he drew her hand to his lips and brushed a kiss over her knuckles. "Ace told me that he'd hired someone, but he failed to mention how pretty you are."

"Oh, for crying out loud," Ace groused. "Quit your flirting, Rory, and get over here and get this kid."

Shooting her a wink, Rory gave her hand a parting squeeze, then moved in front of Ace. His eyes widened in surprise, when he got his first look at his brother. "Whoa. What truck ran over you?"

Ace averted his gaze, obviously embarrassed to admit how he'd received the injuries. "Dang horse pitched me off."

"I told him he should see a doctor," Maggie said, "but he refused."

Rory shook his head. "That's no surprise. Ace has a powerful fear of doctors."

"I do not!" Ace cried.

"I stand corrected," Rory said, bowing. "It's their *needles* that scare you." Chuckling, he glanced over at Maggie. "One time, when we were kids, I stepped on a rusty nail and Ace had to take me to the doctor to get a tetanus shot. Even insisted upon holding my hand while they gave me the injection. One look at that needle, and he passed smooth out. Took two nurses to revive him."

"Shoulda let you die from blood poisoning or lockjaw," Ace grumbled, then snapped, "If you don't take this kid, I'm dumping her on the floor."

Maggie quickly stepped between the two men, fearing Ace would make good his threat.

"Here, I'll take her." She lifted the baby to her shoulder, then offered Ace a hand. "Need some help?"

He slapped her hand away. "It's my ribs that're hurt, not my legs."

But when he tried to stand, his butt only cleared the chair about three inches before he was sinking back down, his face pale, his hand clasped at his side.

Rory moved closer. "Here, Ace. I'll help you."

Ace shot him a murderous look. "I don't need your help. What I need is whiskey. See if there's any in the liquor cabinet in the den."

Rory turned away, biting back a smile. "Sure thing, Ace. Won't take me but a minute."

"If you're in pain," Maggie said worriedly, "I'll get you some aspirin."

"I don't want aspirin. I want whiskey."

"But, Ace—"

"And make it straight," he shouted to Rory.

Rory returned with a bottle and a glass. He splashed two fingers of whiskey into the tumbler, then offered it to Ace. Ace looked pointedly at the glass, then up at Rory. With a shrug, Rory filled it to the top and passed it to Ace.

Ace downed half the drink in one greedy gulp, shuddered, then sank back in the chair with a sigh. "I feel better already."

Rory set the whiskey bottle on the table. "Another shot like that, and you won't feel anything at all."

Maggie pushed the bottle out of Ace's reach. "What you need is food, not whiskey."

"Food?" Rory echoed, his eyes lighting up. "Is there any of Mrs. Frazier's fried chicken left?"

"If there isn't," Maggie told him, "there's plenty more to choose from. If you'll hold the baby, I'll see what I can find."

Rory took a step back, rubbing his hands down the side of his legs. "I don't think so. I've never held a kid before."

Maggie rolled her eyes. "What is it with you Tanner men? She won't bite."

"No, but she might break."

"Oh, for heaven's sake," Maggie fussed, then dragged out a chair and pointed a stiff finger at it. "Sit," she ordered.

Rory sat.

"You'll have to support her head," she warned him. "She's not strong enough yet to hold it up on her own."

He blew out an uneasy breath, wiped his palms down his thighs, then held out his arms. "Okay. Hand her over."

She transferred the baby into his arms, tucking the blanket carefully around her. "There," she said, smiling as she straightened. "That's not so hard, is it?"

Rory looked down at the baby, who was staring up at him in wide-eyed wonder, and grinned. "She's a cute little thing, isn't she?"

"Precious," Ace muttered under his breath, then said louder, "Is anybody going to pour me another drink or am I going to have to get up and get it myself?"

When Rory and Maggie ignored him, Ace set his jaw and dug in his heels, scooching his chair closer to the table. Slamming the empty glass down on its top, he grabbed the bottle and turned it up, gulping whiskey as fast as he could swallow. The liquid burned a path down his throat and hit his empty stomach with a nauseating splash.

Sure that Maggie would have stopped him by now—or at the very least have voiced her disapproval—he lowered the bottle and stole a glance her way. She stood at Rory's side, her arm draped along the back of his chair, her face almost cheek-to-cheek with his, smiling and offering encouragement, as Rory fed the baby the bottle.

For some stupid reason, seeing the two together like that made Ace madder than hell.

"I thought you were going to fix us something to eat?" he snapped.

Maggie leaned to place her hand over Rory's to adjust the angle of the bottle. "I am," she said, as she straightened. "I just wanted to make sure Rory was comfortable with feeding Laura first." She smiled at Rory and gave him a pat on the back. "You're doing great," she said, before turning away.

Ace watched her cross to the refrigerator, a scowl building on his face.

"I don't know what he's doing that's so great," he grumbled. "Any fool can feed a baby."

Maggie pulled open the refrigerator door, then looked over the top of it at Ace. "You ought to know," she said, smiling sweetly. "You managed to do it."

Ace awakened slowly, sure that a woodpecker had set up shop on his forehead and was jackhammering a hole between his eyes. Moaning, he rolled to his back, then sucked in a breath through his teeth, as pain stabbed through his side. Remembering his fall from the horse, he closed his eyes and gulped, willing the nausea back.

When he was fairly certain he could do so without throwing up, he opened his eyes and looked around. Since his last memory was of sitting at the kitchen table, guzzling whiskey straight from the bottle, he was surprised to find himself in his bed and in his room. How had he gotten there? he wondered. Maggie? Rory?

Neither, he decided, scowling. If left up to the two of them, he could've died in that chair and they wouldn't have noticed. They'd been too busy flirting with each other to care what happened to him. Rory he could almost understand, since his brother was a natural born flirt. But Maggie? Hadn't she professed to Ace, only that morning, that she wasn't interested in a relationship with a man, sexual or otherwise?

Hard to believe, after that hot little tango she'd danced with Ace in the kitchen, prior to Rory's arrival. His scowl deepened. Harder still, considering the way she'd latched onto Rory like he was the last living male on earth, preparing him a plate of food and all but hand feeding it to him, while he gave the baby the bottle.

And what had Maggie done for Ace, who was too busted up to stand alone, much less get himself something to eat? Nothing but shoot him dirty looks every time he lifted the bottle for another drink.

You wouldn't be jealous now would you, Tanner?

The question came out of nowhere and had Ace stiffening. Hell, no, he wasn't jealous, he told himself, forcing the tension from his shoulders. He didn't give a tinker's damn if Maggie had the hots for his brother. Why should he care who she fooled around with, as long as she stayed away from him and kept the kid out of his hair?

The bedroom door opened a crack, and he whipped his head around just as Maggie's face appeared in the opening. She looked a little bit too pink-cheeked and cheerful to suit Ace.

"What do you want?" he snapped.

Her smile dipping into a frown, she pushed the door open and stepped inside. "Well, I see that a good night's sleep hasn't improved your disposition any."

Remembering that he was wearing nothing but his boxer shorts, he yanked the sheet across his lower body. "Nothing wrong with my disposition."

Arching a brow, she crossed to the bed. "So you're always this cranky?"

Before he could think of a suitable comeback, she distracted him by leaning to fluff the pillows behind his head. With her body draped across his, he got a whiff of some come-hither perfume and a peek of cleavage that kicked his senses into overload and his hormones into high gear. Down, boy, he told himself, remembering his vow of celibacy where she was concerned.

Straightening, she gave him a stern look. "You owe Rory a big thank-you."

He snorted a disgusted breath. "For what? Feeding the baby her damn bottle?"

"No. For taking you to the emergency room."

He gaped at her. "He didn't take me anywhere."

She smiled smugly. "Oh, but he did. That's just one of the consequences of consuming too much alcohol. It robs a person of whole blocks of time."

Groaning, Ace squeezed a hand at his temples, unable to believe he'd been so drunk he didn't remember a trip to the emergency room.

"By the way," she added. "You'll be glad to know that your ribs aren't broken, just bruised."

"Which is what I said all along," he snapped.

Ignoring him, she went on. "And while you're thanking Rory, you might want to throw in an apology."

"An apology?" he cried. "For *what?*"

"You called him a few choice names, while he was helping you to bed."

Though he was relieved to learn that it was Rory and not Maggie who had stripped him of his clothes, Ace wasn't about to offer his brother an apology. He folded his arms stubbornly across his chest. "Probably deserved it."

"What he *deserves* is an apology."

He eyed her suspiciously, wondering why she was so hell-bent on defending Rory and wondering, too, if it was his brother who had put that pretty shade of pink in her cheeks and left her looking as satisfied as a cat with a belly full of cream. "What time did he leave, anyway?"

She shrugged. "I don't know. Ten or eleven, I'd guess."

"How long before that did he put me to bed?"

"He left right after." She gave him an odd look. "Why?"

Jutting his chin, he looked away. "No reason."

With a shrug, she leaned to press the back of her fingers against his forehead.

He ducked away. "What the hell do you think you're doing?"

"Checking to see if you have a temperature."

"What I have is a headache."

She stooped to pick his clothes up from the floor. "And well earned. You drank enough whiskey to kill a normal person."

He would've argued, but since he felt a little like death, he decided against it. "Get me some aspirin."

She dumped his clothes on the foot of his bed to fist her hands on her hips. "Oh, so you want aspirin now? When I offered them to you last night, all you wanted was whiskey."

His stomach churned sickly at the reminder of the bottle he'd polished off. Or was it two? "Aspirin," he repeated.

With a huff of breath, she dropped her hands from her hips and marched to the adjoining bath. She returned minutes later with a bottle and a glass of water. She shook a couple of tablets onto his palm, then passed him the water to wash them down with.

"Your agent called," she told him while he drank. "He wants you to call him. He said it was an emergency."

Ace backhanded the water from his upper lip. "Everything's an emergency to Max."

She took the glass from him and set it on the bedside table. "He said something about your book being short and your publisher needing more photographs before they can send it on to the printer."

Ace sat bolt upright at the news, then sank weakly back

against the pillows, holding a hand against his bandaged ribs. "What next?" he moaned miserably.

"Do you want me to call him and tell him that you had an accident and can't take care of any business right now?"

"No, I don't want you to tell him any such thing!" He frowned a moment, thinking. "There's a portfolio in the back seat of my truck." He held his hands out, measuring. "About this size and black. Bring it to me."

She lifted a brow. "You might try asking a little nicer."

He set his jaw, knowing she had him between a rock and a hard place, since he wasn't at all sure he could make it to his truck under his own steam. "Please," he ground out between clenched teeth.

She smiled. "All right. But I'll need to check on the baby first. Do you want anything else?"

A break from bad news, Ace thought irritably, but shook his head. "Just the portfolio."

Later that morning, Ace sat propped up in his bed, studying the prints spread in front of him, trying to decide if he could use any for the book. Busted up like he was, making another trip to Wyoming to take additional shots was out of the question.

"Ace?"

He looked up to find Maggie standing in the doorway, the baby in her arms. "What?"

"I'm going to town to buy some supplies for Laura. How do you want me to pay for them?"

He turned his attention back to the photos. "Charge whatever you need. The Bar-T has accounts at every store in town."

"Do you want me to bring you something to eat before I leave? You haven't eaten anything this morning."

Ace's stomach growled at the reminder. "I suppose I could choke down something."

She stepped into the room and crossed to the bed. "I found a lemon pound cake in the refrigerator and there's fresh coffee brewed. How does that sound?"

Without looking up, he waved her away. "Whatever."

He heard a rustling sound and glanced over to find Maggie had moved some of his photos aside and was laying the baby on the bed beside him. "You're not leaving that kid here!" he cried.

"It's just for a minute," she promised, as she hurried for the door. "I can't carry her and a tray, too."

"Wait! I—" Before he could tell Maggie he'd changed his mind about being hungry, she was gone. Scowling down at the baby, he snatched a photo from beneath her foot. "Don't touch a thing," he warned.

She blinked up at him, as if fascinated by the sound of his voice. Curling his lip in disgust, he turned his attention back to his work, determined to ignore the kid.

But a few seconds later, he found his gaze straying back to her.

She is kind of cute, he thought, remembering Rory's comment the night before. But, damn, she was tiny. He touched the tip of his finger against a palm no bigger than a quarter and nearly jumped out of his skin, when she closed her fingers around his. His heart thumping wildly, he tried to pull his finger from her grasp, but she held on tight.

"That's quite a grip you've got there, kid," he said uneasily. Though he wasn't certain, he would swear the little gurgling sound she made was a laugh. He narrowed an eye at her. "So you think this is funny, do you?" He shook his finger, trying to break her grip. His eyes widened in amazement, when he couldn't shake loose. "What are you? Wonder Kid?"

In answer, she lifted her legs and planted her bare feet

against his forearm. He stared at them, astonished at how small they were, how soft.

"If you plan on doing any walking on those things," he told her, "you'd better do some growing."

"She'll grow."

Ace glanced up to find Maggie entering the room, a tray in her hands. Embarrassed that she'd caught him talking to the kid, he jerked his hand back and was relieved the kid chose that moment to release her hold on him.

"She'd better," he grumbled.

Maggie shifted items on the bedside table, making room for the tray. "I wasn't sure what you'd want in your coffee, so I brought both cream and sugar."

Ace reached for the cup and drew it to his lips, all but salivating at the coffee's rich aroma. "Black's fine," he said, before gulping down a swallow. Closing his eyes, he sank back against the pillows with a sigh. "Is there any way you can rig this up to my arm and feed it to me intravenously?"

In spite of her irritation with him, Maggie had to resist a smile at the desperation in his voice. "I don't think so."

While he sipped his coffee, she glanced at the photos spread over the bed. Her curiosity aroused by the black and white shots, she picked one of the photos up to examine it more closely. Captured on the print was a moose, with only its head and antlers visible, peeking around the corner of a weathered barn.

"This is good," she said, impressed by Ace's skill with a camera. "Is this one of the pictures you've chosen to send to your agent?"

He set aside his coffee and took the photo from her. "Maybe," he said, studying it critically. "I haven't decided yet."

Maggie sat down on the side of the bed, absently stroking her fingers up and down the baby's arm, as she looked over the other photos. "What's your book about?" she asked curiously.

"Wyoming." He laid the photo aside and picked up another. "Specifically, the wildlife and domesticized animals found there." He angled the photo he held for her to see. "What do you think of this one?"

The photo was of a little boy and his dog, both dripping wet from a swim in the lake behind them. Charmed by the expressions on the faces of the two, she said the first thought that came to mind. "Best friends."

Ace's eyes sharpened at her response. "Exactly," he said, then tossed the picture aside to pick up another. "And this one?"

Her smile melted as she stared at the picture of an emaciated dog, its ribs protruding grotesquely, digging through a garbage can. In the near distance, a man was pulling a gun from the backseat of his truck. Gulping, she looked up at Ace. "He didn't shoot the dog, did he?"

Ace was too interested in her responses to take time to respond. Dropping the photo, he picked up another to hold before her face. "What about this one?"

Maggie shoved his hand aside. "Please tell me that you didn't let him shoot the dog."

"The dog's fine," he said in frustration, then pushed the photo back in front of her eyes. "What do you see?"

Giving him a doubtful look, Maggie shifted her gaze to the picture and a tender smile curved her lips. "A mother's love."

"That's all?"

She looked up at him, her forehead creasing in puzzlement. "Yes. What was I supposed to see?"

Ace turned the picture around to frown at it. He'd slipped up on the doe in a secluded glen at daybreak, catching the deer lying on a bed of crushed grass, her fawn asleep at her side. He'd snapped the picture just as the doe had turned her head to lick the fawn's face. To him the picture represented peace, tranquility. Nature at its best.

But Maggie had seen only a mother's love.

With a shrug, he set the picture aside. "You put the kid to sleep with all that petting."

Maggie glanced down and was surprised to see that Laura had, indeed, fallen asleep. Smiling, she scooped the infant into her arms and rose. "I guess I better head for town while she's napping."

He dropped his gaze to the photos again, searching for a common thread that would link them together. "Charge whatever you need."

"Do you want me to pick up anything for you while I'm in town?"

He shifted the order of the photos, removed two, then studied them critically. "I need to ship these off to my agent."

"No problem. I can do it for you while I'm in town. I'll need the address."

Seeing the thread he needed, he plucked another picture out of the line-up and tossed it aside, then quickly began gathering the remaining photos and slipping them into protective sleeves. "Never mind. I'll go with you."

Maggie looked at him in surprise. "But your ribs," she reminded him.

He shot her a scowl. "They're only bruised, remember?" He started to whip the sheet back to rise, but caught himself. Holding the sheet at his waist in a fist, he lifted a brow. "Not that I have anything I'd be ashamed for you to see, but you might want to wait outside."

Five

The downtown area of Tanner Crossing was built on the town square concept, with Tanner State Bank sitting dead center. An eclectic mix of retail shops and business offices lined the four streets forming the square, each building's front unique in design and ornamentation, yet blending to create a charming retail center enticing enough to satisfy the shopping needs of visitors and locals alike.

Pushing the newly-purchased stroller down the awning-shaded sidewalk, Maggie glanced wistfully at the window displays she passed, wishing she had time to browse through some of the shops. But Ace's instructions had been specific. One hour, he'd said, and she was to meet him back at the truck. He'd even added the warning that if she was late, he was leaving without her.

Maggie didn't doubt for a minute that he would make good his threat. He was just that ornery.

Fortunately, she'd found most of the things she needed

in the first store she'd stopped at. In less than thirty minutes, she'd purchased a crib, a swing and the stroller, plus filled three huge shopping bags with an assortment of other baby items. But she could never have accomplished so much so quickly if not for the Tanner name. It had barely slipped past her lips, when the owner himself had appeared and had his sales staff all but turning the store inside out in his anxiousness to fill her requests. He'd even agreed to deliver all her purchases to the ranch later in the week at no extra charge.

Still shaking her head over what a difference a name could make, Maggie pushed open the door to the drugstore and carefully maneuvered the stroller over the threshold. Once inside, she stopped to get her bearings and had to blink twice, sure that she'd been catapulted back in time to the '50s. An old-fashioned soda fountain, complete with chrome pedestaled bar stools bolted to a black-and-white tiled floor, dominated the wall on her left. The opposite side of the store held the beauty counter, with cosmetics and perfumes displayed on gleaming glass shelves, and feminine products wrapped in plain brown paper. In between stretched aisle after aisle of merchandise-laden shelving units, the products on each ranging from greeting cards to hand-held massagers. At the rear of the store hung a red neon ℞ guiding customers back to the pharmacy, where a gray-haired man stood on a tall ladder, stocking the shelves with a new shipment of medications.

With a quick glance at her watch to check the time, Maggie pushed the stroller down the aisle marked Infant Care. She quickly selected the toiletries and diapers she needed, placed them on the rack beneath the stroller, then moved on to study the selections of formula and baby food.

"Can I help you find something?"

Maggie glanced over to find a woman bustling down the aisle toward her. Wearing a pastel smock with Samples'

Pharmacy embroidered over the left breast, she moved with a speed that belied her plumpness and snow-white hair.

Maggie offered her a hopeful smile. "You can if you know when it's safe to start a baby on fruits and cereals."

"Safe?" the woman repeated, then huffed a breath. "Honey, you've been reading too many of those new mother books." She gave Maggie's arm a patronizing pat. "But most young folks do with their first."

Before Maggie could explain that Laura wasn't her baby, the woman thrust out her hand.

"I'm Myrna Samples. My husband, John, is the pharmacist." As Maggie took the woman's hand, Myrna leaned close to whisper, "But don't let that fancy title of his fool you. He may know all there is to know about all those little pills that he guards like the national mint, but I'm the authority on babies." She swelled her chest proudly. "Raised four of my own, plus helped raise twelve grandchildren and five greats."

Laughing, Maggie inclined her head. "I bow to your greater experience. I'm Maggie," she said, then gestured to the baby. "And this is Laura."

Myrna stooped to peer beneath the stroller's umbrella at the baby. "Oh, but she's a pretty little thing," she said, then looked up at Maggie. "How old is she?"

"Almost four weeks."

Myrna straightened, her arthritic knees creaking at the effort. "Is she sleeping through the night?"

"No. She usually wakes up between one and two, wanting a bottle."

Myrna pulled a box from the shelf. "Then, you'll want to put a little cereal in her formula. Rice is best, until you've determined if she has any food allergies."

Maggie took the box and added it to the other items beneath the stroller. "Thanks," she said gratefully. "Her formula wasn't seeming to satisfy her any more, but I wasn't sure if I should introduce a new food into her diet this soon, without talking to a doctor first.''

''Go with the gut,'' Myrna said prosaically. ''That's what I always say. A mother knows best what her child needs.''

Again, Maggie tried to explain that she wasn't Laura's mother, but Myrna interrupted her by asking, '' Are you needing anything else?''

Maggie glanced at her list. ''No. That about does it.''

''Then follow me,'' Myrna said and led the way to the checkout. She helped remove the items from beneath the stroller, then stepped behind the cash register and rang up the purchases. ''Cash or charge?'' she asked, when she'd finished.

''Charge,'' Maggie replied, then added, ''To the Bar-T.''

Frowning, Myrna dipped her chin to look at Maggie over the top of her reading glasses. ''The Bar-T?''

Maggie felt a moment's unease. ''Well…yes. The Tanners do have an account here, don't they? Ace said I was to charge whatever I needed.''

Myrna's brows shot high. ''That sweet child is Ace Tanner's?''

Heat flooded Maggie's cheeks. ''Well, no,'' she said hesitantly, unsure if Ace would want the whole town to know about Laura's existence. ''Not exactly. Ace is Laura's…guardian.''

Myrna stared at Maggie a moment, then sputtered a laugh. ''Well, I suppose that's one way of explaining their relationship.'' She hit a register key and a receipt churned out. Tearing it off, she laid it on the counter. ''Sign right here,'' she said, then leaned a hip against the counter and folded her arms over her ample breasts. ''And here I was thinking that Ace had quit cleaning up after his daddy years ago,'' she said, with a regretful shake of her head.

Maggie passed her the receipt. ''Excuse me?''

Myrna flapped a hand, as she tucked the slip of paper into a slot on the register drawer. "Not that I blame Ace, you understand. Buck was nothing but a rounder, and a selfish one at that. Left the raising of his sons up to that poor wife of his. After the cancer got Emma, the old coot didn't show a sign of changing his ways, so Ace stepped in and took over the job." She shook her head sadly. "Poor thing. Wasn't much more than a boy himself, at the time."

While Maggie stared, trying her best to hide her shock, Myrna began to chuckle.

"You should have seen those boys when Ace brought them to town. They'd trail along behind him like a gaggle of baby geese after a mother goose. As they got older, I think they began to resent him bossin' them around. Especially Ry," she added with a frown, then sighed. "But I guess that was to be expected, as he was the closest to Ace in age. But Ace never once backed off from the responsibility he'd taken on, no matter how big a fuss those boys kicked up." She shook her head. "No, siree, he stuck by those brothers of his through thick and thin."

Rearing back, she flapped a hand. "Would you listen to me? Here I am talking your ear off, when I'm sure you've got other errands to run."

Caught up in the glimpse of Ace's past Myrna had woven for her, Maggie had forgotten all about the time. She glanced at her wrist watch and was surprised to see that her hour was almost up. "I really do need to go," she said, panicking. "I'm supposed to meet Ace back at the truck soon. Thanks again for your help, Myrna."

"Anytime, honey," Myrna called after her. "And you be sure and bring that sweet baby back by to see me the next time you're in town, you hear?"

"I will," Maggie promised.

Praying Ace hadn't arrived yet, Maggie all but flew across the street to the spot where she was to meet him.

Not seeing a sign of him anywhere, she heaved a sigh of relief and slowed, pushing the stroller to a park bench beneath the shade of a centuries-old oak tree. Sitting down to wait, she rolled the stroller slowly back and forth, gently rocking the baby, and thought back over her conversation with Myrna.

She tried to picture Ace as a young boy, as Myrna had described him, traipsing through town, with his three brothers in tow. Though the image came easily enough to mind, she couldn't begin to imagine what it must have been like for a boy his age to take on the responsibilities of caring for his three younger brothers—especially after they reached an age where they resented his supervision.

She might have been able to dismiss Myrna's comments as an old woman's rambling, if she hadn't remembered Rory telling her the night before about Ace taking him to the doctor to get a tetanus shot. At the time, Maggie hadn't thought much about the story, other than thinking it was funny that a man as tough as Ace was terrified of needles. But now she realized what a courageous and selfless act that had been for Ace. With no parent around to handle the emergency, he'd set aside his own fears and taken Rory to the doctor, even insisting upon holding his brother's hand while Rory was given the dreaded shot.

Kind. Giving. Compassionate. They were all adjectives that fit the picture of the young Ace Myrna and Rory had drawn for her. But Maggie had a hard time associating those traits with the adult version of that boy.

But maybe that was partly her fault, she thought, trying to be fair. She'd been so blinded by her own grief and so determined that the Tanners should raise Laura, that she'd never once considered Ace's feelings before she'd thrust the baby on him.

In retrospect, she could see why he hadn't exactly welcomed Laura with open arms. In a matter of only a few days, he'd lost his father, assumed the duties of executor of what must be a sizeable and complicated estate and had the guardianship of a half sister, whom he hadn't even known existed, all but dumped on his lap. A lot for any man to deal with, she thought, feeling a stab of remorse for the lack of understanding and compassion she'd offered him.

The sound of approaching footsteps jarred her from her thoughts, and she glanced up to find Ace coming down the sidewalk toward her. He walked with his head down, his hands shoved deeply into his pockets and his shoulders stooped, as if he carried the weight of the world on them.

Emotion tightened her throat. She wanted to believe that it was his slight limp and battered appearance that caused the unexpected swell of emotion. But it was something more than his injuries that had her curling her hands around the edge of the bench to keep herself from jumping up and running to meet him. Something stronger and decidedly scarier that had her wanting to throw herself into his arms.

And that something felt a whole lot like desire.

It was because he'd kissed her, she told herself, even now able to feel the warmth of his hands on her flesh, the smothering, yet captivating heat of his mouth covering hers. He'd made her feel things she'd never felt with a man before. Want things that she hadn't allowed herself to want in years. The memory of that kiss alone was enough to send her heart racing, but seeing him in the flesh made her yearn to experience the thrill of it all again.

Fearing she would give in to the temptation, she gripped her hands tighter on the edge of the bench's seat. *Laura,* she reminded herself sternly. She had to keep her mind focused on Laura and her purpose for being in Ace's home. She couldn't afford to let anything or anyone—especially Ace Tanner—distract her from her goal. Not when she wanted so desperately to convince the Tanners to keep the baby and raise her as their own.

She drew in a deep, steadying breath, then slowly exhaled. But it wouldn't hurt her to be kinder to him, she told herself. More understanding.

Promising herself that she could offer him both, without jeopardizing Laura's future, she forced a smile and rose to greet him. "Did you get all of your errands run?"

He strode right past her, without so much as a glance her way.

She stared after him, her eyes rounded in astonishment. How rude! she thought, her temper flaring at the obvious snub. She knew he'd heard her. How could he *not,* when he'd passed within feet of where she stood?

Setting her jaw, she pushed the stroller to the truck, where he already sat behind the wheel. When she reached for the door, he leaned across the seat and shoved it open, bumping it against her knee.

"Get in," he snapped.

A scathing retort leaped to Maggie's tongue, but she quickly swallowed it, remembering her vow to be more understanding.

Stooping to transfer the baby from the stroller to the car seat, she muttered under her breath, "If I don't kill him first."

Maggie rode in tight-lipped silence for about five miles before she dared open her mouth, without fear of biting Ace's head off. She probably wouldn't have spoken to him then, if she hadn't noticed that he had the truck headed in the opposite direction of the ranch.

"Where are we going?" she asked, trying to keep the resentment from her voice.

"Your house."

She whipped her head around to look at him. "My house? Why?"

"I need to look through Star's personal belongings." He glanced her way. "You do have her stuff, right?"

Squeezing her hands between her thighs, Maggie turned to face the windshield again, the thought of opening up those boxes making her sick to her stomach. "What little she had," she said uneasily, then stole a glance his way. "Why do you need her things?"

"I hired a private detective and he says things'll go quicker, if has something more than a name to go on. I'm hoping to find that something in her stuff."

Maggie tried to remember what she and Dixie had packed into the boxes, when they'd cleaned out Star's apartment. But she'd been so upset by Star's death, she really hadn't paid that much attention.

"There's not much," she said hesitantly. "Clothes. Shoes. A few personal items."

"What about a checkbook or canceled checks?"

She shook her head. "Star didn't have a bank account. She lived on a cash basis and pretty much from paycheck to paycheck."

"There has to be something," he said in frustration.

Though Maggie doubted he would find anything that would offer him a clue to Star's past, she kept her suspicions to herself and rode in silence, that knot of dread in her stomach winding tighter and tighter with each passing mile.

When he pulled to a stop in front of her house, she had to force herself to open the door and climb out. Reaching into the back seat to unfasten the car seat, she hitched it on her hip and led the way to the front door. She passed her house key to Ace, waited while he unlocked the door, then followed him inside. She'd barely made it across the threshold, when he skidded to a stop and she bumped into his back.

"Damn!" he swore, fanning the air in front of his face. "It's like an oven in here."

She quickly set the car seat on the sofa. "Sorry," she murmured and began opening windows. "I don't have air conditioning."

He dragged a sleeve across the perspiration already beading on his forehead. "Are you *that* hard up for money?"

Maggie had to bite her tongue to keep from telling him he ought to try poverty for awhile. Instead, she forced a smile and said, "A penny saved is a penny earned."

He shot her a dark look. "Let's get this over with and get out of here, before we both melt."

As anxious as he to leave, Maggie retrieved a box from her room, set it on the floor in front of him, then left to fetch another.

By the time she returned with the second box, Ace had ripped the tape off the first and was dumping its contents onto the floor. Sinking to her knees opposite him, Maggie sniffed back tears as she watched him sort through the meager pile of Star's possessions.

At the sound, Ace looked up at her. His hand stilled. "What's wrong with you?" he asked impatiently.

She shook her head, her eyes filling. "It's just so sad."

"What is?"

"This," she said, gesturing to the articles of clothing he'd dumped onto the floor. "Twenty-two years, and this is all Star had to show for her life."

Frowning, Ace drew his hands back and rubbed them up and down his thighs, suddenly feeling like a grave-robber. He didn't want to think about the woman who'd owned these things or what her life had been like. And he sure as hell didn't want to think about the part his father had played in that life or what difference he might have made if he'd assumed a more active role.

Setting his jaw, he started stuffing the clothes back into the box. "Possessions don't mean anything. Not in the final count. It's what a person does with his or her life that matters."

"I don't know that Star did anything with her life," Maggie said sadly, "other than give birth to Laura." She glanced toward the sofa, where the baby slept peacefully in the car seat. "But surely that must count for something."

Ace looked over at the baby, then away just as quickly, his frown deepening. "Last I heard, they weren't handing out awards to single women for getting themselves knocked up."

Maggie sank back on her heels to stare at him in horror. "I can't believe you said that!"

He lifted a shoulder. "It's the truth."

"Whether it is or not," she said furiously, "isn't the point. It was cruel and totally uncalled for. When your father refused to marry her, Star could have taken the easy way out and had an abortion. But she chose to keep her baby. I'd think that says a lot for her moral character."

"If she had any morals, she wouldn't have gotten pregnant in the first place."

Incensed, Maggie balled her hands into fists on her knees. "Oh, that is so like a man! Your entire gender is nothing but a bunch of lying cowards. You all go around telling women you love them and promising them the moon and the stars just to get them into bed with you. Then, when the woman winds up pregnant, you turn tail and run, leaving her to deal with the problem alone."

Ace slammed the lid down on the box and faced her. "Not *all* men. I, for one, have never lied to a woman to get her to go to bed with me, and I've never gotten one pregnant, either."

"Yet," she said, pointedly. "And if you ever did get a woman pregnant, I'd hope, for the child's sake, that you *would* turn tail and run."

"And why would you want me to do that?"

"No child deserves a father who's incapable of loving or caring for them."

"Who says I'm incapable of caring for a kid?"

Lifting a brow, Maggie tipped her head toward the sofa and the baby sleeping in the car seat.

Ace scowled. "She's not my kid."

"No. She's your sister."

"Half sister," he corrected.

"And being only 'half' prevents you from loving her or caring what happens to her?"

"Aren't I trying my damnedest to find Star's relatives so that the kid will have a home?"

"You're trying to get rid of her," Maggie told him. "And what happens to Laura if you don't find a relative?"

He opened his mouth, then clamped it shut again. Grabbing the second box, he ripped the top open and dumped its contents on the floor. Confronted with nothing but more clothes and a tangle of shoes, he lurched to his feet. "This is nothing but a waste of time."

As he strode for the door, Maggie stared after him, wincing when he slammed it behind him. Slowly she began to gather the scattered clothes and shoes.

Well, so much for kindness and understanding, she thought glumly.

Maggie stepped back to admire her work, pleased with the way the nursery had turned out. Though she'd deliberated long and hard over how far to go with the room's transformation, she'd finally decided it best to keep Laura's integration into the Tanner household as unobtrusive and subtle as possible. As a result, she'd rearranged the furniture only a bit, creating the space needed for the new crib and changing table that had been delivered that day. She'd taken down the heavy drapes that hung at the windows, but had left the sheers in place. The drapes could easily be rehung, if Ace demanded it—although she sincerely hoped he wouldn't. Without the heavy fabric to block the light, the once dreary bedroom across the hall from Maggie's was now a cheerful, sun-filled space, perfect for a nursery.

Tired, but satisfied with the results of her afternoon's work, she crossed to the crib and reached down to pick up the baby. "And what do you think of your new room, precious?" she asked, turning and holding the infant against her chest so that the baby could see her new room. "Isn't it beautiful?"

Laura opened her mouth in a big, sleepy yawn.

Maggie laughed. "Well, it's a good thing I've got thick skin," she said, as she moved to sit down on the rocker. "Otherwise, your lack of enthusiasm would've hurt my feelings."

Shifting the infant to the crook of her arm, she pushed her toe against the floor and set the rocker into motion. Within seconds, Laura's eyelids, already heavy with sleep, fluttered down, her eyelashes curling tightly against her cheeks. Smiling softly, Maggie traced a finger beneath the furl of lashes, marveling at how much the baby had grown and changed in the few short weeks since her birth. She tried to imagine what Laura would look like as a young woman. Would she have her mother's fragile, waif-like beauty? Or had she inherited her bone structure from the Tanner side and would have high, sculpted cheekbones like Ace?

Ace.

At the thought of him, she dropped her head back with a groan. What was she going to do about him? He hadn't said more than a dozen words to her over the past week.

And when he did bother to speak to her, it was as he was going out the door, telling her not to wait dinner for him. His silence frustrated her almost as much as did his absences. How could she hope to foster a relationship between him and the baby, if he was never around?

Earlier in the week, she'd given serious thought to leaving, thinking that without her there to care for the baby, he would be forced to interact with Laura. But she'd discarded the idea, fearing that, if she did leave, Ace would do something desperate, like turn Laura over to the state's Child Welfare Department, rather than take care of her himself. Maggie shuddered at the thought of Laura being subjected to one of the nightmarish foster homes she'd lived in as a child.

You see yourself in this kid, don't you? Dixie had said. *You think by sticking with her, you can prevent happening to her what happened to you.*

Maggie felt a prickle of guilt, remembering her response. She hadn't denied Dixie's suspicions, thus avoiding a lie, but she hadn't confirmed them, either.

But the similarities were there for any fool to see.

Trisha Dean, Maggie's mother, may not have died after giving birth to Maggie, as Laura's mother had, but for all practical purposes she might as well have. Unfortunately, the parallels didn't stop there. Maggie's mother had led as loose and irresponsible a life as Laura's mother had; maybe even more so.

At fifteen, Tricia Dean was living on the streets, pregnant with Maggie and well on her way to becoming a drug addict. Within six months of Maggie's birth, she'd hooked up with a pimp, who kept her supplied with drugs in exchange for turning tricks for him. Within nine, her baby had been taken away from her and placed in a foster home.

But Tricia had never lost contact with her daughter, in spite of the number of times the social workers had moved

Maggie from one foster home to another. On a few occasions, she'd even convinced the social workers that she was clean and had persuaded them to return Maggie to her care.

But those occasions were rare and never lasted long.

Raised by an ever-changing set of foster parents, by the age of twelve, Maggie was street-wise enough to recognize her mother's drug habit. The runny nose. The shaking hands. The unnatural thinness. What started out as resentment toward her mother, built over the years and slowly festered into hate. Maggie despised the dumps her mother lived in and the men who came and went at all hours of the night. But most of all, she despised her mother's weakness that made her choose a life of drugs and prostitution over one with her own daughter.

In the end, when Tricia was dying, her organs destroyed by the drugs she'd pumped into her system, she'd asked for Maggie. At first, Maggie had refused to see her mother. But she'd finally agreed to visit her, planning to say a quick ''thanks for nothing,'' then split, severing a tie that had never existed in the first place.

But when Maggie had stepped inside the crowded hospital ward and seen her mother lying in the bed, the bitter words had dried up in her throat. There was nothing left of her mother but paper-thin skin stretched over protruding bones and hollowed-out eyes that stared at nothing. Her hair, what was left of it, stuck out in wild tufts that looked fried, as if she'd given herself a home perm and left the solution on too long. Wide, white restraining straps had bound her chest, hips and legs, leashing her to the bed.

Stunned by her mother's emaciated appearance and appalled by the bonds that held her prisoner, Maggie had sunk weakly down on the chair beside the bed. She had no idea how long she'd sat there, before her mother had turned her head on the pillow, and Maggie had looked into eyes the same tobacco-brown as her own. Recognition had flared for a moment in Tricia's eyes, followed by tears that dripped onto the pillow, chased there by a lifetime of wrong turns and regrets.

The sight of her mother's tears shouldn't have gotten to Maggie. Not after all the years of abuse and neglect. But for some stupid reason they had, and Maggie had ended up staying. She'd clung to her mother's hand while Tricia had screamed and fought the restraints, begging for the very drugs that were killing her. She'd wiped her mother's brow and wet her parched lips when Tricia's ranting would cease and she would slip back into a comatose state.

Hours had turned into days and days into weeks, with Maggie remaining by her mother's bedside, nursing her, while watching and praying for her death. As the chilling rattle of her mother's last breaths had echoed around her, Maggie had vowed then and there that she'd never make the mistakes her mother had made, that she'd never allow herself to become so dependent on anything or anyone that she'd sacrifice her life for them.

She'd slipped up once. A small slip that had almost cost her her self-confidence, her pride. Her sanity. But, thanks to Dixie, she'd managed to pull herself out of that dark hole and she'd started her life anew.

Blinking back tears as the memory faded, Maggie looked down at Laura. "But you'll never know that kind of pain," she whispered. "You're a Tanner."

Six

Avoiding someone who lived in the same house wasn't all that easy. Ace managed to pull it off by staying up nights sorting through the files in his father's office, then stumbling to bed in the wee hours of the morning and sleeping until noon each day. When he'd awaken, he'd head straight for town and spend his afternoons locked away in the offices of the family's lawyers and accountants, trying to get a handle on the Tanner assets and holdings. He'd already decided he was getting out of Tanner's Crossing and off the Bar-T as quickly as possible. But before he could, he had to make certain he could fulfill his duties as executor of his father's estate from his home in Kerrville.

From the hours he'd spent with the lawyers and accountants and those alone digging through his father's files, he'd determined that the bulk of the family's assets was comprised of real estate, most of which was raw land. Their holdings also included a number of office buildings, warehouses and a half-dozen or so apartment complexes in town, but those properties were all handled by a management company, so weren't a problem. The balance of the estate consisted of stocks, bonds and other "paper" investments that would require only occasional monitoring, which Ace knew from experience he could handle by phone or fax from anywhere in the world.

That left him with only the ranch to deal with. And until Ace hired a manager, one he could trust, it looked as if he was going to be stuck there awhile longer.

With Maggie.

Sighing, he pulled his truck to a stop in front of the ranch house and killed the engine. Leaning back against the seat, he rubbed a hand absently over his bandaged ribs as he looked over at the house. He knew she was inside, and knew, too, that he couldn't avoid her forever.

He owed her an apology. A big one. The things he'd said about Star…. He shook his head, a week later still shamed by the memory. All that talk about moral character. He hadn't meant a word of it. That had been his anger talking. His resentment. Most of which would've been better directed at his old man.

But without the old man there to take his frustrations out on, Ace had unloaded them on Maggie. He'd hurt her with the things he'd said. He'd known it immediately by the stricken look on her face, the angry way in which she'd lashed back. But he hadn't been able to stop himself.

To her credit, she'd fought back, and valiantly, striking him with blows where, he was sure, she thought she could hurt him the worst. He could still hear the accusation in her voice, the venom, when she'd told him that she hoped, if he ever got a woman pregnant, he'd turn tail and run. Little did she know that he never intended to get a woman pregnant, whether he was married to the woman or not. But she had managed to get in a hit when she'd accused him of not loving or caring for the baby just because the kid was a half sister and not a full sibling.

Half. Full. The degree of blood Ace shared with the kid wasn't what kept him from caring. He didn't *want* to care, didn't want the responsibility or heartbreak of taking on any more of his old man's screw-ups. He'd spent years running riot control over his old man's mistakes, smoothing out the upheaval caused by his father's selfish and careless acts, and he didn't intend to take on that role again. Ever.

But all that didn't matter, he told himself, and pushed open the truck door. Not now, at any rate. He had some crow to eat and putting it off wasn't going to make it any easier to swallow.

He'd expected to find Maggie in the kitchen, preparing the baby's bottles for the next day, as she did about this time every evening. When he didn't find her there, he headed straight for her room, hell-bent on getting his apology said and his conscience cleared before the sun set on another day. But he didn't find her in her room, either. Wondering where she'd gotten off to, he started to leave, but jerked to a stop, when he noticed that the playpen was missing from the foot of her bed.

Puzzled by its absence, he turned back to the hall. As he did, he saw that the door to the bedroom across the hall stood open. Usually closed, the open door was enough of an oddity to have him crossing to peer inside.

The room looked different, he thought, frowning. Lighter. Brighter. And the furniture wasn't where it was supposed to be. The bed, normally standing between the two windows, was shoved up against the far wall, and a crib now stood in its place. A table of sorts was bumped up against one end of the crib, a pile of diapers stacked high on its padded top. Wondering when Maggie had made the changes, he stepped inside.

And that's when he saw her. Sitting in the rocking chair,

her head resting against the chair's pressed back, her eyes closed, the baby asleep in her arms. With the chair angled in front of the window, the fading sunlight streamed across it, bathing both her and the baby in a hazy pool of golden light.

As he stared, a memory seeped slowly into his mind. One of his mother sitting in that same chair, rocking one or another of his brothers to sleep. Usually Rory, as he had always been difficult to settle down for the night. As she'd rock, she'd always sung a lullaby. Ace couldn't remember the words, but the tune played through his mind, as did the sound of her voice. Soft…melodious…soothing. As a youngster, he'd often sat out in the hall, his back to the wall, listening to the rhythmic creak of the rocker and the comforting sound of her voice, wishing like hell he was still small enough to crawl up in her lap to be rocked.

Even now, he could recall the contentment that would steal over him when she'd rocked him, feel the butterfly-soft comb of her fingers through his hair, the whisper of her breath against his cheek. She'd always smelled of roses, her breath of mint. Pleasant scents that, to this day, never failed to bring his mother to mind.

Slowly the memory receded and it was Maggie he stared at in the rocker. He wanted to be there, he realized, his throat closing around the urgency in that want. He wanted to sit in that old, oak rocker, with his hands gripped over the wooden armrests. He wanted to feel the wood's grain beneath his palms, a grain worn smooth by four generations of Tanner hands. He wanted to press his back against the narrow, oak slats carved by his great-great-grandfather and feel the sturdiness of the bowed wood giving beneath the pressure of his spine. He wanted to close his eyes and set the rocker into motion, letting its rhythmic movement lull his mind.

But he didn't want to be alone in the rocker, he realized

slowly. He wanted Maggie there, too. On his lap. He wanted the comforting weight of her head nestled in the curve of his shoulder, the warmth of her body curled against his. He wanted her fingers stroking over his face, her touch feather-light, slowly unraveling the tension from his mind and body. He wanted to feel the moist warmth of her breath on his face, the pillowed softness of her lips beneath his. He wanted to taste her seductive flavor, savor it...

Oh, God, he thought, balling his hands into fists against the need that twisted painfully inside him. He wanted *her*. Needed her more than he needed his next breath.

But Ace hadn't allowed himself to need anything or anyone in years. Wasn't even sure he could handle the level of emotion that kind of need generated, if he dared open himself up to it again. Knowing that, he remained just inside the door, scared spitless to take that first step toward her, yet wanting to so badly, it was a burning knot of pain in his chest.

As he stood, paralyzed by his fears, Maggie stirred and blinked open her eyes. A furrow creased her brow, as she slowly brought him into focus.

"Ace? Is something wrong?"

Her voice, husky with sleep and suffused with concern, seemed to wrap itself around his chest and squeeze. He shook his head, for a moment, unable to speak. "We need to talk."

Her frown deepened. "Now?"

"Yeah," he said, then added, "Outside," thinking, if he could just get out of this room and away from the memories it evoked, he could get a handle on his emotions.

Though she gave him a curious look, she didn't question his request. She simply rose and crossed to put the baby in the crib. After switching on the portable intercom hanging from the crib's top rail, she slipped a small monitor into her pocket and followed him out into the hall.

Ace led the way, acutely aware of the sound of her footsteps a few short steps behind. Once outdoors, he stopped to fill his lungs with the clean, fragrant air, praying it would release some of the tension that knotted his body, chase away the memories that still tangled in his mind.

When it did neither, he released the breath on a weary sigh. Giving his chin a jerk, indicating a field on his left, he said, "Let's walk."

Stuffing his hands in his pockets, he stepped off the porch and started off, leaving Maggie to follow.

By the time he had crossed the field and started up the low rise beyond it, the sun had sunk to a crescent of fire on the horizon that washed the landscape with the muted tones of twilight. At the top of the rise, he drew to a stop before a low iron fence, until that moment unaware that all along his destination had been his family's cemetery.

He heard the gentle fall of Maggie's footsteps behind him, the labored sound of her breathing as she struggled to catch up. When she stopped beside him, her arm brushed his sleeve and sent fractured shocks of awareness skittering beneath his skin. Gulping, he watched as she closed her hands over the finials that topped the iron posts and leaned to peer inside, the curl of her fingers around the delicately carved tops graceful. But he saw the red, work-roughened knuckles, remembered the hard life she'd led.

"Your family?" she asked.

Her voice, pitched low in reverence to the hallowed ground where they stood, whispered over him as gently as the evening breeze that stirred the leaves in the branches overhead.

"Yes." Fearing she would ask him why he'd brought her there and knowing that, if she did, he couldn't explain, he opened the gate and stepped inside.

Tombstones jutted from the ground at odd heights and uneven distances, their haphazard placement and mismatched appearance making them look like a hastily formed troop of untrained soldiers. Some stood straight and tall, while others tilted drunkenly, time and weather having taken their toll. A gray-green moss grew on the faces of the older stones, making the names and dates etched beneath indecipherable.

But Ace knew every name, date and epitaph by heart, having heard the family's history repeated to him over and over again through the years.

"General Nathaniel Johnson Tanner," he said, pointing, as Maggie moved to stand behind him. "'A brave and loyal soldier, mortally wounded leading his Confederate troop into battle.' He wove his way past several tombstones, careful not to step on any of the all but indiscernible graves, then pointed again. "Elizabeth Eddison Tanner and Infant Son Tanner. Left this earth July 20, 1872 and passed into heaven together, with my dearly beloved Lizzy carrying our babe to lay at the feet of our precious Lord and Master."

He walked on, pointing out the final resting places of his Tanner ancestors, his dispassionate tone that of a tour guide who had given this same spiel a thousand times or more.

Puzzled by his odd behavior, Maggie followed, wondering what he wanted to talk to her about and why he'd chosen a cemetery of all places to hold the conversation.

As they reached the newer section, he slowed, then stopped altogether before a mound of freshly turned earth. Assuming it was his father's grave that held his attention, Maggie maintained a respectful distance to give him whatever privacy he needed. But when he turned away to drop down on a stone bench positioned opposite the grave, she realized it was a stone to the right of the mound that had

held his attention. Curiosity drew her close enough to read
the words etched on the pink granite.

Emma Louise Tanner
Wife of "Buck" Tanner

She glanced over her shoulder at Ace. "Your mother?"

His gaze fixed on the tombstone, he slowly nodded.

When he offered nothing more, with a shrug, she joined
him on the bench, assuming that sooner or later he'd get
around to telling her what he wanted to talk to her about.

While she waited, sitting quietly at his side, dusk descended around them, lengthening the shadows of the trees
that bordered the fenced area. In the distance, a coyote
howled, and the eerie sound sent a chill down Maggie's
spine.

Anxious to return to the safety of the house, she thought
a gentle reminder might speed things up a bit. "You said
we needed to talk."

He roused, as if coming from a trance, to look at her.
Frowning, he leaned over to pluck a wildflower from the
ground at his feet. With his forearms braced on his thighs,
he slowly rolled the stem between his fingers.

"About the other day," he began hesitantly.

Maggie knew, without asking, which day he meant. The
afternoon at Star's and the beginning of what she'd come to
think of as "the silent war." "Yes?" she prodded helpfully.

"I—" He stopped, frowned, then tried again. "I'm sorry
for the things I said about Star. I shouldn't have said what
I did."

"No," she agreed. "You shouldn't have. You didn't
know Star."

"Whether I knew her or not, is irrelevant. I was mad
and took it out on you. I'm sorry for that."

Surprised by his apology, for a moment, Maggie couldn't
think of a thing to say. "Who were you mad at? Me?"

Scowling, Ace tossed the flower away. "No. My father."

He jerked his chin toward his mother's tombstone. "You'll notice there aren't any pretty words or touching epitaphs carved on my mother's stone. 'Wife of Buck Tanner,' he quoted, with a sneer. "As far as the old man was concerned, that was her one crowning achievement."

"But she was more than that to you. To your brothers."

Puffing his cheeks, he slumped back against the trunk of the tree. "Yeah," he said, releasing the breath on a shuddery sigh. "A helluva lot more."

In the field below them, a quail sang out its familiar call of, "bob-white, bob-white." For Ace, the sound brought back a wealth of memories that he suddenly found he wanted to share with Maggie.

"When we were kids," he said thoughtfully, "after dinner, Mother would let us play outside for awhile before shooing us all off to bed. She'd usually watch us from the front porch swing, while she rocked Rory to sleep. Sometimes, if she was lucky enough to get him down at a decent hour, she'd come out and play with us. Ring-around-the-rosy. Drop-the-handkerchief. Sissy, childhood games that my brothers and I wouldn't have been caught dead playing any other time. But we'd have played dolls with her, if she'd suggested it, just for the chance to be with her.

"She had a way about her that made even the simplest things fun. In the summer, when the garden was producing, she would ice down a watermelon. That evening we'd sit out on the porch steps and eat it, the meat of that melon so cold, it made our teeth ache. When we were done, she'd challenge us to a contest to see who could spit their seeds the farthest." He shook his head, chuckling, remembering. "Woodrow, Ry and I would just about kill ourselves, trying to outspit each other."

Maggie stared at Ace's profile, astounded by the wistful smile that curved his lips...and envious of his memories. "You must have loved your mother a great deal."

His smile slowly faded. "Yeah. I did."

"How old were you when she died?"

"Twelve. Cancer was what killed her. By the time the doctors found it, there was nothing they could do." He angled his head to look over at her. "Remember when you told me you thought the hospital staff treated your mother differently because she couldn't pay for her care?"

Maggie tensed, unsure why he was bringing the subject up again. "Yes. Why?"

"My mother got five-star treatment. A private room, her own nurse, gourmet meals cooked especially for her. The way I figure it, the wing the Tanners funded for the hospital earned her that kind of care." He looked away, turning his gaze to a darkening sky the setting sun had stained a red, burnished gold. "But there was one thing money couldn't buy her."

"What was that?"

"Time."

Maggie heard the regret in his voice, saw the longing in the face he tipped heavenward, and understood because she'd felt the same emotions when she allowed herself to think of her mother. "Was she in the hospital long?"

"A couple of weeks. Maybe three, if you stacked all the different stays into one. But she didn't die there," he added, glancing her way. "She wanted to die at home and in her own bed."

"That must have been difficult for your father."

"Buck?" Ace snorted. "It might've if he'd been around."

Maggie looked at him in puzzlement. "Your father's business required him to travel?"

"Rarely. He was usually shacked up with his current flavor of the month in an apartment he kept in Tanner's Crossing."

Maggie had heard Star mention the apartment, but she

was surprised that Ace knew about it, as well. That he did perhaps explained some of the bitterness he felt toward his father.

It also raised another question in her mind. "If your father wasn't home to take care of your mother, who did?"

"From six in the morning to ten at night, a private nurse the old man hired. The graveyard shift was mine."

"Yours?" she repeated in surprise. "But you were so young."

He lifted his shoulder in a shrug. "Age wasn't a requirement. In the beginning, I thought the chemo was the worst. After she'd have a treatment, she'd be so sick she could barely lift her head." He shook his head, as if at his own foolishness. "But I soon learned that the worst was the waiting."

"Waiting? For what?"

"Death."

A shiver shook Maggie, as she remembered waiting for her own mother's death, praying for it even, and how endless the nights had seemed, how lonely. When she looked at Ace again, he was staring off into space, as if at a distant memory.

When he spoke, his voice was so low she had to strain to hear his words.

"She was so scared. Sometimes I would hear her crying at night, and I would go to her room to check on her." He huffed out a derisive breath. "As if *I* could do anything. Hell, I was so wet-behind-the-ears, so useless, I didn't know what the hell to do or say. The only thing I could think of was to climb up into bed with her and snuggle close."

Emotion crowded Maggie's throat at the image of Ace comforting his mother. "It was what she needed," she told him. "Knowing someone cared. Having someone with her."

"Whether it was or not, it was all I knew to do."

Maggie's heart broke a little at the regret in his voice. "You miss her, don't you?"

His Adam's apple bobbing convulsively, he slowly nodded his head.

Tears filled her eyes. "Oh, Ace. I'm so sorry."

Ace tensed at the offer of sympathy. *I'm so sorry.* They were only words. Strung together, they were a common sentiment offered to someone who'd suffered the loss of a loved one. He figured he'd heard them voiced a hundred or more times over the last few days alone. But no one had offered them with the wealth of empathy and sincerity that Maggie had…and never with the same results. With those three simple words, she'd managed to reach deep down inside him and dredge up emotion from the vault he'd locked it away in years ago. It filled his throat, a knot of choking pain he couldn't seem to push a word past.

Ducking his head, he swallowed hard, trying to force the emotion back. As he did, he caught a glimpse of Maggie's hands fisted against her thighs, her knuckles now gleaming as white as pearls. In her tightly curled fingers, he recognized the same level of restraint he'd used to govern his emotions for years, the same heart-wrenching pain that had forced him to bury his emotions. Knowing that she'd suffered similarly, perhaps still did, touched him at a depth that nothing had tapped in years.

Reaching out, he covered her hand with his, laced his fingers through hers. Squeezed.

He heard the choking sound she made, felt the desperate clamp of her fingers around his. Angling his head, he saw the tears that flooded her eyes, the quiver of her lips. Helpless to do anything less, he hauled her to him and wrapped his arms around her.

With his hand cupped at the back of her neck, holding

her cheek to his, he felt each scalding tear that streaked down her face, absorbed each sob that racked her body.

But he didn't let her go. Couldn't. And when her tears stopped, he continued to hold her.

From the moment he'd dragged her into his arms, his only thought had been to give her what little comfort a jaded man like himself had to offer. But when her tears stopped, he found himself fisting his fingers in her long hair, drawing her head back, and sliding his mouth to cover hers. On her lips, he tasted the salt of her tears. Saddened by it, he swept his tongue over them to wipe them away. As he did, he felt the tremble that shook her, the unexpected surge of her breasts against his chest and, with a groan, he crushed his mouth over hers.

He kissed her deeply, greedily, taking each pleasure she offered up to him and claiming it for his own. He filled his hands with her hair, knotted his fingers in the dark, silky tresses, then let it slide through his fingers to skim his palms down her back.

With his hands gripped at her hips, he drew her hard up against him and slipped his tongue between her parted lips. He heard her whimper, felt the desperate dig of her fingers around his neck, and gave her more, took more of what she gave up to him.

Time became something indeterminable, the memories that had haunted him moments before nothing but hazy mists that slunk back into the dark recesses of his mind. His world shrank to the bench he sat on, inhabited only by the woman he held in his arms.

When he'd first reached for her, he'd sought only to ease her heart, absorb what he could of her pain. But he found that, somewhere along the way, she'd eased his and left him with a need so strong it thundered through his blood like a herd of wild buffalo, deafening him to all other sound and blinding him to all but her. Maggie.

His response to her stunned him. More, it scared the hell out of him. Holding her face between his hands, he forced their lips apart, until he met her gaze. Passion glazed her tobacco-brown eyes, stained her cheeks. He dropped his gaze to her mouth and to lips bruised from the pressure of his. Shamed by his rough treatment of her, he smoothed a thumb across them to soothe the swollen flesh…and had to wrestle with the temptation to kiss her again.

But Ace wasn't sure, if he did kiss her, he could leave it at that. Not when his body cried out for a much stronger release.

Drawing in a ragged breath, he lifted his gaze to hers. "We'd better head back. Morning's going to come early, and my brothers are due at daybreak to help me round up the cattle."

She gulped, nodded, slowly inching away from him.

As she stood, Ace stood, too, but reached out and caught her hand before she could move away.

"Maggie?"

She glanced back over her shoulder. "Yes?"

"I—" He stopped, searching for just the right words to convey how special he thought she was, how grateful he was to her for listening to him ramble on about a past he seldom allowed himself to even think about, much less share.

Unable to come up with anything that came even close to what he was feeling, he gave her hand a squeeze. "Thanks."

Eyes wide, Maggie lay in her bed, staring up at the ceiling where moonlight and shadows played a mystical game of hide-and-seek. Sleep was the farthest thing from her mind.

Who *is* this man? she asked herself for probably the zillionth time since crawling into her bed. She wasn't sure she knew any longer—if she ever had, at all. That night Ace had revealed to her a side of himself that she'd never dreamed existed. He'd given her a glimpse of a tenderness that she would never in a thousand years have suspected he kept hidden behind that cold and wary guard he kept in place.

And, God help her, she'd discovered in him a passion she prayed she would have the opportunity to experience again.

Pressing her fingers to her lips, she closed her eyes and tried to remember every detail. His masculine scent. The possessive tug of his hands in her hair. The urgent thud of his heart against hers. The burning rasp of his beard against her skin. The satin-like texture of his lips on hers. The seductive power of his touch, his kiss. The restraint she sensed beneath it all.

She recalled in vivid detail each and every breath they'd shared, every touch, every look, the thrill of his kiss, then played it through her mind over and over again.

And when, at last, she slept, it was Ace she dreamed of.

It was still dark outside, when Maggie started breakfast the next morning. Through the kitchen window she could see a hint of pink on the horizon, signaling dawn was quickly approaching, and along with it, the arrival of Ace's brothers.

Unsure if she was expected to feed them all, Maggie pulled a long tray of biscuits from the oven and set them on the island to cool, then turned back to the stove to shovel sizzling patties of sausage onto a platter. As she worked, she found her mind drifting back to the evening before and wondering how she could possibly face Ace again.

"Maggie?"

Startled, she dropped the spatula and whirled to find Ace

standing on the opposite side of the island. Bare-chested, he held a shirt in one hand and a roll of tape in the other.

She pressed a hand to her heart to still its pounding. "I didn't hear you come in."

"Sorry." He held up the roll of tape. "Since I'm going to be riding today, I thought I should wrap my ribs again. Would you mind doing it for me?"

Gulping, she wiped her hands down the skirt of her apron. "Just give me a minute to finish taking up the sausage."

She quickly turned back to the stove, praying Ace would think the flush on her cheeks was due to the heat from the stove.

Taking her time, she shoveled the remaining patties onto the platter. When she'd finished, she caught up a dish towel and wiped her hands, as she turned to face him again. "Now," she said, forcing a smile. "Let's see about those ribs."

He rounded the island and held out the roll of tape. "Something sure smells good."

To avoid looking directly at his chest, she peeled back a strip of tape from the roll. "I made sausage, biscuits and gravy. I wasn't sure if your brothers would have eaten yet, so I cooked enough for an army. You'll need to move your arms."

He lifted them out, holding them at shoulder level. "Probably wise. All the Tanners were blessed with healthy appetites."

As well as gorgeous bodies, she thought, trying not to stare as she pressed the end of the tape against the center of the most gorgeous chest in the world. Ducking under his arm, she began to wind the tape around his upper body.

When she'd circled him four times, she caught the tape between her teeth, starting a tear, then used her fingers to rip it from the roll. "There," she said, pressing the severed end into place. "All done."

He looked down at her and smiled. "Thanks. I couldn't have managed it alone."

Feeling the heat crawl up her neck, she mumbled a barely audible, "you're welcome," and started to turn away. He caught her arm, stopping her, and pulled her back around to face him.

"Maggie…about last night…"

She held her breath, praying he wasn't about to tell her he was sorry that he had kissed her, that it was a huge mistake he now regretted. "Yes?"

Catching her other arm, he drew her to him. "Last night was…special." He gave her arms a squeeze. "*You're* special."

She stared, not trusting her ears.

Ducking his head, he set his jaw, as if he had more to say, but was having a hard time saying it.

"I never talk about my family," he said hesitantly. "I guess because the memories are just too painful. Especially those of my mother." He looked up at her. "You're the first person I've ever told about her. The first one I felt would understand what it was like. I just want you to know how much that meant to me, how much I appreciated you listening."

At the time, Maggie had thought she'd realized how difficult it was for him. Sharing his emotions, baring his soul…that kind of openness would be foreign to a man like Ace. But she understood now what a monumental step that had been for him. She also knew that in talking about his mother and his past, he'd made a giant step toward healing his heart. A heart she prayed would open wide enough to accept Laura.

Hoping to encourage him to continue that healing process, she took a step closer and opened her hands over his chest. "I'm here, Ace. Any time you need to talk, I'm willing to listen."

He nodded. "I appreciate that." He seemed to hesitate a moment, then arched a brow and looked up at her over it. "I was kind of hoping you'd be interested in doing more than just listening."

She tensed, unsure of his meaning.

His smile tentative, he drew her to his chest. "Last night was special for another reason. We'd be good together. I think we both saw the proof of that."

"Y-yes. I suppose we did."

He frowned, as if only now considering the complications. "This could get dicey."

She wet her lips, her mouth suddenly dry. "If we were to allow it to, yes, I suppose it could."

He backed up a step, holding her far enough away that he could see her face. "I'm not looking to get married again."

She gulped, but nodded. "Me, either."

"And I travel all the time, rarely home for more than a week or so before I take off on another assignment."

"My studies keep me busy."

A smile spread slowly across his face. "Sounds to me like we have us a match made in heaven."

Before she could agree or disagree, he dipped his head over hers. Whatever doubts she may have harbored melted at the touch of his lips. Sliding her arms around his neck, she gave herself up to him.

Not only did their expectations align perfectly, she discovered, their bodies did, as well. Lips, chests, hips, thighs. Her curves molded against his body as naturally as if she'd been designed solely for that purpose.

His kiss, tender at first, as if testing, exploring, became more urgent, demanding. He ran his hands down her sides, then up again, bringing her T-shirt up with them. The pressure of his thumbs against the swell of her breasts was a delicious pleasure that made her nipples knot, aching for his touch.

Without warning, he tore his mouth from hers and looked toward the back door.

"Damn," he swore. "They're here."

Dazed, she blinked up at him. "Who's here?"

He reached for his shirt. "My brothers. Remember? They're coming to round up cattle today."

Before she could fully absorb what he was telling her, he dropped a kiss on her mouth, then grinned and shot her a wink. "We'll finish this later."

The back door opened and Maggie whirled, quickly snatching her shirt into place, sure that the word *guilty* was emblazoned across her forehead.

"'Bout time you boys showed up," Ace said, as he tucked his shirttail into his jeans, seemingly unfazed by the fact that his brothers had nearly caught him necking with the nanny in the kitchen. He lifted a hand to point at the first man through the door.

"The ugly one there," he said to Maggie, "is Dr. Ryland Tanner, better known around here as Ry."

Giving Ace a go-to-hell look, Ry peeled off his stained cowboy boot and tapped it against his thigh, as he nodded a terse greeting to Maggie. "Pleased to meet you."

"And this one," Ace said, catching the second one to enter in a headlock before he had a chance to fully clear the threshold, "is Woodrow." With every muscle in his neck standing out in relief as he strained to maintain the hold on his brother, Ace gasped out, "Remember? I told you about him."

Wide-eyed, Maggie stared. "Y-yes. The one who wrote the book on stubbornness."

With a low growl, Woodrow bent at the waist, dragging

Ace across his back, then came up with a bear-like roar, throwing his muscled arms wide.

"Stubborn, hell," he growled, flicking Ace off his back as if he were nothing more than a pesky fly. He hooked a thumb in Ace's direction. "*He's* the stubborn one. Me? I'm just cantankerous."

Rendered speechless by the display of strength she'd just witnessed, Maggie gulped. "I—it's nice to meet you, Woodrow."

He scooped a handful of biscuits from the tray on the island and popped one into his mouth. "Same here," he said around a mouthful, as he strode past her.

Winded, Ace smoothed his hair back into place, then gestured to the man who stood just inside the door, his back braced against the wall. "The shy, quiet one over there in the corner? That's Whit."

Realizing that the attention was directed his way, Whit whipped off his cowboy hat and snapped to attention, his cheeks reddening. "Pleased to meet you, ma'am."

Maggie smiled—warmly this time—enchanted by Whit's shy manners. "The pleasure's mine," she assured him.

Ace glanced over as Rory closed the back door behind him. "And this one," he said, with a careless wave, "you already know."

Relieved to see a familiar face—and a friendly one, at that—in the roomful of strangers, Maggie extended her hand. "Hey, Rory. It's good to see you again."

Rory let out a whoop and, ignoring the offered hand, scooped her up and off her feet.

"Not nearly as good as it is to see you," he cried, all but squeezing the breath out of her in a rib-cracking hug. Planting her on her feet again, he dropped a kiss full on her mouth, then lifted his head and sniffed the air. "Is that sausage I smell?"

Maggie pressed a hand against her forehead, her head

spinning dizzily. "Yes. And biscuits and gravy, too, if you're hungry."

Rory scrubbed his hands together, then pushed his arms out, as if to hold his brothers back. "Stand aside, boys, or be trampled. I'm fixin' to do me some serious grazin'."

He hadn't taken a full step toward the table, when Ace clamped a hand around his arm.

"Not now you're not," he growled. "We're headin' out."

Maggie looked at Ace, surprised by the anger in his voice.

Rory jerked free. "Who put the burr under your saddle?"

Snatching his cowboy hat from the rack by the door, Ace rammed it over his head. "Nobody. Now get your butt movin'. All of you. We've got work to do."

"But Ace," Maggie cried. "What about breakfast?"

Ace snatched open the door. "They came to work, not to eat," he muttered.

Woodrow, Ry and Whit dutifully followed Ace out the door. Rory headed for the island and the platters of food Maggie had left there.

"Who the hell does he think he is?" he grumbled, as he stuffed sausages into a stack of split biscuits. "Tellin' me what I can and can't do like I was still a snotty-nosed kid." He dumped the biscuits onto a napkin and brought the ends of the cloth up, tied them in a knot. "Well, we'll see whose butt is still movin' at the end of the day," he said smugly. Palming the napkin, he turned for the door, but skidded to a stop when he saw Maggie's stricken face.

"Now don't you go worrying that pretty little head of yours," he told her in that slow drawl of his. "I'm not plannin' on killin' him." He crossed to the door, opened it, then glanced back. "But I can't make any promises as to what that horse he's riding has in mind for him." Grinning, he shot her a wink and stepped outside, then shouted, "Hey, wait up! Y'all aren't leaving without me!" and slammed the door behind him.

With a shake of her head, Maggie crossed to the window, watching as Rory jogged toward the barn, where the others were already mounting their horses. As she did, she wondered if Rory's shout of "Y'all aren't leaving without me!" was one pulled straight from his childhood. She could imagine him, the youngest, always having to run to catch up with his older and bigger brothers.

And she could imagine, too, Ace ordering the others to wait while their little brother ran to catch up.

So what was with Ace's anger? she asked herself, still puzzled by it. Why had he been so rude to Rory, even refusing him the time to grab a bite to eat?

Unable to come up with a reasonable explanation, she focused her gaze on the brothers, as they prepared to ride out. Though they all shared a few physical traits in common, each was unique unto himself. Woodrow was definitely the largest, both in breadth and height. Remembering his claim of being cantankerous, she shuddered, doubting anyone would argue the point with him. He *was* cantankerous and scary to boot.

But Ry wasn't exactly Captain Sunshine, she thought, shifting her gaze to study him, though she suspected his surliness was due to impatience. She'd clued into his level of impatience immediately, noticing the tense way he held his mouth and the nervous way he tapped his hat against his thigh. And he was unhappy—or, at the very least, dissatisfied. How she knew that, she wasn't sure. Maybe it was the constant frown he wore. But what she didn't know was what made him unhappy.

A movement had her shifting her gaze away from Ry. Her heart softened a bit, as she saw Whit leading his horse off to the side, still a part of the group, yet slightly removed from the immediate circle of brothers. Was it his status as step-brother that placed him on the perimeter? she wondered. If so, were his brothers the ones who relegated him to the position of outsider or was it Whit, himself, who placed him there?

The dynamics were definitely interesting to consider, Maggie decided, as she watched the brothers turn their horses for the pasture.

She chuckled as she watched Rory swing himself up into the saddle and take out after the others, but grew thoughtful again, as she remembered Ace's rude treatment of him. Ace had greeted the others with a smile and a little good-natured roughhousing. But not so with Rory. The minute Rory had stepped through the back door, Ace had lit into him. And, as far as Maggie had been able to determine, Rory had done nothing to deserve his anger.

Had something happened between the two years before? she wondered. Something they'd never resolved and carried with them into adulthood?

Or could Ace possibly be jealous?

Intrigued by that possibility, she focused on Ace, in the lead. He rode with his hips slightly lifted and the balls of his feet planted firmly in the stirrups, distributing his weight evenly over the horse's back. Though a shirt covered his back now, she could well imagine him without it, her hands splayed over the pads of muscle, as they had been only short minutes before.

We'd be good together...

Shivering, she pressed her fingers against the glass, as if to reach out to him. Touch him.

Yes, they'd be good together, she thought. She didn't have a doubt about that.

But at what price?

She wouldn't allow a man to control her life again, no matter how tempting she found that man. And she would never jeopardize Laura's security and happiness for her own personal gain.

A match made in heaven? she asked herself, remembering Ace's words.

Or one destined for heartbreak?

Seven

Maggie had no idea what time to expect Ace and his brothers to return from rounding up the cattle. Rather than twiddle her thumbs, waiting—or wringing her hands and pacing, which was what she was afraid she might do—she filled her day doing the week's laundry and housework, mundane chores that unfortunately gave her way too much time to think of Ace and his last words to her.

We'll finish this later.

Since, prior to him making the comment, they'd been locked in a kiss, she had to believe that by *this* he'd meant the kiss. What haunted her was *how* he intended to finish it. The possibilities were endless, and each one she considered left her shivering in anticipation.

But as the clock slowly clicked away the minutes and hours, doubt crept in, her emotions running the gamut from breathless excitement to gut-wrenching fear.

Did she really want to get involved in a physical relationship with a man? she asked herself, as she rocked Laura to sleep for the night. After ending her disastrous marriage, she'd sworn off men, promising herself she'd never become dependent on another one for as long as she lived. But she was older now, she told herself. Wiser. She was aware of the pitfalls of dependency and knew that the amount of control she allowed a man to have over her life was up to her to establish...or withhold altogether.

But what about Laura? she worried next. How would Maggie's involvement with Ace affect the baby's future? Though she studied the possibilities from all conceivable angles, she couldn't think of a single way a relationship between the two could harm the baby.

With her concerns resolved for the moment, she continued to rock slowly back and forth, Laura having fallen asleep in her arms long ago. Without the lamp on, shadows draped the nursery. Worried that it would be dark soon, Maggie glanced out the window, but couldn't see anything six feet beyond the glass.

Hearing footsteps coming down the hall, she pressed a foot against the floor, stilling the rocker, and glanced toward the door, listening.

Oh, God, she thought, her panic returning. It had to be Ace.

Then he was there. In the doorway. His shoulders filling the space. Due to the lack of illumination, she couldn't see his face. Only his shape.

"Is she asleep?"

His voice, husky and deep, washed over her, a soothing balm to her burning nerves.

"Yes," she whispered. "Did y'all find all the cattle?"

"Most of 'em, I hope. We herded 'em all up to the north pasture where there's plenty of grass and water." He seemed to hesitate a moment, then asked. "Is she ready to put down?"

Maggie nodded, then rose and carried the baby to the crib to lay her down. Her sleep disturbed, Laura whimpered. Maggie leaned over the side of the crib, murmuring softly to her, patting her, until the infant had settled again.

She sensed Ace's presence beside her and glanced up. Their gazes met, her hesitation melting beneath the blue heat of his. Without a word, he took her hand and tugged her with him out into the hallway. Spinning her around, he crushed his mouth over hers and, with his body pressed against hers, backed her against the wall.

She tasted the need in him, the heat, saw it in his eyes, when, at last, he lifted his head to look down at her.

Smiling ruefully, he cupped a hand at her face and rubbed a thumb across the moisture he'd left on her lips. "I've been thinking about that all day. Kissing you. Nearly drove me crazy."

Mesmerized by the huskiness in his voice, the soft smile that curved his lips, she whispered, "Me, too."

He lifted both hands to her face, his expression turning earnest. "I want to make love with you, Maggie. I spent a hell of a lot of time thinking about that, too."

She closed her eyes, trembling, as he slid his hands down her arms and laced his fingers through hers.

"I thought about touching you," he whispered, brushing his lips across hers. "Kissing you, holding you." He dipped his nose into the curve of her neck and inhaled deeply. "Your scent haunted me," he murmured. "Roses." He opened his mouth and stroked his tongue over her flesh. "But you taste like sin."

Weakened by the seductive pull of his words, her body on fire from his touch, Maggie could barely stand. "Ace…"

Leaning into her, he slipped a knee between her legs. "Tell me that you want to make love with me, too."

The pressure of his thigh at the juncture of her legs sent

need rushing through her. Her mouth dry, her flesh afire, she could manage only a broken, ''Y-yes.''

Hearing the answer he wanted, he dropped his hands to her buttocks and brought her hips up hard against his. She felt the hardened length of his erection against her groin, nearly wept, as he found her mouth with his again. He kissed her passionately, thrusting his tongue deeply into her mouth.

He lifted her higher still, and she wrapped her arms around his neck and clung, as he carried her to his room. At the side of his bed, he stopped and loosened his hold on her, letting her body slide slowly down the length of his. When her feet touched the floor, she had to lock her knees to remain upright.

With a hand behind her neck, he drew back to rest his forehead against her. ''Damn,'' he moaned in frustration. ''I need a shower. I smell like the wrong end of a cow.''

She started to step away, but he tightened his grip on her, holding her in place.

''Take one with me.'' He dropped his mouth to hers and caught the hem of her T-shirt, drew it up. ''You scrub my back, and I'll scrub yours.''

She felt his teasing smile against her lips and couldn't help smiling, too. Fisting her hands in his shirt, she tugged it from the waist of his jeans and walked backwards as he urged her toward the adjoining bath.

He didn't bother with a light, but headed straight for the shower door. With his mouth still locked on hers, he reached around her to twist on the tap, then wrapped his arms around her and gave the kiss his full attention. Steam quickly filled the room, pearling on her already hot skin. He tore his mouth from hers and stepped back, ripping his shirt open.

Dragging in a ragged breath, Maggie stared at his bare chest. Unable to resist a moment longer, she splayed her hands over the muscled expanse, then smoothed them up, catching his shirt and dragging it over his shoulders. Tossing it aside, she carefully pulled off the tape she had bound him with earlier—with his chest bare now, she stepped into him, reaching for his belt as she pressed her lips over his heart.

Their movements became urgent, frantic, and soon they both were naked, their clothes scattered across the tiled floor. Holding up a finger, indicating for her to wait a second, Ace turned to pull open a drawer on the vanity. When he turned back, he held up a condom package for her to see.

''Protection,'' he said, and shot her a wink, then quickly ripped open the package. After fitting the condom over his erection, he caught her hand and guided her into the shower. He stepped in after her and closed the door behind him.

Steam filled the space, fogging the glass door and high window, while multiple showerheads sent hot, stinging streams of water to beat against their skin. With his gaze on hers, Ace took a bar of soap, rubbed it into a lather between his hands, then passed it to her. Maggie did the same, then moved in close, lifting her face to his, as she opened her hands over his chest.

Water streamed down their faces, as their lips met. Soap-slickened hands, combined with the needle-like sting of the water, added another level of sensuality to an already erotic act. Ace slid a hand between her legs, and she broke the kiss to suck in a breath, swamped by sensations she couldn't begin to name.

Murmuring softly to her, he cupped her buttocks and drew her to him, while stroking his finger along the seam of her feminine fold. Trembling, she dropped her head back and closed her eyes, giving herself up to the sensations. To him. She felt his mouth on her throat, the stroke of his tongue along her skin, both pleasure and torture. She gripped her hands at his shoulders to brace herself, as need swept through her in wave after drowning wave. He found her center, swirled his finger around the moist opening, then pushed inside. She arched, gasping, her body clamping down around him and pulsing wildly.

Desperate for him, she curled her fingers around his neck and brought his face down to hers. She drank deeply, thirstily, sweeping her tongue inside his mouth, seeking a satisfaction that she knew only he could give.

"I want you," she breathed against his lips. "I want to feel you inside me."

With a low growl, he lifted her, wrapping her legs around his waist, as he pressed her back against the tiled shower wall. With his mouth on hers, muffling her impatient whimpers, he thrust inside. He held himself there a moment, his body a rigid wall of restraint, giving her the time she needed to adjust to his size and length. He withdrew slowly, only to plunge again and again, setting a pace that Maggie was only too willing to follow. The sound of the water pounding against the tiles blended with the frantic rhythm of their bodies meeting, creating a symphony of sound that roared in their ears. The steam continued to billow around them, its heat pressing against their flesh, beading it with droplets of moisture that gleamed like diamonds in the mist.

Maggie felt the pressure building inside her, an impatient beast that paced and clawed, demanding release. Sure she would die if she didn't find relief soon, she locked her arms around Ace's neck and pushed her hips down against his. She felt the powerful lance of his manhood spear through her, the glorious explosion of her release, the pulsing throb of his…and melted weakly against his chest, her heart thundering against his.

Reaching up, she pushed her fingers through his hair and

turned her cheek to rub against his. "That was wonderful," she murmured.

He drew back to stare at her in disbelief. "Only wonderful?"

Laughing, she licked at the droplets of water that dripped from his chin. "Okay. Stupendous. Mind-blowing. The best sex I've ever had."

"Shoot," he scoffed. "That was nothin' but foreplay." Bracing her back against the tiles again, he dipped his head to capture a nipple between his teeth. He rolled his tongue around the stiffened orb, then released it to grin up at her. "I feel it's only fair to warn you. Tanners are known for their endurance."

She arched a brow. "Oh, really?" She slid her hand between their bodies, circling her fingers around him at the point where they joined. "Well, we'll see who outlasts who."

By Monday morning, Maggie was exhausted—if sated—and willing to call it a draw. After stepping from the shower Saturday night, she and Ace had dived into his bed and made love for what seemed like hours. Afterwards, they'd slept—not much longer than a nap, really—then made love again. And again. And again. And again. Sunday was a repeat performance, with breaks taken only when Laura was awake and needing Maggie's attention.

Shaking her head at the memory, Maggie scooped golden pancakes from the griddle and shoveled them onto waiting plates. She jumped, startled, when Ace slipped up behind her and wrapped his arms around her waist. Sighing, she sank back against him, as he nuzzled her neck.

"Good morning," he murmured sleepily.

Setting aside the spatula, she turned, looping her arms around his neck, as she smiled up at him. "Good morning to you, too."

He gave her a bone-melting kiss, then drew back and smacked his lips. "Mmm-mmm. You taste almost as good as those pancakes smell."

Laughing, she turned to switch off the burner beneath the griddle, then picked up the plates and led the way to the table. "Since I'm rather proud of my pancakes, I'll take that as a compliment."

He pulled out a chair and sat down opposite her, dragging a napkin over his lap. "Good. 'Cause I meant it as one." Picking up the syrup pitcher, he turned it up.

Maggie watched, her eyes rounding in amazement, as he drowned his pancakes in the thick sauce. "Would you like some pancakes with that syrup?"

Ace glanced up, then grinned and set the pitcher aside. "What can I say? I like sweets. I guess that's why I like you so much."

"Me? Sweet?" She choked a laugh. "That'll be the day."

He cut a triangle from his stack of pancakes and popped it into his mouth. "You are sweet," he said, then swallowed and added, "most of the time."

Jutting her chin, she poured syrup over her own pancakes. "Well, at least you're honest."

He leaned across the table and laid a hand over hers. "But you taste sweet all the time."

She narrowed an eye at him. "Are you trying to seduce me back into bed?"

"Is it working?"

Laughing, she waved her napkin in his face, shooing him back. "No. I've got too much to do to spend another day lazing around in bed with you."

Sulking, he sank back in his chair. "What do you have to do that's so all-fired important?"

"Well, for one, I have to take Laura to the doctor."

The color drained slowly from his face. "Is she sick?"

Maggie shook her head. "No. But it's time for her one-month check-up."

He blew out a breath and picked up his fork again, obviously relieved. "Tell 'em to send me the bill."

Maggie watched him sink his fork into another triangle of pancakes. "Ace?"

He glanced over at her. "Yeah?"

"Would you mind going with me?"

He dropped his fork to his plate and pushed out his hands. "Uh-uh. No way. You're not getting me anywhere near a doctor's office."

"But, Ace," she begged. "You're her guardian. Without you there to sign the necessary forms, they might refuse to see her."

Knowing she was probably right, Ace dropped his face into his hands, with a groan. "All right," he muttered and lifted his head to scowl at her. "But I'm not hanging around. Once I give whatever permission they need, I'm getting the hell out of there. Understand?"

Ace sat slumped in a chair in the clinic's waiting room, holding a fly fishing magazine in front of his face and trying his damnedest not to breathe any more than necessary. The antiseptic smell was already getting to him, making his stomach greasy.

Seemingly unaware of the sickening odor, Maggie sat beside him, cuddling the kid and whispering to her that there was nothing to be afraid of, that the doctor and nurses were her friends.

"Yeah, right," he muttered under his breath. "Try convincing the kid of that after they've poked and prodded her a few times."

The door beside the reception desk opened and the doctor stepped out, a manila file folder in his hand. "Laura Cantrell," he read from the folder's bright red tab.

Rising, Maggie called, "Over here," then stooped to gather the diaper bag. "Come on, Ace," she whispered. "It's our turn."

"Ace Tanner?"

At the sound of his name, Ace lowered the magazine to find the doctor looking at him curiously.

Frowning, Ace tossed the magazine onto the coffee table and stood. "Yeah. I'm Ace."

A smile slowly spreading across his face, the doctor started toward him. "Well, I'll be damned. Ace, I haven't seen you in a coon's age."

His frown deepening, Ace tried to place the guy. Slowly recognition dawned. "Tubby Clark?" he said in disbelief.

Wincing at the nickname, 'Tubby' glanced quickly around to make sure that no one had overheard. "Please," he begged. "It's taken me years to outlive that god-awful nickname. I prefer Ed or Doc."

"Doc, huh?" Grinning, Ace clasped Ed's hand, giving him a slow look up and down, as he shook. "Well, I reckon the name 'Tubby' doesn't fit anymore, anyway."

Chuckling, Ed smoothed a hand over a wash-board-flat stomach. "Medical school tends to do that to a man." Sobering, he slung an arm over Ace's shoulder and drew him toward the door. "I was sure sorry to hear about Buck, Ace. What a shock."

"Yeah. It was a shock, all right."

Ed opened the door, holding it for Ace and Maggie to pass through, then followed them. Indicating an examining room on his right, he led the way inside. "So what can I do for y'all?" he asked, obviously ready to get down to business.

Ace tipped his head toward Maggie and the baby. "The kid needs a check-up."

Ed blinked. "Damn, Ace. I didn't know you had any kids."

Scowling, Ace shook his head. "I don't. She's Buck's."

Ed stared a moment, then chuckled. "Looks like age didn't slow old Buck down any."

"No," Ace agreed, then gestured toward Maggie. "This is Maggie Dean, the kid's nanny. Whatever bill she runs up, you send to me."

Smiling at Maggie, Ed took the baby from her. "A nanny, huh?"

Maggie lifted a shoulder. "For the time being."

Figuring he'd done his duty, Ace headed for the door. "I'll wait out in the truck."

"Ace?"

His hand on the door, Ace glanced back to find Ed studying him critically. "Yeah?"

"Are you wearing a girdle or is that the outline of a bandage that I see beneath your shirt?"

Ace touched a hand to his ribs. "I ran into a little trouble with a horse."

Ed passed the baby back to Maggie. "Did the horse give you that cut on your face, too?"

Ace touched a self-conscious hand to his cheek. Though the wound no longer required a bandage, it hadn't healed completely. "Yeah. Must've landed on a rock or something when I fell. It's a lot better now, though."

Ed closed the distance between them. "Let me have a look at that." He poked at the skin surrounding the wound. "Who tended this?"

"Maggie. She's a nursing student."

Ed glanced over his shoulder at Maggie. "Really? We could use another good nurse around here. Are you interested in a job?"

"She *has* a job," Ace reminded him sourly.

Ed shrugged. "Doesn't hurt to ask." He motioned for Maggie to bring him the baby. "Here," he said to Ace, and passed the infant on to him. "You keep an eye on the baby, while I show Maggie around the office."

"Wait! I—"

The door closed behind the two, cutting Ace off. Muttering a curse, he strode to the examining table and laid the baby down. Bracing a hand on her stomach to keep her from falling off the table, he glared at the door.

Seconds later, it opened, and a nurse breezed in.

"Hi," she said cheerfully, as she placed a tray of supplies on the counter beside the examining table. "I'm Betty, Dr. Clark's nurse."

Ace eyed the tray warily. "Ace Tanner."

Giggling, she shifted his hand from the baby and began to unfasten the snaps on the baby's romper. "I know who you are, Mr. Tanner. Everybody does."

"Hey!" Ace cried, as she pulled the romper over the baby's head. "What do you think you're doin'?"

She gave him an absent pat. "Now, now. There's nothing for you to worry about. I'm just removing her clothes so that we can get an accurate weight measurement."

Lifting the baby, she laid the infant on the paper-lined tray above the scale and noted the weight. "Nine pounds," she told Ace, as she returned the baby to the examining table. "I'll take a quick blood sample, then we'll have her all ready for the doctor."

Ace paled. "Blood sample? Why do you need a blood sample?" Betty plucked a lancet from the tray, then caught the baby's heel and swiped it with an alcohol-soaked gauze pad. "The doctor requires one for all new babies."

Wedging himself between the nurse and the table, Ace bodily shoved her out of the way. "You're not sticking this kid with any needles," he told her, then lifted his head and yelled, "Maggie!" at the top of his lungs.

She made a tsking sound. "Now, Mr. Tanner," she

scolded, "there's no need to cause a scene. It's just a little prick."

"Little prick my ass," Ace muttered, then yelled again, "Maggie! Get in here!"

In spite of her diminutive size, Ace discovered that Betty was surprisingly strong…and quick. In the blink of an eye, she'd shouldered Ace aside, caught the baby's ankle and pricked the heel with the lancet. While Ace watched, too paralyzed to do anything more than stare, she squeezed, catching on a specimen slide the droplets of blood that bubbled from the small cut.

Laura let out an indignant wail.

With a growl, Ace snatched the baby up. Cupping a wide hand behind the infant's head, he turned his back on the nurse and hugged the baby to his chest. "It's okay, precious," he soothed. "Ace isn't going to let that mean old nurse hurt you again."

Fisting her fingers in the hair on his chest, Laura buried her face in the curve of his neck and sobbed pitifully. Ace gulped, mortally afraid that he might cry, too.

The door flew open and Maggie rushed in. "What's wrong?" she cried in alarm.

Ace spun to look at her accusingly, the baby held protectively against his chest. He jerked his chin toward Betty who cowered in the corner. "That crazy woman stabbed the kid and made her bleed."

Maggie couldn't decide which shocked her more: seeing Ace standing with the baby clasped against his chest, or the fact that he was standing at all, and not lying on the floor in a dead faint. Drawing in a careful breath, she moved to ease the baby from his arms.

"The nurse was only doing her job," she said quietly, in an effort to calm him.

"Since when is bloodletting a job?"

Ed stuck his head in the door. "Are y'all ready for me yet?"

Setting his jaw, Ace marched to the door. "Do you know what that damn-fool nurse of yours just did?"

Oblivious to what had transpired during his absence, Ed looked from his nurse to Maggie, then back at Ace. "No. What?"

"She stabbed the kid's foot with a needle the size of a first-grader's pencil."

Biting down hard on his lip to keep from laughing, Ed took Ace by the arm. "A first-grader's pencil, huh?" he said, as he pulled Ace out into the hall.

"You think this is funny?" Maggie heard Ace cry before the door closed behind the two men.

Still shaken, Betty looked over at Maggie. "Does he always act this crazy?" she whispered.

"Unfortunately, no."

At Betty's confused look, Maggie shifted the baby to her shoulder to give the nurse a reassuring pat. "Believe me. For Ace, this kind of crazy is a *good* thing."

Later that evening, Maggie set up the infant tub on the vanity in the bathroom off the nursery and proceeded to give Laura her nightly bath.

"So what do you think of your new tub?" she asked the baby, as she drizzled water over the infant's tummy. "Beats the heck out of that old kitchen sink at my house, huh?"

Squealing, Laura kicked her feet, splashing water on Maggie's face.

Laughing, Maggie tickled the infant under her chin. "You little scamp," she scolded playfully. "You're the one who's supposed to be getting a bath, not me."

She reached for a towel to blot the water from her face, but froze when she caught a glimpse of Ace's reflection in the bathroom mirror. He was standing in the doorway behind her, watching.

At some point during the evening, he'd shed his shirt, boots and socks, which left him wearing only his jeans. He'd left the top button on the jeans undone and, standing as he was with his hands braced high on the jamb and one knee cocked, his jeans rode low on his hips, accentuating the V of dark hair that arrowed down his abdomen and disappeared beneath the waist of his jeans. A patch of denim to the left of the jeans' fly was worn a lighter shade of blue.

"Is she okay?"

Realizing that she was staring—and *what* she was staring at—Maggie gulped, then gave him a reassuring smile. "She's fine."

He dropped his arms and moved to look down at the baby.

"No sign of any infection?"

Chuckling, she caught Laura's foot and lifted it up for him to see for himself. "You can't even tell where Betty pricked her with the needle."

He placed a hand over his stomach, blanching at the word "needle."

"Please," he begged.

Laughing, she drew Laura from the tub and quickly wrapped her in a towel. "You should be proud of yourself," she told him, as she led the way back into the nursery.

"Proud? Of what?"

She laid Laura down on the changing table and began to dry her off. "You didn't faint today at the doctor's office."

Scowling, he passed her a diaper. "I wish to hell Rory had never told you that story."

"I'm glad he did," she said, as she slipped the diaper beneath Laura's bottom. "I thought it was kind of sweet."

"Sweet?" He snorted a breath. "More like humiliating."

"Look at it this way," she told him, as she pressed the plastic tabs into place, securing the diaper. "A few more trips with Laura to the doctor, and you'll probably lose your fear of needles altogether."

"Yeah, right."

"It's true," Maggie said, as she guided the infant's arms through the sleeves of a gown. "It's a proven fact that the more often a person experiences something, the less frightening it becomes." She picked up the baby and pressed her against Ace's chest. "Here. Hold her a minute while I rinse out her tub."

Ace looked down at the baby, wondering how he'd ended up with the kid. Frowning, he trailed Maggie into the bathroom. "Do you think she's running a fever? She feels awfully warm to me."

Maggie tipped the tub over, dumping the soapy water into the sink. "If she feels warm, it's probably from the bath." She flipped the tub upside down over the sink to dry and turned to Ace, wiping her hands across the seat of her pants. "Would you like to give her a bottle, before I put her to bed?"

Ace opened his mouth to say no, but closed it and nodded his head instead. "Why not? You could probably use the break."

Hiding a smile, Maggie headed for the door. "It'll take me a minute to warm it up," she called over her shoulder. "Make yourself comfortable."

Ace glanced around. Not seeing any place in the bathroom to sit other than the commode seat, he walked back into the nursery and sat down on the rocker. "What do you think?" he asked the baby. "Is this comfortable enough for you?"

Laura squealed, flapping her arms wildly. Ace panicked, fearing he'd done something wrong.

"Now don't turn on the waterworks," he said nervously. "If you don't like this chair, I'll find us someplace else to sit."

She stilled and stared up at him, as if hanging on his every word. He gave his chin a jerk. "Well, you're going to like it even better once we get snuggled in." Careful not to startle her, he shifted her to a more comfortable position, then eased back, settling his spine against the rocker's bowed slats. "Now," he said, releasing the breath he'd been holding. "That's even better, isn't it?"

Yawning, she brought a fist to her eye and rubbed.

"Are you sleepy?" he asked. "Want me to tell Maggie to speed that bottle up?"

"No need," Maggie told him, as she entered the room. "I've got it right here." Smiling, she handed it to Ace, then sank down at his feet, watching as he offered it to Laura.

"She won't last long," she whispered, noticing that Laura's eyelids were already growing heavy. "She's had a pretty exciting day."

Ace nodded, fascinated by the tiny fingers that curled around his over the bottle. He lifted one of his fingers and carried three of hers up with it. Shaking his head, he lowered it back to the bottle. "She's so damn tiny."

Maggie laughed softly. "Most babies are."

"I suppose, though she seems exceptionally small."

"Dainty," Maggie corrected.

"More like fragile," he said, frowning down at Laura.

Chuckling, Maggie reached to blot a drop of drool from the corner of the infant's mouth. "Don't let her size fool you. She's tougher than she looks."

Ace snorted. "You're going to have a hard time convincing me of that." He lifted his finger again, drawing

Laura's entire hand up with it. "Just look at the size of that, will you? I've seen dolls with bigger hands."

"She'll grow," Maggie assured him. "She's already almost doubled her weight."

"Doubled!" he repeated, then winced, when Laura released the nipple and let out a cry. "Sorry," he murmured, as he guided the bottle back to her mouth. When she'd settled and began sucking again, he looked over at Maggie. "Doubled?" he said again, but more quietly this time.

Maggie nodded. "She weighed a little over five pounds at birth, and today she weighed in at nine pounds."

Ace blew out a breath. "Man. I had no idea she weighed less than five pounds at birth. That's small."

"Dainty," she reminded him.

"Fragile," he insisted.

With a shrug, she conceded the point. "All right, have it your way. But, like I said, she's tougher than you think."

"Look," he whispered. "She's already asleep."

Maggie rose to her knees and eased the bottle from the baby's mouth. "You can put her to bed now."

He looked up at her. "Me?"

She pushed to her feet and gave him a droll look. "It isn't as if you haven't done it before," she reminded him.

He looked down at the baby. "I did, didn't I?"

Careful not to wake her, he rose and crossed to the crib. He patted her back a moment, listening for her burp, then leaned over to lay her down. As he slipped his hand from beneath her, a hint of a smile curved the sides of the baby's mouth.

"Look," Ace whispered. "She's smiling."

Maggie draped an arm over his shoulders, as she peered down at the baby with him. "She's talking to the angels," she said softly.

He glanced over at her, his brow creased in puzzlement. "What?"

She shrugged. "It's something I heard somewhere. Supposedly, when a baby smiles while she's sleeping, it means she's talking to the angels."

Bracing his arms along the rail, Ace stared down at the baby. "Whether it's true or not, it's kind of a neat thought." He reached down to tuck the blanket more securely around her. "Do you think she's warm enough?"

Chuckling, Maggie hugged him against her side. "Will you quit worrying? She's going to be just fine."

Eight

At some point over the last two weeks, Maggie's plan to keep Laura's integration into the Tanner household as unobtrusive and subtle as possible had fallen by the wayside. Now a person couldn't take a step without dodging some type of infant gear. Another visit to town had produced a new playpen that had taken up permanent residence in the den. Baskets filled with an assortment of stuffed toys, teething rings and rattles were scattered all over the house, making the search for an item with which to entertain the baby as simple as reaching out a hand. On the floor of what Maggie considered Ace's office, a quilt was spread, its colorful squares embroidered with caricatures of different farm animals.

The biggest surprise of all, though, was that it was Ace who was responsible for the majority of the additions. He rarely made a trip to town that he didn't return with something new for Laura. An adorable chenille teddy bear for her to sleep with. A rubber rattle shaped like a dog's bone for her to chew on. A storybook constructed from fabric squares and illustrated with colorful felt appliques. With each new addition, Maggie silently prayed that it was a sign that Ace was moving closer to accepting the baby.

She was sending up a similar prayer one evening, when the doorbell rang. Her hands in dishwater, she lifted her head, listening to see if Ace would answer it. Not hearing a sound from his office, she quickly grabbed a dish towel and dried her hands as she hurried for the door.

Opening it, she found a delivery man on the porch. She looked at him in surprise. "It's rather late for a delivery, isn't it?"

"Not when we're transporting perishable goods." He glanced down at the clipboard he held. "The invoice is addressed to an Ace Tanner and requires a signature."

Since Ace hadn't responded to the doorbell, Maggie assumed he was busy and didn't want to be disturbed. "He can't come to the door right now. Is it okay if I sign for the package?"

The man handed over the clipboard. "Makes me no never mind. Personally, I'll be glad to get rid of the dang thing."

She quickly signed her name, then passed it back, frowning. "Why? Is it heavy?"

He snorted a breath. "Heavy and *loud*. The mutt hasn't shut up since I loaded the carrier into my truck."

Maggie's eyes bugged. "Mutt! Ace never said anything about buying a dog. Are you sure you have the right address?"

The man thumped the back of his hand against the clipboard. "Says it right here in plain black and white. Ace Tanner, Bar T Ranch, Tanner Crossing, Texas."

"That's the correct address, all right." Catching her

lower lip between her teeth, she strained to look around him. "Is the dog very big?" she asked uneasily.

He snorted a breath, as he turned and jogged down the porch steps. "Depends on what you call big."

Maggie watched as he slid open the truck's side door and disappeared inside. When he reappeared, he was stooped beneath the weight of a pet carrier large enough to contain a full-grown mountain lion. Maggie crossed to the edge of the porch. "Leave it there," she said, fluttering a hand at a spot on the sidewalk a good ten feet from the edge of the porch.

He groaned, straining, as he set the carrier down. "With pleasure." Dusting off his hands, he turned for his truck. "And good riddance."

Her gaze on the carrier, Maggie slowly descended the steps. She sank to her knees and stooped to peer inside. A yelp from the dog, had her jerking back. Placing a hand over her heart to still its beating, she stooped again to peer inside. A long, pink tongue snaked out and, before she could dodge it, licked her full on the mouth.

Curling her nose in disgust, she drew back, dragging the back of her hand across her mouth. "If I'd wanted a kiss," she complained to the dog, "I'd've asked for one."

His response was a pitiful whimper.

Her heart melting at the heartbreaking sound, she reached for the carrier's latch. "I bet you're tired of being inside of that old cage, aren't you, buddy? I'll let you out, but you've got to promise me you won't—"

Before she could finish the warning, the door flew open and a mountain of fur shot out, striking her against the chest and knocking her flat on her back. With her eyes squeezed shut, Maggie pushed at the dog, who seemed determined to thank her for rescuing him by licking her to death.

"Get off of me!" she cried, shoving at the dog. "You weigh a ton!"

"Not quite a ton, but close."

Hearing Ace's voice, Maggie flipped open her eyes, just as he collared the dog and pulled it back.

Afraid that he intended to punish the dog, she pushed up to her elbows. "He didn't mean any harm," she said, in the dog's defense. "He was just being friendly."

"'He' is a 'her,' and I've never laid a hand on her." He hunkered down and gave the dog's head a brisk rub. "Have I, girl?"

Maggie watched, her eyes widening as she recognized the dog. "That's the dog from the pictures you took for your book on Wyoming wildlife!" she cried.

Laughing, Ace tipped his head back, trying to dodge the dog's tongue, as it frantically licked at him. "This is her, all right…though there's a whole lot more of her. I left her with a buddy of mine in Kerrvile when I got the call that the old man had died. Since it looks as if I'll be here awhile longer, I asked him to ship her to me. Down, Daisy," he ordered sternly. Trembling with excitement, the dog immediately sat back on her haunches, her brown eyes fixed adoringly on Ace.

With a woeful shake of his head, Ace stood and offered Maggie a hand up. "Sorry about the exuberant greeting. She usually has better manners than that."

Maggie stared up at him, as he pulled her to her feet. "You had the dog all along," she said in disbelief. "Why didn't you tell me?"

He lifted a shoulder. "You didn't ask."

Before he had a chance to prepare himself, Maggie threw herself at him. With her legs wrapped around his waist and her arms around his neck, she peppered his face with kisses.

"I just *knew* you were hiding a heart somewhere in that gorgeous chest of yours."

Ace drew back to look at her askance. *"Gorgeous?"*

Maggie ducked her head, blushing to the roots of her hair. "Well…it is to me."

Dropping his head back, Ace hooted a laugh. "Gorgeous," he said again, then laughed even harder. "I don't think anyone's ever referred to my chest as *gorgeous* before."

Scowling, she squirmed, trying to get down. "I don't see what's so funny."

"I do. Gorgeous is a word used to describe a woman's looks. You know, like, 'Maggie Dean is one gorgeous chick.'"

She stopped squirming to look at him in wonder. "You think I'm gorgeous?"

"No. It was just an example."

"Why, you—"

Laughing, he dodged the fist she swung at his head. "I was only kidding!"

She eyed him skeptically. "Double-dog swear?"

"Triple-dog swear." He slowly eased her to her feet, but kept his arms locked around her. "Forgive me?"

"I don't know," she grumbled, unsure if she was ready to forgive him yet.

"Where's the kid?"

"Asleep."

He swept her up into his arms. "Good. That means I've got plenty of time to convince you."

"Ace!" she cried, clinging to his neck. "What about the dog?"

He stopped at the door, whistled and the dog came bounding up the steps.

"Stay, Daisy," he ordered, and the dog immediately flopped down on the porch and dropped her head between her front paws.

Maggie stared at the dog over Ace's shoulder, as he carried her inside. "Amazing," she murmured.

"I've always thought I was."

She bopped him on the back of the head. "Not you, goofus. The dog."

Reaching his room, Ace dumped her onto his bed, then dove in after her, wrapping his arms around her and pulling her over him, as he rolled to his back. "While I'm convincing you to forgive me, I guess I'll just have to convince you that I'm amazing, as well."

Enchanted by this playful side of Ace she had never seen before, Maggie planted an elbow on his chest. "And how do you intend to do that?"

"I could start by dazzling you with my magic skills."

She eyed him dubiously. "What magic skills?"

"I can make things disappear right before your eyes."

"What kind of things?"

He caught the hem of her T-shirt. "My specialty is clothing. Shut your eyes," he instructed.

She narrowed them at him instead. "You said '*before* my eyes.'"

"Semantics. Now close 'em."

Maggie obediently closed her eyes. In a flash, Ace ripped her T-shirt up and over head.

"You can look now."

When she did, he opened his hands before her face and turned them this way and that.

"See?" he said smugly. "No shirt."

She feigned a bored look. "Impressive, but not particularly amazing."

"Well, what about this?"

In the blink of an eye, Maggie was beneath him and the remainder of her clothes—as well as his—were on the floor.

"Now," he said, as he settled between her legs, winded by the effort. "What do you have to say about that?"

Smiling, Maggie slid her hands over his buttocks and urged him to her. "I'd say you're a master magician."

He fumbled a hand in the drawer of the bedside table, found a condom and put it on.

She gasped, tensing, as he pressed his erection against her center, then hummed her pleasure, melting around him as he slipped inside.

"Now *that*," she said, "is truly amazing."

She felt his smile against her neck, the rasp of his tongue as he stroked it down.

"Baby, you ain't seen nothin' yet," he said, just before he caught her nipple between his teeth.

She arched high as he suckled, then strained higher still, as she closed his hand around her opposite breast, mimicking with his fingers the seductive pull of his mouth on the other. Sensation churned inside her, gathering in speed and intensity until they melded into a single bolt of lightning that ripped through her body, piercing her low in her belly and creating an explosion that sent her flying over the edge.

She clung to Ace, her hands trembling, her heart thundering in her ears. "Ace!" she cried.

He chuckled and began to move inside her. "Like I said. Baby, you ain't seen nothin' yet."

A baby's cry tugged Maggie away from her dreams. Responding instinctively to the sound, she pushed back the sheet and started to rise.

A hand on her shoulder stopped her and pulled her back down.

"I'll check on her," she heard Ace say.

Murmuring gratefully, she snuggled her cheek into the pillow and dragged the sheet back to her chin.

When she awoke the second time, the first faint rays of sunshine were seeping through the drapes. Unwinding the tail of the shirt that was twisted around her knees, she smiled, remembering growing cold in the night and Ace getting it for her. Touched by his thoughtfulness, she stretched, rolled...then froze. Ace lay next to her, his face relaxed in sleep, his body curled protectively around the baby, who slept between them, a pacifier dangling from the corner of her mouth.

She gulped, swallowed, emotion crowding her throat. *Oh, Ace,* she thought, touched by the sight of them sleeping together. *Please, please, please let this be a sign that you've decided to keep her.*

Reaching out, she shaped a hand over his cheek and smiled as he blinked open his eyes to look at her. "This is a bad habit to start, you know," she warned.

He glanced down at the baby, then covered Maggie's hand with his and closed his eyes. "She was lonely."

Maggie chuckled and snuggled closer. "She said that?"

He shook his head. "No, but I could tell."

Her heart melting, Maggie leaned to press her lips to his. "You big softie."

"Uh-uh. Lazy. It was easier to stick her here, than have to stay up and entertain her."

Laura stirred between them, and the pacifier slipped from the corner of her mouth. Scrunching up her face, she let out an indignant wail.

Ace pulled his pillow over his head. "Your turn," he mumbled from beneath it.

With a rueful shake of her head, Maggie rolled to her knees and gathered the baby into her arms. "It's okay, precious," she soothed, as she scooted from the bed. "Maggie'll have you a bottle warmed before you can say scat."

"Scat."

Maggie glanced back to frown at the bed. "Very funny, Ace. Keep it up and you'll be the one doing the warming."

A snore came from beneath the pillows.

Chuckling, she headed for the door again. "You big faker."

The next two weeks passed in a blur of activity for Maggie. She spent one entire weekend doing nothing but cleaning the bunkhouse in preparation for the arrival of the three ranch hands Whit had managed to locate. The second she spent cooking and cleaning up after the hands, Ace and his brothers, who he had called home to help work the cattle. The men had worked from dawn until dusk on both Saturday and Sunday, first moving the cattle to the corral, then checking them over, doctoring those that needed it and castrating a dozen or more bull calves that—from the fuss they kicked up—weren't too crazy about the idea of being neutered.

On the weekdays in between, she cared for Laura and, in her spare time, helped Ace clean out his father's office and bedroom. She discovered that, for a man with such extensive holdings, Buck Tanner kept pitifully few records. Ace said it was because Buck didn't trust anyone, including his sons. Whatever his reasons, Buck had left few paper trails for Ace to use as a guide.

From the ranch hands Whit had located, Ace had learned that Buck had fired them all more than three months before his death. As to his reasons for doing so, the ranch hands didn't have much to offer, saying only that Buck had changed, turning meaner than was considered normal for even him, and had taken to sticking fairly close to the ranch.

In spite of all the extra work, Maggie had never been happier. She had Laura and she had Ace, the two people she'd grown to care about more than she'd ever expected to care about anyone again. The two people she was slowly beginning to think of as her family.

She knew it was wrong, dangerous even, to think of them in those terms. But she couldn't help it. She was sharing a home with them, cooking and caring for them, providing for their needs the same as a wife and mother would those of her family. And she slept with Ace. Shared his bed. Made love with him.

Granted, she'd told Ace from the first that she wasn't interested in getting involved in a relationship again and, later, that she wasn't interested in remarrying. For the most part, the last was still true.

Or was it?

She stole a glance at Ace, who, at the moment, sat slumped on the den sofa beside her, watching a movie, the fingers of his right hand laced with hers, his stockinged feet propped alongside hers on the coffee table. Did she want to marry Ace? she asked herself honestly. She mentally gave herself a shake and turned her gaze back to the TV. No. She couldn't think like that…not when he'd said nothing to make her believe he'd changed his feelings on the subject.

Yet, the question continued to niggle at her.

"Ace?"

His attention on the movie they were watching, he drew her hand to his lips. "Yeah?" he said absently.

"What will you do when you…well, when you finish up here?"

He moved his shoulder against hers in a shrug. "Go home, I guess." He turned to look at her. "Why?"

She looked quickly away and shook her head. "I don't know. I was just wondering."

He stared at her a moment, then turned to watch the movie again.

Maggie assumed he'd forgotten all about the question, until later that night, when they were in bed, and he asked, "Are there any nursing schools near Kerrville?"

She tensed, not daring even to breathe, knowing that Kerrville was his home. "I don't know," she said, praying her response came across with the indifference she tried to inject into her voice. "Why?"

He rolled onto his side and draped an arm over her waist, tugging her close. Pressing his lips to her temple, he murmured, "'Cause I was thinking you might want to consider transferring there and moving in with me."

She let the breath out slowly, her heart thundering within her chest. "I think there's a school in San Antonio, but I'm not sure."

He nuzzled his nose against her hair, then settled his head on the pillow next to hers and slid his foot between hers. "Wouldn't hurt to check it out."

"No. I suppose it wouldn't."

He yawned, then brushed his lips across hers. "'Night, Maggie."

She gulped, then whispered, "Good night, Ace." She listened as his breathing grew rhythmic, wondering how he could possibly sleep after making such a life-changing suggestion.

Sleep, for her, didn't come for hours.

At the sound of the phone, Maggie glanced up from the box of papers she was sorting. "Want me to answer it?" she asked Ace.

Sighing, he closed the drawer he was digging through. "That's okay. I'll get it."

Stretching across the desk, he plucked the receiver from the base. "Ace Tanner."

He listened a moment, a frown furrowing his brow. "Are you sure?" he said into the receiver, then listened again. He glanced toward Maggie, his frown deepening. "I don't know," he said slowly. "I'll have to do some checking and get back to you."

Replacing the receiver, he sank back in the chair, templing his fingers thoughtfully against his mouth.

"What?" Maggie asked, her curiosity aroused.

Dropping his hands, he shook his head. "That was the detective I hired to trace Star's family. He said the name 'Cantrell' was assumed."

"What!" Maggie cried. "But Star said—"

He patted a hand at the air. "I know. She told you her name was Cantrell. But the detective thinks she changed her name. He said he's traced her back to Las Vegas, but the trail dries up there, which makes him think she assumed the name there. He's following up on that theory now."

Maggie stared, unable to believe that Star had lied to her about her identity.

"What about Dixie?" Ace asked. "Wouldn't she have to have some kind of proof of Star's identity for her employment records? A social security number or something?"

Maggie pressed a hand against her forehead, trying to absorb the fact that Star had lied to her. "Yes. I suppose. Do you want me to call and ask her?"

Ace shook his head. "No," he said, rising. "It might be best if I talked to her in person."

Carrying the baby, Maggie led the way into the bar. Though it was still early in the afternoon, several customers already sat at the bar, nursing drinks, their eyes glued to the television anchored high on the wall in the corner. Donnie Gay, the announcer for the televised rodeo, was giving a play-by-play of a bull rider's eight-second ride.

Maggie spotted Dixie weaving her way through the tables toward them and offered a smile.

"Hey, Dixie," she said, as Dixie reached her.

Scowling, Dixie took the baby from Maggie's arms. "Hey, yourself." She glanced at Ace, gave him a quick once-over, then turned to Maggie without ever acknowledging his presence. "What are y'all doing here? Slumming?"

Surprised by Dixie's rudeness to Ace, Maggie glanced over at him. "Hardly." She turned to look at Dixie again. "Ace wants to talk to you. About Star," she added.

Dixie snorted. "Figured he'd get around to questioning me about her sooner or later." She nodded her head toward the hallway and her closed office door. "Let's talk in there where it's quieter."

She called out greetings to some of the guys at the bar, as she led the way to her office, with Maggie and Ace following behind.

She waited until they were seated on the sofa, then closed the door and moved behind her desk to sit down. Shifting the baby to her shoulder, she eyed Ace suspiciously. "Okay. So whaddaya wanna know?"

Ace leaned forward, bracing his forearms on his knees. "The detective I hired says Star's name wasn't really Cantrell."

Dixie lifted a shoulder, seemingly unsurprised by the news. "I figured she'd lied."

Maggie gaped. "You did? But you never said anything."

Dixie hooked a leg over her knee and settled the baby in the V she'd created between her legs.

"The girl was all smoke and mirrors. Shows up on my doorstep, carrying this beat-up suitcase and giving me this hard-luck story about a soldier she'd met in Vegas, who'd talked her into coming to Killeen. Claimed he was deployed before she ever got here, leaving her high and dry." She flapped a dismissing hand. "Hell, I've heard that story so many times, I could probably dance a tune to it."

"Are you suggesting that there was never a soldier?" Maggie asked.

Dixie shrugged. "Who knows? You couldn't pin Star

down on anything. She'd feed you a line of bull you would swear was the truth and smile the whole time you were swallowing it.''

Maggie gulped, suddenly feeling sick. ''But what about her family? Star told me they were killed in a car wreck when she was a teenager. Was that a lie, too?''

Dixie lifted a shoulder. ''Could have happened, I guess. Who knows for sure?''

''What about a social security number?'' Ace asked, re-directing the conversation to the purpose of their visit. ''Surely she had to give you some kind of legal ID, before you could hire her?''

''Oh, she had a social security card, all right,'' Dixie told him. ''I wouldn't have hired her without it.''

''And?'' he prodded.

She shrugged again. ''Probably a fake. They're easy enough to get, if you know who to ask and are willing to pay the price.''

Groaning, Ace fell back against the sofa, pressing the heels of his hands against his forehead. After a moment, he dropped his hands with a frustrated sigh. ''Without a positive ID, we might never know who she really was.''

''Any private detective worth his salt could do it,'' Dixie informed him. ''It's just a matter of turning over the right rocks and crossing the right palms.''

''I've hired the best there is,'' Ace informed her.

''Since when does a Tanner settle for anything but the best?'' she asked him, then eyed him speculatively, ''Even when the best was at home waiting on him all along.''

''Dixie!'' Maggie cried at the obvious slur.

Ace held out a hand to silence Maggie, but kept his gaze leveled on Dixie. ''I'm sure you have your reasons for saying what you did, but know this. I'm *Ace* Tanner, not Buck Tanner, and don't ever make the mistake of confusing the two.'' Rising, he crossed to the door, muttered to Maggie, ''I'll be in the truck,'' then slammed the door behind him.

''Now don't go getting your panties in a twist,'' Dixie warned Maggie. She jutted her chin defensively and lifted the baby to her shoulder. ''I was only testing the man's worth.''

Maggie dropped her head to her hands. ''Oh, Dixie,'' she moaned.

''Doesn't sound to me like he's changed his mind.''

Still reeling from Dixie's rudeness, Maggie lifted her head. ''About what?'' she asked in confusion.

''The baby. He's still chasing after Star's family. That tells me he hasn't changed his mind about keeping the baby.''

''Not necessarily. In fact, he's asked me to move to Kerrville with him.''

''The baby, too?''

Maggie paled at the question, not having considered that Laura wouldn't be going to Kerrville with them.

Sighing, Dixie rose and rounded her desk. ''Well, there's always the chance that high-priced detective of his won't find any of Star's relatives.''

Maggie drew in a deep breath, grasping at that possibility. ''Yeah. There's always that chance.''

Placing a finger beneath Maggie's chin, Dixie drew her face up. ''Prepare yourself for the worst, but pray for the best. That's what I always say.''

Maggie forced a brave smile. ''This is going to work out, Dix. You'll see. This is going to work just fine.''

The trip home was made in silence, with Ace frowning at the road ahead and Maggie staring at the windshield, her hands fisted tightly in her lap, trying desperately to push back the doubts that Dixie had placed in her mind.

She wouldn't give up hope, she told herself. She

couldn't. Without hope, how could she survive? What would happen to Laura, if she were to give up? Who would care enough about the baby to see that she had a good home, a family to love her?

She stole a glance at Ace. She'd thought he cared, that he'd changed his mind about Laura, had grown to love her. Could she have been that wrong about him? No, she told herself. She'd seen proof of the changes over the last several weeks. Ace had warmed to Laura, bought her toys and silly little gifts. He'd even started helping Maggie with her care, feeding Laura her bottle when Maggie was busy doing something else or rocking her to sleep at night, while Maggie sat at his feet, watching, her heart nearly bursting with her love for the two of them.

She drew in a deep breath and forced her fingers apart. Ace loved Laura, she told herself firmly. He cared. This need of his to locate Star's family was probably nothing more than a formality, perhaps even a requirement he'd discovered he needed, before the courts would officially name him her legal guardian.

But she wouldn't ask him, if that was the case. Couldn't. If she did and he denied her suppositions, what would she have to place her hope in, then?

Forcing the tension from her shoulders, she reached over and laid a hand on Ace's thigh. At her touch, he glanced her way. She smiled and gave his thigh a squeeze.

"What would you like for dinner tonight?" she asked, hoping to return a sense of normalcy to what had turned into a nightmarish day.

Nine

Ever since the first night they'd made love, Maggie and Ace had slept together in his bed. It wasn't something they had discussed, an agreement they'd reached after laying down specific ground rules. It had just happened. When bedtime arrived each night, Ace would simply seek Maggie out and walk with her to his room, his arm draped along her shoulders. Often, but not always, they would make love before going to sleep, the mood of their lovemaking varying from a sweet and tender loving to hot and steamy sex.

After their visit with Dixie, they continued to sleep together…but they didn't make love any longer. Something happened that day, something intangible that left a barrier between the two that neither seemed willing to address. Yet, Ace still slept with his body curved around Maggie's, his head nestled against hers on her pillow, his feet twined with hers. He still held her hand while they watched television in the evening and dropped kisses on her mouth at moments when she least expected him to…

But he didn't make love with her again.

Though reluctant to approach Ace about the change in their relationship, Maggie worried about it, wondering at the cause, what it meant. She worried, too, about the change she noticed in his relationship with Laura. He seldom held her any more, and on those rare occasions when he did, it was because Maggie forced the baby on him. And he always seemed to disappear at Laura's bedtime, naming one task or another that required his immediate attention, thus avoiding rocking the infant to sleep.

More than the changes in her own relationship with Ace, Maggie was concerned over the changes she saw in his and Laura's. From the beginning, she'd hoped to convince him to keep Laura, raise her as his own, prayed, even, for that to happen. But with each passing day, that hope grew dimmer and dimmer, until one day it was snuffed out altogether.

The day it happened, Maggie was in the laundry room, folding a load of clothes she'd just taken from the dryer, when she heard the telephone ring. She paused, waiting to see if Ace would pick it up. After the second ring, she heard the muffled sound of Ace's voice coming from the kitchen and resumed her folding, knowing he had answered it.

"Montgomery?"

Frowning at the question Ace placed in the name, Maggie paused, listening.

"Dallas?" he said next, his voice carrying a note of surprise, then, "Damn. Here I had you chasing all over the country, when her relatives were in our own backyard the entire time."

Maggie fisted her hands in the towel she was folding, knowing it was the private detective Ace talked with.

"When you do," she heard Ace say. "Let me know. I'd think it'd be better if my brothers and I made the initial contact."

Squeezing her eyes shut, Maggie blocked out the sound of Ace's voice, not wanting to hear any more. The detective had found Star's relatives. There was no doubt about the purpose of the call. But knowing that and accepting it was a different matter altogether.

"Maggie?"

She stiffened at the sound of Ace's voice, unaware until that moment that he'd entered the laundry room and now stood behind her.

She gulped, trying to swallow back the fear that held her in its grip, her gaze fixed unseeingly on the dryer's control panel. "The detective found someone?"

"Not yet, but he knows now her name was Montgomery and he's narrowed the trail to Dallas."

Maggie dropped her chin to her chest. "You're going to give Laura to them when the detective finds them, aren't you?"

She felt the weight of his hands on her shoulders, the dig of his fingers into her flesh, as he squeezed.

"Maggie—"

She turned to face him. "Ace, please," she begged. "Don't do this. Keep her with you."

"Maggie," he said sternly, "I told you from the start that this was only a temporary arrangement."

She pressed her fists against her temples and shook her head, tears streaming down her face. "No," she cried, shaking her head. "You said you didn't know how to take care of her." She fisted her hands in his shirt and looked up at him. "But I'm here, Ace. I'll take care of her. We both can. I'm not suggesting that we get married. I know you don't want that. But we can live together, the three of us. We can give her a home, a family."

He tightened his grip on her shoulders and gave her a hard shake. "Maggie, listen to me. I don't want any kids. I told you that. Mine or anyone else's."

"No!" she screamed. She pounded her fists against his chest, desperate to make him deny his words. "You love her," she sobbed. "I know you do. You can't just give her away to a complete stranger. You can't!"

At the word *love,* he stiffened, his fingers digging painfully into her shoulders. Gulping, Maggie watched his lips flatten, his face turn to stone, his eyes turn that hard, brittle shade of steely blue she remembered from the first time they had met. She wanted to reach up and touch him, lay a hand against his cheek…but she was afraid if she dared touch him, the razor-sharp edge of the mask he'd slipped into place would slice her finger to the bone.

Frightened by the change in him, devastated by it, she backed away from him, hugging her arms around her middle, as if to ward off a chill.

"I won't stand by and watch you give her away," she told him. "I…I can't." Choked by a sob, she spun and ran from the room.

Maggie folded the soggy tissue and blotted at the tears that continued to stream down her face. "I can't believe he's really going to do it, Dixie."

Dixie plucked a fresh tissue from the box and pressed it into Maggie's hand, her face creased with concern. "Ah, honey. I know it hurts. It's gotta. But there's nothin' you can do to stop him. By law, Ace can do what he wants to with the child."

Maggie shot up from the couch. "Law," she repeated, venom all but dripping from her lips at the word. "I'm sick to death of people using *law* as an excuse for their behavior. What about duty? Huh? What about love? Why doesn't anyone ever base their actions on either of those things? Why do they always have to fall back on what the *law* says? Why can't they listen to what their hearts say, instead?"

Dixie caught Maggie's hand and pulled her back down on the sofa beside her. "Now, Maggie," she scolded gently. "You're just getting yourself all worked up again, when what you need to do is calm down."

Maggie balled her hands against her thighs. "But I'm so mad, Dixie. Furious! Every time I think about Ace giving that precious baby away, I want to hit something. Him! How can he be so blind that he can't see that he loves her? So heartless that he can't see that she needs him?"

Dixie patted her knee. "Now, honey, I know that you think you know what's best for the child. But are you sure you aren't the one who's having difficulty seeing? You forged a bond with that baby the minute Star placed her in your arms. But does that give you the right to dictate the child's future? To decide what's best for her and what's not? Star asked you to take her to the Tanners and that's what you did.

"Maybe you need to open up your own eyes and see what's really behind this anger of yours. You've been living out on that ranch with Ace, for what? Close to a month? I'd imagine, by now, you're sleeping with him."

Dixie didn't need confirmation from Maggie to know she was right. The stricken look on Maggie's face was enough.

Sighing, she gave Maggie's knee an understanding squeeze. "I figured as much."

"I love him."

Frowning, Dixie nodded. "I don't doubt that for a minute. You'd never have crawled into bed with him, if you didn't. But what about him? How does he feel about you?"

Maggie balled the tissue in her hand and rubbed a thumb at the fist she'd made. "I don't know. I thought he did...or at least that he cared." She turned to look at Dixie, tears filling her eyes. "He wouldn't have asked me to move to Kerrville with him, if he didn't care for me, would he?"

"Only Ace can answer that. He's the one who knows

his heart. But I imagine once he suggested you move in with him, you started fancying yourself a family. Mama Bear. Papa Bear. Baby Bear. A big, fine home for the three of you to live in.'' She lifted a brow. ''Am I right?''

Maggie stared, amazed at how accurately Dixie had depicted the sequence of her emotions, her thoughts.

Dixie reared back to look at her. ''What? You think you're the first woman to let her dreams run away with her?'' She shook her head sadly. ''Honey, if I was to stand up behind you all the women who'd made that same mistake, the line would stretch for miles.''

''Knowing that doesn't lessen the hurt.''

''I doubt it does. But this isn't the end of the world, so don't you start acting like it is. You've hit a little rough spot, taken a spill. But you'll survive. That's what we women do. We survive.''

Gulping back tears, Maggie leaned to rest her head against Dixie's. ''Oh, Dix. What would I do without you?''

Dixie wrapped an arm around her and gave her a hard squeeze. ''Oh, you'd do all right. You've got a good head on your shoulders. A good heart. You'd find your way.''

Sniffing, Maggie blew her nose. ''Eventually, I guess.'' She angled her head to look at Dixie. ''You know, Dix,'' she said thoughtfully. ''It's a shame you never had children. You'd have made a wonderful mother.''

Dixie snorted a laugh. ''You're just saying that to butter me up. Probably want your old job back.''

Chuckling, Maggie blotted the last tears from her eyes. ''No, but I'd sure like to have it, if it's still available.''

Dixie pursed her lips, as if considering. ''I suppose by now you've forgotten all I taught you. How to tote a loaded tray without strainin' your back. How to dodge a strayin' hand without insultin' the man whose hand did the strayin'.''

Laughing, Maggie hugged Dixie against her side. "No. I haven't forgotten."

"Then I suppose you're back on the payroll."

Dixie stood at the rear entrance of the Longhorn, watching as Maggie climbed into that rag-tail car of hers. She'd been tough on the girl, she thought with regret. But Maggie had needed a good shaking up, to jar her out of the doldrums before they swallowed her all the way up.

It hadn't been easy for Dixie to give her that shaking, though. Not when what she'd wanted to do was wrap her arms around the child and soak up all her pain. But Dixie had discovered long ago that you couldn't spare another from hurt, no matter how badly you wanted to or how hard you tried. Sometimes you just had to sit back and watch 'em take the fall. Oh, you could pick 'em up and dust off their knees, afterwards. Slap a bandage on the hurt. But you couldn't spare them the pain. Life had a way of getting in its blows no matter how good you got at duckin' and dodgin' 'em.

Star was to blame for all this, Dixie thought, trying to stifle the resentment that came with the thought. Saddling Maggie with the responsibility of her baby. Another person would've delivered the kid, as Star had requested, then walked away and wiped her hands of the matter. Not Maggie. She'd taken on the responsibility as if it was her life's work and now suffered a tremendous guilt because she thought she'd failed.

But if anybody understood that kind of dedication, Dixie supposed she did. She'd made a similar promise a few years back, one she still felt bound by today.

She'd made the promise to Patricia Dean.

Maggie's mother.

Ace sat slumped over the kitchen table, his chin resting on its edge, a bottle of whiskey between his hands, turning it slowly around and around, while he tried to work up the enthusiasm to pour himself a drink. It wasn't his brand. Not that he had a favorite. The truth was, he'd never particularly cared for the taste of whiskey.

But he did have a hankering for the escape it promised.

Scowling, he shoved the bottle away and flopped back in his chair.

Hell, he couldn't get drunk. Not with a baby in the house and him the only adult around to take care of it.

But remembering that didn't take away his hankering for escape. It only served to remind him that Maggie was gone.

Slumping lower in the chair, he folded his arms across his chest, his anger with her returning. Packing up her stuff and tearing out like the devil himself was chasing her. What the hell was wrong with her? It wasn't as if he'd lied about his intentions. He'd told her from the get-go that he wasn't keeping the kid. So why had she turned on the waterworks and begged him to keep her?

Frustrated that he didn't have an answer to the question, he heaved himself up from the chair. "Women," he muttered.

At the sink, he twisted on the tap and sent hot water splashing over the bottles and nipples he'd left in the sink. Maggie should be doing this, he thought, as he squirted a generous stream of dishwashing liquid over the bottles. She'd always washed and prepared the baby's bottles for the next day. Not him. And she'd done a lot of other things that now fell to him. Things like feeding the baby, playing with her, giving her her baths.

The hell of it was, he didn't begrudge Maggie the work she'd left him to do. What he resented was that she'd left at all.

Daisy barked at a sound in the hall, startling Ace from his thoughts. He whirled, sure it was Maggie returning, figuring that she'd realized she'd made a mistake. That she'd finally reconciled herself to the fact that Ace was turning the baby over to Star's family.

When it was Rory who appeared in the doorway, not Maggie, Ace turned back to the sink to hide his disappointment.

Snatching up a bottle scrubber, he growled, "What do you want?"

"A man has to have a reason to visit his family home?"

Ace rammed the brush into the bottle and scrubbed furiously. "Funny to me, you never cared about visiting until Maggie showed up."

"So *that's* what's been eating you."

Ace rammed the brush hard into the bottle, then swore when it busted through the opposite end, sending shards of glass flying over both sinks.

"Now look what you've gone and made me do," he complained.

"I didn't make you do anything."

"You damn sure did. You made me break the bottle."

Rory moved to Ace's side and looked down at the shattered glass. "I didn't make you do that. Your jealousy did."

"Jealousy!" Ace cried. "And who am I supposed to be jealous of? You?" He snorted a breath. "In your dreams, little brother. In your dreams."

"Then explain to me why you acted like an ass the night I took you to the emergency room to have your ribs X-rayed?"

Ace tensed. He didn't remember much of anything that happened that night...not after about the fourth glass of whiskey he'd drunk. Had he said something to Rory about Maggie? He remembered Maggie telling him the next morning that he owed Rory an apology for cussing Rory when he'd helped him to bed. But what had he said to Rory at the emergency room?

Deciding a defensive stance the safest to take, he said, "Probably because you provoked me."

"Which proves my point."

"And what point is *that?*"

Smiling smugly, Rory braced a hip on the counter and folded his arms across his chest. "You're jealous."

Ace yanked his hands from the dishwater and snatched up a towel to dry them. "What would you have that I'd be jealous of?"

Rory curled his fingers to study his nails. "It's not what I have. More like what you're afraid I might get."

Ace turned for the table and the whiskey bottle he'd left there. Twisting off the cap, he arched a brow in warning, as he lifted the bottle to his lips. "You try stealing my dog, little brother, and I'll kick your butt all the way to Dallas and back."

"It wasn't your dog I was thinking of stealing. I was thinking more along the lines of Maggie."

Ace slammed down the bottle, without ever having taken a drink, and leveled an accusing finger at Rory. "I knew it!" he cried. "I *knew* you had the hots for her all along."

When Rory only smiled, it angered Ace all the more. He dug down in his arsenal and selected a weapon sure to draw blood.

"What's wrong, Rory?" he taunted. "Aren't there enough women in San Antonio to satisfy your sexual appetite? Or have you grown bored with them all?" Snorting a laugh, Ace turned away. "You're so much like the old man, it's scary."

"Why, you—"

Rory was across the room, before Ace knew he'd even moved. Grabbing Ace by the arm, he spun him around.

"You've been lookin' for a fight for weeks," he said

angrily and gave Ace a shove. "Well, bro, you just found yourself one."

Ace squared off, ready to go head-to-head with Rory, but a wail from the monitor he'd left on the table had him dropping his hands.

"Now look what you've done," he snapped. "You woke up the kid."

Rory took a taunting jab at Ace's shoulder. "Let Maggie get her. You and me are going to settle this once and for all."

Ace turned away, heading for the hallway. "Maggie's gone."

Rory slowly lowered his hands to stare. "Gone?"

When Ace kept walking, Rory took off after him. "What do you mean she's gone?"

"As in vamoosed. Skedaddled."

"Where'd she go?"

"Back where she came from."

Opening the nursery door, Ace reached to turn on the lamp, then moved to the crib.

"Hey, kid," he murmured softly, as he leaned to pick Laura up. "What's the matter? Huh? You hungry?"

"Hungry?" Rory repeated. "Haven't you fed her?"

Ace gave him a withering look. "Well, of course I've fed her. What do you take me for? An imbecile?"

Rory lifted a shoulder. "Well, you let Maggie go."

Scowling, Ace moved to the changing table and laid the baby down. "I didn't *let* Maggie do anything. She got mad and quit."

"Mad about what?"

Wishing he'd kept his mouth shut, Ace gestured for Rory to pass him a diaper. "The detective thinks he's close to finding a relative of Star's."

Rory handed him the diaper. "Why'd that make her

mad? I'd think she'd be tinkled pink, Star being her friend and all.''

Frowning, Ace held up the baby's feet, doused her behind with some powder, then lowered them to snug the diaper into place. ''She wanted me to keep the kid.''

''You?'' Rory hooted a laugh. ''Is the woman crazy? You don't know anything about raising kids.''

Ace turned his head and gave him a long look up and down. ''You look like you survived the experience without too many scars.''

''Well, yeah,'' Rory said. ''But I'm a guy. I was easy.''

''Easy?'' Ace snorted and picked the baby up. ''You were a royal pain in the butt. All of you were.''

With the baby draped over his shoulder, Ace headed for the door, leaving Rory to trail behind.

''Is that why you never wanted to have kids?'' Rory asked.

Ace slammed to a stop, then turned to look at Rory. ''Who told you I never wanted to have kids?''

''Sheila.''

''When did you talk to my ex?''

Rory held up his hands. ''Uh-uh. I'm not walking into that one. Next thing I know, you'll be accusing me of hustling your ex-wife.''

Scowling, Ace headed for the kitchen again. ''Like she'd be interested in you.''

''Is that what busted up your marriage?''

''You? Hardly.''

''No,'' Rory said in frustration. ''You not wanting any kids.''

Ace pulled a bottle from the refrigerator and popped it into the microwave, set the timer. ''Among other things.''

Hooking his thumbs through his belt loops, Rory hung his head. ''Man, Ace. I feel really bad.''

''About what?''

"Ruining you for fatherhood. If not for me and the others, you might've had kids."

"You didn't ruin me for anything," he told Rory, then added, "well, not entirely, anyway."

"If not us, then what did? Sheila said you were emphatic about not wanting any kids. Said you'd even talked about having a vasectomy."

"Did she discuss our sex life with you, too?"

The microwave dinged, saving Rory from having to answer. Holding the baby against his shoulder, Ace removed the bottle and tested the milk's temperature on his wrist, as he moved to sit at the table.

Noticing Rory's hangdog expression, Ace heaved a sigh. "Look, Rory. Sheila and I had problems before the question of kids ever came up. That's not what ended our marriage."

Rory twirled a chair around and straddled it. "I don't get it, Ace. Why don't you want to have kids?"

Ace looked down at Laura and shook his head. "I don't know. A combination of things, I guess. Mostly the old man." He frowned, then glanced over at Rory. "Haven't you ever wondered what kind of father you'd be? A good one or a bad one? Or like the old man? Invisible?"

Rory pursed his lips thoughtfully, as if considering. "No, I can't say that I have."

Ace blew out a long breath. "Well, I have. And there's enough doubt there to keep me from testing the theory."

Rory reared back to look at him in disbelief. "You gotta be kidding me! You'd make a great father, Ace."

"Yeah. Right," Ace said wryly.

Rory pushed up from the chair. "No. I'm serious. Ask Woodrow or Ry or even Whit. They'd tell you the same damn thing. I know we were pains in the butt and acted like ungrateful jerks most of the time. What kid doesn't?

But you were there for us, Ace. When we needed you, you never let us down.

"We may have resented you bossing us around, but we would've resented you for that even if you'd been our real father and not just a stand-in. And just look at you," Rory said, gesturing toward Ace and the baby. "You're taking care of her. You've got what it takes to be a father. You're a natural."

As Ace stared down at the baby, Maggie's words rose up to taunt him.

No child deserves to have a father who's incapable of loving or caring for it.

Was he incapable of loving the kid? he asked himself. Unsure of the answer, he shook his head. "No. I can do the basics. Meet a kid's physical needs. But that's it. A kid need someone who can love 'em and that's where I come up short."

"Like hell you do!" Rory shouted. "Who held my hand when I had to have my stomach pumped, after I swallowed an entire bottle of headache pills?"

Ace snorted a laugh, remembering. "I did."

"And who taught me how to ride a horse and rope a steer?"

"I did. But—"

"And who let me crawl in bed with him in the middle of the night, when a storm blew in and I was too scared to sleep in my own bed?"

Grimacing, Ace muttered. "I did."

Rory dropped a hand on Ace's shoulder and hunkered down to look him square in the eye. "If those weren't acts of love, bro, then you tell me what is."

Ace lay on his side, his head propped on his hand, staring down at the baby who slept beside him. This was the fourth night in a row that he'd had to put the baby in bed with him in order to get her to go to sleep.

Maggie had warned him, he remembered. She'd told him he was starting a bad habit when he'd put the baby in bed with them that first time.

But how the hell was a man supposed to get any rest with the kid screaming her lungs out?

Screaming her lungs out? his conscience prodded.

Well, maybe not screaming, he acceded grudgingly. Probably more like crying.

Crying?

Okay, already! he thought in frustration. So it was a whimper. But what was I supposed to do? The kid was lonely in that big old room all by herself.

Who was lonely?

Groaning, he dropped his hand and let his head fall to rest in the bend of his elbow. Me, he admitted miserably.

"But I'm not the only one who's lonely," he murmured. Reaching out, he brushed a finger over the baby's cheek. "You miss her, too, don't you, kid?"

At his touch, Laura shuddered a sigh, then smacked her lips, as if searching for the missing pacifier.

Ace plucked the pacifier from the pillow he'd propped up on the other side of the baby and rubbed the nipple across her lips. She latched onto it, sucked furiously for a moment, then her jaw went lax and the pacifier slid to dangle from the corner of her mouth. It was a game they repeated several times a night. The baby makes a sucking sound; Ace fetches the pacifier; the baby sucks a minute, quits; the pacifier falls out of the baby's mouth; the baby makes another sucking sound, sometimes a whimper; and the game starts all over again.

Ace felt something cold nudge the back of his leg and looked over his shoulder to find Daisy staring up at him.

"No way," he said. "I may be a sucker, but I'll be darned if I'll let you sleep with me, too."

The dog dropped her chin to the edge of the mattress and whined pitifully, looking up at him with sad brown eyes.

Swearing under his breath, Ace patted the bed. "All right, you big baby. Get up here."

Daisy bounded onto the bed, then flopped down at Ace's feet.

"And stay there," he warned the dog. "I don't want you waking up the kid."

Catching the end of the sheet, Ace pulled it up over his shoulder and settled his head onto his pillow, closed his eyes.

But even with all the company, sleep was still a long time coming for Ace.

It was Maggie he wanted with him in his bed.

Ten

Ace awakened slowly. Blinked, then flipped his eyes wide. Jackknifing up, he looked frantically around. The baby was gone. The dog was gone. Whipping back the sheet, he vaulted from the bed and ran from his room.

At the doorway to the kitchen, he skidded to a stop. Rory sat at the table, calmly feeding the baby a bottle, the dog sprawled at his feet. Bracing a hand on the jamb, Ace placed the other over his heart to still its wild beating.

Rory shot him a grin. "Mornin', Ace."

Ace sank weakly down onto a chair and dropped his head into his hands. "Damn you, Rory. You nearly gave me a heart attack."

Rory bit back a smile. "Why? Did you think somebody had kidnaped the kid?"

Ace lifted his head to scowl. "Hell, I didn't know what to think." He snatched up a dish towel from the table and used one corner to catch a milky drop of drool that leaked from the side of the baby's mouth. "Scared the pee-waddly-doo out of me, though, and that's a damn fact."

Rory gave him a disapproving look. "You probably shouldn't cuss like that in front of the kid." He looked down at the baby and smiled. "A pretty little thing like her? It'd be a shame if the first word out of her mouth was a four-letter one."

Ace snorted a breath. "By the time she starts talking, I won't be around to influence her, good or bad."

Rory glanced up at Ace. "Are you sure you want to turn her over to Star's relatives? I mean, think about it, Ace. You don't know anything about these people. They could be ex-cons, for all you know."

Ace pushed away from the table. "And they might be good, law-abiding folks," he argued stubbornly, as he headed for the sink.

"What about Maggie?" Rory asked. "Why doesn't she adopt her?"

The question hit Ace square in the back, stabbing so deep it pierced his heart, releasing a memory he'd buried there. Though his gaze was fixed on the window above the sink, it wasn't the view of the backyard he saw beyond the glass. It was Maggie he saw. Standing on the front porch the day she'd brought the baby to the ranch, her face ravaged with regret, her eyes swollen with tears, her voice trembling as she'd told him she'd wanted to keep the baby herself, but couldn't.

She deserves more than I can give her.

He shook his head, not trusting his voice. "She can't."

"Why not? It's obvious she's crazy about the kid."

Ace squeezed his eyes shut, trying to shut out the images that flashed through his mind. Images of Maggie holding the baby, rocking her. The love that filled her eyes each time she looked at the child.

Gulping, he forced open his eyes to stare blindly at the

window. "Maggie wants her to have a family. One that will love her and take care of her."

"You could do that, Ace. You and Maggie together could give the kid that."

Ace shook his head. "Maggie could. But not me."

"That's bull, Ace, and you know it. You love Maggie, don't you?"

Ace gripped his hands over the sink, as the reality of that hit him. He hadn't intended to fall in love with her. Couldn't even remember at what point his feelings had changed, grown into something stronger.

"Don't go trying to deny it," Rory warned, "because I know better. Twice you wanted to fight me because I flirted with her. In my book, that spells jealousy with a capital J. And, if you're jealous, that means you've staked a claim on her, which is fine with me, 'cause I like Maggie and wouldn't mind having her for a sister-in-law."

Ace gulped. "Maggie doesn't want to get married. She told me so."

"Well, she either lied or changed her mind, because last night she told me that she did and was willing to marry you."

Ace's heart stuttered a beat. Slowly he turned to stare at Rory. "You saw Maggie?"

"I damn sure did and it wasn't to flirt with her, so don't go swelling up like a bullfrog and trying to pick a fight with me again. I went to talk to her, to try to figure out what the hell was going on between the two of you."

Ace pressed his hands to his head to still the dizzying sensation, trying to absorb what Rory was saying. "She told you that she loved me?"

"Not right off. I had to fish a little first."

"She never said anything," he said dully. "Never told me how she felt."

"Did you tell her?"

Regret burned through Ace that he hadn't, that it had taken losing her to make him realize that he did.

Rory shook his head sadly. "Bro, you may be older, but you sure as hell aren't wiser. Not where women are concerned. Maybe I should give you a couple of pointers."

Ace started for the door. "Stay with the baby. I'll be back as quick as I can."

"Hey!" Rory cried. "Where are you going?"

Ace twisted open the door and started out. "To get Maggie."

"Wait!" Rory shouted.

Ace stopped and looked back. "What?" he snapped in frustration.

"You might want to put on some pants first."

Ace looked down and groaned when he realized that he was wearing nothing but his shorts. Closing the door, he ran for his room.

"Watch out for Dixie," Rory called after him. "Judging by the fuss she kicked up last night when Maggie told her I was your brother, I figure you're probably pretty high on her hit list right now."

When Ace didn't find Maggie at home, he drove straight to the Longhorn, figuring he'd find her there. Sure enough, he spotted her beat-up car in the parking lot beside the building. Parking his truck next to it, he climbed out and headed for the front entrance. He tried the door but found it locked. Framing his hands at his temples, he pressed his face against the glass, trying to see inside. The place looked empty, but he'd swear he heard music.

Lifting a fist, he pounded on the door. "Maggie?" he shouted. "It's me. Ace. Open the door."

He waited a moment, listening, then lifted his hand to pound again. Just as he did, the door opened and Dixie stepped out.

She narrowed her eyes at the fist he managed to halt short inches from her nose.

"Hit me," she snarled, "and I'll have the cops on you so fast it'll make your head spin."

Ace dropped his hand. "I'm not planning on hitting anyone. I want to see Maggie."

"And why would she want to see you?"

By the bitterness in the woman's voice, Ace figured Rory had been right. He was pretty high on Dixie's hit list. Probably on Maggie's, too.

"I don't know that she does," he told her, trying to keep the frustration from his voice. "But I'd appreciate it if you'd tell her that I'm here."

"And why would I want to do that?" Dixie challenged. "Appears to me you've hurt her enough as it is."

At the end of his patience, Ace closed his hands around Dixie's arms and bodily picked her up. He stepped through the doorway, then kicked the door closed behind him.

"Now," he said and plopped her back down on her feet. "You can either tell me where Maggie is, or I can tear this place apart looking for her. Either way, I'm not leaving until I talk to her."

Dixie aimed a finger at his nose. "You hurt that girl again and you'll have me to deal with. Understand?"

Ace caught her hand, pulled it down and pushed his face up to hers. "Perfectly. Now you understand something. I love Maggie and I intend to marry her, if she'll have me, so you better learn to deal with that *and* me, because I'm not going away. Ever. Understand?"

"Ace...what are you doing here?"

He whipped around to find Maggie standing behind the bar. All he could do was stare.

A slap on the back had him stumbling forward a step.

"Well, you said you wanted to talk to her," Dixie snapped. "So? There she is. Talk."

Ace angled his head around to give Dixie a murderous look. "In private, if you don't mind," he grated out between clenched teeth.

Dixie tossed up her hands. "Well, why didn't you say you wanted privacy, 'stead of standing there staring at the girl like a mute."

Muttering under her breath, she stalked to the back hallway and slammed her office door behind her. "Okay!" she shouted from behind the closed door. "I'm in my office now! That's as private as you're gonna get, so talk!"

"Ace?"

Taking a deep breath, he turned back to face Maggie. But, at the sight, his throat closed up around the words he'd come to say to her. He walked slowly toward the bar, braced a hand on its top and vaulted over. With his gaze on hers, he took her hands in his and brought them to his lips. He watched the tears fill her eyes, felt the burn of them behind his own.

"You said you wanted Laura to have a family who loved and cared for her."

She squeezed her eyes shut, dipped her head. Nodded.

"I think I've found the perfect family for her."

Her desolation was obvious, evidenced by the droop of her shoulders, the lifeless relaxing of her hands within his, the tear that leaked past one lid to trail slowly down her cheek.

"They'll be good to her," he promised. "Good for her. They'll give her everything she needs, everything she could ever possibly want."

A sob slipped past her lips and she tried to wrench her hands free.

But Ace hung on, refusing to let her go.

"It's what you wanted, isn't it?" he asked quietly. "A home for Laura, a family to love her?"

She lifted her head, her eyes flooded with tears. "Yes,

that's what I wanted," she cried tearfully. "But I wanted *you* to be the one to provide that home for her, *you* to be the one to love her." Hiccuping a sob, she jerked her hands free and dropped her face onto her palms. "Not just anyone, Ace," she sobbed. "I wanted it to be you."

"I can't do that, Maggie," he said softly. "Not alone. Not without you. Maggie...." He pulled her hands from her face to hold in his. "Marry me, Maggie. Help me create that home for Laura. Help me remember how to love."

She gulped, staring. "Oh, Ace..." She gulped again. Swallowed. "Do you mean it? You're really going to keep her?"

He guided her arms around him, then wrapped his around her. "That's my plan." Reaching up, he thumbed a tear from her cheek. "But Star has family. We know that now. They may want Laura, too."

He felt the dig of her fingers on his back, saw the fear that flashed in her eyes, and wanted desperately to reassure her. "I don't know what the laws are," he told her. "Whose rights for guardianship prevail in a situation like this. But I promise you this. I will do everything within my power to see that Laura remains with us."

She sagged against him, clutching him to her. "Oh, Ace," she cried softly. "She has to. She just has to."

He held her close, slowly rocking her back and forth, his lips pressed against the side of her head. "I love you, Maggie," he whispered. "More than I even dreamed possible."

She leaned back to look up at him, her eyes filled with tears. "And I love you, Ace."

"Marry me, Maggie." He thumbed a tear from her cheek, then dropped his mouth to hers. "Marry me and we'll work through this together, start building on that home you want for Laura."

Smiling through her tears, she framed his face with her hands. "Yes. Together. Oh, Ace..." She flung her arms around him, hugging him tight. "This is going to turn out all right. I just know it will."

"It will, Maggie. The three of us belong together. We're family."

Epilogue

Epilogue

It was almost two months to the day from their father's funeral that the four Tanner brothers gathered in their father's office again. As they had during that first meeting, Woodrow and Rory sat on the leather sofa opposite their father's desk. Ry stood to the left of the desk, his arms folded across his chest, frowning out the window.

In addition to the four brothers, two others were present for this meeting. Whit, who had missed the first meeting, stood on the far side of the room next to the door, his back braced against the wall. Maggie, the newest addition to the Tanner family, was present, as well, and stood at her husband Ace's side, before the desk.

A third person was present, as well. Laura was there and currently being passed from brother-to-brother and—according to Ace—at risk of becoming terminally spoiled.

When the baby finally made it back to Maggie, Ace draped an arm along Maggie's shoulder, and addressed his brothers.

"I think all of you are aware that the private detective I hired has discovered that Star's real name was Montgomery, not Cantrell, and that he's traced her family to Dallas."

Receiving nods of affirmation from his brothers, Ace went on. "Well, now it looks as if he's located a family member. Specifically, a sister."

Rory shot from the sofa, his eyes wide in alarm. "But you and Maggie are keepin' the baby, right? This sister can't take Laura away from us, can she?"

His expression grim, Ace shook his head. "I don't know. That's what we've got to find out. None of the lawyers we have on retainer practice family law, so they're having to research the laws pertaining to guardianship and custodial rights, in situations where both parents die, leaving a child behind. Since neither Star nor the old man left behind a will or specific written instructions pertaining to Laura's welfare, for now we are going to have to assume that Star's sister has the same rights to Laura as any of us do."

Rory dropped weakly back down on the sofa. "Then what?" he asked, lifting his hands helplessly. "I mean, if this sister wants Laura, who decides who gets to keep her?"

Releasing a long breath, Ace withdrew his arm from Maggie and hitched a hip on the corner of the desk. "I guess the courts will."

"Oh, man," Rory moaned. "That could get ugly."

"I'm hoping to avoid that," Ace informed him.

"How?" Rory asked, clearly puzzled as to how they could circumvent a court ruling.

Ace pushed off the desk and began to pace. "As far as we know, this sister doesn't even know Laura exists. My plan is to get to her as quickly as we can, explain the situation to her, then hopefully persuade her to let Maggie and I adopt the baby."

Rory flapped his hands, as if urging them out the door. "So go! The sooner we get this settled, the better, as far as I'm concerned. I know, I for one, will sleep a hell of a lot better once the kid's name is officially Tanner.''

''Maggie and I have discussed this,'' Ace told him, ''and we both agree that we shouldn't be the ones to make the initial contact.''

Ry glanced over his shoulder to look at Ace. ''Are you sending one of our lawyers?''

Ace shook his head. ''No. I think it would be better if a member of the family met with her.'' He glanced at Rory. ''What about you? You're personable, yet I know you can be pretty damn persuasive when it suits you. Would you be willing to do it?''

''Oh, man, Ace,'' Rory said miserably. ''You know I'd do it in a heartbeat. But I'm leaving tonight for Wyoming. I've got meetings scheduled all week with a group of Western artists whose work I want to carry in my store. If you could give me a couple of days—''

''No,'' Ace said, frowning. ''A couple of days is too long to wait.'' He turned to Ry. ''What about you? Do you think you could squeeze a trip to Dallas into your schedule?''

''Sorry,'' Ry said. ''The funeral and my trips here to help out on the ranch have thrown me way behind. I have surgeries scheduled back to back all day, starting at six in the morning. My whole week's like that.''

''What about you, Whit?'' Ace asked, shifting his gaze to the back of the room where Whit stood.

Whit paled. ''Not me, Ace, please. I wouldn't know what to say. What to do.''

''I think Woodrow should be the one to go.''

Four heads spun to stare at Maggie in disbelief.

Woodrow made a choking sound. ''Me?'' he croaked.

Maggie gave her chin a decisive nod. ''You're the perfect choice.''

''But I hate big cities!'' When Maggie merely lifted a

brow, he looked around the room, desperately searching for support. Finding none, he appealed to Ace. "Come on, Ace. You know what my negotiating skills are like. It's my way or the highway."

Ace felt a bump against his arm and turned, taking the baby Maggie pushed into his arms. Wondering what she was up to, he watched her cross to Woodrow and sink down at his feet.

"You can do it, Woodrow," she said confidently. "I wouldn't allow you to represent us if I didn't think you were capable of handling the job."

He drew back, shaking his head slowly. "You don't know me like the rest of 'em do. I don't deal well with people."

She laid a hand on his knee. "You love Laura, don't you?"

"Ah, Maggie," he complained. "That's fightin' dirty. You know I'm crazy about the kid."

"Yes, and because you love her, I know you will fight as hard to keep her as Ace or I would. Will you do this for us? Please? For Laura?"

He glanced over at the baby, gulped, then dropped his chin to his chest, his shoulders sagging in defeat. "All right," he grumbled, then lifted his head to narrow an eye at Maggie. "But if I screw this up, I don't want anyone blamin' me. Understood?"

Laughing, Maggie rose to throw her arms around his neck. "You won't screw this up, Woodrow. You're the perfect man for the job."

Late that same night, Maggie and Ace lay in bed, the lights out, but both wide awake.

"He *could* screw this up," Ace said for the umpteenth time since his brothers had left. "Woodrow's people skills are a little rough around the edges."

Maggie laced her fingers through Ace's. "He won't," she said confidently.

"But he could, you know. To folks that don't know him, Woodrow comes across as abrasive."

"Yes," she agreed. "His size alone is intimidating. One look at him, and Star's poor sister will probably run and hide."

"Oh, God," Ace moaned. "Maybe I should call and tell him to forget it."

When he leaned to reach for the phone, Maggie tightened her grip on his hand. "Don't you dare," she warned, then softened the scolding with a smile, as he laid back down beside her. "Woodrow will do just fine," she assured him. "You'll see. He loves Laura as much as we do."

Pulling his hand from hers, Ace slid it beneath her shoulders and pulled her to his side. "You're right," he said, hugging her close. "All my brothers are crazy about the kid. Not just Woodrow."

She laid her head on his shoulder. "Everything's going to work out all right, Ace. Laura was meant to be with us. I feel it in my heart."

He turned his lips to her forehead. "You'll make a wonderful mother, Maggie. And I want to be a good father to her. Better than my father was to me."

She lifted a hand to cup his cheek, emotion filling her throat. "You already are, Ace. You love her. That's what's most important."

Covering her hand with his, he smiled down at her. "I'm one lucky man to have you as my wife. I love you more than I ever thought was possible."

"And I love you, Ace."

He snuggled close and bumped his nose against hers. "How do you feel about giving Laura a couple of brothers or sisters?"

"Oh, Ace," she said tearfully. "I think that would be wonderful!"

He pressed his lips to hers. "Think we ought to start working on that now?"

She drew back to look at him in surprise. "Now?"

He shrugged. "If we don't hurry up and get another baby for those brothers of mine to spoil, they're going to ruin Laura for sure."

Laughing, she looped her arms behind his neck. "In that case, I guess we better not waste any more time."

* * * * *

EXPECTING BRAND'S BABY

BY
EMILIE ROSE

Emilie Rose resides in North Carolina with her college sweetheart husband and four sons. Her love of romance novels started when she was twelve years old and her mother hid them under the sofa cushions each time Emilie entered the room. Emilie grew up riding and showing horses and her hobbies include quilting, cooking (especially cheesecake) and anything cowboy. Emilie is an avid baseball mum, and during the season can usually be found on the sidelines watching one of her kids play. When she can spare time for TV, she enjoys the Discovery Channel's medical programmes, *ER* and *CSI*. She loves country music because she believes there's a book in every song.

Thanks to my mom, for being the greatest cheerleader a girl could ever have, and to my husband for keeping me in the game when I was too discouraged to continue. I want to thank my kids for learning to cook. I guess you had to, since I forget to feed you when I'm writing. ☺

A special thanks to Sarah Winn, my pioneering friend, who isn't afraid to give me a kick in the pants when I need it.

One

She'd save the ranch tonight—even if she had to do it flat on her back.

Toni Swenson chewed her lip and studied the stream of people wearing jeans and cowboy hats flowing toward the National Finals Rodeo. Somewhere inside the arena there had to be a man with the kind of genes she needed. Genes, which would contribute the love of horses, cattle and open spaces to her son.

And it had better be a son, she thought, wiping her brow.

Toni herded along with the rest of the crowd. She swallowed to ease her dry mouth and wiped her damp palms on her jeans. Her heartbeat thundered like a stampede, nearly deafening her. Glancing wistfully back toward the exit, she took a shuddery breath, trying to pull oxygen past the invisible lariat tightening around her neck. Familiar scents and sounds surrounded her: barbecue and nachos, dirt and livestock. A combination unique to the rodeo.

Memories of happier times with her grandfather rushed

at her and pulled her forward when her feet wanted to drag. Why had he died? The ache in her heart increased. And why had he felt the need to put this metaphorical gun to her head and force her to do something totally against her moral beliefs? He, more than anyone, knew why she didn't trust men.

Sliding into her hard-backed aisle seat, Toni wiped her eyes and wondered how she could have stayed away from the sport of rodeo so long. Vet school had been difficult, but surely if she'd tried harder she could have found the time to attend a rodeo or two with her grandfather. Year after year her grandfather had brought her here, put her in her seat and ordered her not to move. A bitter smile twisted her lips. She'd rarely obeyed that directive. Once he'd disappeared toward the chutes, Toni had followed, staying out of his line of vision.

Cowboys and livestock fascinated her. Always had. Tonight, a rootless cowboy who carelessly used and discarded women was exactly what she had to find. It wasn't as if she had a choice.

A whiskey-rough voice drew her gaze to a pair of cowboys coming down the aisle. "Remember the basics. Shoulders square. Free hand in front of you. Run like hell when you hit the ground. You'll do fine."

The dark-haired one with the bedroom voice slapped the younger man on the back. Thick muscles shifted in his forearm. Toni shivered. Arms like that could do serious damage in a fit of rage. He paused in the aisle beside her, waiting while his companion spoke to someone in the stands.

Black leather chaps framed the best backside Toni'd ever laid eyes on. She could scarcely miss the firm glutes and lean thighs parked just inches from the tip of her nose. All those tight muscles were wrapped in denim so snug he might burst a seam riding tonight. And he would ride. The number between his broad shoulders marked him as a competitor. The intensity of his voice labeled him as the winner even before the contest began.

He turned, allowing someone to pass. Toni sat back and shifted her gaze upward. It was either that or look at... something a lady shouldn't stare at. Of course, a lady wouldn't be planning the kind of encounter she had in mind for tonight, either. But if she wanted to hold on to the ranch she'd forget her principles.

The cowboy's gaze brushed over the crowd, landing on her with the force of a hoof in the stomach. She couldn't breathe and wondered if she'd pass out before he looked away. Those dark eyes beneath the brim of his black hat made her heart misbehave and her midsection flutter. His lean face could've jumped straight out of her fantasies. Sharp angles, square jaw, and high cheekbones. This was a devil of a good-looking cowboy. A man in control. Definitely *not* what she'd come for tonight.

She broke eye contact and looked past him toward his young, blue-eyed companion. Now, *that* was the kind of guy she needed. Someone carefree and careless, whose happy-go-lucky manner was as apparent as the dark cowboy's take-charge attitude.

The blonde glanced her way. Toni forced her lips into what she hoped was a come-hither smile and fought the nervous urge to puke into her popcorn box. Blushing furiously, the young man turned away. Toni frowned and peeked at the dark cowboy. He'd witnessed her strikeout and was scowling at her. Heat flooded her cheeks. She'd bet Tall, Dark and Gorgeous had never struck out. Charisma oozed from his pores. No doubt he knew it.

Toni studied the scuffed toes of her boots and pulled in a deep breath. *Remember what's at stake. Remember the mission.* The ranch meant too much to her to back down now. She set her jaw, thrust her shoulders back. She stood, intent on introducing herself to the younger man, but the black-haired devil had already hustled her quarry down the aisle toward the stairs.

With an admiring look at his retreating derriere, she shook her head. No man should look that good. It wasn't fair to the female population—especially the ones like her, who wanted someone easier to handle. Toni gritted her teeth and followed. She couldn't—wouldn't—chicken out tonight. Looks weren't the only things passed along on the DNA. She needed cowboy genes.

A rueful smile twisted Brand's lips. He adjusted the brim of his hat. *Brandon Lander, you're getting too old for this business.* That li'l buckle bunny had barely spared him one glance from her baby blues. She'd been too busy flirting with Bobby Lee. Hell, Bobby was barely nineteen, still a virgin, and planning to stay that way until he married his high-school sweetheart after Christmas. He wouldn't know what to do with a woman like her.

Glancing over his shoulder as he turned toward the chutes, he spotted the blonde tailing 'em. Looked like she had designs on the kid's virtue. Least he could do was help the kid resist temptation. He gave Bobby Lee a shove. "Hustle up. You'll be late. I'll be along directly. I don't ride for a while yet."

Wiping the smile from his face, he turned to confront the woman who seemed determined to lead a young man down the road to hell. With all those curves, it'd be a scenic trip. She was a tiny one, probably weighed little more than a good saddle. She looked fragile, the type some men would want to coddle and protect. But not him.

Fat, buttery curls floated over her shoulders to the tips of her breasts, framing an angelic face. Skin as smooth as the magnolia blossoms growing beside the front porch back home made his fingers itch to touch. No doubt her mouth would've looked like a rosebud if she hadn't mashed it into such a determined line. It irked Brand more than a little that her huge blue eyes looked straight past him and locked on Bobby Lee's back.

The fierce concentration on her features surprised him. She looked like a woman on a quest. He'd seen the same intense expression on many a bull rider just before they left the chute to face a ride that could mean life or death. But what kind of quest would lead a pixie like her behind the chutes? Determined to find out he stepped into her path and tipped his hat.

"Hello, li'l lady. Where you headed?" If her scowl was any gauge, Brand figured she didn't like being called little.

"Excuse me." She tried to step around him, but he widened his stance and looped his thumbs in his belt. She glanced briefly at his World Championship belt buckle. It didn't seem to impress her. She stepped right and Brand sidled left, blocking her. She moved again, and he countered like a good cutting horse.

"I need to pass." Those rosy lips pinched tighter and her face flushed. She gave her curls a toss. "Move, cowboy."

"Can't let you back there, darlin'. Bull riders only." Damn, she was pretty. He took a minute to savor her sweetly curved form, working his way from her tapping toes to the sparks shooting from her eyes. There'd been a time when he'd let himself be distracted by a morsel like her, but not anymore. Her kind spelled trouble. In capital letters.

"Then there are a few riders not listed in my program."

"Aw, darlin', those are just wives and girlfriends. You with one of the fellas?" She wasn't. Bull riders were a close-knit group, and if she'd belonged to any one of his buddies, they'd have been braying like a jackass, wanting everybody to know.

She swallowed hard and stiffened her shoulders. Some of the pink faded from her cheeks. "Not yet."

The news shouldn't have pleased him, but it did. *Which only goes to show you where your brain is tonight, Romeo.* "Look, darlin', we're fixin' to ride. Why don't you head on back up to your seat before you distract somebody and get 'em hurt."

Her face flushed and her chin lifted. "Why don't *you* move before you get hurt?"

Brand coughed to cover his chuckle. So she wanted to play tough? "Do you honestly think I'd be intimidated by a hundred pounds of fluff when my job is to ride a ton of crazy beef?" He faked a shudder. "You got me shakin' in my boots, darlin'."

She eyed his crotch—not in a complimentary way—and shifted her weight. She looked angry enough to end his reproductive years before he put 'em to good use. Brand rolled to the balls of his feet, prepared to dodge her knee.

"Wish me luck, Brand." Bobby Lee's yell distracted her and gave Brand a chance to shuffle back a step or two.

Keeping a wary eye on the angel with an attitude, he gave Bobby Lee a thumbs-up. The kid, one of the lowest scorers to make the finals, waved and turned toward the chute. It was a matter of pride that as the high scorer, Brand would be riding last. Still, he had a lot riding on his last go and couldn't afford to be distracted by a spunky angel. He considered asking one of the ushers to show her back to her seat, but hesitated, somehow reluctant to turn the spitfire loose.

Toni scowled at the broad-shouldered man blocking her path. Thanks to him, she'd missed her chance to meet the potential father of her baby. Another clean-cut cowboy sidled up, but the band on his ring finger disqualified him. She sighed. Lady Luck was not with her and time was running out.

"Hey Brand, a bunch of us are gettin' together to down a few later. Bobby Lee's coming. How 'bout you?"

Toni straightened when he named the bar of the hotel where she was staying. Maybe all was not lost.

Dark eyes narrowed on her for a moment. "I'll be there."

Toni fought the urge to squirm beneath the challenging stare. The announcer called Bobby Lee something-or-another's name. Toni shifted her gaze to her quarry in an attempt to break free of the devil's spell. If the young cowboy in the chute was going to father her child, she ought to know his last name—if for no other reason than to avoid him after tonight.

The metal gate opened with a clang. Hooves, arena dirt and bull exploded into the air and the crowd went wild. Toni caught herself looking at the pushy dark-haired cowboy instead of at Bobby Lee. He moved closer to the ring, staring intently at the bull and rider. His right hand clenched in front of him, as if he were holding the rigging and living the ride himself. Something about his total concentration on bull and rider, something about *him* held her attention. Powerful muscles bunched and shifted in his forearm and beneath his shirt and jeans.

The noise of the crowd drowned out her pounding heart. *Leave while the devil is distracted.* Her feet didn't move. She blamed her strange fascination on the fact that the cowboy's thick drawl and lazy attitude hadn't seemed to fit the intelligence and the intensity she'd seen in his eyes. She didn't want to notice that anymore than she wanted to admit he was easily the sexiest man she'd ever laid eyes on.

Remember the mission. He isn't what you need tonight, or any other night for that matter. He's too big, too strong, too physical. A man like him could seriously hurt a woman. The hairs on her arms rose. She needed the easygoing cowboy clinging to the back of the bull bounding around the arena. And she only needed *him* for about thirty minutes.

Toni took a step back. Maybe Providence had smiled on her plan after all. It was the right time of the month for her to conceive this child her grandfather's will insisted she bear, and the man who could help her do it would be coming straight to her hotel. She could meet him in the hotel bar—only twelve floors away from conception.

She *would* succeed tonight. Tomorrow she'd leave

Las Vegas carrying the seed of her future and her link to the past.

It was the only way to hold on to her sanctuary.

Watching the door, Toni tore her cocktail napkin into thin strips. She sipped her drink and considered slinking off to her room alone. All too soon the boisterous cowboys came through the swinging doors with Mr. Wrong leading the way. Her stomach lurched. Toni leaned forward in her seat to see if Bobby Lee was in the pack and there he was. Suddenly, she felt nauseous. Women followed the men, enlarging their number to nearly a dozen.

The dark cowboy—Brand, they'd called him—seemed to be the center of attention. People patted him on the back as he passed. Hooking an arm around Bobby Lee's head, he gave him a playful noogie.

He glanced up, his dark gaze locking onto hers with the intensity of a bull preparing to charge. She struggled to pull air past the knot in her throat and tugged at the low-cut neckline of the tacky black dress she'd bought in the hotel boutique. Brand's eyes shifted downward. She wanted to cover her overexposed cleavage, but fastened her hands around her glass instead. The dress was a necessary costume for the role she had to play tonight. Seductress was a new one for her.

Brand said something, and the group shifted like a herd of cattle and headed in her direction. The moment of truth had arrived. Toni's heart thumped. She had to do this. *Had to.* She chased the lump in her throat with another sip of margarita and forced herself to look beyond Brand to Bobby Lee.

She smiled, even though it felt as if it would crack the makeup she'd shoveled on, then patted her upswept hair. One sneeze would have the whole mess tumbling down. Toni fought to subdue the hysterical giggle squirming in her chest and aimed for a take-me-to-bed expression.

Brand bent his head toward Bobby Lee. Whatever he

said caused the younger man to blush and drop back a step. Long before she was ready, the group hovered beside the semicircular booth. Brand winked and flashed her a heart-stopping grin.

"Hello, darlin'. Thanks for savin' us a table." Without waiting for an invitation, he gestured for his friends to sit down and slid into the booth beside her. He stretched his arm along the back of the banquette.

Another cowboy scooted in on Toni's left, crunching her against Brand's hard thighs and into the crook of his arm. Heat seared her. She jerked forward.

With a calloused finger, Brand traced a light pattern on her bare nape. A shiver skipped down her spine. Toni stiffened and tried to shift away, but another bump from the man on her left hemmed her in. Trapped.

She glared at Brand and hissed, "Give me some room."

His teeth gleamed, straight and white. As potent as a caress, his gaze drifted from her eyes, to her lips, to her cleavage. Toni's nipples peaked in betrayal. She wouldn't make a scene by screaming at the pushy cowboy. That wouldn't gain her any points with Bobby Lee who obviously worshipped the jerk. She inhaled slowly, hoping to calm her racing pulse.

Brand smelled of cinnamon and cedar rather than the sweaty bull and arena dirt she'd come to expect from rodeo cowboys. He'd traded the bold striped shirt he'd worn earlier for another, this one resembling an American flag.

She wouldn't let a nice-smelling cowboy with a penchant for loud shirts distract her from her mission. She surveyed the others, dismayed to see Bobby Lee far down the table. With several people between them, she couldn't speak to him without yelling. Brand and the beefy man had her boxed in, so moving closer was out. How in the heck would she woo Bobby Lee with her new Wonderbra from this distance?

Damn. Her first attempt at seduction shot down.

The waitress appeared and nodded toward Toni's empty glass. "What'll ya have, hon? Another one of those?"

No matter how much Dutch courage she needed, she wouldn't accomplish tonight's chore if she passed out first. She shook her head. "Iced tea this time, please."

After giving his order, the beefy cowboy to her left leaned over her, practically pushing Toni into Brand's lap. Obviously, *he* enjoyed the effects of her new lingerie. "What? No champagne, Brand? You ain't celebrating?"

"How many is that now? Three?" A woman with artificial everything reached across the table to scrape an acrylic nail across the back of Brand's hand.

Toni gripped her glass. It wasn't like her to be bitchy, but she'd bet good money that neither the woman's hair nor breasts were compliments of Mother Nature.

"Four." Brand drew his hand out of the talon's reach and threaded his fingers through Toni's. She startled and tried to extricate herself from his warm, calloused grip, to no avail. Sparks hopped and skipped up her arm. His hands were huge with a multitude of tiny scars across the backs and knuckles. Like a fighter's. She hated the telling tremor invading her limbs.

The mission.

The waitress returned. She winked at Brand and set a tall glass in front of him on a cocktail napkin that had a phone number scribbled in the corner. "The bartender sent over something special for you, Champ. Here's your tea, hon."

Toni waited for Brand to acknowledge the blatant invitation in the waitress's smile. When he didn't, the waitress distributed the rest of the order.

"You gonna quit now?" Silence fell over the table after Bobby Lee's question.

Brand drummed the fingers of his free hand on the table. "Might. If I can find a place I can run by myself."

"Tired of taking orders, huh? How many brothers you got back home bossin' you around?" Bobby Lee asked.

"Too many, and damn straight, I'm tired of taking orders. Between them and my dad the ranch is at least a decade behind the times." Brand raised his glass.

Bobby Lee grinned. "How about if I send some of my sisters down to meet your brothers? I know Mom and Dad would be happy to have at least a couple of 'em out of the house."

Toni grimaced into her glass. She knew genetics, and this wasn't good news. If Bobby Lee came from a predominantly female family, her chances of having a son with him were slimmer than say…if she bedded a fella with brothers. A major hitch in her plan.

She couldn't think of an alternative—couldn't think period, because from shoulder to knee, Brand lived up to his name. Surely, there would be singe marks along her side. She tried to move so that at least some part of her wasn't plastered against lean, hard cowboy.

Another cowboy hailed them from across the room. He joined the group, squeezing into the booth. The gap she'd fought to put between her and Brand vanished. To make matters worse, Brand hooked his arm around her shoulder and pulled her even closer. She held her breath and arched as far away as possible.

Distracted by the strength of the hand cupping her shoulder and the cinnamony breath stirring the curls on her neck, Toni missed nearly all of the names bandied about. Hyperventilation threatened. She tried to shrug him off.

The thickheaded devil gave her a squeeze and shifted his fingers to massage her neck with a deft touch. "Loosen up. You've got knots the size of my fist back here."

Her traitorous spine nearly melted. Toni lifted her glass and downed half of the cloudy liquid. It burned going down like no iced tea she'd ever had. Maybe the water was different in Vegas? She sniffed the glass. Was that bourbon in her drink or was it the beefy guy's breath? He was drooling over her cleavage again. She put an elbow in his ribs.

Nursing her drink, she searched for a way out of her predicament. Should she risk fouling up the plan with Bobby Lee or look for another sperm donor with a predominantly male family?

One like Brand.

No, no, no, he was definitely not what she was looking for. No doubt he'd make the ordeal ahead memorable— heaven knows his fingers on her nape were addling her brain—but something in those sharp eyes of his told her he didn't have a careless bone in his body, despite his profession. He wouldn't forget something as important as protection. She set her glass down. It rattled against the table. What a mess. Her ranch was on the line and her hormones were in an uproar for *the wrong man.*

She'd loved dear old Gramps, and she missed him terribly, but he'd landed her in a mess. Under the terms of Gramps's will she could lose her legacy, her sanctuary, land that had been in her family for generations, because she was female. Her grandfather had insisted a male inherit. A husband or a child. Toni had neither. She loved kids, but a husband…no way.

What if she ended up with a husband like her father, who had proved his point with his fists, or one who'd take the ranch from her if the marriage failed? Her lawyer had joked during their hasty phone call that settling the estate would be a lot easier if Toni were pregnant. The idea had taken off like a wild pony and led her here. She'd do anything to hold on to the one place where she'd always felt safe—even sleep with a stranger.

The beefy guy winked and leered. "I'm a calf roper, sweetheart. I'm fast with a rope and good with my hands. I like to tie 'em up."

From the gleam in his eyes she didn't think he meant just calves. She scowled at him over her glass. Brand glared and the man shrank back.

"You left." Brand's whiskey-rough voice murmured in her ear.

Toni choked on her drink and jerked her head around to find dark eyes just inches from her own. She wheezed. Brand patted then stroked her back. The fire licking up her vertebrae had nothing whatsoever to do with the liquid she'd consumed.

"You mean you didn't see Brand ride?" somebody at the table asked before she could catch her breath. Or her wits.

The hovering waitress offered Toni a sympathetic smile. "Probably couldn't stand it, could you, sugar?"

Somehow these people were under the impression that she and Brand were a couple. Since he was wrapped around her like kudzu, it wasn't a far-out conclusion. To get any closer, he'd have to be a tattoo. If she wanted to end the night in bed with Bobby Lee, she had to straighten them out. "Look—"

"What'd you say your name was?" the silicone woman asked.

"Ah…Toni. But—"

"Brand's sure kept you a secret," she interrupted.

"That's because—"

Brand put a finger to her lips. "We wanted to lock ourselves in the hotel room once the rodeo was over. Not coming out for a week." His waggling brows drew snickers from his friends.

Stunned, Toni swiveled. The damned devil had just ruined everything. He snatched his finger away before she could bite him. "What did you say?"

He grinned. "Sorry, I let the cat out of the bag. I'd get down on my knees and beg you to take me on up to bed, darlin', but it'd be kind of painful. Caught one of 'em on the gate."

His eyes weren't black, she discovered. They were the color of dark Godiva chocolate with lighter flecks of milk chocolate drizzled over the top. Good thing Godiva was out of her price range. Chocolate was the one thing she couldn't resist.

"You…I…" The tug of an unwanted attraction erased whatever she'd been trying to say. She closed her eyes. *Too big. Too strong. The mission.*

"You're right. I should've kept our secret." He shrugged his impossibly wide shoulders and stroked a calloused finger over her cheek. Toni turned into a vessel of rampant hormones. What was it about him that did this to her? "I'm just a dumb cowboy, darlin'."

His humility was patently insincere. She stifled the urge to dump the rest of her drink in his lap and pressed the cold glass to the fire he'd left on her cheek. If he'd wanted to spoil her chances with the other cowboys, he couldn't have chosen a better way than marking her as his. Even if she could ditch this irritating bull jockey, she no longer stood a chance with Bobby Lee or any other man at the table—except maybe the beefy calf roper. She grimaced and downed the remainder of her drink. She might be desperate, but she wasn't that desperate. She wanted a few words with this Brand character for screwing up her carefully thought-out plan. *"Out!"*

"You're wanting to test the mattress already?" Innocence personified, Brand batted his ridiculously lush eyelashes.

She'd kill him. "Let me out!"

"All right, darlin', but it's no rush. We've got all night." Capturing an errant curl, he twined it around his finger and added in a sexy whisper, "I promise I'll be worth the wait."

Fury vibrated through her. Awareness made it difficult to think. Damn the devil's sorry hide. She shoved him hard enough to move a horse. Brand didn't budge, but her fingers ended up buried in his chest. His firm, warm muscles contracted beneath her fingertips and Toni felt an insane urge to dig in. "I said, let me out."

"Well, folks, the li'l lady wants me naked. Thanks for

the party, but drinks are on me tonight.'' Brand stood, pulled out his wallet, and tossed a couple of hundred-dollar bills on the table. He tipped his hat, then grabbed Toni's hand and tugged her out of the bar to a chorus of raucous comments.

Cursing him under her breath, she stumbled after him. Her knees seemed to be working without direction from her head and when he stopped she fell into him. She wasn't drunk, but she was as close to it as she'd ever been in her entire life.

''Are you crazy?'' She planted her feet in the lobby.

''It's not me that's crazy, darlin'. You're eyeing Bobby Lee like a starving dog eyes a bone. He's not on the menu.''

Was this macho jerk in the tacky shirt calling her a dog? She ought to kick him in the—

''He's engaged and staying that way.'' Another group of cowboys burst through the front door of the hotel. One called his name. Brand swore and scooped her into his arms.

Her head spun. Afraid he'd drop her, Toni clung to his broad shoulders. He didn't stop moving until they were behind a bank of plants beside the elevators. The doors pinged open. Brand ducked inside and dropped her legs. She slid against him until her feet touched the floor. Toni couldn't turn him loose. The elevator whisked upward, leaving her stomach behind. Grasping his thick leather belt, she struggled for balance. She lifted her head to give him a piece of her mind, but choked back the words when the doors opened again. Several couples crowded inside.

One of the men gestured to the unlit numbers on the panel. ''Which floor?''

Toni gave her floor number automatically and immediately regretted it when Brand gave her a smug smile. Fine. She'd take him to her room, tear a strip off his obnoxiously overconfident hide, then she'd go back downstairs and do what she had to do. If she couldn't have Bobby Lee, there were a dozen other cowboys to choose from. With any luck she'd find one with an abundance of brothers.

She'd bet the ranch—and essentially that was what she was doing—that she could find a cowboy who'd let her have things her way. One who would be careless. And she'd start looking for him just as soon as she ditched this hardheaded bull rider.

The doors opened and Toni stepped out. Brand caught her elbow and followed closer than her shadow until she stopped in front of her door. With an irritated glare over her shoulder, Toni tried to stuff the key card through the slot but her hands were shaking too much. Brand took the card from her and reached around her to insert it into the lock. He crowded her, enclosing her in his scent, his heat. When he opened the door, Toni raced through, praying Brand wouldn't follow.

No such luck.

Two

Brand followed the hell-bent angel into her room, unable to stop himself from admiring the delicious curve of her backside in the tight dress and the first-class set of legs below the short hem. He blew a silent whistle. Toni might be petite, but everything was in the right place.

She wanted sex. No doubt about it. A woman didn't dress in fabric tight enough to reveal the dimple of her navel if she didn't want a guy to go peeling it off her. *Real slow.* His fingers flexed in anticipation, but he reined in his maverick thoughts. He wasn't here for a horizontal two-step.

Evidently, she had a thing for bull riders. He'd seen and resisted women like her dozens of times over the past ten years. Buckle bunnies weren't his thing, but for once, he wished they were, because this one…. Whew. Pure temptation.

He nudged back his hat and scratched his brow. So why in the hell had he followed her up here? Was his pride tweaked because she'd ignored him? Probably. Women usually swarmed him like flies on a fresh cowpie. Was it the need to let off some steam after winning his fourth world championship? Nah, if that was the case he wouldn't have left his friends in the bar.

Was he really trying to save Bobby Lee from her clutches? He had a soft spot for the kid who reminded him a lot of his youngest brother. Bobby Lee had the same idealistic view of life, the same certainty that everybody was a kindhearted soul. He'd be easy prey for a woman on the make, regardless of his fiancée, and Toni had all the markings of a woman on the make.

Brand rubbed the prickle at the back of his neck. He had a feeling he was here for purely selfish reasons. Like the need to taste her lips. Were they as soft as they'd looked before she smeared that red lipstick on 'em? Or was it the need to test the silkiness of the magnolia skin she'd hidden beneath a truckload of makeup? His hands tingled with the need to take the pins from her buttery curls and feel them drag across his bare chest. He wondered if the heady scent of dew-covered roses was stronger between her breasts, between her legs.

He wanted her, dammit, in a way he'd never wanted before.

She stalked halfway across the room and back. A pint-size bundle of dynamite. He'd swear that beneath all the stuff on her face, her cheeks were flushed. Her breasts rose and fell swiftly, nearly bursting from the low neckline of her dress. Brand hoped she'd breathe a little harder.

She flung her tiny purse onto the sofa and parked her clenched fists on her hips. "You are a total jerk."

Not exactly the invitation to her bed he'd expected, but he could handle 'em feisty. He fought a grin. "Who me?"

"You. You've ruined everything with your buttinsky ways."

She sounded near tears. Brand's heart twisted. He couldn't stand a woman crying. "Look, darlin'—"

"I am not your darlin'. You are not what I'm looking for, and I want you to get lost." She paced to the window and back.

Tears streaked mascara down her cheeks.

"Look, dar—" She sucked a sharp breath and almost popped out of the dress, distracting him so much he nearly missed her glare. He pulled off his hat and tossed it onto the dresser, then shoved his hands through his hair. "Ah, Toni? Bobby Lee's a good kid. He wouldn't know how to handle a woman like you."

"And I suppose you would?" She wiped a hand across her face, smearing her mascara in an inch-wide trail. When she caught sight of the black on the back of her hand, she gave a startled cry and looked in the mirror. Cussing like a cowboy, she hustled toward the bathroom.

The lady had an interesting vocabulary. Brand shook his head. Over his chuckles, he heard water running. When Toni came back into the room, her smooth skin was free of makeup. She still wore the hooker's dress, and her hair still looked like she'd spent a long, hot night in some lucky man's bed.

"Go. Away." She sank onto the edge of the bed and buried her face in her hands. "I have something to do tonight, and you're messing it up."

Brand studied the defeated droop of her shoulders. "If I leave, are you going back downstairs?"

Her shoulders squared and she lifted her chin. When she met his gaze it was pure grit and determination he saw in her baby blues. He wondered what put it there. "I have to."

He ought to leave, but he couldn't seem to get his feet to head out the door. Against his better judgment, Brand sat beside her on the bed and twined a curl around his finger. He tugged until her lips were within an inch of his. "And if I don't go?"

Her eyes rounded. He heard her breath catch and his did the same. It locked in his chest with a painful burn. She exhaled, her breath sweeping across his lips like a butterfly wing. Brand's head spun. His heart and groin throbbed in tandem. He wanted to blame it on the drink he'd had downstairs, but Toni'd had him on his ear back at the arena when she hadn't been wearing a bucket of makeup, and he'd been stone-cold sober.

"You should leave." Her voice was a whisper, but her eyes focused on his mouth. His lips tingled, anticipating the kiss he couldn't do without. Brand traced a path from her silky shoulder to her slender wrist with a surprisingly unsteady hand. He captured her fingers and spread them over his pounding heart.

"Yep, but I sure don't want to." He tugged the curl, closing the distance between her lips and his. Soft as a rosebud. Sweet as a sugar cube. She hit him like the dose of pure oxygen the medics gave after a nasty toss. He brushed her lips once, twice. Already he was addicted to the taste of her. He had to be out of his mind because there was no way he was leaving.

"Darlin', there's nothing you can find downstairs that I can't give you."

She drew back and studied him for several unblinking moments. Unshed tears glistened in her eyes. And secrets. Brand drew back a fraction.

"You married?" He wouldn't sleep with another man's woman.

Her eyes widened. "No."

"Me, neither. And I don't aim to get that way. Ever." She swallowed, then nodded. "Me, neither."

Brand pulled a pin from her hair. When she offered no resistance, he threaded his fingers through the silky strands, removing the rest of the pins and dropping them on the floor. The fat curls wrapped around his wrist and tumbled over her shoulders as he ran his fingers through the tangles. Her head lolled back, baring her throat.

Brand bent and pressed his lips to the rapidly beating pulse at the base of her neck. If he had good sense he'd get the hell out of here. His good sense wasn't listening. "You know what I want, don't you, Toni?"

He drew back to look at her flushed face. Her lids lifted slowly. Desire slumbered in her eyes. She nodded and moistened her lips.

"I want to make love to you. I want to taste every inch of you, starting right here." Brand nipped her earlobe. She pulled in a shuddery breath then exhaled on a sigh. He stroked his palm across her smooth cheek. She nuzzled into it. "You want that, too?"

"Yes."

Brand felt a moment's hesitation at the surprise in her voice. If she hadn't wanted him, then why had she brought him to her room? She pressed her lips to his palm and suddenly, it didn't matter. Tugging his wallet from his jeans, he withdrew a string of foil packets and tossed them on the bed. He'd picked 'em up for one of the other guys, but…tough.

Toni's mouth opened then closed, as if she'd had something to say then changed her mind. She fisted a hand in his shirt. Brand forgot all reason and lowered his head.

He overwhelmed her with his soft, experimental kisses. Toni thought she'd turn into a blazing inferno if he did that thing with his tongue again. He did and she nearly combusted on the spot. Alarmed by her body's enthusiastic response, Toni pushed him away and stared at him. What she was doing was wrong. She shouldn't enjoy it this much, but the way he made her feel was…incredible. He was so gentle and yet his hunger for her was unmistakable.

"Easy, darlin'. Take it easy." Brand nuzzled her neck, and nibbled on her collarbone.

Breathless, Toni grasped for sanity, for control. Her fingers tangled in his hair. When his tongue traced the neckline of her dress her reasons for resisting toppled like a row of dominos. She forgot about holding back. Instead she arched her back and held him close. "Oh…Brand."

He caught the fabric in his teeth and tugged it down to

reveal her strapless black satin bra. Afraid he'd be disappointed because the bra promised more of her than there actually was, Toni tried to cover herself. He caught her wrists.

"I need to taste you, Toni. In the worst kind of way."

She hesitated, but the desire blazing in his eyes convinced her to lower her hands. She felt peculiar, as if every nerve ending she possessed hungered for his touch. He scorched her mouth with another incendiary kiss.

"Zipper?"

She shook her head.

"I just peel it off?"

"Mmmmm."

Suiting word to deed, he scrunched the dress around her waist. With a flick of his fingers, the bra dropped. He cupped her breasts, thumbing her nipples. Sparklers blazed from his calloused hands straight to her womb. Toni closed her eyes and let her head fall back. The man had magical hands.

"You can touch me, too." He pulled his shirttails from his pants and yanked the snapped placket apart. Within seconds, the shirt lay on the floor.

Brand had a marvelous chest. A smattering of dark hair dusted his clearly defined pectorals and bisected his taut belly. Toni reached for him, then drew back, afraid her touch would unleash the animal in him. She'd been this far before and been scared out of her wits by her partner's loss of control. She'd ended up locked in the bathroom until he'd gone home.

Brand caught her hand and pressed it to his breast. A flat male nipple prodded her palm like a branding iron. He closed his eyes and inhaled deeply. "Oh, yeah."

His touch remained gentle. He didn't go wild and crush her into the mattress. Tentatively, she tunneled her nails through the dark curls, testing the texture, and loving the way the hairs tickled her palms.

He hissed and pulled her hand away. "Maybe we better wait till next time for that."

Brand didn't give her time to ask why. He bent her over his arm and captured a nipple in his mouth, suckling until she squirmed on the bed. He transferred his attention to her other breast. Like a content cat she clawed the sheets, his hair, his back—not to get free, but in ecstasy. When his lips left her breasts to travel down her abdomen in the wake of her dress she nearly cried. Then the dress was gone and she lay before him in nothing but thigh-high stockings, tiny panties and spike heels.

His gaze poured over her like melted chocolate, evaporating her momentary flash of nerves. Brand made her feel desirable. Sexy. Needy. He stood and leaned against the wall. He shucked one boot, then the other. His socks followed. When his hands fell to his championship belt buckle, Toni closed her eyes. Watching the man undress was more excitement than she could bear. Fabric rustled. Something heavy hit the floor.

Her mouth watered. Her skin tingled. Anticipation of what he'd do to her next left her panting. *You shouldn't be enjoying this.* The thought scattered with the touch of his lips on her ankle. She opened her eyes to find him kneeling beside the bed. Naked. This is where she should panic, but Brand did nothing to alarm her. He removed her shoes, rolled down her stockings, then gently eased her thighs apart. He tasted his way past her calf, her knee, her thigh, to the part of her screaming for his attention. She knew what he planned to do, had read about it in one of her college roommate's erotic novels. She'd even touched herself, but nothing, *nothing* could prepare her for the lightning strike of his tongue. She cried out and slapped a hand over her mouth.

He nipped her thigh. "Don't. I want to hear you scream."

"I—I don't scream." Not in pain or in pleasure.

"You will and you'll love it." He sucked the point of

her desire into his mouth and set her off. Roman candles careened through her bloodstream, and she promptly proved his words.

"That's it, darlin'. Now let's see if you can do it again."

She did, several times. Brand knelt on the bed and reached for a condom. By then, Toni didn't care that he was preventing the very thing she sought. Nor did she fear the size of his enormous erection. Hungrily, she reached for him. He braced himself above her to plunder her mouth, but it wasn't enough. Toni wrapped her legs around his waist and urged him on. Thus far, he'd been gentle, but she no longer needed gentle. He'd done something to her, freed something inside her that she didn't understand.

"Easy, darlin'." He nibbled her ear and the cords of her neck. "We have all night."

"Now."

He chuckled. "Yes, ma'am."

With one deep thrust, he filled her. Toni arched off the bed at the unexpected stab of pain. She'd ridden horses before she walked. She hadn't thought there'd be any sign of her innocence left.

Brand bowed back in surprise. Rolling over without disconnecting their bodies, he cradled her against his chest and stroked her back, her hair. "Relax. Let me know when you're ready."

His sensitivity to her discomfort amazed her. The pain receded and the hunger resumed. Beneath her ear, Brand's chest rose and fell rapidly, his heart raced, but he didn't force her. Tentatively, Toni shifted.

Brand sucked in a sharp breath. His jaw clenched, his hands tightened on her waist. "Good to go?"

"Yeah."

"I wish I could promise you slow, darlin', but—" he shook his head "—you've got me triggered."

He lifted her and eased her back down, filling her again and again. Toni picked up the rhythm until she couldn't move fast enough to satisfy the need in her. When her legs gave out Brand flipped her over and rose above her as they raced toward completion. Toni imploded and Brand followed.

She lay there for a moment trying to figure out how she could have given up control and loved every minute of it. The man had her pinned to the bed. Why wasn't she clawing her way out from under him? Her eyelids grew heavy and she stretched like a satisfied cat. She'd figure out why in a minute…or ten.

Brand rolled to her side. He nuzzled her forehead and kissed her brow. One calloused palm skated down her spine to cup her bottom. He whispered into her ear, "Woman, you ought to be wearing a warning sign."

Toni fell asleep with a smile on her lips.

Her head pounded. Cotton wool filled her mouth. For several seconds, Toni considered burrowing into the warmth behind her and going back to sleep. *Warmth? In December?*

Cautiously, she opened her eyes. A muscle-corded arm pinned her to the mattress. Her heart jolted in panic. Oh, God, she'd done it. Nausea swirled in her stomach. She clapped a hand over her mouth, then checked to make sure she hadn't woken her oblivious partner in crime. Brand. *Brand who?* She didn't even know the man's last name. Shame swept through her.

She eased from beneath the tanned hand cupping her breast. Keeping a wary eye on the occupant of the bed, she gathered jeans and a shirt from the back of the chair. Her bedmate rolled to his back, throwing his arms wide. Toni jumped, but relaxed when his eyes remained closed.

Rumpled hair. Stubble-darkened chin. Thick thighs and muscular calves tangled in the twisted linens. Against her will, her eyes swept over his broad chest and down his flat stomach to the corner of the tumbled sheets covering the crucial parts. She didn't need visuals to remember the silken hard flesh which had brought her so much pleasure

throughout the night or to recall how gentle those big calloused hands had been each time he'd reached for her.

Squeezing her eyes shut, Toni swallowed hard. *Mission
accomplished.* The knowledge gave her no satisfaction.
She'd done the unthinkable to hold on to the ranch. *And
she'd enjoyed every single sinful moment of it.* What kind
of woman did that make her?

She crept into the bathroom and pulled on her clothes,
then studied the woman in the mirror. Other than the reddish mark on her neck and the panic in her eyes, she
looked the same, nothing like a woman who'd seduce a
man into forgetting to use a condom. She stuffed her tooth-
brush and paste into her bag because she didn't want to
risk waking the cowboy by running the water. She had to
leave before Brand awoke. She could barely face herself.
She knew she couldn't face him. What she'd done last
night contradicted her moral beliefs. She'd shared her body
with a stranger and stolen something more personal than
money from him. Something much more important.

Easing open the bathroom door, Toni peeked into the
room. On the floor beside the bed, her clothes and his
embraced each other, as tangled together as their bodies
had been last night. Her womb tightened with the memory
of the way Brand had tutored her. Her one-night cowboy
had made a tawdry night beautiful. For that, she'd never
forget him.

How could she have enjoyed it? She cursed her wanton
soul. How could she have forgotten—even for one second—why she was doing what she'd done? She felt a moment's regret for what might have been had they met under
other circumstances. But no, she didn't want to give a man
control of her life again. She'd learned the hard way that
nothing was more important than independence.

Still, there was a heaviness in her heart over how she'd
used the man in the rumpled bed. He didn't deserve it. It
didn't matter that the ranch was the only place she'd felt

safe in her life. She'd used Brand, and now she intended to toss him aside.

Toni hefted her suitcase. Tears burned her throat. It was too late for regrets. She opened the door and stopped cold. Brand's face stared up at her from the front page of the complimentary newspaper lying on the floor outside her door. She held her breath and picked up the paper. The pages rattled in her hand.

Brand Leaves His Mark in Vegas, the caption above the photo said. Toni's hand fluttered to her heart as she read the article below.

Brandon Lander clinched his fourth world championship in bull riding last night. The twenty-eight-year-old cowboy from McMullen County, Texas, has been on a hot streak during the finals. He not only rode all ten bulls, but his final ride on Detonator, a bounty bull unridden all season, netted him a twenty-five-thousand-dollar bonus.

Friends close to Lander say the champ is considering retirement. Lander could not be reached for comment, but turning his back on the sport could cost him a bundle. His endorsements alone total well into the six-figure range.

"Brand's a friend and mentor to a lot of us younger guys," says Bobby Lee Garrison, a fellow competitor and son of Democratic Senator Garrison from Oklahoma. "What he don't know about a bull ain't worth knowing. He's got years of good riding ahead of him."

Toni clutched the paper to her chest. She'd made a huge mistake. Not only had she ended up with a take-charge kind of cowboy, she'd picked a famous one who lived less than two hundred miles from her grandfather's ranch. Of course, Bobby Lee, a senator's son, would have been worse.

She ran for the elevator as fast as she could. She'd known Brand was trouble from the moment she'd laid eyes on him. He'd drawn her attention from the job at hand. She should have steered clear. She should have known better.

She should have stuck with her plan. Damn. Double damn. She punched the call button again and paced beside the elevators. She'd wanted a rootless man who wouldn't care that he'd forgotten to use protection that last time. She had a feeling Brand wasn't likely to forget.

She'd had every intention of kicking him out last night and going back downstairs to find someone else, but with one kiss, Brand had changed her mind. She was twenty-six years old and had been kissed quite a few times, but she'd only gotten close to becoming intimate with one man. He'd scared her to death by turning into a rabid octopus after a couple of hot kisses and hurt her in his enthusiasm. When she'd asked him to stop he'd turned nasty. She'd decided intimacy wasn't worth the risk.

She hadn't been afraid last night.

Toni squashed the thought. The elevator doors opened and she leaped inside. When Brand didn't appear before the doors closed, she sagged against the wall. Her grandfather's ranch had never seemed more like a refuge. She couldn't wait to get to the only real home she'd ever known.

Brand awoke with a smile on his face. He snuggled deeper into the pillow, inhaling Toni's scent. Damned if the sweet little angel hadn't worn him out. He hadn't been able to get enough of her, nor she of him it seemed. Her hungry kisses and sexy little mews had kept him hard all night.

His chest expanded with pride that she'd allowed him to be her first lover. He'd done his best to make sure she didn't regret it. Despite his concern that she'd be sore, she'd been hungry for him again and again. They'd made love more times than…Brand rocketed up in the bed.

More times than he'd had condoms. "Hell."

The space beside him was empty. Toni's dress lay crumpled on the floor where he'd tossed it. He threw back the covers and stalked into the bathroom to find her. The bathroom was empty and her junk wasn't on the counter. A knot formed in his gut. Swearing, he returned to the bedroom. Her suitcase was gone. With his heart pounding, Brand grabbed the phone and dialed the front desk.

"Miss Swenson checked out."

Brand clenched his fist and rubbed his forehead. "She forgot to leave me a forwarding address. Could you get that for me?"

"I'm not at liberty to release that information, sir."

"Lady, I'm calling from her room. She'd want me to have her address."

"I'm sorry, sir."

Slamming the phone down, he jabbed his hands through his hair and yanked on his clothes. "Ow, ow, ow." He rubbed his tender knee and threw his boot across the room. It hit the wall with a satisfying thunk. He'd been had. How many times had he warned the younger guys about just such a thing? And he'd been stupid enough to forget protection at least once.

From the beginning, he'd thought the woman was on a quest. He'd seen the determination in her eyes and the set of her delicate chin. But had he paid attention? *Hell, no.* It had been a damn long time since he'd had a woman, and he'd let his hormones lead him straight into trouble.

What did she want? Money? He pulled out his wallet and counted the stack of bills. All there. No, that didn't make sense, anyway. If she'd wanted money, why had she been gunning for Bobby Lee? Why not him? With all his endorsements, he was worth a hell of a lot more than Bobby Lee. He pulled on his boots. Maybe it wasn't

money she was after. More than one of Bobby Lee's relatives held an elected office. Did she want to cause a po-
litical scandal? Brand scrubbed a hand over his beard-
stubbled face and cradled his head. She hadn't gone to bed
with Bobby Lee.

What in the hell did it mean? What did she want?

Shoving his hat on his pounding head, Brand let himself
into the hall. Too antsy to wait for the elevator, he headed
for the stairs, banged-up knee and all. Ignoring the pain,
he raced to his own room three floors up and burst through
the door.

"Wha— What is it?" Bobby Lee sat up in bed and eyed
him groggily. Man, the kid didn't even need to shave every
morning. What could she have wanted with such an innocent?

"Have you heard from Toni this morning?"

Bobby Lee blushed and studied the sheets. "Nah, I
thought she was…that you had…you were, like together."

"We were. I need a private detective." Brand started
flinging off his clothes as he headed for the bathroom.

"What for?" The kid rubbed his eyes like a two-year-
old.

Naked, Brand paused in the bathroom doorway. "Toni
lit out of here. I need to find her."

"She steal your wallet or something?"

Brand's stomach clenched and bile burned the back of
his throat. She'd taken more than his possessions. The
woman was carrying his seed. It was a damned old-
fashioned way of thinking, but he was going to track her
down and make sure that he hadn't made her pregnant. If
he had… He rubbed his face. If he had, then the Lander
family history was going to repeat itself. "Or something."

Bobby stretched his bowlegged, bony frame. "My dad
has a P.I. he uses every now and then. She'll find your
man, uh, woman."

Bobby Lee talked to his father and scribbled across a
piece of hotel stationery. He hung up the phone and passed

the paper to Brand. "You gonna marry her once you find her?"

To Bobby Lee, sex and marriage went hand in hand. Brand hated to disillusion the kid. Why had he gone to bed with Toni? He hadn't intended to. He'd just wanted to spoil her chances with any other slobbering cowboy. Now there was the possibility of a pregnancy. And marriage. He headed for the shower.

"Damned if I know, kid."

Three

Toni drove from Vegas to her apartment. After a few fretful hours sleep she loaded her belongings into a rented trailer and turned in her keys. If things went according to plan, she was going home to the Rocking A for good. No more packing or hiding.

She refused to consider the possibility that she might have failed in her mission. After what she'd done, she had to be pregnant with Brand Lander's child. A son, she hoped. A daughter wouldn't be loved any less, but it wouldn't solve her problem. Her stomach lurched. The next few weeks were going to be an agony of waiting to confirm the pregnancy and there'd be an even longer wait to see if she carried a dark-haired boy with irresistible Godiva-chocolate eyes.

Toni took the fork in the driveway that led past Granddad's house and parked in the rear. Only company parked out front. With a satisfied sigh she turned off the car. Home, at last.

Matthews, her grandfather's foreman, came out to meet the car. Toni wondered at his weaving gait until he exhaled. The man was drunk at ten o'clock in the morning? Two more hands stumbled out of the bunkhouse, neither looking any more sober.

Their scowls made her feel about as welcome as a swarm of mosquitoes. She summarized her conversation with the lawyer—less a few personal details. "So, I'm moving in."

"We know how things is run round here. Don't you fret yer little head about it, girlie. Me an' the boys'll handle it. Jus' like we been doing since the old man dropped dead."

Toni flinched at the foreman's callous remark. "Would you help me unload the trailer?"

Matthews spit out a wad of chewing tobacco. "We got business to tend to." He turned on his heel and left. The hands followed.

Dumbfounded, Toni stared after them. Things weren't starting out well, but at least she was home. Hefting a box, she lugged it from the tiny U-Haul trailer to the screened back porch. She pulled open the door and propped it with the box. An unclean smell assaulted her.

Beau, the old basset hound her grandfather had given her the summer before she'd gone off to college, rolled off his bed in the corner and lethargically crossed the porch to greet her. Toni dropped to her knees and hugged the dog. His less-than-enthusiastic response concerned her. He usually greeted her with an eardrum-splitting howl.

"Beau? What's the matter, boy? Aren't you glad to see me?" Toni stroked his head then studied his dull brown eyes and dry nose. His ribs showed through his coat. "Beau?"

The dog tried to bark, but only a scratchy sound emerged. Toni glanced at his food and water bowls. Both were empty. Judging by the condition of the back porch the men hadn't let Beau out often enough. She clenched her jaw.

"Are you thirsty?" The black tail thumped once. "Hungry?" The tail tweaked again. "Well, let's see what we can find."

Stepping into the kitchen was like coming home. After filling the dog's bowls, Toni stood back and watched Beau lap the water as if he hadn't had any in days. Anger spiraled inside her. The lawyer had assured her the hands would take care of things. Toni felt another flash of anger over such cruelty.

By the time she'd finished cleaning the porch and unpacking her trailer, she was too tired to study the ranch journals. The stress of the day and two nearly sleepless nights had caught up with her. Exhausted, Toni crawled between the sheets of the bed she'd used since childhood. And dreamed anything but childish dreams about a dark-haired cowboy.

Toni sprang out of bed, looking forward to her first day in charge of the Rocking A. After hustling through breakfast, she rushed out the back door. A much happier and healthier Beau greeted her with a howl and a swinging tail.

"You look better today, boy." He'd damned well better. She'd have shot someone if Beau hadn't responded to the TLC she'd given him yesterday. "Feel like a walk?"

Beau woofed and followed Toni on her survey of the property. In the bright sunlight everything looked faded, run-down. Yesterday she'd been so thrilled to be here she hadn't noticed the disrepair of the buildings. "Oh, Granddad," she moaned.

The sense of loss overwhelmed her. Toni sank down on a bale of hay and let the tears go. She missed coffee on the back porch with Gramps. Missed hearing him hand out orders to the crew from the stoop. Missed the challenge of tagging along and trying not to get caught. The corner of her mouth turned up. He'd always insisted she stay in the compound surrounding the house and outbuildings, but Toni had loved the open spaces. She'd tailed him like a faithful Indian scout.

With her crew nowhere to be found, Toni and Beau headed for the barn. She greeted and fed one horse, then another. The horses had been neglected almost as badly as the dog. They needed a farrier and a vet. She'd call the farrier to tend the hooves. With Granddad's journals and her veterinary training, she didn't doubt for one moment that she could run this ranch, and she was eager to get started. Whistling for Beau, she jogged back to the house to go over the books.

Hours later Toni slumped in the leather office chair. The books looked bad. The ranch didn't have a mortgage, but the amount of cash in the account was pitifully small. There'd be no income from selling cattle for months. She pulled the calculator forward and went through the records once more, figuring her monthly expenses and hoping she'd miscalculated.

Brand climbed into his truck. It had taken a long, frustrating week for the P.I. to get two names and addresses in his hands. He'd filled the time by giving interviews and shooting ads for his sponsors, but his mind wasn't on his work. His thoughts were with the woman who'd made him forget his number-one rule. Don't fool around on the road. And his second rule. If you're stupid enough to fool around, don't do it without taking precautions.

He read the slip of paper in his hand. Antonia Allison Swenson had an apartment near the A & M campus, but the address she'd used at the hotel belonged to a Will Anderson, recently deceased, of the Rocking A Ranch in Texas. Brand started the engine then drummed his fingers on the steering wheel. Where would she be? Her apartment or the Rocking A? He headed south. Arizona and New Mexico blew by in a blur of traffic and hastily eaten truck-stop meals.

What had Toni wanted from him? he asked himself again. She didn't have the look or the experience of a buckle bunny who wanted to start sleeping with cowboys for no other reason than to add another notch to her lipstick case. To be rid of her virginity? Nah, there'd been genuine hunger in her eyes and in her touch. He wasn't bragging to admit that much. *So what did she want?* It irritated him that he hadn't figured it out by the time he crossed the Texas state line. He pulled into a fast-food place, hoping caffeine and food would fuel his brain.

Had she been as caught up in their lovemaking as he'd been and simply forgotten to use protection the last time? Or did she want to get pregnant? The thought exploded into his head with the subtlety of a grenade. She wouldn't be the first female to try that trick, but it didn't make sense. If she'd wanted to get pregnant why pick on a kid like Bobby Lee?

It hit Brand like a sucker punch that he'd been second choice. She'd wanted Bobby Lee, but she'd settled for him. His ego staggered. He tossed his half-eaten burger into the trash. "Why are you so determined to find a woman who used and ditched you, fool?"

Because she might be pregnant, you irresponsible idiot.

He'd never been careless before, and didn't aim to start now. Not when he was so close to his dream of getting out of this career he hadn't wanted and into one he did. His heart wasn't in the rodeo. Never had been. Gold buckle or no, he'd considered making this his last year of competition. He was sick of living out of a suitcase. Tired of having no place to call home. Crooked Creek, the family ranch, didn't count. There, he was no more than an unpaid hand. He did what he was told and had no say in the operation. His father and his oldest brother, Caleb, made all the decisions. He needed more than that.

But he'd be damned if there'd be a little Lander wandering around that he didn't know about. He'd seen it happen to his buddies. A cowboy rode into town, celebrated with a lady and lit out for the next rodeo. Sooner or later, the guy got a registered letter demanding child support or a female demanding a golden ring. It had happened to his older brother and to a few of his friends, but it wasn't going to happen to him. He didn't aim to give it all away because of one foolish night.

It had been one hell of a night. His groin throbbed with remembered passion. Good night or not, if he'd made a kid he was responsible for it. No kid of his would be dumped like garbage.

Muttering a chorus of cuss words, he pulled the truck back onto the highway. The Rocking A Ranch was on his way home. He'd stop and see if Toni was staying at her grandfather's place. If she wasn't, he'd head on to her apartment. On second thoughts, he'd call. Pulling off the highway at the next exit, Brand located a pay phone and got information to dial the number to her apartment.

"The number you have dialed has been disconnected."

Brand slammed the phone into the cradle and dialed up the Rocking A. No answer. Damn. He hoped like hell she was on the Rocking A or, at least, that somebody there knew where to find her. If not, the P.I. was going to get another chunk of his winnings—the part he'd set aside for one particular bull he was itching to buy.

Toni returned from putting fresh flowers on her grandparents' graves. Generations of Andersons had lived on this land and been laid to rest in the family cemetery. Unless fate was on her side, Grandpa Will could be the last. She stopped abruptly at the sight of the three men loitering in the yard. Obviously, they had no intention of following the instructions she'd handed out this morning. "Is there a problem with fixing the fence in the east pasture?"

Matthews wiped his red nose and pursed his lips around a toothpick. Toni smelled alcohol on his breath again. Either he hadn't sobered up from last night, or the man started drinking at sunrise. She was beginning to believe the latter.

"Nope, but I figure we'll work in the west today. Probably be shifting the herd thataway in a day or two anyhow."

Toni shoved her fists in her pockets and ground her teeth. The man's open defiance this past week had driven her pretty darn close to firing him. If she did, she knew the other hands would follow. She couldn't run the place by herself, so she bit her tongue, then repeated her orders. "As I explained this morning, the west pasture needs reseeding. We'll move the cattle to the east pasture next week after they've been inoculated."

All three of them stared at her as if she hadn't spoken English, then turned toward their horses. Impotent fury made Toni stomp her foot. "I want that fence fixed today, Matthews."

Without acknowledging her orders, the men mounted up and turned their horses west. They hadn't gone more than a few yards when a voice stopped them.

"She said east. You need a compass?"

Toni spun toward the whiskey-rough voice. Her hand fluttered to her throat. Her heart stuttered to a stop, then raced in panic. The heat of humiliation fired her face. She'd stolen from the man and then sneaked off like a rustler in the night. She blinked, hoping this was another one of those dreams that had haunted her nights for the past week, but when she opened her eyes, her one-night cowboy was heading her way.

Brand wore black jeans again, but this time a black-and-teal shirt stretched across the breadth of his chest. A large belt buckle winked in the sun with every long stride that covered the yard. He showed no trace of the injury that had turned his knee black and blue. The unwanted memory of how she'd bathed his bruises with her tongue bloomed in Toni's mind.

She tried to speak, but couldn't. She had no idea what

she'd say anyway. He'd found her. She had no contingency plan for that.

Tipping back his hat with a lean finger, he said, "Hello, darlin'. Miss me?"

Some corner of her mind registered the men muttering about Brand's championship belt buckle, but the majority of her synapses focused on the angry golden sparkles in Brand's eyes and the sarcastic edge to his voice.

His clenched jaw didn't look as if it had seen a razor in days, and he didn't look pleased to see her.

He knew what she'd done.

The knowledge chilled her. How would he react? Would she have to physically defend herself? It wasn't likely that she could count on the clowns behind her to help. She remembered the strength in Brand's thickly muscled arms and her stomach knotted with fear.

A mournful howl came from the back porch. Brand looked away, giving her a chance to gather her thoughts. Toni welcomed the distraction. While Beau approached cautiously to sniff out the visitor, Toni considered her options. Running wasn't one of them, but she didn't know the limits of Brand's anger or how far he'd go to punish someone who'd crossed him.

"Hey, you're the one that just won the finals, ain't ya? What brings you out here? You looking to buy this ranch?"

Brand let the dog sniff and lick his hand before straightening to face the men. "That's between her and me. Now I'd suggest you mend the fence in the east pasture like she said."

Matthews's face darkened and his lips compressed, but he kept his objections to himself. He turned his horse toward the eastern pasture. The men followed.

Toni didn't know whether to be thankful for Brand's help or panicked because he'd tracked her down. Panicked, she decided, because if the hard glint in his eyes was anything to go by, this wasn't going to be pleasant. She wiped her palms on her jeans and swallowed the lump in her throat. "Why are you here?"

He looked her up and down, as if searching out her secret. "We have unfinished business."

Beau parked himself between them, his tail thumping in welcome. Her dog had betrayed her and she couldn't blame him. What she'd done was despicable. Toni studied the man she'd wronged and wondered if he'd understand her motives. When the sun hit his face she noticed he looked drawn and paler than she remembered. His lips, the ones that had caressed every inch of her body, were set in a hard line.

Her heart fluttered in fear. "Come inside."

Brand stepped around the droopy basset hound to follow Toni toward the house. He'd seen her naked, but until now, he'd never seen her butt in a pair of jeans. She had a first-class behind. He turned away from the tempting sight and yanked his ear. His hormones were leading him astray when he needed to hold on to his anger.

The house, like the outbuildings, needed repairs. Beneath one of the sheds sat a tractor with a good portion of its parts spread on the ground beneath its belly. Brand pulled the door of the screened porch open for Toni. It gave an ungodly screech worthy of a horror flick. The dog waddled through and settled with an almighty sigh on a pillow in the corner. Brand was tempted to swipe the scattered bits of tack and the jar of saddle soap from the faded cushions of the old wicker sofa and sleep for a week. Exhaustion pulled at him after countless nights of worrying over this mess he'd gotten himself into. He stepped inside the house. Although it looked clean, it wasn't in much better shape than the outside.

"Sit down." Toni pointed toward the scarred wooden table.

Just ask her and leave. It wouldn't take two minutes to clear this mess up then he could hit the road. Brand removed his hat, hooked it on the rack just inside the door, and sat down. He ran a hand through his hair, suddenly nervous for some damn fool reason. Then he noticed the tired droop of Toni's shoulders and the downward curve of her lips. She looked as ragged as he felt.

She brought him a cup of coffee then perched on the edge of a chair. A second later she jumped back up and paced to the window where she hovered like a hummingbird.

"Why are you here?" Toni asked again as she wrung a dish towel in her hands. Brand could see tension and fear in her eyes, but he couldn't afford to be sympathetic.

"Are you pregnant?" His words came out harshly, baldly, as an accusation. Dammit, he'd meant to lead up to the question with a little more finesse, find out why she'd chosen him.

She flinched and paled, leaning back against the window frame as if she'd fall down without its support. Her eyes shifted away, then back. The hairs on the back of Brand's neck stood up.

"I don't know yet," she whispered. Glancing away again, she bit her lip.

Her words hit him like a blow. Whatever he'd expected to hear, he wasn't prepared for that. He'd expected her to laugh, to tell him he'd been fretting over nothing, that she was on the pill, anything but *that.* "Did you plan it?"

He sucked a slow breath, hoping—praying—she'd deny it. Seconds ticked past, each one like another nail in the coffin holding his dreams. *Deny it,* he pleaded silently.

She stared at the floor then slowly lifted her head. "Yes."

Air gushed from his chest, like blood from an arterial wound. *She was trying to trap him.*

"Why me?" It hurt his throat to say the words. Hell, he ought to give her credit for honesty, but anger at her and disappointment in himself nearly choked him. God help him, he'd thought her different from the other women who used a man for sport. How wrong could he be? Hadn't he learned anything about the true nature of women from his mother and ex-sister-in-law? They wanted to be kept, given a free ride, and they'd lied, cheated and stolen to get it.

He'd thought he was smart enough not to fall into the trap.

She twisted the towel, then tossed it down and squared her shoulders. "Look, I'm sorry for involving you. It wasn't… personal."

His mouth dropped open. He slammed his cup to the table and jumped to his feet, ignoring what looked like fear in her eyes. "Not personal! Lady, I was *inside you* and I'm the only man who's ever been there. That's pretty damned personal."

She held her hands up and backed away a few steps. "I guess I just didn't think it through. I never expected a guy would care as long as I didn't ask for support or anything. I'll sign a paper waiving you of any parental obligations." She turned her head away, but he could still see the blush on her cheek.

"The whole point of going to bed with a stranger…was that he—*you*—weren't supposed to know if there were consequences. And you don't have to know, Brand. Go. Leave. Drive away."

"Not until I know for sure." *And then what will you do, sucker?* Damned if he knew. Other than his little brother, he hadn't been around kids much, didn't even know if he liked 'em. But without a doubt he wouldn't abandon any child of his, not after the way he'd been raised.

He needed time to think, time to plan his next move. No matter what she said he wasn't about to leave. He searched for a safer topic while his mind scrambled for answers. "Your foreman always give you that much trouble?"

The vibrant, feisty angel he'd made love—had sex with—he corrected, had wilted. Toni shifted uneasily, looking fragile enough to break in a gentle breeze. *No sympathy, dammit. The woman has robbed you.*

Toni sighed and wiped a trembling hand across her pale forehead. ''Yeah.''

The tenderness he felt over her vulnerability angered him. It was probably an act.

''Sit down before you fall down.'' Brand pulled out a chair. After a moment's hesitation, Toni collapsed into it. He crossed to the draining rack and picked up a mug. Filling it with the fragrant coffee, he set it on the table and straddled a chair in front of her. ''Why were you trying to get pregnant?''

Toni straightened her spine. Her color came back in a rush. ''It's none of your business.''

Brand leaned forward. ''If it's my kid, it sure as hell is my business.'' She flinched and he realized he'd yelled. He made an effort to soften his voice. ''I'm not leaving, so start talking.''

Her chin lifted to a challenging angle. He expected her to tell him to go to hell any minute, but her gaze fell. He thought she might be pouting, until he saw her chin wobble. ''My grandfather died.''

His heart twisted at the pain in her voice. *No sympathy.* ''Yeah, I know. Sorry.''

Her head jerked up. ''How—''

''I hired a private detective to track you.'' He could tell by the tightening of her lips and the way she strangled her cup that she didn't like that tidbit. ''What's that got to do with what happened in Vegas?''

Again she studied the coffee as if the answers to all her problems resided in the dark brew. ''He wouldn't leave the ranch to me. I'm female.''

''I noticed.'' Sparks shot from her eyes at his sarcasm.

''He didn't believe a woman has any place on a ranch. At least not outside the house. He was…protective.'' She shoved her mug away and fisted her hands on the table. Small, delicate hands, but strong. She'd clenched them in his hair and held him to her breasts. Those slender, short-nailed fingers had dug into his buttocks, raked across his chest and back. A flash of heat ricocheted through him. Brand shot to his feet and paced to the window.

"Granddad wasn't just chauvinistic. He honestly didn't believe I could handle the responsibility of a ranch alone. I'm a vet, for crying out loud, but he didn't think I could manage the herd. Stick to puppies and kitties, he said."

Brand turned with a jerk. Perhaps his angel wasn't the bit of fluff he'd believed. "You're a veterinarian?"

"Yeah. I graduated this past summer. I'd talked to Grandpa before he died, but he never mentioned his plans for the place or I'd have…" She shook her head and gave a dispirited sigh and rubbed her temple. "I have to produce a husband or a male child within the year or the property will be sold."

Her crazy plan was starting to make sense. Brand's gaze dropped to her flat stomach. The mere thought of his child growing inside her made it difficult for him to breathe. "What happens if you're not pregnant or if you have a girl?"

Toni's hands trembled until she clasped them tightly around her mug. "Plan B. I'll hire a temporary husband."

Her words lit the fuse of his anger, but at least she wasn't talking about getting rid of the kid if it was female. "Is this place worth it? You're sacrificing an innocent baby and selling yourself to get your hands on a chunk of dirt and a few run-down buildings. Let me guess, I'd be getting a call in about nine months."

She shot to her feet and glared. The surge of red into her pale cheeks made her look closer to spitting mad than passing out like she had a minute ago. He shouldn't have cared.

"You made your feelings clear in Vegas. I would never call you, Brand. You don't want to be married. Well, neither do I, but I listened to my grandfather spin yarns about this place for as long as I can remember. I know how prosperous it once was and it will be again.'' She jerked her thumb to her chest. ''With me at the helm.

''As for the child...'' Her face and voice softened. ''Boy or girl, I'd love it and do my best for it. How could I do any less?'' She rubbed her temple as if fighting off a headache. ''But life would sure be easier if it were a boy.''

Brand noted the tears in her eyes before she blinked them away. He reluctantly gave her points for not turning on the waterworks. His mother had been a master at that.

''Toni, the place is falling apart. From what I saw, most of the buildings need structural repairs, and the fences look like they'll fall with the first strong breeze. You have boards and roofing that need replacing and everything needs a coat of paint. Do you have the cash for that?''

She crumpled into her chair and put her head in her hands. Her hair fell forward to reveal the tender nape of her neck. Brand had to jerk himself back to the matter at hand.

''I barely have enough to make payroll for the next few months. I can't fire that good-for-nothing crew because they're cheap. To get better help, I'd have to pay better wages, and I just don't have...'' She bit her lip, looking as if she regretted telling him her problem. ''Maybe when I've sold some cattle...''

''You're talking a hell of a lot of money, Toni. More than a few head of cattle will bring. You'd probably have to sell your entire herd to raise that kind of cash. Next year you'll be in the same bind, but you won't have any stock to sell.''

Her eyes narrowed on him in appraisal. ''You sound like you know ranching.''

Brand shrugged. ''Grew up on one. What if you're pregnant? How will you work the ranch and raise a baby by yourself?''

She pinched her lips and squared her shoulders. Brand had to admire her grit. Even if she was ignoring the obvious. ''I'll manage.''

"You need a partner with capital." He watched her weigh the idea, then her chin jutted out in what was already becoming a familiar gesture. Seconds ticked past. He couldn't blame her for wanting to hold on to the place. The buildings might need work, but from what he'd seen driving in, the land looked good. Judging by the number of fence posts he'd passed, it was a pretty good-size spread.

Resignation settled over Toni's features. "Maybe a silent partner."

Brand frowned and stroked his brow. She'd skipped town, trying to steal his child from him once already. Would she do it again? No doubt about it. There was only one way he could guarantee himself legal rights to his child if she decided to bolt.

Marry her.

"Fifty-fifty. Your ranch. My money." He heard the words leave his mouth and wondered if he'd lost his freakin' mind. He'd always sworn he'd never tie himself to a woman. They demanded too much and were never happy. His father and brother had nearly killed themselves trying to keep their wives happy and what had happened? The women had left anyway, but not until the money had run out.

Toni looked as if she, too, doubted his sanity. He hadn't thought it possible for her eyes to get any bluer, her skin to get any paler. He'd been wrong. Her hand fluttered to her throat, but not before he saw her pulse pounding there. "What if I'm not pregnant?"

Hell, at least he'd get her back into his bed for however long the marriage lasted. For some reason Toni Swenson got to him in a way no other woman had. Might as well figure out why. He shrugged. "You said you'd inherit if you got married?"

She nodded hesitantly.

"Then, you will. To me."

Her eyes and lips rounded. Her throat worked convulsively. "I...I don't want to get married," she whispered.

"Me neither, darlin', but I'll be damned if you'll take my kid and run off." He didn't need to add *again*.

The cornered look was back on her face. She paced toward the door and back a couple of times, stopping in front of him with that determined glint in her eyes. "I'd insist on a prenuptial agreement. I'm not losing this place to a man who decides to go off and search for..." she shifted uncomfortably and glanced away "...greener pastures."

Brand leaned against the edge of the counter, crossed his legs at the ankle, and hooked a thumb through his belt loop. So she wanted to make demands, did she? "What makes you think I'd ever find a woman who's better in bed than you?"

He'd shocked her. Well, hell, he'd been trying to. So why did he feel like a jackass? Her pink lips parted. Her eyes widened, and her face turned beet-red. She looked everywhere but at him. Her voice squeaked. "I'd still want a prenup—"

"Fine. It'll take a few days to get the license and for my family to get here. If you can have it drawn up by then, I'll sign it." He curved his finger around her chin and turned her until their eyes met. "Fifty-fifty, Toni. I'll take nothing less."

Her nearness immediately made him start thinking of things he shouldn't be thinking. Brand straightened and put some space between them. "One more thing. When you leave, I get sole custody of the child—if there is one—and first right of refusal on your share of this ranch."

"And if you leave?"

Brand nearly snorted. It wasn't the man who cut loose. "Same deal."

Toni's knees felt rubbery, and she had to clench the counter for support. How had all her meticulous planning backfired? And why would Brand make such ridiculous demands? Didn't he know a mother would never willingly give up her child?

Movement in the backyard drew her attention away from the crazy cowboy she was seriously considering marrying. The ranch hands loitered by the bunkhouse. Her foreman lifted a flask to his lips then passed it to the next man who took a swig and passed it on. Toni sucked an angry breath. Brand stepped behind her. Too close. She could feel his breath on her nape and the heat radiating from his body.

He slammed a fist on the counter and Toni nearly jumped out of her skin. "Cut their checks. I'm going to fire the crew."

"But… What'll I do for help?" She stopped him with a hand on his arm. His muscles clenched beneath her fingers and she jerked her hand away. How could she be considering marrying a man with such powerful arms and big hands?

He leveled his dark eyes on her. "I know plenty of cowboys who need work off-season. Soon as I put the word out we'll have 'em lining up." Brand settled his hat on his head and strode out the back door.

Toni closed her eyes and rubbed her temple. Things were going from bad to worse with the speed of a twister ripping through her life. She stumbled into her grandfather's office and sank into his old leather chair. It smelled of him. Usually, it soothed her to sit here, made her feel safe, but today her fingers still burned from the contact with Brand and her hands shook so badly she could barely write the checks.

She laid the pen down and buried her face in her hands. What had she done? Had she made a bargain with the devil? She could already be pregnant with a stranger's child. She touched her belly. She didn't know how to be a mother. She'd never even been a baby-sitter. Now, she'd agreed to become a wife to a man she didn't know other than in the biblical sense. A big man. A physical man.

Tying herself to him terrified her, but there wasn't another option. Her gaze fell on the letter beside the blotter. The bank had refused her loan request. Toni looked at the last entry in her grandfather's journal. Two of the wells had run dry and the barn roof leaked like a sieve. He'd been worried that the first big rain could destroy all the feed stored under a tarp in the loft.

The unexpected expenses she dreaded were already adding up. Worse, if she'd counted the herd correctly, her grandfather had been running fewer cattle than he should have been for a ranch this size. Brand was right—there wouldn't be enough money for all the repairs if she sold every steer and every piece of equipment on the place.

Being a qualified vet was fine and dandy, but if she didn't have the money to buy the supplies she needed she couldn't care for the animals. Add in feed costs, salaries, her college-loan payment, and the day-to-day operating expenses and the result was a negative number. She wouldn't ask her parents for the money. There would be strings. Her father always had strings.

She had to take Brand on as a partner. And as a husband. But how could she be sure he wouldn't try to take the place from her? How could she be sure he wouldn't hurt her? Toni stiffened her spine. She could protect herself and her baby, and she'd have her grandfather's attorney draw up an airtight legal document to protect her land. Losing this ranch to some itinerant rodeo bum was not an option. As for his thinking she'd leave and he'd get custody of her child…

Well, *she* wouldn't be the one leaving.

Four

Brand surveyed the buildings with a critical eye as he crossed the yard, making a mental list of supplies he'd need and the amount of time and labor the work would require. It was a long list. Nearly as long as the list of reasons why he shouldn't be marrying Toni, and he had to be plumb loco even to consider it. Still, he'd do it and take on the challenge of getting this ranch back into prime condition—if for no other reason than the kid she might be carrying.

His kid.

Brand stopped in front of the foreman. The hands picked at their tack, trying to look busy. ''You have trouble finding the east pasture?''

''Nah. We'll move the herd in a few days. There's no need to waste time on that fence right now. That li'l girl don't know squat 'bout cattle.''

''You disobeyed a direct order. Pack your gear. You're fired.''

"You can't fire me, boy." The foreman puffed up his chest and advanced.

Brand planted his feet and watched the drunk. He was used to men who threw their weight around. "Clear out."

"Me an' Will had an agreement. I'm staying."

"Nope, you're going."

He'd expected the punch. Brand caught the meaty fist, twisted it and had the foreman flat on his back in the dirt. The other men either weren't drunk enough to fight him, or they had better sense. Disgusted, Brand headed for the house. He heard a grunt and turned. The foreman shot to his feet. Fast and agile for a man of his girth and alcohol content, he caught Brand in a chest-crushing squeeze, pinning his arms to his sides. "Let's teach this here bull rider a lesson, boys."

The other two men clenched their fists and approached. Before he could curse his stupidity for turning his back on the man, Brand heard a *crack-ping*. The metal tractor sign on a light pole above their heads rocked. There was a bullet hole dead center on the tractor tire in the picture. He yanked his gaze toward the house.

Toni stood on the back steps, staring down the sight of the rifle propped on her shoulder. She pointed it straight at the foreman. "Pack and leave. The sheriff's on his way."

The arms bruising Brand's ribs dropped and the foreman stepped away, muttering a few ripe words. The men hustled into the bunkhouse as she crossed the yard.

"I don't like this," she said, putting the safety on the rifle. Brand noticed the trembling of her voice and the white line around her lips. The confrontation had definitely spooked her. "He might make trouble."

"I'll take care of it."

"Excuse me?" she protested huffily. The look in Toni's eyes reminded Brand of the way she'd looked at the rodeo. Determined.

"We'll keep an eye out." Brand noted the competent

way she handled the weapon. "You're going to have to tell me your secrets, darlin'."

She eyed him warily.

"The marksmanship." How many other secrets did she have?

A sheriff's car pulled off the highway and headed up the dirt driveway with enough speed to throw a rooster tail of dust in its wake. It slid to a halt a few feet away. A young man flung the door open and climbed out. "I had a call about a disturb— Toni?"

"Josh?"

His brand-new fiancée dashed across the yard to hug a man who looked more like a landlocked surfer than a deputy. The burn in Brand's gut had nothing to do with jealousy—he hadn't known Toni long enough for that, and he damn sure wasn't ever going to like her enough to be jealous. The woman was not to be trusted.

The deputy sheriff glanced from the rifle tucked under Toni's arm to Brand. His hand settled on the butt of his pistol. "This man giving you trouble?"

"Brand? No. He...I...we..."

"I'm Brand Lander, Toni's fiancé." Brand stepped forward, stuck out his right hand, and snaked his left around Toni's waist, pulling her against his side.

"Josh Keegan." The deputy hesitated then shook Brand's hand. Toni looked less than happy about the situation. She held herself stiffly against him—a far cry from the way she'd melted all over him in Vegas. Her gaze darted between him and the deputy.

"So what's the disturbance?"

"We're firing some hands. They're not in a hurry to leave," Toni told him.

"You mean your grandfather left the place to you after all? I can't believe the old coot finally relented. He forget you're a girl?"

"Not exactly." Toni squirmed, but Brand refused to let

her go. "Josh, I'm worried that my ex-foreman, Matthews, might cause trouble. He already tried to hurt Brand."

"Pressing charges?" Keegan flipped open his notepad.

"Not this time. Just noted," Brand answered.

Nodding, Josh jotted the details down as Brand gave them. "Wouldn't be the first time your foreman's been in trouble. He gets into a bar fight in town at least once a month."

The men came out of the bunkhouse, tossed their gear in the back of a pickup truck and peeled out of the driveway. Keegan took down the license-plate number and the men's names. Business completed, he studied Toni again as if she were the best thing since homemade ice cream. Brand didn't like it.

"It's great to see you. What've you been doing?"

She smiled at the lawman in a way she'd never smiled at Brand. He didn't like that, either. As a matter of fact, Brand decided, he didn't like one damn thing about Deputy Keegan. Not his pretty-boy face. Not his friendly attitude. Especially not the way he eyed Toni. Territorial was something he'd never been before.

It's because she might be carrying my kid.

"I finished vet school. You want to come in for coffee, Josh?"

Brand glared at the lawman. "I'm sure the deputy needs to get back on patrol, darlin'."

Josh shot Brand a cautious glance and backed toward his patrol car. "Well…uh…I really should be going. I'll stop by another time and take you up on that invitation, Toni."

The car disappeared in a cloud of dust. Toni stepped away.

"How dare you be so rude to Josh." Despite her bold words, Brand thought she watched him warily. She stood on the balls of her feet as if ready to move fast or dodge. He frowned.

"The deal goes both ways. I don't cheat. You don't cheat."

She practically sputtered with anger. "For Pete's sake, Josh is like a brother to me."

"Tell him that. Did your grandfather pay his foreman enough for him to be able to buy a thirty-thousand-dollar truck?"

The fire in Toni's eyes turned to suspicion. Her brow puckered. "I don't think so."

"There's a lot that needs to be done here. Let me tell you where I want to start." Brand headed toward one of the barns.

Toni parked her hands on her hips and ground her teeth. "Listen, Lander, this is supposed to be a partnership, not a dictatorship. If this is going to work we need to discuss expenses beforehand."

Toni had a feeling the battle lines had just been drawn in the dust beneath her feet. Brand stopped abruptly and slowly turned. One hand fisted, the other shifted his hat. "Would you care to show me around so we can discuss the repairs? I have a few suggestions."

His words dripped sarcasm and his eyes held the warmth of a polar ice cap. She rubbed her forehead and the doozy of a headache announcing its presence in her brow. Battling wills with a hardheaded cowboy wouldn't improve it any—especially not when he was angry. There was no doubt in her mind that Brand Lander was powerful. More powerful than her father. She'd seen his strength when he'd stopped Matthews's punch.

Keep your distance. Use reason. Reason sometimes works.

She inched cautiously toward him. "More important than the outbuildings are the two dry wells, the downed fences, and the pastures that need reseeding. We can't increase or maintain the herd without those."

Surprise flashed in Brand's eyes. He nodded to acknowledge her point. "Can we take the truck or do we need to saddle up?"

Toni waved toward the old truck parked in the side yard. "We can drive, if we can get a vehicle running. My car won't make it through the fields."

"I'll look at the truck later. We can take mine."

Toni followed Brand around the front of the house. A white king-cab truck sat beneath the oak tree. Brand held open the door, and Toni climbed in. "This isn't exactly the overloaded boy toy I'd expect a four-time world champion to drive."

Bracing his arms on the door opening, Brand said, "I need a reliable ride to get from one rodeo to the next— not a chick magnet. I bought this truck and another one for my dad with my first big check. The majority of my winnings, I've put in the bank or invested."

His calluses scraped gently along her jaw. Toni caught her breath as awareness arched between them. Brand lowered his head.

Toni leaned back. "Don't."

"Don't?"

"I'll marry you, but I'm not—I'm not sleeping with you."

Brand stepped back, frowning. "I don't remember you saying no in Vegas."

She didn't want to say no now. "We hardly know each other."

"We were good, Toni. Better than good."

"I know, but…I need time."

"How much time?"

"I—I don't know. I don't love you and I—" She'd never expected to enjoy making love with a man she didn't love.

"It wasn't love you wanted that night. Hell, it wasn't even *me* you wanted. You wanted Bobby Lee."

She'd stung his pride. "No, no, I didn't want Bobby

Lee. I wanted a cowboy who wouldn't follow me home. He seemed the type. You on the other hand..." She shrugged. No need to state the obvious.

"Don't mention the baby to my family," Brand said the following day without looking up from the supply list on the table in front of him.

Coffee splashed over the rim of Toni's cup, burning her fingers. She snatched them back. "Brand, I may not be pregnant. It was just one night."

One long, passionate night. Toni blew on her stinging fingers and concentrated on regulating her breathing. She'd spent the morning pretending Brand didn't look fabulous in his tight jeans and his brightly patterned shirt. Attraction would cloud the issue. A clear head was crucial.

Brand was beside her in two strides, examining her hand then thrusting it under cold running water. Toni jerked away. "I'm okay."

Grabbing the plate of pancakes he'd left for her on the stove, she sat at the far end of the table. Not that she expected to eat. She was too nervous. It was her wedding day. "It's not like I'm going to greet your family with 'Nice to meet you, I might be pregnant.' So tell me why you felt the need to warn me."

Brand sat down and focused on the paper in front of him. The sun shining in through the window glistened on his hair and lit the tiny nick on his clean-shaven jaw. Darn the man for looking good first thing in the morning when she felt about as energetic as a wet mop after tossing and turning all night.

"My brother Caleb was trapped into marriage by a woman claiming to be carrying his child. Not only was the baby a piece of fiction, his marriage was two years of hell for all of us."

Toni set down her fork and tried to ease the lump in her throat. She was marrying a stranger and acquiring his fam-ily—a family that was likely to hate her when they found out what she'd done. "What other land mines do I need to avoid?"

Brand drummed his fingers on the table. Toni thought he wasn't going to answer. His usually sensuous lips looked as tight as his shoulders. "Let's just say my family shares your grandfather's opinion that a woman doesn't belong on a ranch."

"I'm perfectly capable—" Anger choked off her words. Were all men this sexist? Toni slammed her cup down on the table. "What is wrong with a woman running a ranch?"

Something in the depths of Brand's eyes dried up her arguments. He blinked and the look was gone. "My mother split when I was eight. Guess she got sick of being stuck in the house all day with sniveling brats."

Bitterness and hurt hardened his voice and twisted his lips. Toni's heart ached for the lost little boy he must have been. "I guess I'm not going to be welcomed with open arms."

He snorted. "Hardly."

Appetite gone, she shoved her plate aside. "Why'd you leave home?"

Brand crossed the room to put his dishes in the sink. "I was tired of busting my butt and not having any say in the ranch. There were a lot of things Dad could've done different, but he wasn't willing to change or to listen to a smart-mouthed kid's ideas." He clenched his fist and stared out the window. "And then there was the rodeo."

Toni had a feeling there was more to it than that, but he obviously didn't want to share. "Tell me about the rest of your family. How many brothers?"

Brand rinsed his mug. "Three. Caleb's ten years older. Patrick, eight. Cort is six years younger than me." His tone and face softened. "He's in medical school at Duke."

"Oh my gosh, he was only two when your mother left."

Brand shoved his hat on his head and turned toward the door. "I have things to do. Ring the bell if I'm not back when they get here. Your turn to cook breakfast tomorrow.''

He snatched up a leftover sausage link and carried it out the door. Beau, the traitor, waited, his tail thumping.

Brand saddled up the most ornery mount in the barn, a young sorrel gelding with more buck than brains. Trying to stay on the back of a horse determined to feed him dirt ought to keep his mind occupied. Wrong. His mother's voice rang through his head as clear as if she'd left yesterday. He remembered sitting on her bed, an unwilling confidant, watching her pack. Cort had been crying in his crib in the next room.

''I have to go, Brandon. I'd sooner put a gun to my head than stay. Your dad, Caleb and Patrick will take care of the ranch. You take care of Cort. That's your job. I can't do it anymore. When things settle down, I'll come for you and Cort.''

He'd been eight years old. It had taken a while, but he'd figured it out. When the going got tough, the women got going. There was nothing like the emptiness he'd felt standing on the porch juggling his squirming and screaming two-year-old brother and watching his mother drive out of sight. She hadn't come back.

Sooner or later, kid or no kid, Toni would bail out, and, like his dad, he'd be left to struggle with the land and his kid. The difference was that he wouldn't need to work his kids like slaves to make a living. He could afford to hire help. The Rocking A was a fine piece of land to raise a kid on. Whenever Toni decided to leave, he'd offer her a fair price.

Between now and then he wasn't going to make the mistake his dad and brother had of falling in love with the women they married and getting his heart ripped out.

Toni smoothed her hand down the fitted bodice of the wedding dress Brand had bought her and opened the door to three big, sour-faced men. All had the same dark hair and eyes as Brand, but none had his easy smile or his lean build. Somber in their Sunday best and slicked-down hair, they looked better suited to attending a funeral than a wedding.

"Hello, I'm Toni Swenson." Her voice came out a little weak. To compensate, she plastered on a big, fake smile and extended her hand toward the oldest man.

He sized her up before he took her hand in a meaty grip. Judging by his scowl, she hadn't fared well. "Jack Lander. My sons, Caleb, Patrick and… Where the hell is the boy?"

"Over here." A younger man straightened from petting Beau and headed her way. "I'm Cort. You must be Toni. Damn, Brand's got good taste. Ditch him and run away with me, darlin'." He winked and Toni had to laugh. Cort had Brand's smile and charm, albeit a less potent version.

"Stuff it, brat." Brand said behind her. The hair on her neck immediately rose. He snaked an arm around her waist and reached past her to give Cort a playful noogie.

Toni wondered if Brand planned to pretend this was a love match. She eased away from his scorching grip and glanced his way for a clue. Her mouth dropped open. In a dark suit Brand was positively breathtaking. The Western-cut jacket emphasized the breadth of his shoulders, while the white banded-collar shirt accentuated his tan.

The phone rang and Brand said, "I'll get it. I'm expecting a call."

Toni eyed the men. An uneasy silence settled over them. With the exclusion of Cort, the Lander men studied her as if she were a new and fatal strain of virus. "Come in. I'll uh…make coffee."

Caleb Lander scowled at her. "You knocked up?"

She nearly tripped over the hem of her dress. The rest of the family didn't appear to be surprised by his rudeness. No doubt their hasty marriage had been speculated over. "I—"

Brand scowled as he reentered the room. "That's no way to greet my fiancée."

"Just looking out for you, little brother."

"I can look out for myself."

Turning to Toni, Brand put his hands on her shoulders and squeezed. "Did I mention you look beautiful?"

His thumbs circled at the base of her neck, smoothing out the knots of tension. The man had magical hands. Toni would have purred if she hadn't been nervous enough to throw up.

Luckily, his brother broke the spell.

Cort pulled a check from his pocket. "Brand, you sent too much money in the tuition check again."

"Keep it. I don't want you working *and* going to school."

"It's just more that I'll have to pay you back," Cort argued. "I can get financial aid—"

"I don't want the money. Let's go."

Toni's stomach lurched, her heart beat erratically and her knees refused to work. She thought she might pass out. Brand pulled her from her chair. She flinched when she saw his hand coming toward her face, but all he did was tip her chin with a calloused finger.

"You all right?" The concern in his eyes looked genuine, but he could have been acting for his family's benefit. After all, he *had* bought her this exquisite gown. Swallowing her nausea, she nodded and let him propel her out the door. The long full skirt of her satin wedding dress blew in the breeze.

Brand suspected that meeting his family wasn't easy for Toni. Her skin was magnolia pale—almost as pale as her dress—and she acted more skittish than a new filly. He probably shouldn't have bought something so low-cut that he'd be distracted by the curves of her breasts, but the dress had reminded him of the black thing she'd worn in Vegas. It looked virginal and sinful at the same time. He opened the truck door for her.

"Can I ride with you?" Cort asked. Brand motioned him to the rear seat before helping Toni get her dress all tucked in. The others followed in the family pickup.

Cort asked a hundred questions about the NFR finals. Brand was thankful for the distraction. He was more nervous than he'd been before he'd mounted his last bull at the finals, and it had nothing to do with the money riding on the deal.

Toni's lawyer had been out of town, but his partner had drawn up the prenuptial agreement. She'd leave him with no more than she came with, and he had first option to buy her out. She'd even put in the custody clause he'd requested. His mouth twisted with bitterness. What kind of woman would sign away her child? *Any kind,* he reminded himself. Women, with few exceptions, were quitters.

He'd decided late last night that he wanted his family to believe they were marrying for love. One day his son or daughter might ask questions. Brand wanted the kid to know that he'd done everything he could to keep Toni around. He'd blamed his father for not finding some way to make his mother stay, and he didn't want his child blaming him for Toni's desertion.

If there is a kid.

Maybe he was jumping the gun by refusing to wait a couple more weeks and find out, but he couldn't risk Toni bolting. Brand shrugged his tight shoulders. It didn't make sense that he was getting superstitious now when he never had been on the circuit—heaven knows bull riders were a superstitious bunch. His gut instinct told him there'd be a baby. He couldn't believe something as earth-shattering as his night with Toni could pass without some visible effect.

"So how'd you guys meet?" Cort asked.

"At a rodeo." Brand glanced at Toni's chalky face. She knew what she wanted and went for it. He was that way himself. It was a little too easy to admire her strength, tenacity and levelheadedness. Hell, she could look at a situation and sum it up in a couple of words while he was still studying the angles. In other circumstances he could like her.

"So, was it love at first sight?"

"What do you think?" Brand answered.

Toni chewed her lip.

"You don't drag your feet when you know what you want."

"Yep." Brand pulled the truck into a parking spot.

Toni came out of whatever trance she'd been in to say, "We need to park closer to the courthouse."

Her pallor combined with the white dress made her blue eyes almost luminescent, and she'd painted her lips with a pale pink. He liked them better bare and didn't resist the impulse to lean across the seat and kiss her lipstick off. It had nothing to do with convincing his family.

Her lips parted beneath his. Need slammed him as hard, if not harder, than it had in Vegas. The woman was as heady as a straight shot of tequila on an empty stomach. He swept his tongue inside her mouth to taste her. The urge to lay the truck seat back and make love to her right here beneath the church steeple surprised him. Releasing the catch of her safety belt, Brand pulled her closer.

"Get a room." Cort laughed and punched his shoulder.

Brand drew back reluctantly and felt a little embarrassed. Toni's flushed face and erratic breathing mirrored his own. She'd turned him into a hormone-driven adolescent. Toni scooted toward her door as if she couldn't get away from him fast enough. He caught her hand. "This the church where your parents married?"

She nodded. "I thought we were having a civil service."

Brand shook his head and got out of the truck. He opened her door. Toni's teeth dug into her bottom lip so hard, he expected to see blood. With his thumb, he rescued her lip from the nip of her teeth. Her cold hands trembled in his. Evidently, she didn't want to do this any more than he did. For some damned reason, that irked him. "Let me get the camera for Cort. He's our photographer today."

Toni headed up the walk.

"So, *is* she pregnant?" Cort asked.

"Won't be for lack of trying if she's not."

"Do you love her?"

Brand's gaze tracked her. No doubt about it, his new wife-to-be had him hooked. But love? Uh-uh. "What do you think?"

"Come on, give me details, or I'm gonna make up my own."

Brand grinned. "You do that."

He followed Toni up the walk. For as long as it lasted, he and Toni would be one hell of a team. In bed and out.

Five

Toni walked toward the church, her nerves knotting tighter with each step.

She had to be crazy. She didn't even know if she was pregnant. But what if she was? Or wasn't? What if she had a precious baby girl instead of the boy she so desperately needed? She had to do this. Marrying Brand would guarantee she wouldn't lose her ranch. Once the estate was probated and the deed was in her name, she and Brand could go their separate ways.

How could she be contemplating *divorce* before the ceremony? Except in extreme cases, like her parents, marriage should be forever. Her throat ached with unshed tears. Another strong conviction bites the dust. First she had sex with a stranger. Now she stood in front of a church wearing an exquisite wedding dress and contemplating divorce.

Brand stopped beside her. The man was absolutely gorgeous. He'd left his hat at home. The light wind ruffled the thick, dark strands and left a curl across his forehead.

Toni twisted her purse strap around her fingers to keep from brushing it back. Gentleness from a man was something she didn't understand. Hatred? Yes. Fear? Certainly. But thus far she had no reason to feel either of those debilitating emotions for Brand.

"How'd you know about the church?"

He shrugged. "Saw the picture of your parents in the living room. I recognized the place when I came to town for the license. The preacher remembers you and your folks."

She could hear the question in his voice, but she didn't want to explain why she hadn't invited her parents. She'd told Brand they couldn't make it and refused to elaborate.

Her eyes stung. She didn't want him to be gentle or kind or thoughtful. She didn't want to know he was paying his brother's tuition or that he'd bought his dad a truck. She wanted Brand to be a macho jerk she could easily resist and forget.

"It's bad enough that you're getting married, but in a church?" Grimacing, Patrick jerked a thumb toward the weathered stone building. "Damnation, Brand, when was the last time you stepped inside one of these for anything but a funeral?"

Brand ignored him, cupped Toni's elbow, and led her into the vestibule.

Mrs. Betts, the preacher's wife, met them inside the door. She hugged Toni, then pressed a bouquet into her hands. "Toni, it's nice to see you on a happy occasion this time. You look lovely, dear."

Toni stared at the flowers. "Mrs. Betts, you didn't have to—"

"Brand asked me to pick them up," the woman interrupted with a wink in Brand's direction. "White roses, you said, but I remembered how much Toni used to love the daisies we planted out front. She used to pick one every Sunday when Will wasn't looking. I hope you don't mind that I asked the florist to add a few to the bouquet."

Brand dipped his head. "Not at all, ma'am."

Surprised, Toni turned to Brand. His lips quirked up in his trademark grin, but his eyes remained serious. "A bride has to have flowers, darlin'."

Her heart did a swan dive. His charm was lethal. She'd had a nearly toxic dose of it and was going down for the count. Was this what had happened to her mother?

"Everything set?" Brand asked.

"We're ready whenever you are." Mrs. Betts beamed. "You have the license?"

Brand handed over the papers and guided Toni into the silent sanctuary with a hand at her waist. Reverend Betts turned to greet them. Toni barely heard what he said. Candlelight, flowers, stained glass. *What was she doing?*

The reverend positioned them at the end of the aisle. Mrs. Betts stood on one side and Brand on her other. Brand's father and brothers stood behind them. *Trapped.* Toni strangled her bouquet until Mrs. Betts pried it from her fingers. Everything seemed to go into slow motion. Brand took her hand in his. The preacher asked for the rings. Toni's heart stuttered. *She hadn't bought a ring.* Cort winked, dug into his pocket and withdrew two wide gold bands. The vows were the ones young girls dream of making, but to Toni it seemed wrong to be saying them when she didn't believe in love and didn't expect to be tied to this man "till death us do part."

Toni tallied her sins. She'd slept with a stranger and deceived him to get pregnant. Now she stood before an altar and lied. She'd go to hell, for sure. Panic put a lump in her throat. She couldn't breathe, couldn't swallow, couldn't speak.

Brand's steady gaze locked with hers. He repeated his vows, his voice deep and even, then he slid the band onto her finger. His hands were steady. Hers shook so much she nearly dropped the ring before she could push it over his scarred knuckle.

"You may kiss your bride, Brand."

He cupped her face and covered her lips, branding her as his. He angled his head and slid his hands down her back, deepening the kiss and pulling her flush against him. Toni lost all sense of time and place. Brand's heart pounded beneath her hand. His scent and taste invaded her bloodstream like a narcotic. She felt the heat of his desire against her belly. An answering warmth flooded hers.

"Jeez, Brand, save it for tonight." Cort's teasing words severed the connection with the cool precision of a new scalpel.

Toni's hand fluttered from Brand's chest to her own. She'd added lusting in church to her sins.

Cort kissed her hot cheek and winked. "I'm telling you, Toni, you shoulda held out for me."

She tried to laugh, but couldn't. She'd tied herself to a man who made his living with his muscles.

The preacher led them into an alcove and passed her a pen. *Antonia Swenson Lander,* she signed. Her stomach felt like the middle of a beehive.

"You'll fax a copy of this to the attorney?" Brand asked Reverend Betts after signing his name.

"He'll have it in five minutes." Reverend Betts passed the marriage license to his wife who bustled off. "You made a lovely bride, dear. You just let me know when we'll need a christening."

Toni darted a startled glance at the clergyman. Brand squeezed her hand. "We'll do that."

Outside the church the clouds had given way to sunshine. Cort rode with his family, leaving Toni and Brand to cover the miles home alone. Her heart hammered with the enormity of what she'd done. She'd never wanted to marry, never wanted to give a man that kind of power over her, and yet the sunlight bouncing off the golden bands on their hands told her she had. Brand had not only saved her ranch, he'd given her the kind of wedding the tight-knit community could accept. "Thank you."

Brand shot her a curious glance. "For what?"

"The dress, the flowers, the church, the pictures. It seems…real."

"This *is* a real marriage, Toni. Don't doubt it." The gleam in his eyes left her in no doubt of his meaning. Her nerve endings sizzled. Her stomach knotted. The truck cab suddenly seemed airless.

"Brand—" Dozens of cars lined the ranch driveway. Only a barn or house fire brought this kind of crowd. Toni threw open the door. "What's going on?"

The Landers' truck and the Bettses' car pulled in behind them. Brand helped Toni down from the cab. Mrs. Betts bustled over and squeezed Toni's hand. "I hope you don't mind, but so many people remember you from your visits to your granddad. We all wanted to welcome you and your groom home. I'm just sorry your mother couldn't make it."

Toni cringed. She hadn't invited her mother because her mother wouldn't come alone, and there was no way to predict how her father would react. It was best to put off that confrontation as long as possible. It might be the coward's way, but she had Brand and maybe even their baby to consider now.

Brand ground his teeth and smiled. His wife was dancing with the deputy. All he wanted to do was cut in, but each of his new neighbors seemed to have a story to tell, including the man who now had him cornered by the punch bowl.

"Toni spent every summer and every Christmas holiday with Will for as far back as I kin remember. T'was good for her to get away from—" The man's wife elbowed him. He cleared his throat.

Brand frowned. What did Toni need to get away from?

The man tugged at the collar of his dress shirt. "I'd say Toni ran circles round Will, with the help of that foreman of his. It was Rusty who taught Toni to ride and shoot like a reg'lar ranch hand. Said she needed to learn to stick up for herself if—'' Again the wife's elbow interrupted him. ''Can't say Will liked her being a tomboy, but he did love that girl.''

Brand's face ached from smiling, and his mind churned. What didn't the woman want him to know? The sound of Toni's laughter drew his gaze across the yard. Excusing himself, Brand decided to reclaim his wife. He turned off the stereo and grabbed a couple of glasses of champagne punch. Everyone halted midstep. He caught Toni's gaze and lifted a glass.

''I'd like to propose a toast to my beautiful bride, the only woman I know who could make me give up the rodeo.'' Brand heard the exclamations of surprise, but what interested him most was the dismay on Toni's face.

Caleb yelled out, ''Why you wanna do a dang-fool thing like that when you could go for another world championship?''

Brand strolled across the yard, not once breaking eye contact with Toni. He pressed a plastic champagne flute into her hand and captured the other, tugging her away from Keegan. She watched him warily, and Brand couldn't blame her. He had a sudden urge to kiss his bride and not turn her loose until she lay exhausted in his arms. *Like she'd been in Vegas.*

Brand tried for a besotted expression. ''Toni and I want to start a family real soon. Can't do that if I'm never home.''

Objections bubbled in her eyes. Brand planted a swift kiss on her lips to keep her from voicing them. ''I always figured I'd quit once I found the right place to settle down.''

''And the right woman,'' added Cort.

Brand lifted his glass in agreement rather than correct his mistake. Cort would be disillusioned soon enough.

A rickety van pulled to a halt in the drive. The doors opened and cowboys spilled out. Brand grinned and nodded toward the van. ''Crew's here.''

"What crew?" Toni caught his sleeve.

"I hired some of my buddies to help out."

"Brand, we didn't discuss this." The sparks shooting from her eyes were hard to miss.

"We agreed on the basic stuff. These guys'll get it done."

"The basics—" Her nostrils flared as she took a deep breath. "I should have been in on the interviews."

Her breasts rose and fell rapidly. It was distracting as hell and made him feel like a hormone-driven adolescent again.

"There were no interviews, darlin'. I've known these guys for years. I gave 'em a call and here they are." What was the fuss about? Any crew was better than the one she'd had.

"And where do you think they'll sleep?"

"The bunkhouse."

The triumphant look in her eyes made him uneasy. Had it been a trick question? "I guess you haven't been inside the bunkhouse since the last crew left. They trashed the place, Brand. It'll take weeks to get it repaired."

Brand said a word that made her flinch. "Why didn't you say something, or call your buddy, the deputy, and report 'em for vandalism?"

"I did tell Josh, but we can't prove Matthews did it. I only discovered it yesterday. Neither of us went into the bunkhouse before the crew left."

Brand slammed his hand into his fist. Toni shrank away. It wasn't the first time the fear in her eyes contradicted her gutsy behavior. What was she afraid of? "Toni—"

"Trouble in paradise already?" Caleb's bitter tone asked for trouble.

"Take a hike, Caleb."

Toni stepped between them. "No, it's all right. Brand didn't realize we'd have to let his new crew share our house until the bunkhouse is repaired. I'm…upset at having a honeymoon for six." She wore a conciliatory smile, but her grip on Brand's hand could very likely break his bones.

Caleb grinned and Toni's grip loosened. "Not so bright, little brother. Can't they bunk in the barn or camp outside?"

Toni shook her head. "The weatherman is calling for rain, the tack room is overrun by rats, and the loft is full of hay. We have houseguests. Excuse me."

Toni looked from the elaborate three-tiered wedding cake one of her neighbors had labored over to the table laden with gifts. Unless she wanted to tell the guests that her marriage was a sham, she and Brand would be sharing a room. She scanned the happy faces and shook her head. These people had stood by her during some really rough times. She wouldn't disappoint them.

She felt queasy just contemplating sharing Brand's bed again. Their relationship was a temporary necessity, a means to an end. She wouldn't let it become more. She'd seen firsthand that love was a trap loaded with mental and physical pain.

Toni slipped into the house to move her things into Brand's room. She pulled out an armful of hangers. The ranch was her family's heritage. *She* was going to get it back into prime working order and keep right on running it once the wanderlust hit Brand again. Despite his unexpected announcement today, she didn't believe he'd give up the rodeo.

"Need some help?"

Toni yelped and spun around, scattering clothes in the process. Brand leaned against the doorjamb of her bedroom. He removed his suit coat and tossed it on the bed, then unfastened several buttons of his shirt. The exposed sliver of chest made Toni's hands tingle from the memory of firm flesh beneath her fingertips and the tickle of dark curls against her palms. He came toward her, jolting her heart into a dangerously fast pace with his slow, measured steps. Toni gathered her clothes and held them like a barrier between them.

"I'm moving my things to your room, but I can manage." In the intimacy of the bedroom she was afraid to lift her gaze higher than the middle of his chest. The room felt crowded and airless. This ridiculous hormonal reaction was exactly why she'd avoided Brand as much as possible over the past few days. When he entered a room, she left it. Now he blocked her path.

"I don't doubt it, darlin'. You seem capable of just about anything, but I'll help." Brand wrestled the clothes from her, his knuckles brushing her breasts in the process. He turned and disappeared into the hallway as if he hadn't heard her gasp.

Toni closed her eyes, inhaling and exhaling slowly. She tried to ignore the tingle of her nipples. She couldn't let him get to her. Grabbing more clothes, Toni headed for the master bedroom. Brand hung her things in the closet beside his own. Toni took one look at the wide bed, dumped her burden on it and bolted back to her room.

With her eyes closed she leaned back against the dresser, and tried to gather her shattered composure. This wasn't going to work. She couldn't pretend indifference when every hormone in her body had been on red alert since she'd spotted one dark-haired cowboy in that arena in Vegas. She'd broken her cardinal rule when she'd had sex with Brand, and he was tempting her to break it again. But she wouldn't. She'd vowed long ago not to get tangled up with another controlling, *physical* man. Her father had been enough to last a lifetime.

"Toni?"

She jerked her eyes open, surprised by his nearness when she hadn't heard him approach. Brand stood scant inches from her, his brow wrinkled in concern, his dark gaze intent on hers. Toni plastered herself against the dresser, gripping the edge until her knuckles ached. "Wh-what?"

She saw something in his eyes that looked like regret. "I won't lie to you and say I don't want you back in my bed, but I don't intend to force you." Toni flinched when he lifted his hand, but he only stroked a stray wisp of hair from her cheek. He noticed her involuntary gesture. She could see the questions in his eyes and cursed herself for revealing her fear. The delicate scrape of his fingertip had all her nerve endings clicking their heels in attention.

"We were good together, Toni." His husky words and those darned chocolate eyes sent her heart racing.

"I won't sleep with you." Who was she trying to convince with that quivery statement? Him? Or herself? It didn't matter. Neither one of them was listening. She frowned and pushed at his wrist. He resisted. Toni felt the strong, rapid beat of his pulse drumming beneath her fingers. It beat nearly as fast as her own. "I mean…I will *sleep* with you, but I won't…I…oh, hell."

Brand's other hand joined the first in cupping her face. With his thumbs, he tilted her chin until her eyes met his.

He stroked his thumb over her bottom lip and Toni's knees threatened to go on strike. "Making love is a lot like bull riding. It's as much a mental thing as it is a physical thing. Unless you're with me, it's not going to be any good." His gaze followed the path of his thumb, then returned to hers even hotter than before. "You were with me in Vegas, darlin', and it was damn near earth-shattering."

His head lowered, pausing with his mouth a scant inch away from hers. His breath fanned her lips. "Are you with me, Toni?"

She was. Despite all reason and fear. Beneath the heat of his gaze and the touch of his hands, she couldn't think, couldn't breathe. His deep voice mesmerized, beckoning her back to the ecstasy of that night. Toni's lips parted. She flushed hot then cold and wanted out of her clothes. She tightened her grip on his wrist. "Ye—"

Roy, the beefy calf roper, stood in the open door. "Hey, Brand, where you want us to stow our gear?"

Muttering an earthy curse, Brand dropped his hands and stepped away. Toni closed her eyes and silently thanked the blundering cowboy for interrupting what would have been a colossal mistake. What was wrong with her? Had she lost her mind?

"Starting the honeymoon already?" Roy leered and winked at Toni. The scowl on Brand's face had Roy throwing up his hands and backing out of the room. "Sorry."

"We'll finish this later," Brand promised before leading Roy down the hall to the spare bedroom.

Toni collapsed against the dresser. She was in trouble. Big, big trouble. She absolutely could not fall for Brand's potent charm again. In Vegas he'd worked his sorcery on her and made her forget all about finding an easygoing, irresponsible cowboy. Look how badly that had turned out. She now had a husband she didn't want and an entire town to witness her falling on her face.

Brand lay on the bed, his arms behind his head, striving to appear relaxed when he was anything but. The last of the wedding guests had vanished, leaving him with an overload of anticipation humming through his veins. Toni was in the bathroom. She'd turned the water off a good fifteen minutes ago, but he hadn't heard a sound from beyond the door since. He had a hunch she wasn't preparing for their wedding night, but he could hope. As a matter of fact, he'd bet his Finals check she was avoiding him. It wasn't a flattering thought for a guy who'd always had women chasing after him. Not that he'd taken advantage of the buckle bunnies, safety being an issue and all. That was probably why Toni had his hormones in an uproar. He'd been without a steady woman too long.

He checked the clock again. Why would she hide out in the bathroom? Their lovemaking in Vegas had damn near stopped his heart. He couldn't see any possible reason to avoid repeating something that incredible. He'd been gentle with her, even taken extra care to make sure her first time was a good experience.

Hell, it had been a fabulous experience. For both of them.

Hadn't it? Brand's gut twisted with doubt. Had Toni been faking it? Hell, no. She'd been wet and breathless. Her heart had pounded just as hard as his. He'd felt it beneath his hands and lips. Brand grew more tense as the minutes ticked by until he began thinking she might be sick or something.

Toni admitted she was stalling. She sat on the vanity counter and lectured her reflection. ''Do not go out there and make a fool of yourself by crawling all over the man. It doesn't matter that he gave you the kind of wedding day dreams are made of—other people's dreams, that is. He's a heap of trouble in a Resistol. You are not going to get involved with him under any circumstances.''

Her gaze dropped to her stomach, which she covered protectively with her hand. She was already in over her head, but she couldn't afford to let him get any closer. He'd leave, or he'd take over. Her child. Her ranch. Her life. She'd sworn she'd never give another man the power to hurt her.

Toni shivered. She'd been able to run to Grandpa Will before, but she couldn't run anymore, because she had no one and no place to run to. This time, she had to handle the situation on her own. Not only was her life at stake, so was her child's—if there was one.

Focus on the mission. Where had she gone wrong? Conceiving should have been as emotionally detached as visiting a sperm bank, only with a guarantee that the male contribution came from a real cowboy, not just some guy who lied and said he was one. But it hadn't been clinical. Brand Lander had reduced her to pleading and begging in a way she'd never anticipated. He'd made her weak and weakness was something she couldn't afford.

He'd been right, damn his sorry hide. She'd been with him. Every breath. Every whisper. Every touch. The memories of how gentle he'd been could still make her pulse flutter and her belly tighten. It wouldn't do. It just wouldn't do. Toni squared her shoulders and glared at her flushed face in the mirror. She had a plan. All she had to do was execute it.

"Don't look at him. Don't touch him. Just sleep. Piece of cake. You sleep every night of your life. Tonight's no different." Pulling in a deep breath, she reached for the door.

"Toni?" Brand rapped on the door.

She nearly jumped out of her skin. "Uh... Yeah?"

"What in the hell are you doing in there?"

Toni yanked open the door, intent on telling him to get off her case. The words dried up. Brand wore nothing but underwear. Very *brief* briefs, which left little to the imagination. His hair stood in spikes, as if he'd been raking his fingers through it. A lone curl, the one she'd twined around her finger in Vegas, flopped across his forehead. Her hormones rioted.

"You all right?" He rubbed a hand across his bare chest. Toni's fingers tingled as if she could actually feel the wiry curls herself. The man had a magnificent chest.

Dragging her gaze from his pectorals, she focused on the crooked lampshade beyond his shoulder and reminded her lungs that they had a job to do, because they weren't doing it well. She felt light-headed. "F-fine. I'm fine. Just sleepy. Very sleepy. Good night."

She sidled around him and headed toward the bed with the determination of a salmon swimming upstream. *Oh, bad analogy. Salmon went upstream to reproduce.* She didn't even want to think about that right now.

"Whose shirt is that?" Brand's hand on her shoulder stopped her. It sent a flash of heat clear down to her womb.

For precious moments, Toni fought the urge to turn in his arms and put his hands on her aching breasts.

Go to sleep before you get yourself in trouble, you idiot. She inhaled slowly and turned to face him, but she kept her eyes focused on his. She would not look at his broad chest or the flat nipples she knew were as sensitive as her own. She would not notice the way the dark triangle of hair narrowed until it became a thin line leading from the navel she'd tickled with her tongue to his—

Toni jerked her head back up and cursed herself for doing exactly what she'd promised herself she wouldn't. Her heart beat so hard she was sure he could hear it. "M-my grandfather's. I d-didn't have anything else to s-sleep in."

Brand's jaw dropped. Closing his mouth and eyes, he dropped his head back and groaned. The hand on her shoulder tightened—not enough to hurt—then dropped away. "You sleep in the raw?"

Toni felt a blush climbing from her toes clear up to her ears. She may have renounced the prissy ways her parents had tried to force on her, but she hadn't been able to dismiss her love for silky underthings. She didn't own a single piece of lingerie that was anything less than an invitation to any man who saw it. She certainly wasn't wearing that kind of thing to bed with Brand because he wasn't the type to ignore the invitation. Despite the lecture she'd given herself, she wasn't sure she could resist if he pushed. Toni rubbed her temple. As a matter of fact, she was pretty sure she'd cave then hate herself in the morning. "I'll be comfortable in this."

"That's not what I asked," he said, tugging her chin around until their eyes met. "What do you usually sleep in?"

Toni couldn't think with his hand sliding down her arm to capture and stroke her fingers. He did it with such gentleness. His eyes glistened. *Get in that bed and go to sleep, Antonia Swenson. Lander.* She lifted her lids, which seemed determined to close, not because she was sleepy, but because her blood had heated to a thick ooze. Yanking her hand away, she opened a drawer, grabbed the nightie on top and flung it in his face. "I usually sleep in this."

While he gaped, she dived into bed, yanked the covers up to her chin, and hugged her edge of the mattress.

Brand caught the scrap of lace as it struck his face. Seeing Toni in another man's shirt had irked him. The shirttail flapping against her bare thighs had his groin throbbing with the memory of Toni wearing his shirt in Vegas. They'd awoken hungry and ordered a middle-of-the-night buffet. Afterward, she'd wrapped those shapely thighs of hers around his waist while he slowly unbuttoned... Oh, man.

The silky pink material slipping through his fingers only exacerbated his desire. Darned if he wouldn't have been better off thinking she slept naked rather than picturing her in this peek-a-boo piece of sin.

He was hard and hurting. And it looked as though he'd stay like that if the way Toni clung to her edge of the bed was anything to go by. She sent out more cold than a chunk of dry ice. He tossed the gown back into the drawer.

"Dammit, Toni. This is ridiculous." Easing her legs out of the way, he sat beside her.

She scowled. "I did not want a husband. You're the one who insisted we marry." Rolling over, she presented him with her back.

Brand stroked a knuckle down her stiff spine. Even though she stiffened up, he didn't miss her shiver or the hitch in her breathing. "There's nothing to say we can't make the best of the situation."

She glared at him over her shoulder.

Brand sighed and stood. He wasn't going to beg. He adjusted his briefs and circled the bed to crawl beneath the covers. Rolling to his side to face her, he propped his head on his elbow. Their eyes met for one brief moment. He dragged a fingertip along her arm. For some reason he couldn't help touching her petal-soft skin. "Toni, there's so much more I could teach you about making love."

"It wasn't making love, Brand. It was sex. Procreation. Pure and simple." She squeezed her eyes shut.

Brand snorted and lay on his back, folding his hands beneath his head. "Darlin', there was nothing pure or simple about that night in Vegas. We were about as sinful and tangled up as a man and woman can get."

She yanked the covers up to her ears. From the flush on her skin and her unsteady breathing, Brand knew he could probably change her mind with a little effort, but he wanted her willing.

Toni tried holding her breath, but it didn't work. She might not have to look at him, talk to him or even touch him, but she could *smell* him. For crying out loud. He'd showered before her. It was bad enough that his scent had hung in the bathroom when her turn had come, invading her space when he wasn't in sight. Now, in the cover of darkness, with nothing more than a shaft of moonlight crossing the bed, his woodsy scent again invaded her space, her mind. It made her ache. She pulled the sheet over her nose and chased sleep.

Her resistance weakened. It *had* been good in Vegas. Brand had been an ardent lover. She hadn't known that a man could make magic with his hands, his mouth, his body. She hadn't known that the rough groan of a man's voice, urging her to climb the peak one more time, could be so sexy. She hadn't known that lovemaking could be fast and urgent, slow and tender, or any number of variations in between.

She'd never known a man could be so gentle.

After her father's last tirade, the counselors had assured her that not all men were violent, but she hadn't believed them. Could they be right? Brand hadn't raised his hand in anger. *Yet,* her mind cautioned. She eased onto her side. For precious moments she let her hand hover over Brand's chest, anticipating the feel of him, the taste of him, the weight of him.

Down the hall the bathroom door squeaked open as one of the ranch hands got up. Toni jerked her hand back. Brand was a man. Of course she couldn't trust him.

Six

Déjà vu. A muscle-corded arm pinned Toni to the bed and a tanned hand cupped her breast. Brand's hard thigh fit intimately between hers, and his body heat seared her from her ankles to the back of her neck. His breath teased her hair, causing goose bumps to chase across her skin and her nipple to peak beneath his palm.

Toni gritted her teeth against the bud of desire unfurling in her belly and eased onto her back. First job of the day: extricating herself from the bed without waking her husband.

Her husband. She lay back and swallowed. Brand muttered something in his sleep and contracted his fingers. Toni gasped as lightning shot from her breast to her womb. Even in his sleep he knew what to do with a woman!

Brand jerked awake. He blinked once, twice. A slow, sleepy smile curved his lips. His eyes went from foggy to fiery in a nanosecond, and Toni's heart rate doubled just as fast.

"Mornin'," he said in a voice as raspy as his face. His thumbnail scratched over her nipple, finding it easily through her grandfather's chambray shirt. The place between her thighs tingled. *Danger* flashed in her mind like a street sign.

"Let me up, Brand." Was that her voice? That husky plea? Dear heavens. Toni put her hand on his thigh, determined to shove him off her and bolt for the bathroom. She hadn't counted on his hot skin scorching her palm or his wiry hairs tickling her nerve endings until she forgot all about running. Forgot everything but the feel of his skin next to hers.

Brand's arms banded around her and with an easy flip, he had her tucked beneath him. The heat of him scorched her through the tangled sheets. His mouth hovered, then brushed lightly against hers. Toni struggled with her need for safety and an overwhelming hunger to touch him, to stroke the hot, satiny skin of his back, to feel him inside her.

Rap. Rap. Wade, the youngest of the new crew, stood in the open bedroom door staring at the ceiling. His face and neck were nearly as red as his hair. "Uh…boss, you gonna get up? We're waiting for orders. It's nearly eight, and you said we needed to get going ASAP," he said, his tone apologetic.

Embarrassed beyond belief, Toni tried to hide beneath Brand.

"Be right down," Brand told him. Once the footsteps faded Brand closed his eyes and flopped back onto his side of the bed with a groan. "I know I shut that door last night," he growled irritably, then threw the covers back.

Toni started counting the stripes on the sheet to keep herself from watching Brand dress. Squeezing her eyes shut, she acknowledged it wasn't fear making her heart race. She cleared her throat and picked at the pillowcase. "The lock won't catch, so the door won't stay shut."

"I'll fix it. But first, I'm gonna warn those yahoos about

interrupting us. I swear I'll castrate the next one." He sounded angry enough to carry out the threat. Toni's eyes flew open. Brand had on his jeans and was stuffing his arms into another one of his flashy shirts. This one was white with a vivid herd of horses galloping across the sunset depicted on his back.

"Brand, don't you have any…work clothes?" She bit her lip and tried not to wince when he turned and she saw the front was twice as bright as the back. But at least she'd distracted him from his anger. She was very good at defusing anger. She'd had to be from an early age.

He glanced at his shirt and shrugged. "These *are* my work clothes. My sponsors give me the clothes, boots and hats, and pay me to wear them. If I'm dressed, darlin', I'm working. You'll get used to 'em eventually. I did." He grinned and Toni's breath hitched. "Best I remember, it took a while though."

He stepped into the bathroom. When he came out he put on his hat and turned for the door. "I'm going to get the boys started on the bunkhouse."

He left and Toni threw his pillow at the door. Darn it, she didn't want the bunkhouse fixed. Twice now, one of the men had kept her from doing something stupid.

Shoving aside the covers, she crossed the room and shut the bedroom door. She used one of the boxes of Brand's belongings his family had left behind yesterday to block it closed. She'd just tugged off her nightshirt and panties when the bedroom door opened. Toni squealed and tried to cover herself with her hands.

"What the he—" Brand looked up from the box he'd kicked aside and his words stopped. His gaze narrowed, raking slowly over her with bone-melting thoroughness. Stepping inside, he removed his hat, closed the door, and kicked the makeshift doorstop back into place.

"The men are working outside." His voice was rough. Toni's skin heated beneath his scrutiny. She kept one arm over her breasts and the other over her lap. "Y-you should kn-knock."

"On my own door?" His nostrils flared. After another lingering perusal of her nudity, his gaze met hers.

Toni squeezed her eyes shut and turned away from the invitation in his eyes. She heard him move closer and every muscle in her tensed. "P-please leave."

"Look at me," Brand's voice commanded in her ear.

She could feel his closeness, his heat and his breath stirring her hair. Reluctantly, she obeyed. In the mirror, she saw him behind her completely clothed, while she was totally naked. Her insides tightened. Her breath shuddered. She felt vulnerable. And weak. And aroused. And powerful. How did he do that? How could he exude such strength and yet make her feel strong at the same time?

He lifted his hand, and Toni braced herself against the touch she saw coming but was unable to resist. Brand dragged a fingertip down her arm, setting off an explosion, like a string of firecrackers in its wake.

His beard-roughened kiss on the sensitive spot beneath her ear electrified her. His hands settled on her waist, pulling her against him. "Let's go back to bed."

The denim of his jeans felt rough as he pressed himself against her bottom, while the pearlized snaps of his shirt felt cool against her spine. Toni's eyelids grew heavy.

"We can't." She exhaled the words. Brand nipped her earlobe. Her resistance faded beneath the sensuous glide of his hands over her hips, back up to the outer curves of her breasts. The reasons why they shouldn't be doing this burst like balloons.

He slid his tongue down the tendons of her neck. "Let me love you, Ton—"

A door slammed downstairs. One of the crew bellowed, "Brand! Time's a wastin'. Let's head out."

Brand muttered a curse and tightened his hands on her waist. "I used to like that man." Compressing his lips, Brand put a few inches between them. "You're right.

Now's not the time. I'm heading for town to pick up supplies. Need anything?''

Toni could barely remember her name, let alone her shopping requirements. ''I have a list on my desk. We need to repair the wells and reseed the pastures before the weather changes.''

''Toni—'' A horn blew outside. Brand heaved a sigh and settled his hat on his head. ''I'll see you in a few hours.''

Then he was gone. Toni sank onto the chair, her body still quivering from his caress. *Idiot. You didn't last five seconds with him once he turned on the charm. All he had to do was breathe on you.*

Toni cleaned the debris from the bunkhouse and piled it in the side yard for burning. She mucked the stalls and fed all the horses. She'd just finished reloading the mouse-traps when Brand returned. A delivery truck bearing the Farm and Ranch Supply logo followed his truck. She greeted the driver, whom she'd known for years, then walked alongside the flatbed, looking for seed, pump parts and barbed wire. All she saw was building materials. Next she searched the bed of Brand's truck. Groceries. Horse feed. No pump. No fencing. No seed. Her temper stirred. Hands on hips, she faced him. ''Brand, where's my stuff?''

Brand nudged his hat back and hooked his thumbs through his belt loops. ''We'll get it after we get the bunkhouse repaired.''

''We agreed. The wells and pastures are top priority,'' she pointed out. ''The cattle dip and inoculant are next.''

His jaw firmed. ''As of this morning, the bunkhouse became top priority.''

Toni felt her cheeks heat as the men listened attentively. ''Getting the crew out of the house will not change things,'' she whispered angrily.

''If you say so, darlin'.'' Brand's lips tilted up in a naughty grin. Hot sparks radiated from his eyes.

The urge to smack the know-it-all look off his handsome face stunned her. She'd *never* felt violent toward another person—not even her father. "Brand, we agreed to fix the wells and fences first."

"No, darlin', we didn't."

"I... You..." She was so angry she was sputtering. If she didn't get away from him, she *was* going to hit him, and hitting was never the answer. This was her ranch, she reminded herself. Brand was only a temporary investor here. Once he had his fill of solitude and hard work, he'd go back to the excitement of rodeoing and adoring buckle bunnies.

She turned on her heel and stomped into the house, determined to find the money somewhere to buy the pumps and fencing. An hour later, the bottom line still read broke, or at least near it. She wasted a moment wishing her grandfather had converted his records to computer, but at least he wrote legibly. Although he'd never gone beyond sixth grade, his letters were carefully printed in the proper school-taught style except for a few sloppy entries on the last few pages. Toni stuck her pencil behind her ear and frowned. Why hadn't she noticed that the last time she went through the ledger? Because she'd been crying then.

Toni bent over the pages and felt a surge of guilt. Had Granddad's illness caused the change in his handwriting? She should have been here to help out, but she'd been finishing school and training her replacement at the vet's office.

Half an hour later she sat back in dismay. The bank statement showed a large sum of money had already been withdrawn from the ranch account. The amount matched the estimate she'd found on well costs. Only there weren't any new well pumps or rolls of fencing. She and Brand had covered every inch of the property. She would have seen the items lying around if they'd been purchased, or she would have found the cash when she packed up her grandfather's clothes. Double-checking the dates and the handwriting, Toni noted that the sloppy entries came just days before her grandfather's death. Where was the money if the equipment hadn't been bought?

She called the bank and asked for the manager.

"Your grandfather's foreman made the withdrawal for him, Mrs. Lander. Your grandfather wasn't feeling well, and he couldn't make the trip to town. I checked with the Billings brothers before releasing the money. They verified that the parts had been ordered."

Toni sat up straighter in the chair. There was no work order from Billings Brothers' Well-Drilling Company. "Did the withdrawal slip have my grandfather's signature on it?"

"Are you suggesting he didn't authorize the withdrawal?" The man's voice chilled considerably.

"I'm saying, Mr. Richards, that the money was withdrawn for repairs, and the equipment to make them is not on the ranch. Neither is the cash. Mr. Matthews is not listed on the account."

He put her on hold. Toni impatiently thumped her pencil on the desk. She wouldn't put it past Matthews to rob a dying man.

"Miss Anderson, the signature doesn't seem to be…as neat as your grandfather's. I've also spoken with Lettie Billings. The well parts haven't been paid for or picked up."

"And if the signature is forged?" Hope flickered within her breast. It wasn't enough to bail out the ranch, but it would help her get the upper hand with one pigheaded cowboy.

"Then the bank will cover the funds, and we'll prosecute the forger. It's a federal offense to obtain money under false pretenses. We'll do our best to rectify the situation." Now the banker sounded overeager to please. Funny how her mistake had made him hoity. His mistake made him simper.

Toni ended the call and went in search of Brand. She

found him in the bunkhouse, stripped to the waist, a new tool belt hanging low on his hips. *Sexy.* The word popped into her brain before she could squash it. Muscles flexed and bunched beneath his sweat-slickened back as he pounded nails into a sheet of paneling on the wall.

"Brand?" Her voice was breathless and weak. She had to repeat herself to be heard over the hammering.

He lowered the hammer and faced her. "Yeah?"

Sweat tricked over his stubbly jaw, down his chest, and over his lean abdomen to dampen the waistband of his jeans. One droplet disappeared into his navel—the navel she'd dipped her tongue into. He cleared his throat, wiped his arm across his forehead and arched a dark brow.

Toni dropped her eyes to the paper crushed in her palm and pulled in a slow breath, willing the vision of rippling muscles to vacate her brain. Her blood raced and it had nothing to do with fear. "I…I think I've discovered where Matthews found the money for his new truck."

Brand slotted the hammer into his tool belt. "Show me."

Toni led him back to the house and into the study. She bent over the ledger, pointing wordlessly to the sloppy entries, because she couldn't find her voice. Brand leaned over the desk, his hands bracketing her body. The clean scent of fresh perspiration and the heat of his body filled her senses.

"What can we do about it?" Brand didn't draw back. He merely turned his head. His breath fanned her cheek.

Toni cleared her throat and focused on the scratches in the surface of the old desk rather than on the curve of Brand's lips. "The bank manager said the bank would have to make the money good if it's their mistake."

Brand nodded, his expression thoughtful as he straightened. He squeezed her shoulder. "Good job."

"As soon as it's cleared, I'm going to have the wells repaired and buy the seed." Taking one step back then another, she thrust out her chin and dared him to dispute it.

Brand sighed and scraped a hand across his face. "I'll get those, Toni. Put the money aside. You might...need it."

"Why?" She frowned.

"In case one of us doesn't hang around." Brand turned on his heel and left.

Toni scowled after him. A chill skipped down her spine. He had that right. One of them definitely wasn't the settling-down kind, but it wasn't her.

"What in the hell are you doing?"

The hammer slipped from Toni's fingers. She dug her nails into the roofing felt to keep from following the tool down the steep slope to the ground. "Stop creeping up on me."

Brand stood at the top of the ladder. "You have no business up here. Get down."

As hot as it was on the black tar paper, the temperature shot up another dozen degrees under his glare. "Wrong, cowboy. This ranch and anything on it is my business. Go bother somebody else."

"Get down." Brand knelt on the blacktop, as immovable as a gargoyle, but not nearly as ugly. Unfortunately. His sweat-soaked white T-shirt clung to his chest, as transparent as wet tissue. It was distracting, to say the least, to a woman who didn't want to topple to the ground below.

Golden sparks shot from his deep brown eyes and he'd thinned his luscious lips to an angry slash. And his jeans... She blew out a breath. With the way they clung and cupped him, her balance was in serious jeopardy. "Go away, Brand. I need to finish before the rain starts."

"Get down or I'll carry you down." The words were quietly, but adamantly spoken.

"What's the matter? Can't stand to have a woman above you?" Toni knew from the sudden glint in his eye, that she should have kept her smart mouth shut. What was wrong with her? Provoking someone was something she usually avoided at all costs, but it seemed she had a subconscious wish to push Brand until he snapped. At least then she'd know his limits.

"I have no problem with a woman over me or under me, darlin'. You should know. You've been both."

Heat flashed through her like a lit match. Toni told herself she had to get off the roof to get her hammer anyway. It had nothing to do with the sudden light-headedness she experienced when he turned on that bedroom voice and reminded her of Vegas.

Brand stayed one rung below her while she descended the ladder. She didn't know whether to be irritated that he coddled her or touched over his concern. Once she had both feet on the ground, she turned, intent on going to work in some Brand-less location. His hands still gripped the ladder on either side of her shoulders, trapping her between the metal rungs and hard, muscled cowboy. Reluctantly, she met his gaze.

"Let the guys do the dangerous stuff. It's what I'm paying 'em for." With a nod of his head, he was gone.

Brand figured the woman was going to give him a heart attack. Despite her pint size she seemed determined to take on jobs clearly better suited to a man. A part of him said let her break her dang-fool neck. The other part wanted her doing less hazardous chores. Hell, she didn't have to prove her worth to him. He'd already figured out there wasn't anything on this ranch she couldn't handle. There was something about a woman who looked as delicate as an angel but was as tough and determined as a veteran bull rider that set him on his heels.

In the meantime, between her escapades and the fact that she looked like every cowboy's dream in her tight jeans and tank tops, it didn't look like his heart was ever going to catch its normal rhythm again. He'd probably keel over before he saw this place running smoothly. It was a shame she wouldn't stick around. They could've been quite a team.

He was acting like a spoiled kid who wanted what he couldn't have, and he knew it, but Toni made him ache for something he couldn't put a tag on. Part of it was the memory of that night in Vegas, but part of it was... something else.

He found himself looking forward to their shared cup of coffee each morning and again after dinner. He liked the easy way she teased the men, keeping 'em in line with an arch of her brow or a fist on her hip. She might be a little slip of a thing, but the men all liked and respected her. Problem was, he was beginning to, too. She was smart and funny. If they'd met under different circumstances... Nah, he didn't believe in marriage because he'd seen it fail too many times. If he hadn't *had* to marry her, he wouldn't have.

He stepped into the shade of the bunkhouse porch, mentally counting the days since Vegas. When would she know if she was pregnant? Would she tell him or would he have to pry it out of her? His stomach did a funny twist. The possibility of being a father to a tiny helpless baby scared him spitless, but it also left him with a determination to do right by his kid. He'd seen enough happy families on the circuit to know a kid needed more than three square meals a day. A kid needed to know he was loved— doubly so if one of the parents had taken off. A kid needed to know he was more than just free labor and an obligation.

And a kid needed hugs. He couldn't remember the last time somebody had hugged him. *His* kid would have hugs.

The screen door slammed. Brand nearly dropped the new door he and Roy were hanging on the bunkhouse when Toni came off the back porch wearing a dress. He'd forgotten she had a first-class pair of legs, a tiny waist and a great set of— "Yeeeeow, damn it all to hell, Roy. You dropped the door on my foot."

"Sorry, Brand." Roy flushed and lifted his side of the door. His appreciative gaze shifted back to Toni. "Ya sure married you a looker."

The wind caught Toni's skirt, ballooning it up and out and giving him a peek at her sleek thighs. The view sent a flash of heat to his groin. That woman's legs were meant to be worn like a belt—around his waist. Shame was, she didn't agree.

Brand heard more than one wolf whistle and glared at his crew. "Put your eyes back in your heads. Roy, hold that door level. Wade, take over for me here." Brand passed the drill to the blushing kid and jogged over to meet Toni at the car.

"Where you headed?" She looked fabulous, and he wanted to drag her straight to bed. She'd put on her pink lipstick. The familiar urge to smear it with his mouth hit him just before the flowery scent of her perfume nearly knocked him to his knees.

Toni stepped around him and headed to the car. "I'm going to the bank to get the money straightened out."

"I'll come with you."

She frowned and glanced at her watch. "I have a nine o'clock appointment. I don't have time to wait for you to get ready."

Brand glanced at his clothes. He had on one of his sponsor-provided shirts. It had red lightning bolts on a black background. The colors were a little loud, but both the shirt and his black jeans were clean. "There's something wrong with what I'm wearing?"

Toni's gaze swept slowly over him. His blood headed south under her slow perusal. If the wave of pink flush creeping up her neck was any indication, she'd noticed his response.

"Let's go." She slid into the driver's seat of her aged sedan and fired the engine.

Brand knew without a doubt if he didn't drop his tool belt pronto and get in, she'd leave him behind. One thing he'd learned about Toni was that she didn't waste time when something needed doing. He tossed the belt to Aaron and settled in the seat.

Inside the bank, employees stepped forward to congratulate them on their marriage. One woman dragged Toni off to her desk to see a picture of her latest grandchild. Brand felt a frisson slither down his spine. Toni had roots here. Would she leave as soon as he expected? Sure, she would.

Toni beckoned him from an open office door. "Mr. Richards is ready for us."

Richards was a typical banker. High-dollar suit, wire-rimmed glasses and slicked-back hair. Brand would bet the man had never sipped from a longneck bottle in his life. After shaking Brand's hand with his soft palm, he gestured to the chairs opposite his desk, and closed the door before launching into a suck-up monologue.

Brand interrupted. "Let's cut to the chase. We want the money back in the ranch account with all due interest. Toni and I'll need our names on the signature card and new checks printed." Brand sat back in his chair. "If you can handle that, I'll transfer my personal accounts to your bank."

As expected, the man squirmed like an overeager puppy. "I'll get the forms immediately." He hustled out of the office.

Toni rolled her eyes. "I haven't seen that much brown-nosing on a new calf searching his momma for his first meal."

"Don't take it personally. It's my money he wants."

Richards bustled in, fanned out several signature cards and an assortment of forms across his desk. He pointed to the first two. "These are the signature cards for the Rocking A accounts. If you'll both sign those where marked?" He shifted several other cards. "These will be for your new accounts…unless, of course, you'd like to deposit all of your funds into the ranch account?''

"Nope." Brand shook his head. "Keeping it separate."

Richards nodded. "So all we'll need to do is transfer your funds to this bank and add Toni—" he flashed Toni a fond smile "—Mrs. Lander's signature to your signature card."

"This'll be my personal account." There was no way in hell he'd give the woman a chance to clean out his money.

After a moment of uncomfortable silence the banker said, "Of course, Mr. Lander. Many young couples keep separate accounts these days. I should have asked instead of assuming."

Despite the quick recovery of the banker, Brand knew from the starch in Toni's spine that she wasn't happy. After concluding their business, Brand followed her from the bank. She climbed into her car without waiting for him to open her door. Brand had to hustle around the trunk and jump in as she shifted into reverse.

Toni reached the end of the city limits and hit the gas pedal. The deputy merely waved when the blue sedan blew past him at the speed of light. If there was a decent bone in the man's body, he'd have pulled her over. A few miles down the road, she swung the car into the Farm and Ranch Supply parking lot.

"Toni, my rodeoing is a separate business," he said, unclenching his fingers. "For tax purposes—"

She threw open her car door, slammed it in his face, and marched for the steps. Why in the hell did he feel so bad for doing the right thing? Brand swore and hustled to catch up. He grabbed her arm and spun her around. She jerked back as if she expected him to hit her, which angered and confused him even more. How could she think he'd hurt her, or any woman for that matter?

"You'll get the money you need for the ranch. Hell, I'm

going to deposit your half of the property value in the account as soon as the appraiser's report comes back.''

Fire shot from her baby blues. How he'd ever thought she looked angelic, he didn't know. She looked positively lethal.

She pushed his hand away. ''What I wanted was not to be totally humiliated by my husband. You might as well have taken out a front-page article in the weekly paper announcing that you didn't trust me with *your* money. It's the only bank in town, Brand. The one place everyone has in common. It's also the biggest source of gossip.''

He thought he saw tears sparkling in her eyes, but she turned from him and threw open the glass door to the store. Everyone inside looked elsewhere. Brand swore again. Two stops in town. Two strikes against him.

Toni stepped to the counter and greeted the clerk by name. After a few minutes of chitchat she handed the man her list. ''Brand forgot to pick up these the other day. Would you please have them delivered to the ranch tomorrow?''

She pulled out her checkbook and started writing. Brand stepped forward to remind her that he was supposed to be paying, but he held back. Making an issue of the money in front of the store personnel and customers was not the way to handle it. He'd deposit the amount of the check in the farm account next time he came to town.

''Mr. Lander?'' the clerk called. ''That fencing you ordered will be in tomorrow. Do you want us to deliver it with Toni's supplies?''

Toni frowned. ''What fencing material? You said you didn't get anything on my list.''

''The bull pen.''

''We do our breeding by insemination.''

Brand ran a finger under his collar. He'd meant to discuss his plans with her, but…well, with the way his hormones had been in an uproar, he'd forgotten. He glanced at the eavesdropping clerk and customers, then back to

Toni. "I'm building a corral and chutes for bucking bulls. I've bought a couple, and they'll be delivered within the week."

Color ran up her cheeks. It didn't stop until it reached her hairline. Her mouth opened and closed, then she pressed her lips together. Toni positively vibrated with anger. He wouldn't have been surprised if she'd taken a swing at him. "The Rocking A is a beef-cattle operation."

"I know, and we'll get back to that, eventually, but right now I want to give lessons to the kids coming along, Toni. Might even try to raise a few head of Brahma for the circuit."

Toni stared at him. Without another word, she walked out. Brand hustled behind her and hopped into the car. He had a feeling she'd like to leave him behind. A few miles down the road, she swerved to the shoulder.

Toni turned to him with a jerk. "Thank you for your repeated displays of confidence. First—" the gesture displaying a single finger was not a polite one "—you hire hands without consulting me. Second, you ignore my supply list in some mistaken belief that getting your buddies out of the house will have you sharing more than just my mattress. Third, your humiliating lack of confidence in me at the bank, and now this." She smacked the steering wheel. "Fifty-fifty, you said. When do I get a say in how *my family's ranch* is run?" Her voice had risen several decibels.

"Toni—"

"Get out," she said quietly. Her hands tightened on the steering wheel until her knuckles turned white. He figured she'd probably rather wrap 'em around his neck.

"What?" Brand shoved back his hat and laughed, thinking she was joking, but her glare could have set a dry field ablaze.

"Get out."

Brand got out.

Toni drove down the road a couple of miles and pulled

over. She shook so badly she could barely put the car in Park. If she hadn't made Brand get out of the car she would have hit him. *Hit him.* Never in her life had she met anyone who could arouse her to this degree of anger. *You are not your father,* the counselors had told her. She had to wonder. Today, she'd almost decked a cowboy.

She hadn't known Brand was considering raising bulls or teaching bull riding, because he hadn't bothered to tell her. High-handed. That's what he was. Devious and conniving. At least about the ranch. He was pretty darn honest about wanting more sex. With the crew he was kind, compassionate, loyal and generous. But with her....

She'd had enough negativity from her father, who'd been a firm believer in keeping the women in his life in the dark and under his thumb. According to him, a woman's role was to look good and support her husband's career. Her grandfather had offered her a safe refuge, but he'd also believed a woman's job was to support her man. Well she didn't want to support a man. She wanted to support herself.

If it hadn't been for her grandfather's former foreman, she wouldn't have been allowed out of the ranch compound. Rusty had sneaked her out on the trail. He'd taught her how to ride, rope, shoot, brand and just about everything else that needed doing on the ranch. He'd never held her back because she was female. He'd treated her like one of the hands. In the process he'd gifted her with a confidence in herself and her abilities, something she'd sorely lacked.

All she'd ever wanted was to come home to the Rocking A. If Brand thought he was going to take over, then she'd straighten him out pretty darn quick. And if she couldn't do it by herself, she'd find old Rusty. What that man could do with an unruly cowboy was legendary.

Seven

Brand kicked a rock and added another yard to the blue streak he'd been swearing along the roadside. Women were a pain. He'd be damned if he knew why men put up with them.

A memory of Vegas steamed his brain cells and ignited his groin. All right, he knew why. He'd put up with a lot to get Toni back in his bed. Or to see her face over his coffee mug each morning. He could talk to her. Didn't matter whether it was feed rations or baseball. She didn't fuss about clothes, breaking a fingernail, or getting dirty like other women. And her ideas for the ranch blew his mind.

As if his day hadn't started out bad enough, the deputy sheriff's car pulled to a stop beside him. "Need a ride?"

The ranch was a good ten miles down the road. Except for that one night, he'd never been stupid. Brand swallowed his pride, opened the cruiser door, and climbed in. "'Preciate it."

They rode in silence for several minutes. Josh cleared his throat. "I know you don't want to hear this from me, but Toni has a hard time with men who try to boss her around. She had more than her share of that from her dad, and Will near 'bout smothered her. From what I've heard, either you didn't know or you don't care."

Brand digested the information. It explained a lot about some of the things that set Toni off. He turned in the seat, propped his elbow on the door, and eyed Keegan suspiciously. "You playing marriage counselor?"

Josh grimaced. "Nah. I just want Toni to be happy. If you're the one who makes her happy, then…" He shrugged.

Brand narrowed his eyes. "And if I don't?"

Keegan turned into the ranch driveway. Once he'd parked the cruiser behind the house, he turned off the ignition and faced Brand. "Then somebody else will."

Brand felt his territorial hackles rise. "Thanks for the warning, but Toni is *my* wife."

Again Josh shrugged. "If you can keep her. See, folks around here know things about Toni that you don't."

"And I know things about her that *you* don't. Thanks for the ride, Deputy, but stay away from Toni."

The aromas coming from the kitchen made Brand's mouth water and his stomach growl. He hung up his hat as Toni set lasagna, salad and crusty bread on the table. The hands were grumbling good-naturedly, but loading their plates with everything, including the veggies Toni insisted they eat.

She did more than her share of the kitchen duties and for that he gave thanks. He and the men knew how to cook steak and hamburger, hamburger and steak. All of it medium rare. And none of it with anything green near it except maybe a pickle.

"Hey, darlin'." She sidestepped his kiss. Brand shook his head and picked up a plate. Obviously she wasn't interested in making amends.

Toni seated herself at the far end of the table from him and addressed the ranch hands. "Can any of you drive the John Deere? I'd like to get started on the seeding while the weather's cooperating, and if a couple of you could help me with the fencing I'd appreciate it."

Deke frowned at Brand. "I thought the bull pen was next."

"Right after the bunkhouse, you said," Aaron insisted.

Wade watched wide-eyed, as if expecting an explosion. Roy smirked.

Brand looked at Toni's stiff shoulders and tight features. "Toni, the bulls have already left Cheyenne. I need Deke and Aaron to help me build the pens and Wade and Roy to help with set-up."

"Fine." She stood, scraped the food she hadn't touched into the trash, then headed for the office and quietly shut the door.

Four sets of eyes studied him as if he'd just drop-kicked a puppy. Brand growled, "Eat your damn dinners."

Toni sank into the leather chair, and put her head in her hands. Brand didn't trust her. She didn't even think he liked her. How could they have a marriage, even a temporary one, without those basics to build on? And if there was a baby, how could she bring it up in such a combative atmosphere?

The ranch wasn't her refuge anymore. It was a war zone with each of them trying to score hits off the other. So far, the hits had been verbal, but what would it take to push Brand over the line?

She reached for the phone to do the chore she'd been avoiding. "Mom—"

"Toni, good heavens child, where are you?" Without pausing for an answer she swept on, "We've been expecting you to come home as soon as you closed up Daddy's place. Your father has already contacted a Realtor about selling the ranch."

Toni counted to ten. "Mom, I'm staying here at the ranch."

"But Antonia, you can't handle that place alone, and I—I'd like to have you near."

Toni felt a stab of guilt. Maybe she should have stayed and stood up for her mother instead of running away, but the counselors had assured her that she had to get out while she could, before her father's brainwashing convinced her that she deserved the abuse. Still, leaving her mother behind had been difficult. She'd always regret it.

"Mom, I called to tell you that I got married last week."

"Without your father meeting him first and making sure he was an acceptable husband? What were you thinking?"

She bit her tongue on the retort that sprang to her lips and sighed. Fighting with her mother wasn't why she'd called. "His name is Brand Lander. You may have seen his picture in the paper. He's the National Finals Rodeo bull-riding champion this year."

"You married a man who rides bulls for a living!"

Why did talking to her mother always give her a headache? "Look, Mom, I've got to go…tend to a horse. Talk to you later."

Toni hung up on her mother's sputtering and pressed her fingers against her temples. That hadn't gone well. Not that she'd expected it would. She could only hope that her call to Rusty Jackson, her grandfather's previous foreman, would go better. She reached for her grandfather's Rolodex and crossed her fingers.

Perspiration rolled down Brand's face, but his skin felt clammy. His heart hammered triple-time. Inching backward, he never took his eyes from the snake coiled beside the wall on the far side of the stall. He heard someone enter the barn.

"Brand?"

He'd expected a confrontation, but he couldn't handle

it *now*. He had to warn her, but it was difficult to get anything past the terror clogging his throat. ''Get out.''

''What?''

''Snake. Get the hell out.'' He tried to talk without moving his lips.

He felt her presence directly behind him. ''What kind?''

''A live one, dammit. Now move.'' She leaned past him. Crowding him. *Blocking his escape.* Every cell in his being tensed. Brand slowly spread his arms and tried to shield her. He eased backward. One step. Two.

Toni clasped his waist and planted her feet.

He braced himself, clenching his jaw. At this point his brothers would have shoved, and he'd have landed either on or too damn near the reptile.

Toni didn't shove. She squeezed his waist and said, ''Brand, it's only a barn snake.''

''What in the hell do you mean it's 'only a barn snake'? That SOB's six feet long.'' He wished he wasn't too busy to enjoy the press of her breasts against his back.

''He'll eat a lot of rats.''

''Toni, I only have one rule about snakes. That a live one needs to be a dead one.'' Short of turning his back on the snake—which he would not do—and tossing Toni over his shoulder, there was no way for him to get them both out of the barn. *And he wouldn't leave Toni behind.* That was as sobering a thought as he'd ever had. He'd risk a snake for Toni.

When Toni backed off, Brand exhaled. Now he could get out of here. His ego had taken a hit. He'd shown his yellow streak in front of his wife. He inched backward.

The stall door opposite him opened. Toni stood framed in the sunlight. ''Shoo him my way, Brand.''

''No way.'' His throat knotted again at the thought of putting her in danger. His heartbeat thundered in his ears.

''Brand, we need to get him out before the crew brings the horses back in for the night. Shoo him out the door.''

''I want a shovel or a gun. I want him in pieces.''

Toni stepped out of sight. The snake eyed Brand. It eyed the open door. He hoped like hell it chose the door. He'd embarrassed himself enough already without running for the exit.

Toni came in behind him and elbowed him aside. With nothing more than a broom she approached the monster, shooed him outside, then closed the stall door. Was she crazy? Brand found himself rigid with fury that she'd risk herself over a snake. He grabbed her shoulders and pressed her against the wall.

"Are you out of your freakin' mind?"

Eyes wide, Toni shrank away from him. He felt her trembling beneath his hands and didn't understand it. She'd shown no fear of the monster. Why was she shaking now that it was gone?

"It was a *snake*. A big snake. He could have bitten you."

"B-barn snakes don't b-bite." He released her, but she remained wary. "Our—our tack room is overrun with mice. A dozen barn snakes that size would be nice right about now. I've handled snakes much larger than that one before."

Brand's eyes bulged and his gut pitched. "You pick 'em up?"

She shrugged and put a couple of steps between them without talking her eyes off him. "It's my job. I specialized in large animals, but I studied everything else. I had a part-time job with a small-animal vet. He treated reptiles."

Brand suppressed a shudder. Once more, Toni's delicate image bit the dust. If the woman could handle snakes, she could handle anything. So why had she been shaking after the fact? She didn't give him time to ask.

"Why are you terrified of snakes?"

What was left of his ego curled up and died. He shoved his hands in his pockets and turned away. He wanted to spit or scratch or do one of those obnoxious guy things that proved he wasn't a sissy. But he didn't. He had a feeling Toni would see right through it. "You mean why am I a coward?"

"That's not what I asked. A lot of people are afraid of snakes, Brand. I'd say you were more than just afraid."

Brand scraped up a pile of shavings with his boot, then spread 'em back out. Toni waited. Resigning himself to telling the tale, Brand leaned against the stall.

"When I was six, my best friend and I were swimming in the creek. We knew we weren't supposed to swim after a hard rain, but we did anyway. He got into a moccasin bed and was bitten more times than you can count. He died. Right there on the bank."

A picture of Dan's punctured body flashed in his mind. As if it were yesterday, he could hear his best friend struggling for his last breath. A shudder racked him.

Toni curled an arm around his waist and she hugged him. *Hugged him.* He'd vowed that his kid would have hugs, but he didn't know how he was supposed to respond to one. He took a deep breath and cleared his throat. Tentatively, he put his arms around her waist. It felt right to be standing here in her arms in the dimly lit barn.

"Ever since I haven't…liked snakes much. My brothers knew it and used every opportunity to scare me. If there was a snake around, you can bet they'd catch it and put it somewhere for me to find. Boots, lunch boxes, toilet. You name it. Patrick was bitten when he tried to catch a rattler to torture me with. We weren't sure he'd pull through."

Toni gasped and tightened her arms. "That's horrible. Why would they do that?"

Brand shrugged. "They're my brothers. Brothers do that kind of thing for fun."

He'd expected ridicule, not compassion. Was Toni ever going to do what he expected? Brand studied his boots. "Toni, I'm sorry I embarrassed you at the bank today. I should have explained beforehand that I want to keep my rodeo business separate."

The sympathetic softness left her eyes. They went from the soft blue of a baby's blanket to the hard silvery blue of an ice chip. Her arms fell from his waist and she stepped away.

"You made your point, Brand. You don't trust me. I can't say I blame you. We've known each other less than two weeks, and I didn't exactly start off on the best foot. Just don't expect me to extend my trust to you when I'm getting nothing in return."

Brand watched her stomp off toward the bunkhouse. He'd let her go work with Roy. She needed time to cool down, and maybe by tonight he'd find the words to make her understand.

One thing was for sure, next time he had her curled against him he'd just shut up and kiss her.

Toni held the sink against the wall while Roy tightened a piece of pipe beneath it. The bunkhouse renovation was nearly complete. As far as she was concerned that wasn't good news.

"So how'd you lasso him?" Roy's question nearly caused her to drop the sink on his head.

"What?"

He cranked the socket wrench another time and heaved his bulk out from beneath the porcelain. "How'd you catch Brand? He never fools around during the season. Lives like a danged monk."

Toni squirmed inwardly, certain that if Roy heard the truth she'd have another crew that hated her guts. "I—I don't know. It just sort of…happened."

"You can let go now. It oughta hold." Roy scratched his head and plunked on his hat. "Ain't no secrets on the circuit, but nobody knew 'bout you 'cept Bobby Lee. An' all he'd say is you left Vegas and Brand hired somebody to find you."

He started packing away the tools. "Never thought Brand was the marrying sort. He's had a thing going with some li'l gal—name of Megan, I b'lieve—at Coyote Western Wear, y'know, one of those sponsor companies, for the last couple of years, but he's never been serious about nobody." His gaze caught Toni's. "Until he up and married you."

Unexpected jealousy made it difficult to get a word out. Toni gave herself a mental kick. She had no claim on Brand prior to Vegas, and if she'd had her way, she wouldn't have one on him now. *Liar.* All right, for some reason the thought of Brand with another woman bothered her. Unclenching her fingers from the basin, she tried to sound unconcerned. "He has a girlfriend?"

Roy snapped the latch on the toolbox and faced her. "Last I heard, he did, and it wasn't you." He patted her on the shoulder. "Nothing for you to be worried about since he put a ring on your finger. Brand ain't the cheatin' kind. I'm heading out to help the boys."

"Right. Nothing to worry about." Toni forced her lips into a smile and sank down on the edge of the bed Aaron and Deke had assembled that morning. Her husband had a lover. She should be happy. No, *thrilled.* Certainly he'd want to sell out and spend more time with her. This was good news wasn't it?

Then why did it make her so…miserable?

A quick rap on the bedroom door drew Toni's gaze. Brand entered, closed the door and locked it. His gaze drifted over the skin bared by the sagging neckline of her oversize sweatshirt. She yanked up the material, folded her arms, and tried to ignore the prickle of awareness his slow perusal caused. She focused instead on how much his distrust hurt.

The day had been long and unpleasant beginning with the embarrassing scene at the bank and ending with the news that Brand had a girlfriend the last couple of years. Add in the call to her mother and the confrontation in the barn and she wasn't up to more heartache now. She was cranky and short-tempered and she just wanted to be left alone.

Toni turned away. After a minute, she heard the bathroom door shut. She was angry with Brand and even more with herself. The crew had told her so much about Brand's generosity over the last few days—things she should have known before going to bed with him and totally ruining her plan. If she'd tried, she couldn't have chosen a man less likely to turn his back on his child. She didn't want to like the man she'd married, but it was too late. Brand Lander was truly a nice guy who didn't deserve what she'd done to him.

The water stopped splashing in the sink and the door opened. She faced him. "Why didn't you tell me this job was putting food on the table for Aaron and Deke's huge family? Or that Roy is battling alcoholism and you offered him a job and a place to dry out?"

Brand wiped his face on a towel, looking a little uncomfortable. "They're my buddies, Toni. I'm helping out the only way I know how."

"And Wade? That poor kid's older brother used to get high and beat him up. He told me he ran away the day he turned eighteen and ended up with you. For him, you're like a father and hero rolled into one. He bends over backward to impress you."

Brand shrugged. "He's a good road partner. Likes to drive."

"So why didn't you just tell me instead of ramming your friends down my throat? Didn't you think I'd understand and back you one hundred percent?" She reached for him, but lowered her hand before making contact. Touching him would only complicate things. "You're doing a good thing, Brand."

She turned to stare at her reflection in the darkened window. She'd done her best to forget Vegas, had even tried blaming that crazy rush of sensation on hormones and alcohol. She knew she lied. From the moment she'd set eyes

on Brand Lander, he'd mesmerized her. At the most in-
convenient times she caught herself recalling his taste and
the feel of his calloused fingertips skipping along her skin.
In Brand's arms she'd felt womanly, wise and wonderful,
not cold-blooded and calculating.

His gentleness and his obvious concern for her pleasure
had shocked her. All her life, no one had ever cared
enough to find out what made her tick. She'd gone looking
for a bum and ended up with a man who anticipated her
desires before she recognized them herself.

The gentle touch of his hands on her shoulders made
her jerk in surprise. With his thumbs he pressed soothing
circles along her spine and beneath her shoulder blades,
untangling knots of tensions. She bit her lip, battling the
urge to lean into him.

"I don't know how to be a husband, but I am working
on it." Brand murmured the words against her nape, stirring the fine hairs along her neck and shoulders. Heat
crackled down her spine and pooled in her abdomen. The
man dissolved her good sense and made her want so much
more than the solitary life she'd planned.

"Sex won't solve anything," she whispered. But heavens, he made her feel good. When Brand held her close,
being female didn't mean being powerless or victimized.
It meant an equitable giving and receiving of pleasure. In
his arms, she had a power she'd found nowhere else. *And
it didn't hurt.*

Brand turned her to face him. The hot promise in his
eyes lured her, tempting her to take a risk. "Maybe not,
but we have to start somewhere. Find some common
ground with me, Toni."

He slid his hands down her arms and stroked a hypnotic
pattern on her wrists, her palms. Tiny shocks of sensation
radiated from his light caress to the pit of her stomach.
With slow, deliberate movements Brand lifted her hands
to his shoulders. He cupped her waist and feathered se-

ductive, tender kisses along her hairline, her jaw. Her lids grew heavy.

This wasn't a good idea and she knew it. If she had half a brain she'd end this madness before it consumed her. It was important to keep her distance, because Brand would leave. Suddenly, it didn't matter. What mattered was now.

His teeth tugged her earlobe. Toni's breath hitched. He traced the shell of her ear with his tongue and her knees weakened. Afraid she'd collapse at his feet, she dug her fingers into his broad shoulders and let her head fall to the side. Brand took advantage by opening his mouth and swirling his hot tongue over her erratic pulse. He nuzzled her neck band aside and nibbled on her shoulder, her collarbone.

She was sinking fast into a white-hot pool of sensation, but some part of her sanity held on. "I won't share."

Brand drew back, confusion mingling with the desire in his gaze. "Share what, darlin'?"

"You."

The possessive flash in his dark eyes held her captive, and the sexy curl of his lips destroyed the last of her resistance. "You won't have to."

For a moment Toni battled her conscience, then she surrendered to her need to get closer to Brand. Her eager fingers fumbled with the buttons of his shirt.

"Easy, darlin', we have all night." Brand's hands swept beneath her baggy sweatshirt, skimming up over her ribs to cup her bare breasts. The calloused pads of his thumbs scratched erotically over her pebbled nipples with a touch so delicate it nearly made her weep. Had it not been for his strong thigh thrust between her own, she might have sunk to the floor in a mindless puddle of need.

Brand whisked her shirt over her head, scooped her up. He carried her to the bed and set her down in the middle of the mattress. He left her long enough to yank off his shirt, then he knelt over her again. The crisp curls on his chest tickled her breasts like a thousand tiny fingers while he finger-combed her hair across the coverlet.

"When I close my eyes at night I see you like this."

He captured her surprised gasp with his lips, kissing her long, slow, deep, as if he had all night to devote to making love to her mouth. With his tongue, he explored the recesses and invited her to do the same to his. Toni accepted the invitation. She tested the softness of his lips, tasted the silky cavern. He closed his lips around her tongue and sucked. Rational thought fled. Her fingers were hungry for the satiny skin and taut muscles of his back. Clasping her thighs around his, she arched shamelessly against the ridge of his arousal, fitting him tighter to her aching center.

Brand reared back with a sharply indrawn breath. "Whoa, darlin'. Don't rush it."

He lowered his head and nuzzled her breast with the rough stubble of his chin, then followed it up with the silky, slick heat of his tongue. When he suckled her deep into his mouth, Toni could only moan and dig her fingers into his hair as the vortex of pleasure pulled her under. He licked and nibbled his way across her abdomen to the opposite breast. Her blood became lava. Her heart pounded harder in an effort to push the thick liquid through her veins.

Brand tugged the sweatpants from her and nuzzled the sensitive skin on the inside of her thighs. In Vegas, he'd shown her exquisite pleasure with his intimate kisses. He'd made her lose control and she hadn't minded. Tonight was no different. Desire curled and tightened, centering all her thoughts, all her feelings, on the stroke of his tongue. She clutched his hair, his shoulders, the sheets, as he brought her to peak after peak, not stopping until she whimpered, "No more."

His husky chuckle vibrated against her belly like the purr of a cat. "Oh, darlin', we have barely even started. Undress me."

It was only then that she realized Brand still wore his

jeans and boots. She felt a moment's embarrassment over her nakedness, but he gave her time for no more than that before he scorched her with another hot kiss. When they broke for air she scooted down the bed, anxious to get him bare. She grasped a boot and tugged, but it didn't budge.

"Stand at the foot of the bed," he instructed, his voice rusty and full of promise. Toni slid off the bed, eager to do anything he suggested if it meant getting him naked, getting him inside her. "Now turn around."

Never crazy about the width of her bottom, she hesitated, but the fire in his eyes told her to risk the exposure. She turned and saw the stranger from Vegas in the mirror on the dresser, a wanton woman with disheveled hair and glowing eyes. Whisker burn marked her breasts, her neck, her thighs. Brand's tanned hands framed her waist. His boot appeared between her legs.

"Now bend over and pull," he instructed. Toni grasped the boot and felt the sole of the other on her bare buttock. He pushed, she pulled. The boot came off in her hands. She tugged off his sock and tossed it away. Brand switched legs, and she repeated the procedure.

She tried to turn. His hands tightened on her hips and held her in place. The warmth of his breath brushed over her sensitized skin. He pressed kiss after kiss over her rounded behind. His lips held her captive, marking an upward trail on her vertebrae as he stood to shove off his jeans. He kicked them aside and sat back down. Brand pulled her back, opening her legs over his. Suddenly, swiftly, unexpectedly, his arousal filled her, pushing the air from her lungs and all thought from her mind.

"Ride me, Toni." Rough words, groaned against her back, sent an electric charge to her womb. She caught Brand's reflection in the mirror. Streaks of color swept his cheekbones. His eyes were closed and his jaw clenched. His Adam's apple bobbed. His hot, harsh breath blew against the fine hairs on her skin. Each follicle acted like a lightning rod, accepting a charge and relaying it until her body hummed like a tuning fork. He lifted his lids and the heat of his dark chocolate eyes melted over her.

As if feeling his possession wasn't erotic enough, Toni saw it all in the mirror. Brand shoved her hair over one shoulder and buried his mouth against her neck. She saw it coming, but nothing could prepare her for the sensual prickle of his evening beard or the scorch of his tongue. She witnessed tanned hands cupping her pale breasts, rolling her peaked nipples and it multiplied her response tenfold. His hands stroked downward, spreading her pale thighs wider. Golden curls mingled with nearly black. Then his biceps bunched in a raw display of power as he lifted and lowered her. She saw herself, open and vulnerable to his possession.

And she wasn't afraid.

Planting her feet on the floor, Toni lifted then lowered, following the rhythm Brand demonstrated with a firm grip on her waist. One of his big, scarred hands parted her feminine folds to caress the heart of her with a touch so delicate it amazed her. Her blood sluiced through her veins. Her heartbeat nearly deafened her. Before her eyes, her body swallowed his length while his hands stroked her magically. *Gently.*

The thick muscles in his arms and legs contracted. Instead of the fear she expected, the strength of his body fascinated her. She couldn't resist tracing the raised veins on his forearms to the backs of his hands. When she dragged her nails lightly over his thighs, Brand bowed his back and smothered a groan against her neck. He nipped her shoulder, his face tightening, as if he were in agony.

But he didn't hurt her.

Even lost in the throes of passion he was careful. He bucked again, nearly unseating her, and surged into her harder, faster. And together they watched his body, slick with her dew, sliding into hers again and again.

Lightning struck. The tingles began at her toes and shot upward in a shower of sparks. She jerked against him, her back arching. His arms tightened around her, but never to the point of pain. She heard Brand groan her name, felt his own cataclysmic explosion. And then all was still except for the sound of their labored breathing.

Slowly, Toni's heart rate approached normal. Her thighs ached and her body felt tender. She couldn't have supported her own weight. She sagged into the heat of Brand at her back and looked at the two of them in the mirror. How could she find such abandon in a man's arms, and how could she trust a man so lost in passion not to injure her? But she did. She trusted Brand and she was afraid she might be falling in love with him.

His chin rested heavily on her shoulder, and his chest still heaved. He met her gaze in the mirror and a drowsy smile quirked the corner of his mouth. Keeping her anchored against him with one hand, he used the other to brush the hair from her eyes and stroke a droplet of sweat from her cheek.

"Darlin', if we're half as good at running a ranch together as we are at this, the Rockin' A will be the best damned spread in the country."

Toni felt her lips curl in a sad smile. If only it were that easy. She'd finally found a man she could trust not to hurt her physically and he had the power to destroy her mentally by taking away the most important thing in her life—her sanctuary.

"I'm behind you, Toni." His tone implied more that just his present physical location. "We can make this work. I don't know how, but we will."

Brand helped her to her feet, turned her to face him, and pulled her between his thighs. His eyes were intent as he dragged a knuckle along her jaw. "I'll help you get this place the way you want it to be, but you have to work with me, not against me."

The pad of his finger drifted from her collarbone to her nipple. Formulating a reply took too much effort. "It's difficult to work with you when you're the only one who knows what you're doing.''

Brand nodded. ''Tomorrow, after we set the men to work, you and I'll sit down and talk. The bull pen can wait until after lunch.''

Toni bristled at the reminder. ''I don't like bucking bulls.''

Brand sighed. ''I can walk away from competing, Toni, but I can't just toss out years of my life. I've learned a hell of a lot, and I want to share it with the kids coming up.''

Toni understood goals. Vet school had been one step toward her goal of independence. ''I did a lot of work in animal husbandry in school specifically with the goal of trying to crossbreed for leaner beef. I don't know anything about raising bucking stock.''

''But that's what I do know.'' Brand's hand stroked the skin between her navel and her tight golden curls. ''What about our breeding stock? When will you know?''

As if his hand were a magnet, the iron in her blood pooled beneath the warmth of his palm, distracting her from the determined tone of his voice. ''Another week or so, I guess.''

His eyes held hers. ''I want to know as soon as you do.''

Toni swallowed the knot in her throat. Was it caused by fear or longing? She didn't know. What she did know was that the thought of carrying Brand's baby, of being tied to this man for the rest of her life through a child, didn't terrify her the way it once had. ''Okay.''

He yawned hugely. ''Right now, I want to curl up next to you and get some sleep. You've worn me out, darlin'.'' He winked then bent forward to suckle her nipple. ''Course, it might take me a while to get to sleep.''

Eight

Brand heard the truck long before he saw it.

He tightened another bolt in the section of the metal bullring he and the crew were assembling. Toni was up on the roof of the barn, determined to reshingle it herself. Short of putting his foot down and hiding the ladder, he hadn't had a choice but to let her do the job. Nobody in town was interested in working on the Rocking A. Wade was afraid of heights. Roy was just too damn big and awkward to be that far off the ground. Aaron and Deke were the only ones who knew how to install a bull fence.

The old El Camino rust bucket came to a shuddering halt beside the ring. The engine backfired and Toni squealed. Brand's blood ran cold. With his heart in his throat, he spun toward the barn, expecting to see her tumbling from the roof. Instead she skidded from the apex on her behind, clambered down the ladder at breakneck speed and sprinted across the yard to launch herself at the driver of the truck.

Beau came out of the barn howling as if in mortal pain. Brand glanced away from Toni long enough to make sure the dog hadn't been bitten by that damned barn snake. The mutt streaked toward the newcomer. It was the first time Brand had seen the dog move faster than a snail.

The man climbing from the truck not only looked like Santa Claus, his booming laugh sounded like him, too. Toni wrapped her arms around their visitor's wide middle and gave him a hug. Beau squirmed and wiggled beside them like an overeager puppy.

Brand put down his tools and headed in their direction. That burn in his gut was hunger, not jealousy. So the guy made Toni laugh. Big deal. And Beau liked him. So what?

The visitor's light blue eyes glittered a warning as Brand approached. The closer he got, the stiffer the man's spine became and the more his chest swelled.

"This the one?" When Toni nodded, the Santa impostor planted his broad self in front of Brand and glared. "You been messin' with my girl?"

The guy had him by at least sixty pounds, but Brand had him beat by a few inches in height, not to mention thirty years or so. Brand glared right back. "You talking about my wife?"

Toni squeezed between them. "Rusty, this is Brand Lander. Brand, Rusty Jackson, Granddad's old foreman."

"Watch who you're calling old, gal." The warmth in the man's pale blue eyes when he looked at Toni softened the harsh words. They turned back to ice before settling on Brand.

Toni smiled at the old man, her love clear for all to see. It hit Brand hard. She hadn't smiled at him like that. Not even after last night. The realization that he wanted her to winded him.

"Brand, Rusty's here to help us turn this place around." She clutched his forearm and squeezed. The look in her eyes told him how important his response was to her.

Brand looked at Toni then at Jackson and back to Toni. "You've hired him to be foreman?"

Toni took a deep breath and tilted her chin. "Yes."

Maybe they should've talked this morning after all, but they'd sent the crew off and gone back to bed. He wondered if she would have told him about the old man. She'd hired someone without consulting him, exactly as he'd done to her. He didn't like it any better than she had, but he remembered her words about trusting. It stung him to do so, but Brand offered his hand. "Welcome."

The man's shoulders relaxed. "Thanks."

"The men finished the bunkhouse this morning. Let's move in your gear." His acceptance of the new foreman earned him one of Toni's smiles. He grabbed the back of her neck and pulled her forward to plant a hard kiss on her lips. "That all right?"

She hugged him then saluted, clicking the heels of her boots together. "Yes, sir."

Toni was frisky and happy. He didn't know if he'd ever seen a more lethal combination. And she'd hugged him again. He could get used to that. Although he wanted to linger over her smiling lips, he turned away and grabbed a suitcase from the bed of the truck. He led Rusty to the bunkhouse. Toni followed.

"Choose your bunk."

"Toni didn't tell you about me?"

Brand sensed wariness in the old man's attitude, despite all his blustering outside. Before he could answer, Toni did. "Not yet."

"I can do the work. What I can't do I can explain real well, so's the younger ones can learn. I may be old, but there's a lot of life stored up here." Rusty tapped his head.

"There's easier jobs than ranching," Brand pointed out.

Rusty nodded. "Yeah, but there ain't no challenge in handing out smiley stickers and shoppin' carts at SuperMart." Toni patted his arm.

Jackson and his father were about the same age. He

didn't think his dad would survive without the ranch. "Did you and Toni agree on a salary?"

The man's cheeks flushed. He and Toni shared a grimace. "I was so danged glad to hear from her, I didn't think to ask. I just quit my job and packed my gear." Rusty looked at his scuffed boots.

Brand's gaze followed. He'd seen his dad in broken-down boots, and he'd put a stop to it as soon as he'd started earning serious money.

"What did Toni's grandfather pay you?"

Rusty named a pitifully low figure. Brand managed to conceal his wince, but Toni didn't. Even five years ago that was low. Brand named a figure more in keeping with the current market. "There'll be health insurance in addition to that and a bonus if we turn a profit."

Relief flashed in the man's eyes. "You won't regret it, Mr. Lander. I'll earn every penny." It was worth every cent he'd pay the man to see the approval in Toni's eyes.

"Call me Brand. Mr. Lander is my dad. What size boots do you wear?"

Rusty looked away, red scorching his cheeks, but mumbled his size.

Toni looked uncomfortable. "Brand, I—"

"You wear the same size as me. I have a sponsor who gives me about two dozen pairs of boots a year. If you'd test-drive a pair or two for me I'd appreciate it. Let me know what you think of 'em, and I'll pass the word on to the manufacturers."

Rusty studied Brand for a moment as if trying to decide whether it was a legitimate offer or charity. He glanced at Toni and she shrugged. "All right. Long as you don't make me wear none of those funny-looking ones." He pointed to Brand's hand-tooled ostrich boots.

"Can't talk you into a red pair, can I?"

"Not while I'm still breathin'. I ain't no poster boy."

There were days Brand felt the same way, but he wore what he was paid to wear. The money was putting food on his family's table and paying Cort's tuition at one of the finest medical schools in the country. Sure, he could wear regular boots and clothes when he wasn't making public appearances, but it seemed stupid to waste money buying something he already had.

"We'll leave you to get settled." Capturing Toni's hand he led her outside. She glanced at him quizzically as he led her across the yard.

"Inside."

She nodded and continued toward the house.

In the kitchen she faced him. "I'm sorry. I should have told you I'd called Rusty, but after yesterday at the bank…I just needed someone on my side."

He was sorry his distrust had hurt her, but what was a man supposed to do? He had to protect what was his or risk losing it all the way Caleb had. His brother's wife had cleaned out the family's savings before leaving town. "Is he the right man for the job?"

Toni bit her lip. "Granddad swore Rusty was the best foreman in the state, but he had to leave about five years ago to take care of his brother who was dying from lung cancer."

Brand pulled her into his arms. She'd surprised him again with her concern for others. Obviously, Rusty needed the job as much as she needed him here. "Next time, we hire as a team. Now let's go introduce the foreman to his temporary crew.

"We'll set the men to work, and then we'll come back inside—" he waggled his brows "—and take a nap."

From the flush spreading across her cheeks, Brand knew she understood that sleep was the last thing on his mind. Even though he ought to be working on his bull pen, he'd rather spend the next hour holding Toni than holding a wrench. The thought worried him for about two seconds. When Toni's gaze heated and her lips curved with sensual promise he forgot about his bulls. Wrapping an arm around her shoulders, he nibbled her earlobe, and whispered what he wanted to do with her. Once Toni's face was as flushed as his felt, Brand led her outside.

Brand forked another load of fluffy omelet into his mouth and passed Toni the plate of Texas toast. Rusty Jackson was one heck of a cook.

"I carried the boys' breakfast out to the bunkhouse." Rusty set himself down with a heaping breakfast.

Toni huddled over her coffee cup as if eight hours of uninterrupted sleep could be found within the strong brew. Her lids were heavy, her lips slightly puffy. Buttery curls hung over her shoulders, reminding him of how they'd felt dragging across his chest last night. She'd never looked sexier. He wanted her. Again.

He squeezed her knee beneath the table and traced the seam of her jeans along the length of her thigh. He loved watching the color rise in her cheeks.

What had she done to him to make him want to forget everything except the feel and taste of her? Right now he didn't give a horse's behind about what was going on outside the ranch house. He wanted to grab his wife and drag her back upstairs. If he had his way they wouldn't see the light of day for weeks. That could be a serious problem. When a man started thinking with something besides his head he stood a good chance of taking a nasty toss, but he figured the intense sexual attraction was a temporary thing. Might as well enjoy it for the short while it lasted.

Of course, Toni had other plans. She'd dragged him out of bed for this little meeting. "Rusty, you're more familiar with the limitations of the land than either Brand or me. We'd like to run some ideas by you." Toni glanced Brand's way. He winked.

Beneath the table Toni caught his hand and transferred it back to his own thigh. Brand refused to release her, and he knew she wouldn't struggle and risk Rusty catching on to the shenanigans beneath the table. He pressed her fingers to his thigh and gave her a smug smile.

She blushed and turned back toward Rusty. The fighting angle of her chin should've warned Brand that he wasn't in control of the situation. Her hand under the table wreaked havoc with his concentration. She pulled her thumb free and scratched her fingernail over the worn denim beneath his fly. His temperature skyrocketed and his brain short-circuited when his blood headed south. He and Toni were great together in bed, but she'd never initiated anything before.

She smiled sweetly, but he saw the mischief in her eyes and the flush staining her neck. "I trust you to be unbiased."

"Gal, just cause I nearly wore you in my hip pocket for years, don't mean I'll let you run the place into the ground."

"I studied genetics in vet school with the intention of raising a crossbreed of cattle that's leaner than the strand Granddad was running. The Rocking A has always been a beef-cattle operation." She made a circle over a particularly sensitive area. Brand tried to steady his breathing.

Rusty nodded. "That it has."

Brand tried and failed to focus on the complicated genetic discussion going on while Toni explained her research. What she proposed would take years of measuring and charting the changes in the herd. He didn't expect her to be around long enough to see it through, and he didn't have the training or the inclination to take over once she left.

He pressed his thighs together, trapping her trouble-making fingers. He needed a clear head if he planned to win this argument. "Beef prices are down. It'd be more profitable to raise bucking bulls. Rodeo's hotter than ever. Demand's up. I also want to open a rodeo school. I'll need to add on an arena and access roads that'll eat into your pasture space."

Her hand stilled. There was genuine concern in Toni's

eyes and voice. "Wouldn't you have to demonstrate to teach?"

Other than Cort, his own family never seemed concerned with the risks he took to put money in their bank account. Did she actually care if he got hurt? Her life would be easier with him out of the picture.

He laced his fingers with hers. "Toni, it's my job. I'm damned good at it."

She pulled free and stood. "It doesn't matter how good you are, Brand. Accidents happen all the time—especially around unpredictable bulls. You could be injured or…or worse. Would you want to leave your child without a father?"

The fluffy eggs turned to bricks in his stomach. The woman fought dirty. "We don't know if there is a baby yet."

"We don't know there's not."

Her earnest blue eyes wrenched his heart. His gaze dropped to her flat belly. Would his plans change if he had a son or a daughter? Would he risk never seeing his child ride a pony or a school bus? He'd been the one to break the news to his buddy's wife and two small kids when his buddy had been pronounced dead at the scene of a rodeo wreck. Would he put his kid through that? He felt his dream and his promise slipping from his grasp.

"I can do most of the work from the ground."

Rusty held a hand up, stifling Toni's protests. "Not ever' man is as careless as Josh Keegan was, Toni. His mind was on courtin' you, not on what he was doing.

"The boy got hisself gored 'bout ten years ago," he said to Brand. "Didn't think he'd pull through. You'll have to promise Toni-girl you'll hire bullfighters, wear flak jackets and not take stupid chances."

His gaze holding Toni's, Brand nodded. "I'll be careful."

"Missy." Rusty pointed a finger toward Toni. "You didn't tell me there might be a young'un on the way. If there is, your job's gonna change. None of that roof climbing, for starters."

Toni sputtered. Brand sat back and let the old man lecture.

"Now you, cowboy." Brand stiffened. "There's plenty of land on the Rocking A, and you ought to have enough money to set Toni up and have your bulls, too. Let her do her work while you do yours."

"You're suggesting we run a dual operation?"

"Don't see why not."

"All right. Toni'll have her business and I'll have mine." Dividing the ranch down the middle wasn't what he had in mind, but at least he'd have control over his half of the ranch.

Toni smiled. It slammed Brand with the force of a bull's kick. He found himself grinning foolishly back. He liked making her smile. Not just any smile, but *that smile,* the one that put sparkles in her eyes and a spring in her step.

He knew better than to become attached. His head knew she'd leave, but his heart didn't seem to be getting the message. He kept thinking about what would happen if Toni stayed—the ranch they'd share, the kids they'd have. It wasn't something he'd ever considered with any other woman, and he wasn't real happy to be thinking about it now. Sooner or later, reality was gonna kick him in the teeth.

Toni's brow furrowed. "Is something wrong?" Brand couldn't speak past the tightness in his throat, so he just shook his head. "Then why are you still here? Aren't your bulls due at the train station in an hour or so? You should have left already."

His bulls. He needed his head examined for letting a woman come between him and work. "Yeah, I need to go…Toni, stay away from the bulls, all right?"

She stiffened and the sparkle faded from her eyes. "You don't trust me with your money *or* your bulls?"

Brand silently cursed his clumsy tongue. "No, I don't

want you to be hurt. You said yourself they're unpredictable. Besides, you don't like 'em.''

She was all starch and fire, poker-straight back and flashing eyes. ''I have news for you, Brandon Lander. As the only vet on this ranch, I'll be very close to those bulls and any other livestock on the Rocking A. It's my job and I'm good at it.''

She threw his own words back in his face. He slid his hand from her waist to cup her stomach. ''If you won't think about you, think about the baby.''

She took a step back and hugged her arms across her chest. Her face paled. ''You couldn't possibly believe I'd do something to harm my child.''

He needed to keep his mouth shut. Every time he opened it, he made things worse. He grabbed his hat and headed for the door. ''I need to go, or I'll be late.''

''Brand? Be careful.'' Concern clouded her eyes and she gnawed her lip.

He winked and made a crossing motion over his heart, the gesture of the carefree cowboy he'd been before he met Toni.

Despite what people said, bull riding was a thinking man's game, and usually he was a thinking man. From the moment he'd met Toni he'd deviated from that course, acting and reacting from his gut and not his head. That had to change.

Toni propped her chin on a rail and wondered why Brand had married her on the mere possibility of a child when he could have waited just a few short weeks to be sure. What were the odds that she'd conceived?

She'd thought they had something growing between them, a relationship that might be worth holding on to, until today when the blinders had fallen off. Brand was protective, but not of her. He was concerned for the maybe baby. He wanted her to stay off the barn roof, off the windmills, off the horses' backs and away from the bulls. The list grew daily and it chafed.

Because of the baby. She was a fool. She'd felt cherished when his only concern was for a child that might not even exist. Where would that leave her if she weren't pregnant? Would he leave? Toni's throat tightened. Wasn't having the ranch to herself what she wanted? Now that Brand had agreed to fund her vision of the ranch and keep his own business separate she wasn't sure anymore. It'd be like dividing the property into His and Hers sectors. That common ground he talked about would be limited to the bedroom. She wanted more than just great sex.

She shoved away from the fence. Like it or not, the bulls were on their way and she needed to get ready for them.

She'd just finished filling the water troughs when Brand's truck, towing a long stock trailer, turned into the driveway. Another pickup followed close behind. Toni opened the bull-pen gate and watched Brand back the trailer toward the opening. Nerves knotted in her stomach. Dread stiffened her muscles.

She stared through the iron bars on the side of the stock trailer. A brindle bull occupied the front section, separated from his traveling companion by a hinged divider. The bull in the rear was big, black and ugly. He snorted in her face and charged the bar. Toni jumped back. Bulls had always frightened her—especially after Josh's accident. But Rusty was wrong. It hadn't been her Josh had been trying to impress. He'd been more interested in one of the ranch hands. Josh was gay. But that wasn't her secret to tell.

Brand unlatched one side of the loading ramp. Toni tightened her fingers on the metal gate. She knew she should be helping him unload the beasts, but her feet wouldn't move. She kept seeing Josh flying through the air. She remembered the dust mingling with blood on the ground. Then the picture blurred and it was Brand in the dirt.

Before she could unlock her knees, Craig Stevens, the

local vet, appeared beside her and reached to unlock the side of the ramp nearest to her.

"Hi there, Toni. I ran into Brand in town and came out to look over these bad boys for myself, but I want to talk to you before I leave." Dr. Stevens returned his attention to the restless animals in the trailer. He popped the latch and yelled, "Got it."

The black bull exploded from the trailer, bucking and kicking. Toni screamed a warning to Brand and the bull turned toward her. A hoof connected with the gate and pain exploded her shins, her chest and her forehead. She found herself lying flat on her back in the dirt.

Before she could catch her breath, Brand knelt over her. "Are you all right?"

A shaft of pain shot through her head when she nodded.

"Don't move your head." Brand's hands gently traced her skull then cupped her face. "Tell me where you're hurtin'."

"I...I'm okay. Just winded, I think." She wiped her brow. Warm, sticky blood covered her hand.

Dr. Stevens jumped to his feet. "I'll get some sterile bandages out of the truck."

With one hand, Brand pressed his bandanna to her wound. His other hand swept across her abdomen. His eyes, darkened with concern, held hers. Her heart contracted at the emotion she saw there. "Are you sure you're okay?"

Her head cleared as if he'd dumped ice water over her. The pain in her skull dulled in comparison to the stabbing pain in her heart. Brand's only concern was for a baby that might not even exist. Embarrassed that she'd read him so wrong, she shoved his hand away, clambered to her feet, and nearly bit off her tongue as pain ricocheted through her. Her head spun. It hurt to breathe. She didn't know which injury ached most. But that was nothing. Her heart was breaking.

Brand grabbed her arm. Toni jerked away. She winced

and bent over at the spear of pain the sudden movement caused.

"Where you hurt, Toni-girl?" Rusty tried to elbow Brand aside but Brand wouldn't budge.

"I'm okay." His stern look warned her not to lie. Toni straightened. Carefully. "The gate caught my rib cage. Just a bruise, I think."

Brand supported her with an arm around her waist. "She got hit pretty hard. Knocked her clear off her feet. She needs a doctor. Let's go." Brand herded her toward her car.

"Brand, please. You're making too much of this."

Without a word, he swept her into his arms and carried her toward the car. He didn't stop until he set her down beside the door. "We're getting you to the hospital whether you like it or not, so stop arguing."

The pallor of his face and the genuine concern in his eyes halted any arguments she might have had. She sat down and he bent over her to buckle her belt. "I'm going to lay your seat back."

Brand gently peeled off the blood-soaked bandanna and studied her wound. His hands were shaking when he took an alcohol pad from Dr. Stevens and cleaned the cut. It stung like crazy and she flinched, but through the pain she realized Brand cared.

"Sorry, but I'm not risking an infection." He covered the cut with gauze squares and pressed her hand to the makeshift bandage. "Put pressure on it." She did as he said, but still he didn't move away.

"What's wrong?"

He shook his head. "Nothing a few stitches won't fix, but they'll be hidden by your hair. No scar to mar that pretty face." Still, he lingered for a few more seconds before moving around to the driver's side of the car.

The vet appeared. "You okay?"

"Just dented."

"Good. Because I'm short of help and I came over to-

day to ask you to help me in my practice until that boy of
mine graduates in June.''

"No," Brand said from the behind the wheel.

Toni jerked her head toward him, wincing as pain lanced
her. "He was asking me."

"And you're in no shape to be talking about taking any
more risks."

"Call me next week," she told the vet. She wouldn't
let Brand dictate to her.

Nine

Brand took her to the hospital emergency room. When Toni's lack of health insurance threatened to slow things down, he whipped out his platinum charge card and passed it to the harassed clerk.

"Just get her a doctor." The nurse hastened to obey. "There's no point in trying to convince her you're covered by my plan when we don't have a card yet."

"I—I am?"

He nodded. "I added you the day after we got married."

She shouldn't have been surprised because Brand was always taking care of somebody. Now it was her turn. Did it mean she truly meant something to him? Or was she just another obligation?

A nurse showed her to a tiny curtained cubicle. She poked and prodded and asked innumerable questions, most of which were extremely personal and embarrassing, considering there was only a thin curtain and a half-dozen feet between her and the beds on either side of her. Her answers could be heard by at least ten people—including the man beside her.

The female physician was patient and thorough. "Any chance you might be pregnant?"

"Yes," Brand answered immediately.

"How far along?"

"Two weeks." Again Brand responded before Toni could.

The doctor raised her eyebrows in Toni's direction for clarification. "What was the first day of your last period?"

Heat climbed Toni's cheeks, and she supplied the date. "I'm only a few days late. I—I haven't done the test yet."

"That's plenty of time for an accurate result. We can do a pregnancy test here, if you like. Then we'll know whether it's safe to x-ray you," the doctor offered with a smile. "I'd like to rule out rib fractures and a concussion."

For once, Brand didn't snap out an answer. Toni focused on him rather than her own building panic. She watched him swallow hard and tighten his grip on the bedrail until his knuckles turned white. He looked as nervous as she felt.

"Mrs. Lander?" the doctor prompted.

"O-okay," she croaked out. What would Brand do if she weren't pregnant?

After suturing the cut, the doctor promised to send in a lab tech and left. Brand thrust his hands into his pockets and turned away as soon as the curtain swished closed. His spine was stiff. "You win. The bulls are going back."

Toni's heart did a funny little two-step. She'd never had a man make sacrifices for her. "Why don't you tell me why the bulls are so important to you?"

He turned his back before she could decipher the expression on his face. "I made a promise."

"What kind of promise?"

"When I first started riding, a retired rider saw how bad I wanted to win. He didn't charge me a dime for lessons because he knew I couldn't afford it. His only request was that I give back. Do for some other kid what he'd done for me.''

He faced her. The sadness in his eyes made Toni catch her breath. ''Every year after the season is over I volunteered at his ranch, teaching the way he taught me. He had a stroke last spring, and he's pretty bad off. There won't be a camp this year because his wife sold the ranch. Hell, if I'd known she wanted to sell I'd have bought it, but nobody told me until the deal was done.''

''Then sending the bulls back would be a mistake. I wish you'd told me, Brand.''

He spun to face her. ''I don't want you getting hurt again.''

Toni searched his eyes, hoping that he meant her and not just the baby she might be carrying. ''I was hurt because I made a stupid, rookie mistake. I took my eyes off the animal. It wasn't your fault.''

Brand paced the small cubicle. The pain in Toni's head and shin subsided to a dull throb, and her rib only hurt when she breathed. Her stomach however was a different story. She was worrying herself into an ulcer.

''Brand, sit down and tell me why you chose rodeo in the first place.''

He hesitated before sinking into the chair beside her bed. ''I didn't choose it as much as it chose me. I'd done some riding in high school and won some here and there, but I didn't plan to take it any further. I wanted to go to college.''

''What stopped you?''

''Before she left, Caleb's wife spent every dime we had—including my college money. Riding and *winning* was the only way to hold on to the ranch. Lucky for me I won more than I lost. Still, I didn't start winning fast enough. We had to sell half the ranch to keep from losing the whole spread.''

''Oh Brand, I'm sorry.''

He shrugged it off. "No big deal. Worked out for the best."

The doctor opened the curtain. "Congratulations. You're going to be parents."

Toni's heart nearly beat its way out of her chest. Her gaze met Brand's. His stunned expression no doubt matched her own.

The doctor frowned. "You didn't plan this baby?"

Toni stayed focused on Brand. His face was pale, his eyes glassy. She thought he might pass out. She covered his hand with hers. "Yes, yes I did."

She was going to have Brand Lander's baby. Part of her wanted to laugh with joy. Another part was disappointed because now she'd never know who Brand wanted, her or their child.

Toni was going to have his child. Brand's chest felt tight—kind of like the panic attack a fellow rider had once described. If the baby was a boy, Toni wouldn't need him anymore. She could boot him off the ranch and keep it to herself. And he didn't want to go. Wouldn't go, dammit.

He choked back a curse. He had no idea when or how it had happened, but despite trying to keep his distance, he'd done the unthinkable. He'd fallen in love with his wife.

It could have been in Vegas where the gutsy little angel had stolen his heart. He'd been surprised by the steely determination in such a delicate-looking package.

It could be the way she worked with the crew. Sometimes those guys were as clumsy as the Three Stooges in their attempts to impress her, but not once had she laughed at them.

Then there were the nights… Toni melted in his arms and made him feel like a god. The woman touched him or gave him that smile and he nearly exploded.

On automatic pilot, he helped her into the car and headed home. Damn. He hadn't intended to fall in love and didn't want to think about how he'd deal with it when she left or if she asked him to leave. Now he understood why his heart was in his throat each time she worked on the barn roof or scaled the windmills. If he kept the bulls, she'd insist on treating them. He didn't want to give them up or break his promise to his old friend, but he wasn't willing to put Toni at risk.

Brand scrubbed his hand across his face. He had a wife and now a kid on the way. Less than three weeks ago he'd had neither and hadn't wanted them. He felt as though a rogue bull had tossed him. Trampled. Stunned. And there were no bullfighters coming to his rescue. He was scared spitless.

Toni ached everywhere. With Brand's assistance she eased herself from the car. The ranch hands swarmed them. She was touched by their concern, but mostly she was worried because Brand hadn't said a word to her since the doctor had confirmed her pregnancy. As one, the group of men erupted into questions.

Toni held up her hands. "Just bruised. Relax."

"Let's get you settled inside," Brand said.

Toni looked at him and frowned. He was still as pale as a corpse. She let him lead her toward the house, in part because her head felt as if it were going to explode, but mostly because she needed time to think. *She was going to be a mother. Mission accomplished.* The reality of it terrified her. She was afraid she'd be as bad a parent as her own...or worse.

"You all right, Toni-girl?" At that moment, Toni thought Rusty looked every one of his sixty-two years.

"Just sore and embarrassed to have caused such a fuss, Rusty." She forced a smile for her mentor and squeezed his hand.

Some of the concern eased from his face. He nodded once, then focused a hard stare on Brand. "Your bulls are in the pen, but if they hurt my girl again, they're gonna be on the grill.''

Brand didn't hesitate. ''I like my steak medium rare.''

Wade cleared his throat. ''Ahh…Brand? Whatcha wanna do about that other thing in your truck?''

Toni watched Brand shake his head imperceptibly. Curious, she turned toward Wade and asked, ''What other thing?''

Brand ran a finger under his collar, then hooked his thumbs through his belt loops. He glanced at her briefly then toward Rusty. ''Nothing you need to worry about right now.''

''No time like the present,'' she insisted, not liking the fact that Brand was keeping secrets again.

He seemed to consider her words, then huffed out a breath. ''I bought you a four-wheeler. I'd rather you rode it than a horse if you have to go out into the pastures. You're less likely to fall off and hurt yourself or the baby.''

Toni sucked a hasty breath as pain of a different sort lanced her. Her ribs protested. *The baby.* Again. His only concern was the baby. ''The doctor said it was okay for me to pursue my normal activities.''

His jaw jutted forward. ''The doctor hasn't met that mare you insist on riding.''

Toni sputtered with anger over Brand's high-handed attitude—even if he was right. She had no business on the back of that feisty horse when she was pregnant and she knew it. But to have him take the decision away from her reminded her too much of her past.

Aaron stepped forward before she could protest. ''Wait a minute. Toni's pregnant? Hell, Brand, you didn't waste any time. You gonna keep her barefoot, too?''

Brand kept his eyes on Toni. ''While you're angry, I might as well tell you I also bought cellular phones. I want you to take one wherever you go in case you have a problem. Rusty and I will each carry one.''

"I am not a child who needs to be tracked every moment of the day," Toni snapped. "I'm not going to risk my baby or myself by doing something foolish. Credit me with a little sense, Brand."

"Toni-girl," Rusty stepped between them. His eyes held a wounded look. "This time I'm gonna side with Brand. Forty years ago I lost my wife and the baby she was carrying because she got throw'd from her horse and couldn't get help. She bled to death not two miles from the house. I'm not gonna stand by and let that happen to you when carrying a phone is so easy."

Anger instantly dissipated. Struggling with tears, she stepped into Rusty's embrace. She'd known him for years and she hadn't known this.

Toni met Brand's stoic gaze. "All right. I'll ride the four-wheeler and carry a phone." At least he wasn't trying to confine her to the yard the way her grandfather had. Yet.

Turning on her heel, Toni hobbled into the house. She didn't stop until she'd locked the bathroom door behind her. Turning on the taps, she peeled off her clothes as the tub filled. Already her shin, rib cage and forehead were turning colorful.

Toni sank into the warm water. She felt emotionally numb. Shell-shocked. Closing her eyes, she leaned her head back and let the warm water ease her aches. Would her baby have the melting Godiva-chocolate eyes of its daddy? That mischievous sparkle? The thick, nearly black hair with the recalcitrant curl on top? Would her son have the same swaggering step, the same broad shoulders?

What if it were a girl? Would she have her father's daredevil streak and the same tender heart? Toni stroked her still-flat belly. She knew she'd love a daughter just as much as a son, because it was a part of Brand. One thing she knew for sure, she'd never, *never* let anyone raise a hand to her child. Fingering the tiny horseshoe-shaped scar on her chin, Toni leaned back and closed her eyes. "I'll protect you," she murmured.

After a few words with the men, Brand followed Toni inside. He wanted to see her settled and comfortable. He'd left the ranch earlier without a thought of the bulls he'd been so eager to receive. His only concern had been for Toni. Now he knew why and he wanted to look in her eyes, knowing that he loved her. He wanted to touch her skin, knowing that he'd do anything to make her stay. He wanted to see if there was a fraction of his love reflected back in her gaze.

The closed bathroom door stopped him. Toni obviously wanted privacy and he couldn't blame her. His mind was reeling and his throat felt tight. *He was going to be a father.* He felt proud enough to strut and nervous enough to puke. He and Toni would have to talk, but later, when he'd had time to digest the news.

Back outside, he called the men together. "I'm gonna need your help keeping Toni from doing anything too strenuous. No roofing. No windmill climbing. No heavy lifting. And for Pete's sake, keep her away from the bulls."

Rusty cleared his throat. "You're making a mistake there, Brand. She ain't gonna like it if you try to corral her."

"I'm not corralling her, Rusty. I'm just trying to keep her from hurting herself."

"Her granddad said the same thing, and I'm telling you, you're gonna face a rebellion if you lay down the law. Toni's already told you she wouldn't do anything to hurt the baby. You gotta trust her. You won't have a marriage till you do."

The old man was right, but Brand couldn't trust Toni to look out for herself. There was too much at stake.

* * *

Toni rolled over, groaning as her multitude of bruises made their presence known. Brand's side of the bed was cold and empty. She hugged his pillow to her chest and inhaled his scent. Last night he'd shown her a gentleness she'd never experienced before. Did that make him different from her father?

Shoving back the covers, she stumbled into the bathroom and flinched at the sight of her battered face. Black, blue and purple covered the side of her forehead, stretching down to her cheekbone. Traces of blood still matted her hair. She looked as if she'd lost a barroom brawl. Even her father had never left her this bruised.

She couldn't camouflage this kind of disaster, and the doctor had told her to keep the cut dry. That meant washing the blood from her hair was out of the question.

Tugging on jeans and a sweatshirt, Toni went in search of something to settle her stomach. It felt a little off this morning. The smell of old coffee assaulted her as soon as she entered the kitchen. Her stomach revolted. Toni clapped a hand over her mouth and bolted for the bathroom. Holding her sore ribs with one hand and her hair with the other, she bent over the bowl. With each retch of her stomach, blistering pain burned through her side.

After rinsing her mouth and hands, Toni studied the battered, tear-streaked face in the mirror. A smile tugged at her lips. If she'd needed proof of her pregnancy, her antsy stomach was willing to provide it. She was going to have Brand's baby.

"Toni?"

She frowned, turning toward the voice. Surely that wasn't her mother? *Not now.* Toni stepped out of the bathroom. Her parents stood in the kitchen. "What are you doing here?"

Their horrified expressions stopped Toni in her tracks. Her face was a showstopper—worse than they'd seen before. Her hand covered the tender area. "I had a fight with a gate."

''A gate?'' her father said with a sneer. Toni took a step back.

The kitchen door opened. Cool air and the scent of pine swept in, followed by Brand carrying a large Christmas tree. She'd been so caught up in getting pregnant, married, and renovating the ranch that she'd forgotten all about the upcoming holiday. Brand propped the pine against the wall and shut the door. ''Oh, Brand. You bought a tree?''

''You the man who did this to my daughter?'' Toni recognized the nuance in her father's voice. Before she could warn him, Brand grimaced and nodded. Freeing one hand from the tree, he offered it to her father. Her father plowed his fist into Brand's jaw. Brand dropped the tree and rocked back against the doorjamb, cupping his chin.

''What in the hell—''

''Daddy!'' Horrified, Toni hobbled across the room. She knew the risk she took when she grabbed her father's arm as he drew back to hit Brand again. ''Stop!''

''He hit you. I hit him.'' Toni had seen this side of her father before. He presented his public persona—smooth, suave, patience personified—until someone, usually his wife or daughter, made him angry. Then he lashed out.

Torn between fear of her father and the need to make sure Brand was all right, Toni's glance darted from one man to the other and back again. Brand had widened his stance, apparently ready to defend himself. Toni released her father's arm and stepped in front of Brand. She knew her father would just as soon hit her as anyone else. Tears of humiliation stung her eyes. Shame scorched her cheeks. She hadn't wanted to drag Brand into the sordid mess of her family. Now he knew her secret.

''I told you, Dad, I ran into a gate.''

''Don't lie to me,'' he bellowed. Opening his palm, he drew back his arm. Toni clenched her jaw and braced herself for a blow.

With the swiftness of a striking snake, Brand caught her father's wrist, twisting it up and behind her father's back.

Her father groaned, but ceased his struggling when Brand yanked his arm up another notch. "Keep your damn hands off my wife."

"Nobody hits my daughter," her father threatened through gritted teeth.

"Nobody but you, you mean." The menace in Brand's voice made the hair on Toni's neck stand up. This was a side of him she'd never seen—no matter how hard she'd pushed. And she had pushed.

"Get your filthy hands off me," her father growled, struggling.

Brand yanked his wrist again. "You forgot to warn me about your father, darlin'. You all right?"

"I...you...I'm so sorry." Keeping a wary eye on her father, Toni studied the swelling area on Brand's jaw.

"Call the sheriff, Toni."

All her life, her father had acted out his anger with physical violence, but he'd never, to her knowledge, tried to hurt anyone besides her mother and herself. "Brand, he's my father."

"I don't care if he's your priest. He has no business hitting you. Call the sheriff."

Her mother grabbed her arm. "Don't, Toni, please."

Indecision twisted Toni's insides. The last time her father had hit her, she'd moved out the same night. She'd found a job and freedom, but guilt had burned like salt in an open wound because she'd left her mother behind. She'd known when she left that her mother would have no one to divert her father's anger.

"He needs help, Mom." She hadn't been able to save her mother then, but now... Toni reached for the phone.

"He's been getting help. He's doing better, I promise. He hasn't... We haven't had an incident in over a year."

"Until today," Brand muttered.

"Yes, well, it was a shock for Paul to find out Toni had married and then to see her so...bruised."

Brand flattened his lips. "There's never an excuse to beat up on a woman or someone smaller than you."

"Please, Toni, put down the phone. He's seeing a therapist every week." Her mother's plea made Toni lower the receiver.

The back door opened and Rusty stepped inside. "Came to help with the tree. Miss Allison, Mr. Paul, how're you—" Rusty studied the situation and frowned. "What's going on here?"

"My father thinks Brand is a wife beater, so he—"

Rusty shook his head slowly and said, "You're a real jackass, Swenson. Wassamatter? Don't want anybody else beatin' up on your women?"

Toni's father struggled and cursed Rusty. Brand jerked on his arm. He clamped his lips shut and paled.

"You can let him go, Brand," Rusty stated. "If he takes another swing at anybody, he knows I'll take him out. Been wantin' to for a damned long time."

Brand released Paul Swenson with obvious reluctance. "He needs to be locked up."

Her father huffed, straightened his jacket, and put as much space between himself and Brand as the room would allow. Toni kept her distance.

"Won't do any good." Rusty shook his head again. "Allison'll just bail him out. If she don't, the courts'll let him go."

"He's getting help," her mother insisted a third time.

"It doesn't seem to be working." Brand crossed the room to stand beside Toni.

Toni watched him carefully. He bristled with anger, but his eyes and the arm he looped around her waist were nothing but gentle. Cautiously, she stroked her fingers over his swelling jaw. "You need an ice pack."

He covered her hand with his. The understanding she found in his gaze made her eyes tear.

"Exactly how did my daughter get that black eye,

Rusty?'' her father asked. ''And don't feed me any of that gate garbage.''

''Toni don't lie,'' Rusty said, rummaging through the freezer. He offered an ice-filled plastic bag to Brand. Reluctantly, Toni released Brand and let him apply the ice.

''Ya don't have to worry about Brand, Miss Allison. I'll take out any man who hurts that girl myself,'' Rusty assured her mother. He shot a hard look toward Brand and then her father to make sure the warning was received.

Toni rolled her eyes. ''I can take care of myself.''

Her mother asked, ''Why were you crying when you came out of the bathroom?''

Toni pulled in a shaky breath and glanced at Brand. You couldn't keep secrets around here. Although she would have liked to keep this one a little longer. Say…nine months or so. ''I wasn't crying. I'd had my first bout with morning sickness. Brand and I are going to have a baby.''

If the news of her hasty marriage had surprised them, then news of her pregnancy shocked them. Her father looked ready to take another swing at Brand.

Brand turned her in his arms and brushed a hand across her cheek. ''You all right?''

''The smell of stale coffee upset my stomach, but I'm okay.'' Without a word, Brand crossed the room, grabbed the pot, and emptied it into the sink.

''Toni, you had no business getting married without letting us meet him first.'' Her father said *him* with enough emphasis to make a less confident man cringe. ''You know nothing about men—''

''I know enough to know which kind to avoid.'' Her father bristled. Toni reminded herself it was best not to provoke him, but some habits were hard to break.

''He's a rodeo bum.''

Brand leaned against the counter and studied his in-laws. His jaw hurt. The ice bag was cold. And his heart was breaking. Now that he knew Toni's secret, he wished he didn't. Thoughts of the bastard smacking her around brought out a violence he hadn't known he possessed. If Rusty hadn't walked in, Brand knew he probably would have broken Paul Swenson's arm. Then his face.

Toni's father was a tall man, a couple of inches over Brand's six feet, and whipcord lean. Brand could forgive him for taking a swing at him because he thought he'd hit his daughter, but he couldn't forgive the bastard for hurting Toni. Even now, the jerk talked down to her, questioning her sanity in choosing to marry a rodeo bum and to have a baby so early in her marriage. He'd had enough of the man's destructive barbs.

"Mr. Swenson, I'd suggest you shut your mouth." Brand tossed the ice bag on the table and stepped between his father-in-law and Toni. The room grew silent. "I don't like bullies and from what I've seen, that's what you are. If you have a problem with me or my career, then you talk to me, but get off Toni's case."

Like most bullies, Paul Swenson backed down when confronted. Lips thinned, he sat down in a chair. Toni's mother stood behind him, squeezing his shoulders. Brand had to wonder why she put up with the man. He sighed and ran a hand over his face. This was not the way to get to know his in-laws. The man might be a jackass, but he *was* Toni's father.

"If you have questions, ask me," he repeated. "Toni's not up to an inquisition right now. If anything, you should be concerned about her and the baby, not about whether or not we knew each other's favorite color before we married."

Brand took in Toni's pale face, covered in a light sheen of sweat. Her lips were pinched and pale, and she looked as if she was going to be sick again. "You all right, darlin'?"

Slapping a hand over her mouth, Toni shook her head and bolted from the kitchen. Brand followed. She bent over the toilet and heaved. Brand knelt down to hold her hair out of the way. He'd had a lot of experience with drunk, heaving cowboys. A heaving woman wasn't that different, was it? Only, with his buddies he didn't feel this helpless.

When Toni finished rinsing her mouth, Brand dampened the hand towel and gently wiped her face. The colorful bruise stood out on her ashen skin. Guilt kicked him hard. His bulls. His fault. He'd forced himself on her as a husband and ramrodded his ideas for the ranch down her throat. Was he any less of a bully than her father? He brushed his lips over her cheek. "I'm sorry."

She touched his swollen chin. "Me, too."

The tenderness he felt toward the woman he'd married felt strange, like a pair of unbroken-in boots. It would take some getting used to.

"Sweet tea and toast, coming up. It's what my wife always had to settle her stomach," Rusty called out.

Her father turned when they entered the kitchen. "Did the appraiser come out? He told me he'd get a value and contact the real-estate agent."

Toni's parents wanted her to sell out. A hard knot formed in Brand's stomach. "Toni and I aren't selling."

Toni's father glared in Brand's direction. "We want you to move home with us, Toni."

Brand stiffened and clenched his fists. He wasn't letting this abusive bastard near Toni or their baby. "She *is* home."

"How long have you known this man?" Swenson glared in Brand's direction.

"We met last month in Vegas," Toni admitted quietly.

"And which college did you attend, Lander?"

Brand flexed his fingers under the table and suppressed the urge to knock out the man's teeth. "I didn't."

"Did you even finish high school before you took off chasing rainbows?"

Brand gritted his teeth.

"Dad—"

Her father turned an angry red. "Do you think this no-good cowboy married you for love? Use your head, girl. He married you for your land and that degree of yours. You're his meal ticket. Cowboys know how to spend money. They don't know how to make it.''

Brand put his fist down on the table hard enough to rattle the dishes. Toni nearly jumped out of her chair. ''I married your daughter for several reasons. Money was not one of them.''

''I appreciate your concern, Dad, but I don't need it.''

''You rushed into a marriage with a man you barely know,'' her father said irritably. ''Admit it, you made a mistake. Come home and I'll fix it.''

Toni shot to her feet. She weaved a little and Brand stood to support her. ''I'll never do that and you know it. I'm making a home for my baby here. I want my child to be safe, and I don't think he would be with you.''

Swenson looked livid. He pulled out his checkbook. ''What will it take to get rid of you, cowboy?''

Brand held on to his temper by a fraying thread. Beneath his hands, he felt Toni tremble. ''Mister, you don't have what it takes.'' He steered Toni toward the door. ''Let's go for a walk, darlin'. I think you need some fresh air. I know I do.''

Ten

When they reached the pasture fence, Brand caught Toni's arm and turned her toward him. "Why in the hell didn't you tell me about your father?"

Toni gazed toward the cattle off in the distance and fingered the small horseshoe-shaped scar on her chin. He'd kissed it dozens of times. Brand's gut tightened in anger when he remembered that her father had been wearing a ring with a small horseshoe made out of diamonds on it. The bastard.

"What was I supposed to say? 'By the way, my dad likes to hit women'?" Toni hooked her boot over the peeling white fence.

"Tell me the rest of it."

She looked hesitant, then resigned. "My dad is a control freak. Whenever things didn't go exactly as he wanted, he took his anger out on us. I tried to take the brunt of it. Better me than Mom."

"He should have been locked up. You should have told someone."

Toni turned to face him and the defeat in her eyes hit Brand like a blow to the gut. "I tried to get help. I talked to the school counselors a couple of times and they made noises about calling in Social Services. But the wheels turn slow. Before they could do anything, Dad would change jobs. That meant new states, new schools, losing the few friends I'd made. It got so that he'd move us whenever he thought I was getting too close to anyone. He didn't want to risk me talking."

Brand swore. No wonder Toni was made of steel.

"The moving and physical abuse were his way of keeping Mom and I in line. As long as we had no one else, he was our only security, our only constant. The only place I felt safe was here on the Rocking A." She turned and gripped his arm. Her face was pale and drawn, and he wanted to pull her into his arms and hold her tight. "Brand, he is my father and even though he is a jerk I love him. For a long time I was convinced if I'd been a better daughter, none of it would have happened."

"Toni, he's sick."

"I know that now. The last time he hurt me I ended up in the hospital. It took a persistent counselor who met me on the sly to convince me that it wasn't my fault. She's the one who told me that I couldn't help my mother if she didn't want to be helped. She's the one who convinced me to leave.

"If what my mom says about Dad getting help is the truth, then it's a start. He's never been willing to admit he had a problem before."

"He hurt you." Frustration and anger burned Brand's chest.

"Yes, he did. But what hurt more was that no matter how much my grandfather and I begged, my mother wouldn't leave. She said she couldn't take my grandfather trying to run her life the way he had when she was younger." Toni's laugh held no humor. "What Mom didn't realize was that my father was ten times worse. Granddad may have been bossy and he did like to keep us close to home, but he did it to protect us, not to control us. And he never, ever laid a hand on me in anger."

A lump in Brand's throat threatened to choke him. Toni needed the ranch. She'd told him that before, but he hadn't understood the level of her commitment. Now he did. And did he have it in his heart to force himself on her at the cost of her happiness?

Some of her father's condemning words replayed in Brand's head. What did he have to offer a woman with a graduate degree? Money and a willingness to work hard seemed to be his only assets. He'd never gone to college, never held a steady job other than bull riding. Toni deserved better.

Her parents' car was gone. Toni heaved a sigh of relief and let herself into the house.

Brand followed, carrying an armload of wood. "Let's build a fire and decorate the tree. Rusty said he'd put it in the stand."

The tree filled the corner of the den, its scent permeating the air. Beside it sat the familiar box holding her grandmother's Christmas ornaments. Toni knelt beside the box and lifted the lid. A nostalgic smile tilted her mouth. Most of the ornaments were homemade, some she'd made herself. There were crocheted snowflakes, painted pinecones, and tiny knitted stockings. Each was a symbol of her heritage here on the Rocking A. The ornaments were a legacy she'd pass on to her child.

Brand reached into the box and lifted a jar lid bordered in red ribbon. On the flat side, a picture of Santa had been glued. The inside of the lid framed a picture of Toni.

Brand stared at the photo. "How old were you here?"

Toni wrinkled her nose at the toothless mug shot. "Seven. That was the year I begged Santa for front teeth.

Grandma made one of those each year until she died. There should be sixteen of them.''

''You spent a lot of time here.'' Brand stood to untangle the lights.

''Summers and every long holiday. Dad worked in hotel management and he could never leave the hotels on holidays. He didn't want a child running through the halls disturbing the guests. I later realized my grandparents had me here because Dad was under a lot of pressure during those times and it was better if I wasn't around. I didn't mind. I loved it here, and I don't ever want to leave again.'' Toni sat back on her heels cradling an angel made from the remnants of her great-great-grandmother's wedding dress. ''What did your family do for Christmas?''

Brand dug into the box, his face turned away from her, but the angle of his jaw was tight. ''Not much after Mom left. It was just another day. Stock had to be tended. Stalls needed cleaning. Dad did the best he could, but money was tight.''

He carried a strand of lights to the tree without glancing her way. Toni's heart ached for the little boy who'd had no Christmas. ''What about Santa?''

''He quit coming after Mom left.''

Tears stung her eyes, but the stiffness in his shoulders told her Brand wouldn't accept pity. There was one special gift she could give her husband. Christmas.

Early Christmas morning, Brand sneaked out of bed and down the stairs. Even at 6:00 a.m., the air smelled of roasting turkey. The kitchen counters were covered in pies, cakes and sugar cookies. It had been a long time, but he remembered the holidays before his mother left. Like Toni, his mother had spent days preparing and had risen before dawn to put the bird in the oven.

His gut twisted. He wanted to believe in forever, even felt a flicker of hope that maybe Toni would be different from the other women in his life. But he was afraid to trust the feeling. Afraid to set himself up for another disappointment.

He swiped a cookie while the milk heated. Juggling a thermos of hot chocolate and one large present, he returned upstairs, stopping in the bedroom doorway.

Toni stood in front of the window, stretching. Sunlight shone directly through the sheer nightgown she wore, outlining her curves in a way that had his body responding with enthusiasm. He set the present in the center of the bed and poured her a mug of hot chocolate. "Merry Christmas."

"To you, too. Thanks." Toni took the mug and sipped it.

He pulled his thoughts from his throbbing groin and nodded toward the box. "You might want to open that one right away."

As eager as a child, Toni scampered onto the bed and ripped the wrapping paper. She hesitated when she read the cardboard box then her lips turned up. "You bought me a case of crackers?"

"The lady at the grocery store suggested it. Said crackers were the only thing that settled her stomach when she was expecting."

Toni laughed, opened a box, and started nibbling. "I guess I don't have to feel bad about giving you this then." She reached under the bed, pulled out a flat package, and tossed it to him.

Brand tore the wrapping paper and read the cover of the book. Was she making fun of his cowardice? "It's about snakes."

"The book has every species of snake, whether or not it's poisonous, and where its territory is located. I thought it might help you get past your fear if you knew which ones could hurt you and which wouldn't."

Brand grimaced at the reminder of his disgrace, but at least she wasn't laughing at him. "Uh...thanks."

"You're welcome. The rest of your gifts are downstairs."

Snatching up her robe, she skipped downstairs. She gave him chambray work shirts, socks and a rifle. "In case the book doesn't help," she said with a grin. "Either Rusty or I can give you marksmanship lessons."

Brand glanced at the presents still under the tree. The crew, except for Rusty, had left to spend Christmas with their families. "Who're those for?"

She took a deep breath and blew it out, eyeing him warily. "Your family. I invited them for Christmas dinner."

Brand kissed her because she was giving him and his family back Christmas. Because she was taking time to try to help him with his snake phobia. Because she'd noticed the holey condition of his socks. Toni was like that. She noticed details. Mostly, he kissed her because he loved her. His love was his secret gift to her. He ruffled her hair. "You have another present. I'll get it."

"Brand, you've already given me the four-wheeler and the cell phone and a year's supply of crackers. What else do I need?"

He held up his finger and retrieved the box from the back porch. He set it in her lap.

Toni lifted the lid. Sleeping inside the box were a fluffy butter-colored kitten and a scraggly mostly black tabby. They wore homemade name tags on the bows tied around their necks. "You named the cats Day and Night? Oh, Brand."

"I like these better than snakes to get rid of the rats in the barn," he explained.

"Me, too." Her smile was like sunshine breaking through the clouds after a week-long rain. It warmed him and made his heart miss a beat. More than that, it made him wish for a hundred more Christmas mornings with Toni, and that was a Christmas wish he was pretty damned certain wasn't going to come true.

* * *

Toni opened the front door to the four Lander men. With a sense of déjà vu she noted their somber expressions. Cort came forward with a sprig of mistletoe in his hand. He held it over her head and gave her a peck on the cheek. "Merry Christmas, sis."

The youngest son had the holiday spirit the others sorely lacked. Toni invited them in and introduced them to Rusty.

"Holy smoke. She's invited Santa," Toni heard Patrick grumble. "Where's Brand?"

"Right here," Brand responded. "Bringing in the eggnog. Take your coats off and kick back. Toni won't let us eat until all the presents have been opened."

The men looked pained, but, like children, their eyes lit when they spotted the presents under the tree. It made the effort worth it. Her kittens cavorted amongst the presents, mangling ribbons. When Brand grabbed her hand and pulled her onto the sofa beside him she snuggled into the crook of his arm. It felt right to be here in front of the fire, surrounded by Brand's family—even if Brand's attentiveness could be an act. She hoped it wasn't. The only gift she really wanted was to know that this was the first of many Christmases with Brand.

While they opened presents, Toni discovered that Patrick had a wicked sense of humor, much like Brand's, which slipped out occasionally. Caleb shared Brand's strong sense of responsibility. She especially liked the tales they told.

"Dad was always trying to make our presents, cuz money was tight, ya know," said Caleb. "We tried to do the same thing. I'll never forget the year Patrick got bitten by that rattler he wanted to make into a belt."

"A belt? I thought it was for my lunch box," Brand said.

Caleb and Patrick exchanged chagrined smiles. "We just told you that to scare you. Patrick wanted to make a snakeskin belt for Dad."

"Hell, Brand, we liked to scare ya. We didn't ever intend to kill ya," added Patrick.

While the brothers exchanged insults, Toni stood and walked to the tree. Only one gift remained—the one she'd spent days pulling together. She passed it to Jack Lander. He looked surprised, but peeled off the paper as eagerly as a five-year-old. His large scarred hand swept over the leather binder inside. "What's this?"

"My grandfather had at least a dozen years' worth of rodeo magazines in the attic. I went through them and cut out all the articles and pictures of Brand. I didn't know if you'd kept a scrapbook of his career. One day, I'm hoping you'll show it to your grandkids and tell them what Brand was like growing up."

Jack Lander mashed his lips shut and nodded his head. Toni thought she saw tears in his eyes. After several silent moments, he met her gaze. "I'd like that."

"Kids? Does that mean what I think it means?" asked Cort.

She felt Brand's presence behind her then his arms circled her waist. "It means that we're going to have a baby in the house next Christmas."

Patrick and Caleb exchanged a dark glance. Their lips tightened and their eyes narrowed. Cort, on the other hand, seemed pleased. "Cool. I guess that means you'll get to play Santa again. Just like you did for me all those years."

Toni twisted in Brand's arms and saw the flush on his cheeks. Another piece of the puzzle fell into place and she knew why the youngest Lander still had the Christmas spirit. Brand had kept the tradition alive.

Jack Lander cleared his throat. "Now, can we eat? I'm 'bout starving for some of that cheesecake I saw on the way in."

Toni laughed and turned for the kitchen. "Then I guess we'd better eat."

Brand's father stopped him with a hand on the arm, but

he didn't say another word until the others had left the room. "Your momma would've liked Toni."

Brand couldn't have been more surprised if his father had stripped naked and danced around the tree. "She wouldn't have cared what kind of wife I had."

Sadness filled his father's eyes. "She would've cared. Your momma loved you boys. It was me she couldn't stand. I kept her tied to me when she loved somebody else."

Brand's vocal cords were paralyzed. His father stared at the tree and continued talking. "Your mother and I were just friends. We had too much to drink one night and I got her pregnant. She had nobody else to turn to, so she married me. We had some good years, and I grew to love that woman.

"Once Caleb and Patrick went off to school, your momma got bored stuck at the ranch all day. She took a part-time job in town and she fell for her boss. I knew she was thinking about leaving me." He pulled on his ear which had turned as red as his cheeks. "Your momma couldn't take the pill. I tampered with the condoms and she got pregnant again. She knew her lover wouldn't want her when she was carrying my kid. So she stayed, but she wasn't happy. I convinced her another baby would fix our marriage and we had Cort. But then one day she didn't come home. She'd gone to meet her lover. She left me a note saying she'd send for you and Cort, but she didn't because she and her fella were killed in a car accident down in Mexico."

Remorse etched lines on his face. "Toni seems like a nice girl. Treat her right." He pounded Brand's shoulder and headed toward the kitchen.

Brand couldn't move. His father's words had crumbled his foundations. Everything he'd ever believed about his mother was a lie.

On the day after Christmas, Toni cautiously rolled over in bed, reaching for the crackers on the bedside table even before she opened her eyes. Her head was pounding. On second thoughts, it wasn't coming from inside her head, but from outside the window. She eased herself upright. When the contents of her stomach didn't race for her throat, she shuffled toward the bathroom, munching a cracker along the way. The kittens followed, tripping all over themselves. So far, they hadn't made it out to the barn.

After a shower and toast, she stepped outside to track down the hammering. To her surprise, Brand's brothers were perched on the barn roof. Jack Lander supervised the men scattered around the yard mending the board fence or painting the house.

"Roy, where's Brand and what's going on?"

Roy paused in unloading an armload of paint cans from the bed of Brand's truck. "Your neighbors and in-laws showed up demanding we let 'em help get the place back in shape. Ain't that a kick? Less than a month ago, he couldn't hire nobody. Now that they've seen how much he cares about you—you know, that Prince Charming to the rescue thing when the gate whomped you?—they want to work."

Toni covered the ache that formed in her chest at Roy's words with her hand. Her neighbors and in-laws didn't know it was the baby Brand was really concerned about. If only he cared about her in that way, she would be impossibly happy.

"Brand's down at the bull pen. A couple of boys showed up wanting lessons. Come on. I'll walk with ya." Roy set the cans down and headed for the pens.

Like a flashback, Toni heard the whiskey-rough voice. "Shoulders square. Free hand out front. Concentrate on the basics and you'll do fine."

"I'd sure like to see you ride him, Brand," a boy of perhaps eighteen said with an eagerness that made Toni's stomach clench in apprehension. Would Brand ride? In

Vegas, she hadn't cared about the risks he took, but now...for the baby's sake, *for her sake,* she hoped he wouldn't ride.

"I rode him in Cheyenne for ninety-two points. Be glad to show you the video sometime, but I'm not getting back on him. I've got a baby on the way, Chris, and I plan to live to see the kid through college." Brand slapped the boy's protective leather vest. "Run like hell when you hit the ground."

"Yeah, yeah, I know." Chris turned toward the chute where Aaron and Deke waited with a bull.

As if sensing her presence, Brand turned. His eyes swept her, then he nodded. "Morning, ma'am. You're looking good today." He stepped closer and brushed his thumb over her lips. The heat in his eyes told her he was wishing it were his mouth. So was she. "As a matter of fact, Mrs. Lander, you look *damn* good."

Toni felt a blush warm her and take some of the chill off her heart. "You're looking mighty fine yourself."

"We're ready, Brand," called Deke.

"Gotta go." He pressed his lips against her forehead, then turned toward the chute.

Roy climbed down off the fence and stood beside her while Brand coached the kid from beside the chute. "He's really good with the boys. O'course none of them have made the count, but they're just high-school kids."

The chute opened. Dirt, bull and cowboy flew through the air. Aaron and Deke played rodeo clown, heading the bull off and turning it into the holding pen. Once the bull was penned, Brand climbed over the fence. He coached the kid on his good moves, then pointed out his mistakes. He finished with another positive comment. From the expression on the boy's face, Toni could tell he hung on Brand's every word and left the ring encouraged, not discouraged. She had to admit Brand was a good teacher.

"This bull-riding school of Brand's could be a real moneymaker." Roy narrowed his eyes on her; his usual flirtatious manner was lacking. "That is, if he don't have to give it up."

"I'm not making him give it up."

"Hope not. He's already quit riding for you. I'd hate to see him lose this, too. A woman can only take so much from a man before he ain't the man she wanted to begin with."

Roy ambled away and Toni stared after him. She didn't want to change Brand. She admired his courage, his honesty and his strong sense of responsibility—qualities she hadn't wanted when she'd gone hunting for a cowboy in Vegas. Brand Lander was definitely not the man she'd wanted to begin with, but for whatever reason, he was the man fate had chosen to father her child and steal her heart. She'd never regret their time together.

Brand waved goodbye to the boys, then climbed out of the empty ring. He strode in her direction. Anticipation fizzed through her bloodstream at the look of intent on his face. He caught her hand, dragged her into the tractor shed and slanted his lips across hers in a kiss so thorough it left her breathless and weak in the knees. She clung to his broad shoulders to stay on her feet.

He lifted his head. "Whaddaya say we take a lunch break?"

Heat pooled in Toni's belly at the sensual promise in Brand's eyes. She dampened her lips. "It might be a little tricky slipping away with a dozen or so men in the yard."

His grin widened. "But not impossible."

Someone in the yard yelled. Metal clanged. Brand was out of the shed in an instant. Toni followed one step behind. She made it to the clearing just in time to see the black bull lunge out of the chute with Wade clinging to his pitching back.

"Sonofabitch." Brand launched himself over the fence. Aaron and Deke did the same. A scream lodged itself in Toni's throat. Neither Brand, Aaron nor Deke wore their protective vests. Within seconds, Wade was airborne. He hit the ground hard and the bull turned on him. Brand threw his hat and waved his arms, distracting the bull from Wade. When it turned toward him, he ran toward the rails with the bull on his heels. Toni's muscles locked with fear. When it looked certain the black beast would hook Brand, Deke ran between them. The bull veered after him. Deke made it into the holding pen just yards ahead of the beast and launched himself up the metal fence. Aaron slammed the gate closed and latched it shut.

Toni's heart hammered and her stomach pitched. It had happened so fast. Brand had nearly been gored and then—

Wade released his hold on the rails and stepped back down into the dirt. Toni'd never seen Brand look so angry. In seconds he'd crossed the ring, grabbed Wade by the shirt, and shoved him against the metal rails. "What in the hell were you doing? Are you outta your mind?"

Toni was afraid, afraid of the anger she saw in her husband's face, afraid of what he would do if she didn't divert his rage from the young cowboy. She clambered over the fence and tried to shove herself between Brand and Wade.

"Brand, stop." She grabbed his forearm and pulled with all her might, but she wasn't able to move him.

Brand ignored her. He glared at Wade. "You coulda gotten yourself killed."

"Brand, please." She tried again.

"If you're going to pull asinine stunts like that, then you pack your bags and get the hell off my ranch. I'm not in the suicide business."

"He was trying to impress you," she shouted. Dark brown eyes shifted her way then back toward the cowering Wade.

"You put Aaron, Deke and I—three men—at risk for a joyride. Do you think that's gonna impress anybody?"

Wade cowered.

Brand's face was flushed, but pale around the lips. His body trembled with fury. He looked livid, but still he didn't raise a hand to Wade. Or her. Tension eased from

Toni's shoulders. She relaxed her hold on his arm, knowing she'd probably caused bruises. Even though the young cowboy could have gotten any of them injured or worse, Brand seemed more interested in scaring the daylights out of him than in hurting him.

"I...I'm sorry," Wade stammered.

"Sorry don't mean squat if you can't back it up with action. I can't work with a man I can't trust, Wade."

"Yessir." Wade bowed his head.

"You know the rules. No bullfighters, no rides."

"Yessir. I was stupid."

Brand sighed and rubbed his temple. "You're not stupid, kid. You made one bad choice. Don't let it happen again."

Toni watched the group disperse with no blood shed. Her father had belted her and her mother for far less serious offenses. Were the counselors right? Were there men out there who knew how to control their anger? Was Brand one of them?

Once the ring cleared out, Brand glanced her way. He narrowed his lips. "You thought I was going to hit him."

She considered denying it, but nodded instead.

He swore. "I'm not your father, Toni."

"I'm beginning to see that."

"Is that what you did? Put yourself between your mother and father when they fought?"

"Somebody had to protect her."

He pulled her into his arms and buried his face in her hair. "It should have been the law, not an innocent kid."

Eleven

Toni set down the phone and paced the office. Megan Jeffries from Coyote Western Wear in Houston had just called. Brand's sponsors. Brand's former lover. She wanted him there for an entire week for a product shoot.

Toni's hands were shaking. She felt weak and it had nothing to do with her pregnancy. She'd let herself fall in love with her one-night cowboy, and she no longer wanted him to leave. Instead of counting the days until he lost interest and left her, she now feared he'd do exactly that. She wanted Brand for keeps.

Brand, on the other hand, saw her as a temporary sexual partner, the incubator for his child and the co-owner of the ranch. A necessary evil. He chivvied endlessly. "Don't lift that. It's too heavy. You might hurt the baby. Don't climb that. You'll fall and hurt the baby. Don't forget to drink your milk. It's good for the baby."

He'd taken to reading and quoting books on pregnancy and childbirth. If he loved her and not just the child she carried, Toni would have been thrilled by his interest. She was jealous of her own baby. Add another sin to her growing list.

She sank into the leather chair and put her head in her hands. Her own experiences had taught her that keeping someone under lock and key wasn't the way to hold on to them. She had to let Brand go to Houston. She had to trust him not to break her heart.

Boots rapped out a staccato rhythm on the hardwood floor of the hall. Brand entered the office with Craig Stevens on his tail.

"The doc is back to make you another offer." Brand's voice was flat, his eyes expressionless.

"He's right, Toni. I am here to make you another offer, but first, congratulations on the baby."

"Thanks." Toni put a hand over her abdomen and smiled. Patting the baby was becoming as much a habit as eating crackers. As they always did, Brand's eyes followed the gesture.

Dr. Stevens sat down. "First, I want to assure you both that what I need Toni to do won't be hazardous. I need help in the surgery. I've ordered new laser equipment and don't know how to use it. I'd appreciate some help setting it up and some tutoring. How do you feel about teaching an old dog new tricks?"

Brand saw the excited sparkle in Toni's blue eyes, the pink flush on her cheek. It faded to disappointment and resignation.

"I appreciate the offer, but I want to start a breeding program and I won't be able to spare the time," Toni said.

Dr. Stevens frowned at Brand. "You can't spare her for say…fifteen hours a week?"

Toni answered before Brand could open his mouth. "No, the beef operation is mine. Brand is working with his bulls."

She wanted the job and he wanted her to stay. Hell, he

could handle a little extra work and hire a few extra hands if it would make her happy. "I'll cover for you."

He'd bet that Toni's smile couldn't get any wider. She launched herself at him. He caught her in his arms and squeezed her tight, savoring her joy and hating that he had to let her out of his sight.

A beeping noise pierced the silence. The vet fumbled for the pager hooked to his belt. "Do I take that as a yes, Toni?"

"You bet."

"Stop by the office Monday morning, and we'll get started."

The doctor's bootsteps faded down the hall. As quickly as it had erupted, Toni's smile vanished. She crossed the room and stared out the window. "You had a call while you were out."

Puzzled by her sudden mood swing, Brand propped his hip on the desk and studied her stiff spine. "Yeah?"

"Megan Jeffries wants you to call her at home. She said she'd need you to stay in Houston all of next week."

"Next week? I thought that was…" Time flew when he was with Toni. "I'll call later. Right now I have something more important to tend to."

He caught her hand as she tried to leave the room, pulled her between his thighs. Something about Megan's call had upset her. He wanted to hash it out. Toni squirmed in his hold. She scowled and tugged on her hand, but Brand held tight. He turned her until her back rested against his chest, and then he leaned forward to inhale the sweet scent of her hair, of her.

"You want to tell me what has you all knotted up?" Beginning at her stiff shoulders, he massaged his way down her spine. Whenever Toni worried she knotted up.

"Nothing."

"Uh-huh. Do you have a problem with me going to Houston?"

"Of course not." She was lying through her pretty

white teeth. Toni turned and tried to step away. He snagged a couple of her belt loops with his fingers, trapping her between his legs, and massaged the curve of her waist with his thumbs.

She pretended not to notice, but the flush on her cheeks and the catch in her breath were hard to miss. She reached past him to search through the papers on the desk to his left. If he didn't know better, he'd think she was jealous. But he knew better, didn't he?

"Toni, you don't have to worry about Megan."

She redirected her search to the papers on his right.

"It's been over for a long time." She continued to shuffle through the stack as if she'd lost something vital. "Since before the season started last—"

She held up her hand as if she didn't want to hear more. "I can't find my college-loan payment book. I thought I put it in the desk drawer."

Brand traced a path along the inside of her waistband and up her rib cage. Touching Toni had its usual effect. He shifted her against his arousal. After a quick gasp of surprise, she leaned into him, giving him one of her mindblowing kisses. When her nipples pebbled and poked against her shirt he just had to touch 'em.

"I paid off your loan." He whispered the words against her temple.

She jerked her head up so fast she clipped his chin. He nearly bit his tongue. "Why?"

Brand shrugged and cupped her shoulders. "I wanted to. Didn't make much sense for you to pay interest on the loan when I had the money sitting in the bank to pay it off."

For a moment, he thought she'd argue. Her brow puckered. "Thank you. I'll put it toward your half of the ranch."

He pulled her shirttail free to stroke the soft skin beneath. He wanted to tell her that she was the only woman in his life, and she wouldn't even look at him. "Come with me to Houston."

Her muscles quivered beneath his fingertips. "I—I'm supposed to start work on Monday."

Brand smothered his disappointment. "Yeah, I forgot. No big deal. I'll only be gone a week."

But it was a big deal. He didn't want to leave her. He considered trying to change her mind. This His and Hers business had to stop. They were a team—at least for now.

Toni nibbled his neck and lowered his zipper. Brand sucked a sharp breath and forgot about arguing when she freed him from the restricting denim and took him into her mouth. For precious moments, Brand let her have her way, although the pleasure nearly took his head off. He scooted off the desk and fumbled with the snap and zipper of her jeans. Once he'd peeled the snug denim away, he laid her on her back across the desk and buried himself within her slick heat.

Toni wriggled and wrapped her legs around his waist. He loved it when she played aggressively. As if reading his thoughts, she grabbed his shirt collar in her fists and pulled him down for a kiss. Damn, the woman knew how to kiss. Her lips teased his. Her teeth nipped, then her sweet little tongue swept the inside of his bottom lip.

Some corner of his mind told him there was a hint of desperation in her loving, but when she popped open the snaps of his shirt and scraped her short nails over his chest he lost his train of thought. Brand drew back to return the favor. He flicked open the front fastening of her bra and pulled a pink-tipped breast into his mouth. She was even more sensitive there now and when he nipped her she made the sexiest noise he'd ever heard. He made her do it again.

Shock waves radiated through his body. He clutched her hips. "Slow down. I'm on the edge here."

She writhed beneath him. "Mmm, me too."

Brand leaned over to tease her plump breasts. He suckled and bit in the way he knew drove her wild. With his thumb, he teased the heart of her until she exploded, her body arching off the desk, squeezing him. Brand gave in and rode the crest with her.

While he struggled to catch his breath, he tugged her into sitting position and refastened her bra and shirt. His fingers wandered and it took a little longer than it should have.

"We've got to stop meeting like this." He jerked his head to indicate the office door they'd left wide open. The woman made him forget good ol' common sense sometimes. The men were due in for lunch soon, and he'd rather not have the guys see Toni like this. They were already half in love with her. If they saw her looking this sexy he'd definitely need Toni's marksmanship lessons to keep 'em in line.

Biting her lips on a wicked smile, she slapped the door closed. "You started it."

Brand couldn't help but grin right back at her. He stepped back so she could scoot off the desk. "Who me? I didn't do anything."

She shimmied into her jeans, glancing over her shoulder at him. "Will you not do anything again sometime soon?"

He had to clamp down on his baser instincts. Otherwise, he'd be stripping her right back out of those britches. A mess of work waited for him outside, but he sat down in the chair behind the desk and pulled her into his lap. She laid her head on his shoulder and rested her hand over his heart. It was times like this that made him forget how they'd started and how they'd likely end up. Apart.

"This'll probably be my last trip to Houston." He had enough money to do what he wanted. His contract with Coyote Western Wear was almost up, and he wouldn't renew it. It was time to turn the endorsements over to one of the younger riders who wouldn't mind being away from home—away from family.

"That's good—um, are you sure?"

"Yeah." He stroked a path from her silky lips to her cotton-covered belly. "We'll be busy around here."

Toni ducked her head. "Yeah." She fiddled with the snap on his shirt. "Thanks for agreeing to help with the breeding program."

Whatever it takes to keep you here. He almost said the words aloud.

Toni sat beside Brand as he drove them toward town. She brushed the crumbs off her shirt. She'd been eating crackers to settle her antsy stomach ever since the call from Kyle Williams, her lawyer. Something wasn't right, but Kyle refused to discuss it over the phone. He'd insisted they make an appointment before Brand went out of town. The urgency doubled her nervousness.

The receptionist ushered them straight into Kyle's office. Toni introduced the men and took a seat even though sitting was the last thing she wanted to do. The tight look on Kyle's face didn't bode well. "What's the problem?"

Kyle pushed his glasses up on his nose and steepled his fingers. "As we discussed, you had to have a male heir to gain control of your grandfather's ranch." Toni nodded cautiously.

"Toni, you should have talked to me before taking such drastic measures."

"You were gone a month. I talked to Tom. Your partner drew up our prenuptial agreement."

Kyle shuffled the papers in his hands. "I advised your grandfather against the clause, but he insisted. I'm afraid my partner didn't fully understand the terms when he drew up your prenuptial agreement."

The crackers in Toni's stomach turned to lead. Scooting toward the edge of the chair, she gripped the edge of his desk. "What are you saying?"

Kyle glanced at Brand then fixed his somber gaze on Toni. "Even though you're expecting, the wedding came before the birth of a child. It takes precedence." He paused. Toni's heart did the same. "The deed to the ranch must go into your husband's name." He shook his head. "I'm sorry you didn't get the copy of the will I mailed to your apartment. At least then you might have had a chance to read it before taking such drastic measures."

She could only stare at Kyle in disbelief. This sick feeling in her stomach intensified.

"Toni, I liked and respected your grandfather, but we both know how he felt about a woman running a ranch, or he would have left the place to your mother. Will wanted you to find a husband and settle down. He thought this would hurry you and Josh to the altar."

She might pass out. "What you're saying is that by marrying Brand I didn't gain control of the ranch. *I gave it away?*"

"More or less, yes."

Through the buzzing in her ears she heard Brand ask, "You're saying the ranch is mine?"

"Correct."

A cold sweat dampened her forehead. Spots clouded her vision. She'd sold herself for a piece of land and come up with nothing. She straightened. No, that wasn't right. She'd have her baby. They just wouldn't have a home.

Brand leaned forward in his chair, apparently eager to take it all from her. He wouldn't have to keep her in order to own the land. He'd probably kick her off the ranch and try to take their child away from her, too.

"What you're saying is that I can do anything I want with the property? Sell it, develop it? List the deed anyway I see fit?"

"That is correct." Kyle's tone grew frostier.

This was the payback for all the sins she'd committed. God or Fate or whoever held the cards was playing a cruel trick. Just when she thought she had it all, it was being wrenched from her fingers. She was going to be sick.

Brand leaned back, crossed his ankles, and smiled. That cunning smile made Toni's heart turn over. She'd played the game and lost. She stumbled to her feet and headed for the door. Brand jumped up, but she waved him off. She needed to be alone. "Ladies' room."

Brand stared at the closed door, concern over Toni's pallor making him want to follow. "She has morning sickness at the damnedest times."

"I'll have my secretary check on her."

Still worried, Brand sat back down while the attorney directed his secretary to keep an eye on Toni.

"Brand, I need to know what you intend to do with the ranch."

"Put Toni's name on the deed."

The attorney narrowed his eyes. "If you mean her name alone, then I'd have to point out that wouldn't be a sound move financially. You'd pay inheritance taxes, and then she would be taxed again on the same property."

"Counselor, if you bothered to read the prenup your partner drew up, you'd know Toni and I want a fifty-fifty split. You might not think it was a legally binding agreement, but I signed it and I intend to respect it."

Brand glanced at the door and stood. Toni hadn't come back. "While you're fixing that, we'll need to set up a trust fund for this baby and change my will to name Toni and the child as beneficiaries."

For the first time since their arrival, Brand saw respect in the man's gaze. Kyle stood and offered Brand his hand. "I'll have the papers ready for your signature when you return from your trip. It'll be a pleasure doing business with you, Mr. Lander."

The secretary peeked in. "Mrs. Lander has left. She asked me to call a cab to take you to the airport."

Brand wandered around the arena, surprised that the itch to compete hadn't hit him the minute he'd walked through the gate. His buddies razzed him about tying the knot, and he took it. He'd missed these people, but tonight all he could think about was that Toni hadn't answered the phone when he'd called from the airport.

"Hello, gorgeous."

Brand turned. Megan was as beautiful as ever, but he didn't feel the need to press his lips to hers or grind his chest against her ample bosom. "Hey, Meg."

She twined her fingers around his neck, but he turned his head. Her kiss landed on his cheek. "I can't believe you really did it. I thought it was a joke when you told me you got married. You always swore no woman would ever tie you down."

He had, and he'd meant it. "That was before I met Toni."

"Well, wife or no wife, you're mine for the next week. Your retirement is making the marketing department crazy. We've been scrambling for ways to make the most of it before people forget your name. Let's get you suited up before the check presentation."

She followed him into the dressing room just like she always had. Brand had never minded undressing in front of Megan before. "Meg, if you'll tell me what I'm supposed to wear, you can go check on the rest of the setup."

She dragged a finger down his shirt placket. "Need help?"

"Nope."

"Toni's a lucky woman."

"I hope she thinks so. Is there a phone I can use?"

This was crazy. He loved his wife and he hadn't even told her. Maybe if she knew she'd be willing to give him a chance. He shook his head. He'd never told a woman he loved her before and he wanted to see Toni's face when he said the words.

"Hey, Meg, any chance we can wrap this thing up early?"

* * *

Toni rolled the spool of barbed wire toward the back of the four-wheeler.

"I'll do that." Roy grabbed the wire and headed off.

Dusting off her hands, she turned toward the tractor shed determined to start on the seeding. But Aaron was there before she could fire up the motor. "Which pasture you want done?"

"The west one." He started the tractor and drove off.

Parking her hands on her hips, Toni pursed her lips and frowned after him. What was going on? Deke had intercepted when she'd said she was going to ride out to check the herd, claiming he needed something he'd left at the well yesterday. Wade had developed a sudden urge to muck stalls—as soon as he saw the pitchfork in her hands. The men wouldn't let her lift a finger. Any job she'd attempted yesterday and today had been taken over by someone else.

Rusty glanced up from the bench where he was mending a bridle. "They mean well."

Toni figured her frustration must be plainly written on her face. "What's going on?"

He hesitated then set the bridle down. "Brand asked the crew to keep an eye on you while he was gone." Toni's anger stirred. She clenched her fists and pinched her lips. "Ain't no reason to get riled, Toni-girl. Brand don't understand that he's making you feel penned, but he'll learn—if you're willing to teach him."

"So what *am* I allowed to do? Can I leave the yard? Or do I have to sneak around like I did with Granddad?"

"The boy's lookin' out for you the best way he knows how."

"I can look after myself." Toni spun on her heel and marched toward the house. All her old frustrations rose to the surface. She felt trapped, but sitting and stewing wasn't her way. When her grandfather wouldn't give her anything to do, she'd found jobs for herself. If Brand was determined to confine her to the house, she'd work in the house.

It wasn't as if she didn't have plenty to do to get ready for the baby and no nosy cowboys would interfere.

The house was a run-down dump, but a dump she loved with all her heart. She had a week to turn it into the kind of home a man liked to return to. Then maybe Brand wouldn't leave her.

Toni studied the freshly painted sky-blue walls of the nursery, then the paint cans stacked on the floor. She rolled her tired shoulder muscles and flipped through the magazine to the picture she'd earmarked. She'd never painted clouds or a rainbow before, but she'd go nuts if she had to sit around the house and think of Brand with Megan. Working in the vet's office each morning helped, but the afternoons were long and lonely. Even though Brand called every night, she felt restless without him here. He hadn't mentioned the will and she hadn't asked, fearing he'd tell her to be gone before he got home. If only he'd told her he loved her....

Determined to finish the room before Brand got home at the end of the week she pried the lid off the paint can. In the last three days, she'd painted the den, kitchen and master bedroom. The house was shaping up.

The kittens scampered across the room, skidded on the drop cloth, then darted through her legs and scampered up the step stool. She shooed them back down. "Hey, you two, scoot."

Toni poured the paint into the tray and dipped in the rag. According to the magazine, all she had to do was to blot the rag against the tops of the walls. The result should look like puffy white clouds. Climbing up to the third rung, she daubed the paint into a cloudlike shape, then stepped back down to judge her work. Pretty good. Moving the step stool along the wall, she repeated the process. Up. Down. Up. Two clouds done, probably another dozen to go before she made it around the room.

She daubed another cloud and descended. A terrible screech rent the air, and Toni jerked her foot off the tail she'd inadvertently trodden on. The kitten dodged the same way she did. Toni lost her balance, dropped the rag, and windmilled to no avail. The floor rushed at her and the impact of hardwood floor against her hip knocked the breath from her.

Her first thought was of the baby, but surely nothing could happen. She hadn't fallen far. A blob of paint dripped from her hair onto her nose and cheek. Good grief, if Brand could see her now. She needed a shower.

Shoving herself to her feet, she looked for the kittens, but they'd scampered off. A faint trail of white paw prints marked their path. She took the time to mop them up before peeling off her paint-soiled clothes and heading for the bathroom.

The paint blended with the warm water in a milky-colored mix. She lathered her hair and continued to rinse until the water ran clear. The pink streak swirling the drain was unexpected. Confused, she looked down. A thin trail of red ran down her leg. *The baby.* Panic hit her like a truck. Throwing back the shower curtain, she snatched a towel and hastily dried off.

The baby. Something was wrong with her baby. She had to get to a doctor. She had to find Brand.

Pale and tense, she knelt by the phone because her legs were too shaky to support her. First, she called the obstetrician to tell her that she was coming to the hospital. Next, she tried Brand's hotel room. She waited for the beep and left her message.

"Brand, I'm bleeding. I think it's—" Her voice cracked. Toni tried again. "I fell and I think I hurt the baby."

Toni replaced the receiver and pulled her clothes over damp skin. None of the ranch hands were in the yard. She yelled once, but no one answered. Not wanting to waste precious time she scratched out a note and pinned it on the bunkhouse bulletin board. She drove to the hospital as fast as she could. Pulling up to the emergency-room entrance, she threw her keys to one of the men in scrub suits outside and raced through the doors.

Inside, a nurse whisked her behind a curtain. "Your doctor's on her way. Tell me what happened."

Toni focused on her words, not wanting to miss any significant detail. Panic blurred the edges of her sanity. She'd never forgive herself if her stubbornness had caused her to lose the baby. Losing the baby also meant losing Brand.

Brand paced the hospital hallway. He'd never been so scared in all his life. He stopped and looked through the window in the hospital door. Toni lay on the white sheets, so pale she nearly blended into the fabric. The knot in his throat felt as big as his boot, and his eyes burned something fierce. He felt so damned helpless. He shouldn't have left her. He should have stayed home or made her go with him. He shouldn't have asked the guys to keep her from doing the work she loved. Rusty was right. He'd penned her in and she'd rebelled by painting the entire house.

He should have told her he loved her.

"Mr. Lander, your wife was distraught." Brand tried to focus on the doctor who'd stopped beside him. "I gave her something to calm her down. We're trying to be as thorough in our diagnosis as possible. I'm concerned about the bleeding, but I'm not convinced yet that the baby is in danger. We've run some lab tests and—"

"When—" He had to swallow. "When will you know something?" He wanted to get inside to see Toni, but the petite doctor blocked the door as surely as a dam blocked a river.

"The good news is that in the four hours your wife has been here there hasn't been a single contraction. As soon as we can get her to ultrasound, we'll have a better idea of what's going on. Unfortunately, we have to wait for the critical cases to clear out."

He raked a hand through his hair. "You said she was bleeding. Will she be okay? Toni, I mean."

"We'll know soon."

Not soon enough. "Look, get in there and take care of her."

"The baby appears—"

"Dammit, we can have another baby. Take care of my wife." His words stunned him, as did the tears running down his face. Brand clenched his fists and bowed his head. The baby wasn't nearly as important as Toni. Sure, he already loved the little person he hadn't intended to create, but not nearly as much as he loved his wife. There might be other babies, but there would never, *never* be another Toni.

He'd come home early intending to tell her he loved her. Instead, he'd found a panicking crew. They'd shown him Toni's note. Brand shoved off the wall and stared at the doctor. "I need to be with her."

"She'll probably sleep for a few more hours, but you can go in if you promise not to disturb her. You were so upset earlier that I didn't want to let you in until you'd settled down a bit.

"As soon as the ultrasound is available, we'll come for her. For now, be comforted by the fact that the bleeding was sparse and even that has stopped."

The doctor kept on talking, but Brand barely heard her words. His hand trembled when he stroked a path across Toni's cool, colorless cheek to the artery in her neck. He checked her pulse, not trusting the machine that blinked beside her. Tension eased from his shoulders as he felt the steady beat. "Why's that monitor counting over a hundred when her pulse is only sixty beats a minute?"

"That's your baby's heartbeat."

Brand's knees gave out. His butt hit the chair beside the bed. "I-is it supposed to be that fast?"

The doctor patted him on the back. "One hundred twenty is within the normal range."

His child. Toni's child. He slid his hand down her belly to cradle the baby the way he'd seen her do so many times.

Early-morning sunlight stung her eyelids, but Toni didn't want to waken. In her dreams, Brand had held her all night and told her he loved her. He'd stroked her hair, promised her forever and a dozen kids if she wanted them.

Before the dream had been a nightmare of fear. Blurred images of pitying glances, tubes and needles haunted her. Poking and prodding and blood. She hadn't been able to stop crying and she'd asked for Brand until a nurse had injected something into her IV. It could only mean one thing.

Pain pierced her heart. Emptiness threatened to consume her. Tears slid from beneath her lids and dampened her hair. She'd lost her baby and probably Brand, too, because she was a stubborn, pigheaded fool who had to prove her worth.

"Toni?" She turned her head. Brand, looking as awful as she felt, straightened in the chair beside the bed. His face was pale and drawn beneath the black stubble of his morning beard. His hair stuck up in spikes and his clothes were a wreck. For once he wore a solid-black shirt instead of his usual cowboy duds. The somber color seemed appropriate. "How are you, darlin'?"

Her throat blocked up. She couldn't answer. Everything important to her would very likely vanish today. Her hand fluttered over her stomach. She'd never felt so alone. Fresh tears stung her eyes.

Brand took her hand. "You scared the hell out of me."

"I'm sorry. I know that's not enough, but..." How could you apologize for an act of stupidity that cost a man his child? He must hate her.

"Hey, cut that out. I can't stand to see you cry." He brushed at her tears with his thumbs.

"I can't h-help it."

He sat on the bed and pulled her into his arms. How

could he be so tender when she'd done him wrong since day one?

"Do me a favor. No more trips to the hospital until it's time for this little cowpoke to make an appearance."

Toni blinked and drew back. *What?* "The baby…"

"Look, there's its heartbeat, right there." He pointed at the monitor with one hand and pulled her closer with the other. Toni watched the red numbers flash and tried to comprehend what he was saying.

"We're waiting on the ultrasound machine to get a picture of the little critter."

"But I was bleeding."

"The doc says that's not necessarily a bad thing." Brand cupped her cheek. The emotion in his gaze robbed her breath. She had to remind herself that Brand was being attentive because of their child. Dreams didn't really come true, and that wasn't love she saw in his dark eyes. But she wished it were. She put her fist to her mouth to stymie a sob.

"You need some crackers? I can get some from the cafeteria."

Toni blinked away her tears, but her throat burned from the effort of holding back. She hadn't lost her baby. She hadn't lost Brand. *Yet.* When he found out it was her fault that she was here… "I just want to go home."

"As soon as they do the ultrasound I'll check with the doc to see if I can spring you from this place."

The door opened and a nurse walked in. "We're going to take Mommy down the hall. Come on, Dad. If you're good, I'll let you push the chair."

Twenty minutes later Toni gaped at Brand. He looked as stunned as she felt. "Twins?"

The doctor and the ultrasound tech smiled, then the tech pointed out first one beating heart, then another. "It's too early to tell the sex yet, but you can see the hearts are working fine."

The doctor said, "It looks like you just dislodged a little

clot when you fell. Most women hang on to that until closer to labor. Everything else is in the right place for a pair of identical twins.''

Toni looked at the blurry images then at the man beside her. She must have done something right while she'd been racking up all those sins to deserve this. Now all she had to do was find a way to hold on to it.

After a silent ride home Brand carried her inside as if she were fragile and precious. He eased her down onto the bed so gently it made Toni want to weep. She hadn't tried to explain why she'd done what she'd done because she wanted to pretend Brand's love was real for a few more moments.

He stood, shoved his hands into his pants pockets, and turned toward the window. His shoulders rose and fell as he took several deep breaths. Toni braced herself for his well-deserved anger.

''Brand, I—''

''Dammit Toni, I thought I was going to lose you. I...'' He wiped a hand across his face. She saw his Adam's apple bob. ''I hope the nurse took notes. I made so many deals with God I can't remember half of 'em, but I reckon I'll be busy for a while.''

''I know you were worried about the baby....'' Tears choked off her words. She couldn't go on. Coldness seeped into her limbs. More than anything, she wanted to go back to sleep, back to the happy dream. She clutched a pillow to her chest.

''The baby?'' Brand lifted his head with a jerk and approached the bed in quick strides. He reached out and instinctively, Toni's muscles clenched. She forced them to relax because she knew now that Brand would never hurt her—even though she'd pushed him further than any man ought to be pushed.

He brushed the hair off her cheek and tipped her chin up. ''Didn't you hear a word I said last night?'' He sighed and shook his head. Hesitantly, it seemed, he laced his fingers through hers. "Nah, I guess you didn't."

He eased himself down on the edge of the bed and in his eyes made her heart swell with hope. "I was bargaining for you, Toni. For us. Sure, I want these babies, but if…if we lost them, we could try again. If you wanted to."

He touched his lips to hers as soft as a whisper and when he met her gaze his eyes glistened with unshed tears. "I don't want to lose *you,* Toni." He glanced away and cleared his throat. "I had Kyle put your name on the deed. Fifty-fifty. Just like we agreed."

She shouldn't be disappointed when he'd delivered such good news, but for moment she'd thought he was going to say something else. Hoped he was going to say something else. "Thank you. You can't know how much that means to—"

"I love you." He said the words in such a rush and he looked so anxious she thought she'd misunderstood.

"What?"

Brand inhaled deeply and squared his shoulders. The intense concentration on his face resembled the photos of him bull riding that she'd put in his father's scrapbook. "I love you and I don't want to lose you."

Her stomach took a funny turn. "M-me? You love me?"

One corner of his mouth curled upward. "My bossy, opinionated, snake-handling wife? Sure. Who else?"

"I've done you wrong at every turn. How can you love me?"

The teasing smile faded. "There's not another woman who can rile me or excite me or hug me like you do. I'm not willing to give that up."

Joy filled her until she thought she'd burst, but she was still afraid to believe what she'd heard. With an unsteady hand, she stroked his bristly chin. "I love you, too."

A muscle twitched beneath her fingers. Doubt clouded

his eyes. "You're sure? You're not just saying that 'cause I spilled my guts?"

"I went to Vegas looking for a love-'em-and-leave-'em cowboy, but I think I hit the jackpot instead. There's nothing I'd want more than to make a home here with you—and our kids, Brand."

He cupped her face in his hands and met her eyes with a steady gaze. "I want to spend the rest of my life with you, Toni, and God willing, we can have as many kids as you want. As many as your career will allow. You can open up your own practice. We'll build a clinic right on the ranch, and I'll watch the kids while you work."

"And I'll watch them while you work. We'll be one heck of a team."

"Damn straight."

Toni grabbed him by the collar and pulled him forward until their noses touched. She smiled against his lips. "What do you mean *I'm* opinionated?"

Brand's sexy grin was enough to curl her toes. "I notice you're not questioning 'bossy.'"

He gave her one of those slow-building-but-guaranteed-to-fry-her-brain-cells kisses, and Toni knew the sex of their child—children—no longer mattered.

The cowboy who'd followed her home was here to stay.

*   *   *   *   *

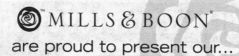

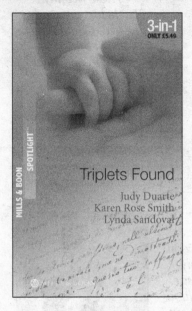

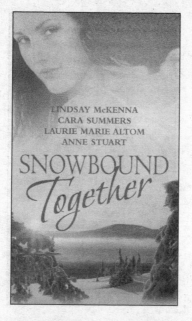

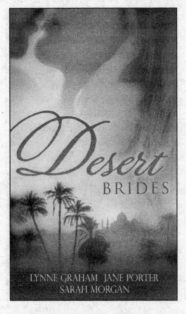

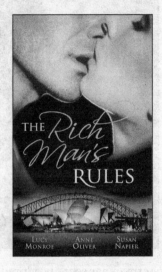

A wanton widow

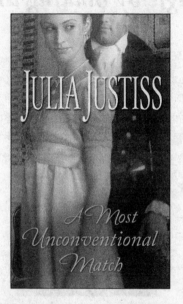

Hal Waterman has secretly adored newly widowed Elizabeth Lowery for years. When he calls upon Elizabeth to offer his help, his silent, protective presence awakens feelings in her that she does not understand.

Elizabeth knows that society would condemn her, but Hal's attractions may well prove too much to resist!

Available 18th December 2009

millsandboon.co.uk Community

Join Us!

The Community is the perfect place to meet and chat to kindred spirits who love books and reading as much as you do, but it's also the place to:

- Get the inside scoop from authors about their latest books
- Learn how to write a romance book with advice from our editors
- Help us to continue publishing the best in women's fiction
- Share your thoughts on the books we publish
- Befriend other users

Forums: Interact with each other as well as authors, editors and a whole host of other users worldwide.

Blogs: Every registered community member has their own blog to tell the world what they're up to and what's on their mind.

Book Challenge: We're aiming to read 5,000 books and have joined forces with The Reading Agency in our inaugural Book Challenge.

Profile Page: Showcase yourself and keep a record of your recent community activity.

Social Networking: We've added buttons at the end of every post to share via digg, Facebook, Google, Yahoo, technorati and de.licio.us.

www.millsandboon.co.uk